THE PRINCE OF STEEL

"Wait!" she blurted. "I have an idea. Let's make a wager. You give me an amount of money, and, if I cannot double it on the exchange within three months, then you're off the hook."

Before he thought better of it, he asked, "How much?"

She shrugged. "You may decide. Five thousand, perhaps?"

He admired her spirit, so he played along. "Too low. Let's make it ten."

"Fine. And when I double it, I'll take the twenty thousand and another fifty to start my business."

"Our business," he corrected. "And you only get three weeks. Not three months." No use making it easy on her.

Her jaw dropped. "Three weeks! I cannot possibly—"

"Then we have nothing else to discuss." He stood and walked around his desk. "Good day, Miss Sloane."

"Fine! Three weeks."

He suppressed a smirk. She would need to learn better negotiation skills for certain. He shoved his hands in his pockets. "Tell me something."

"Yes?"

"What's in it for me?"

"Well, money, of course."

"I've got plenty of money. You'll have to do better than that."

This caught her off guard, and she started chewing her lip. "I . . . There's nothing other than altruism and money in it for you, I'm afraid."

"One unappealing and the other completely unnecessary. What else?"

Joanna Shupe's Wicked Deceptions Series Is the Talk of the *Ton*!

The Lady Hellion

"A beautiful and complex love story featuring a hero who suffers from post-traumatic stress disorder and a heroine with a penchant for saving the day. Shupe is very talented, walking a fine line between Quint's demons and Sophie's charming, almost madcap character. These two sparkle in this wildly entertaining story."
—Sarah MacLean, *The Washington Post*

"Shupe invites readers to sit back and enjoy the terrific chemistry between the unconventional Lord Quint and the exasperating Lady Sophie in the conclusion to the Wicked Deceptions trilogy. With emotional intensity, poignancy, passion and murder, they won't be disappointed."
—*RT Book Reviews,* 4.5 Stars

"Sophie's independent nature makes her a delightful protagonist . . . The romance is delectable as sensual love scenes balance the well-woven mystery subplot."
—*Publishers Weekly*

"I enjoyed this series quite a lot, and am looking forward to see what Shupe writes in the future."
—*Smart Bitches Trashy Books*

"*The Lady Hellion* is a fabulous, wonderful book! Sophie is a superb heroine, the kind little girls dream of being. It is also refreshing that Quint is neither a rake nor a rogue, but he is most definitely a brooding hero, and it is totally relevant to the story arc. *The Lady Hellion* is built upon a very clever premise, and Ms. Shupe crafts an exciting and meticulously researched story fraught with suspense, startling plot twists combined with frissons of sexual tension, and a beautiful, tender love story—and what an ending! Absolutely terrific!"
—*Fresh Fiction*

The Harlot Countess

"With her knowledge of the modes and morals of the Regency era, Shupe delivers a well-crafted novel in this second installment of her Wicked Deceptions series. Steady pacing, delightful characters and an ability to build steamy sexual tension make for a lively love story."
—*RT Book Reviews*, 4.5 Stars

"A good story well told. This is a fun series."
—*Romance Reviews Today*

"An intriguing tale, *The Harlot Countess*, the second book in author Joanna Shupe's Wicked Deceptions series, is an emotion-packed, sexy historical romance that will keep readers captivated right up to the very end. Angst, heartache, vengeance, blackmail, secrets, miscommunication, passion, forgiveness, romance and love all intertwine in a story that readers will not soon forget."
—*Romance Junkies*

The Courtesan Duchess

"The powerful passion in this riveting tale of betrayal and forgiveness will knock your socks off!"
—Sabrina Jeffries

"Joanna Shupe's compelling story of an estranged couple brims with emotion and sensuality."
—Miranda Neville

"Heartfelt . . . This original and alluring novel is a very promising beginning to Shupe's career."
—*Publishers Weekly*

"Shupe's debut Wicked Deceptions tale is passionate and seductive. Her carefully drawn characters and their nicely crafted, poignant love story engage the readers' emotions and will have everyone anticipating the next book in the series."
—*RT Book Reviews*, 4 Stars

"Shupe launches her romance-writing career with a polished Regency-set historical that successfully merges engaging characters, steamy sensuality, and a dash of danger into one captivating romance."
—*Booklist*

"A lively story . . . A naïve, desperate heroine and a thoughtless, rakehell hero mature delightfully as they come into their own in this steamy debut that is the first of a back-to-back trilogy and skillfully sets the stage for more stories to come."
—*Library Journal*

"From its first naughty page, be prepared to be swept away by Joanna Shupe's *The Courtesan Duchess*. Julia will win your heart, and hero Nick's too! This skillful debut reads sure and true, and I can't wait to see what Joanna dreams up next in the series."
—Maggie Robinson

"One of the best debuts I've read in years. Joanna Shupe's *The Courtesan Duchess* is fast-paced, compelling, and super sexy. You won't be able to put it down."
—Valerie Bowman

"Joanna Shupe is a wonderful new voice in historical romance. *The Courtesan Duchess* takes readers on a steamy ride from Venice to London, proving that some happily ever afters are worth waiting for."
—Jennifer McQuiston

Books by Joanna Shupe

Wicked Deceptions

The Courtesan Duchess

The Harlot Countess

The Lady Hellion

The Knickerbocker Club

Tycoon
(novella)

Magnate

Baron
(coming in November 2016)

Published by Kensington Publishing Corporation

MAGNATE

The Knickerbocker Club

JOANNA SHUPE

ZEBRA BOOKS
KENSINGTON PUBLISHING CORP.
http://www.kensingtonbooks.com

ZEBRA BOOKS are published by

Kensington Publishing Corp.
119 West 40th Street
New York, NY 10018

All Kensington titles, imprints and distributed lines are available at special quantity discounts for bulk purchases for sales promotion, premiums, fund-raising, educational or institutional use.

Special book excerpts or customized printings can also be created to fit specific needs. For details, write or phone the office of the Kensington Sales Manager. Attn.: Sales Department. Kensington Publishing Corp., 119 West 40th Street, New York, NY 10018. Phone: 1-800-221-2647.

Zebra and the Z logo Reg. U.S. Pat. & TM Off.

First Printing: May 2016
ISBN-13: 978-1-4201-3984-6
ISBN-10: 1-4201-3984-3

eISBN-13: 978-1-4201-3985-3
eISBN-10: 1-4201-3985-1

10 9 8 7 6 5 4 3 2

Printed in the United States of America

For Sally and Claire:

Never stop dreaming.

ACKNOWLEDGMENTS

The Gilded Age, which falls roughly from 1870–1900, was a fascinating time of innovation, upheaval, and new ideals. This era wrought powerful industry, incredible corruption, and extreme wealth in America. There were social struggles, as waves of new immigrants, the middle-class, and recently freed slaves attempted to find a place in this country. In addition, New York's Knickerbocker families were desperately trying to uphold their rules and traditions while the nouveau riche angled to gain a foothold in the upper classes.

I set *Magnate* in early 1888 for a specific reason. In March of that year, the East Coast experienced one of the worst snowstorms it had ever seen, with over twenty inches of snow dumping on New York City. I couldn't resist using this natural disaster as a plot point. I spent hours looking at real photos of the storm's aftermath as well as reading the news accounts, which were harrowing and, in many cases, heartbreaking.

A great deal of debt is owed to Victoria Woodhull and Tennessee Clafin, who served as part of the inspiration for Lizzie, the heroine in *Magnate*. These two sisters opened the first female-operated stock brokerage firm in 1870. Backed by Cornelius Vanderbilt, the women stormed Wall Street and were an instant success. Interestingly, their offices had a private door in the back that led to a women-only lounge, a system that allowed women to begin to take independent control of their finances. Sadly, their firm only lasted three years, and it would be not until 1967 that the first woman purchased a seat on the New York Stock Exchange.

Many people helped in the writing of this book. First, I

am fortunate to have the dean of a business school as well as an economics professor in my family. So thanks to Denise and Joel, who patiently answered all my stock and finance questions, and provided resources to help with the accuracy of several stock details. Also, a huge thank-you to my husband, Rich, who helped plot out much of this story, then re-plot when things weren't working and my head was spinning.

I owe undying gratitude to my pals Lin Gavin, Michele Mannon, JB Schroeder, and Diana Quincy, who each helped brainstorm on this story, read the manuscript early on, and kept me on track when I faltered. Thanks to Chris Gavin, who patiently answered my stock questions on a trip at the beach. Thanks to both Megan Frampton and Sonali Dev for their comments on the manuscript and general awesome writerly support. And thanks to the other Violet Femmes—Tina, Jaye, Maria, RoseAnn—for reading the first chapter at a moment's notice! You rock!

Also, thanks to Peter Senftleben (who pushed me to up my game on this manuscript), Jane Nutter, and the entire team at Kensington for getting behind my stories, no matter what time period I write in. Thank you to Laura Bradford for being her awesome agent self, as well as doing an early read through on *Magnate* and giving me critical feedback on the characters.

My thanks to Greg Young and Tom Meyers, better known as The Bowery Boys, for their amazing podcast, Web site (www.boweryboyshistory.com), and willingness to answer my questions about Washington Square. If you like New York history, please check them out!

Most of all, thank you to the readers! I am so grateful for all of the support and feedback I get from you. I hope you enjoy the Knickerbocker Club series as much as I enjoyed writing it. All the errors here are my own.

Chapter One

Man cannot do without society, and society cannot be maintained without customs and laws.

—American Etiquette and Rules of Politeness, 1883

Seventy-Fifth Street and Fifth Avenue, New York City
December 1887

If given the choice between bears and bulls, Lizzie vastly preferred the bull. Bears were tentative and sluggish, whereas bulls charged forward and caused things to happen. She had finally decided to consider herself a bull, ready to pursue her hopes and dreams by any means necessary.

Which is how she found herself on upper Fifth Avenue this afternoon, waiting in the largest mansion on Millionaire's Row. The monstrosity belonged to one of the wealthiest men in the world, a steel magnate who had reputedly forged his empire through daring, determination, and sheer grit.

And before Lizzie left his house today, she intended to convince him to take another risk, this time on her.

A noise caught her attention, and she turned as an immense man stepped into the receiving room. "Miss Sloane, I am Emmett Cavanaugh."

Lizzie clasped her trembling hands and tried not to gawk. She'd heard the rumors, of course. Not only was Cavanaugh the owner of the powerful East Coast Steel, but he was also her brother's friend. Still, the bits of news and gossip here and there hadn't quite prepared her for the shock of actually seeing him in person.

He was *huge*—a mountain of a man. Thick and tall, with wide shoulders that could only be borne of physical activity. The breadth of his chest . . . good heavens. His tailor must charge a fortune for the additional fabric required to clothe him.

He did not smile. No welcoming warmth lit his expression, no curious twinkle shining in his eyes. He merely stood watching her, as if taking her measure as well. Her knees wobbled in the weighted silence, uncertainty hollowing out her belly and drying out her mouth. There was a hardness about this man, an edge, like one of the new skyscrapers towering unapologetically over the city's old, elegant buildings.

"Mr. Cavanaugh," she returned, straightening her shoulders. "Thank you for seeing me."

"Of course, though I'm a bit unclear on the rules. I don't normally entertain unmarried ladies in my home. Am I supposed to offer you refreshment?"

Yes, she'd heard rumors of the types of ladies he entertained. All actresses, and the liaisons never lasted long. "That's not necessary. I promise not to take up too much of your time."

"Then by all means, please sit."

Lizzie lowered herself onto a chair and studied him

through her lashes as he assumed the chair opposite. She hadn't expected him to be quite so . . . striking. He had full lips and a finely curved jaw. Stark, slashing cheekbones and slightly long, dark brown hair. A small indent graced the tip of his bold chin, an imperfect mark on an otherwise perfect profile, and her heart began picking up steam, thumping hard in her chest. His handsomeness made her even more unsure of herself, unsure of her decision to come here today.

But what choice did she have? She needed a partner, one wealthy and influential enough to help get her business up and running. Using her talent for stock speculation, she could save her family's finances if given a chance. Unfortunately, no one else would even meet with her. Emmett Cavanaugh was her last hope.

She cleared her throat. "The reason I've called today is that I have a business proposition for you."

One dark eyebrow shot up. "A business proposition? Interesting, though I'm curious as to why you've not taken this idea to your brother. William Sloane does own one of the country's largest railroads."

True, the Northeast Railroad Company was one of the biggest railroads, and Will had served as the president since their father's death. Her older brother never included her in business matters, however. He staunchly refused to discuss any of their financial problems, insisting he had everything well in hand, even when she knew otherwise. *"Stick to your parties and theater, Lizzie,"* Will often said. *"Leave the business side of things to me."*

Why couldn't she do both, as Will did? That precise attitude—that women were narrow-minded creatures incapable of understanding financial matters—never failed to anger her. No one took her ambition seriously, not even her friends. To them, her dreams were merely a temporary fancy, one that would disappear the instant she found the right man to marry. All the more reason to move forward with her plans, quickly and quietly.

"I have spoken with him, yes, but he's proven difficult to convince. I'm hoping you'll be more open-minded."

"Well, that does intrigue me. But what about the Rutledge boy, the one to whom you're nearly engaged?"

Hardly a surprise Cavanaugh had heard the rumors about her and Henry Rutledge. Will was keen on the match, as was Edith Rutledge, Lizzie's good friend and Henry's sister. But Lizzie hadn't yet made up her mind. Henry's views on women in business were far from progressive. "Mr. Rutledge is not in control of his own pockets, I'm afraid, and his father would never agree to what I'm proposing."

"Then I suppose I'm flattered to be approached. You must tell me this radical idea." Cavanaugh moved not a muscle, his focus unwavering yet guarded. She hoped that was a sign of interest on his part.

"I want to open a stock brokerage firm. I am seeking a partner, one to provide working capital to get started. Someone high profile enough to help me lure clients."

No sign of amusement or horror showed on his face. His expression remained unreadable. "Like Vanderbilt did for Woodhull a few years back?"

"Precisely." She relaxed a bit. *He understood.*

"And who will be doing the advising?"

"Me. I will advise on all the trades. I do plan to keep that knowledge from the male clients, however, at least until they're comfortable with the idea of working with a woman."

He tilted his head and stroked his jaw. "You speculate on the exchange?"

She nodded. "Indeed. Of course, I can't trade myself, so I plan to hire a young man to represent me on the exchange floor."

He gave her a long, indecipherable look. She couldn't tell if he was considering her plan or preparing to laugh.

"You are from one of the oldest and wealthiest families in New York, Miss Sloane. Surely you can finance whatever scheme you're dreaming up. Sell a bracelet or two to raise the money. Why bring someone in from the outside?"

This was a sticky, yet not entirely unexpected, question. She couldn't tell Cavanaugh the truth, that she suspected the worst of the Sloane finances. Her brother would not discuss it, but she was certain they were in trouble. Paintings disappearing, servants let go, stock sold . . . Had Will thought she wouldn't notice? Had he honestly believed she didn't pay attention? Yet her offers to help had been refused. So she had decided to do this without Will's assistance.

Moistening her dry lips, she charged on with the answer she'd prepared, one that was not a lie. "I do not come into possession of my trust until my twenty-fifth birthday, which leaves me with very little money to work with before then. However, even if I had the capital, I won't be taken seriously by my clients—the male clients—until I prove that I can earn money."

"And I am to believe you're competent, entrust you with my money?"

She picked up the ledger she'd been keeping for four years, the proof that she wasn't some silly female with unrealistic aspirations. No, in here lay her undeniable abilities in ink. "These are records of the transactions I would have made, had I been allowed." He held out his large hand, and she slipped the volume into his grip. "I read the reports, Mr. Cavanaugh. I follow the markets. You'll see I maintain a healthy balance in the black."

"A fictional balance," he noted, before studying the most recent entries. "Most of these are obvious, sure bets any trader would make." He paused. "What's this, a short sale on Pennington? Did you truly see that price drop coming, when no one else did?"

Not easy to keep the smugness out of her voice, but she managed it. "Over the past three years, I've noticed their second quarter earnings are always delayed. The Pennington stock drops ten percent like clockwork as a result."

"How do I know you didn't write these entries the next day, once you read the papers?"

Heat washed over her skin, like she'd been dipped in a hot water bath. "Are you saying that I am a liar?"

The question seemed to amuse him. His lips twitched as he handed the ledger back. "Why me?"

She lifted a shoulder, trying to appear casual when she felt the exact opposite. "First, you have the means and the influence. Second, I know about your meetings with my brother each month, along with Calvin Cabot and Theodore Harper." She drew in a deep breath and admitted the truth, praying she would not offend him. "And neither Mr. Cabot nor Mr. Harper would see me when I paid a call."

"Well, at least you're honest about my being your last choice," he said dryly.

Cavanaugh's reputation for ruthlessness had factored into the decision to save him for last. Legend held he'd grown up on the streets of Five Points, fought his way out of the slums to a steel mill, which he later purchased to start his empire. Unlike the other wealthy men of business, he didn't involve himself in charitable causes and kept far removed from the social scene.

He surprised her by rising in one fluid motion. "Follow me," he said, and started out of the room.

Stomach fluttering with nerves, she trailed him into the corridor and deeper into the garishly decorated house, passing the two-story entry hall with its sleek pink marble staircase and gold railing. Next came a long gallery, with paintings from Dutch and Italian masters and a carved ceiling decorated with frescoes and rimmed in gold leaf. If she weren't so anxious, she might've found the surroundings impressive.

Cavanaugh walked fast, and Lizzie had to lift the hem of her skirts in order to keep up. Not very loquacious, was he? Or polite, for that matter.

She had no idea where he was leading her. To the safe where he kept his money? A side door, where he'd eject her from his house? For some strange reason, she wasn't worried for her safety. He'd been patient with her, asking intelligent questions and listening to her answers. Moreover, he was her brother's friend.

They ended up in a large room containing a massive desk. Rows of books lined the walls and a collection of modern-day conveniences—telephone, telegraph machine, stock ticker—shared what must be Cavanaugh's office. The space smelled of cigar, lemon polish, and big business. A thrill slid through her as she imagined the deals and fortunes this room had witnessed.

"Colin, leave us," Cavanaugh said, and a young man stood up from a smaller desk in the corner. He wore round glasses, his eyes curious behind the frames as he hurried to the hall. Lizzie guessed not many ladies had ever crossed into this masculine domain.

Cavanaugh continued to the stock ticker, which was churning and spitting out a long white strip. He ripped off the paper, returned to her side, and held out the tape. "Read it. The last five updates."

Taking a deep breath, she lowered herself into a chair, set down her ledger, and smoothed the thin strip of paper between her fingers. Cavanaugh sat as well, thankfully saving her from craning her neck to see him. "Deere and Company down seven and three-eighths. State Street Corporation up two points. Seneca Textiles down twelve points. PPG Industries up six and one-eighth points. Kimberly-Clark up three and five-eighths."

"Very good," he said, though he hardly sounded impressed. "But interpreting the tape is the skill. So tell me, based on what you read, what would you advise your clients to do?"

She didn't even need to ponder it. "I would advise them to buy Seneca Textiles."

"Why, when they've been down steadily since September?"

"Because Easter is three months away, and in a few days, the ladies will begin ordering their bonnets, dresses, gloves, and the like. I also know that Seneca will soon announce an exclusive agreement to import the same Honiton lace as supplied to Queen Victoria."

Cavanaugh glanced away, his brow furrowed. She held utterly still, watching and awaiting his decision. Blunt fingers stroked the rough skin of his jaw, and her attention was drawn to the small indentation in his chin. She imagined tracing it with her finger. . . .

"Not bad, Miss Sloane. Not bad at all. But my answer must still be no."

* * *

Emmett studied her carefully as the news sank in. Christ, she was beautiful. How did a bastard like Will Sloane have such a breathtaking sister?

In a high-necked, blue-and-white-striped shirtwaist and matching skirt, Miss Sloane possessed a cool, untouchable beauty, the kind far removed from the type of women he usually fraternized with. She had the flawless skin found only in the top tier of society—people who'd never worked, toiled in a field, or sweat in the heat of a steel mill. Emmett felt dirty just sitting across from her.

Still, his blood stirred all the same. How could it not? Blond hair, perfect poise, slate-gray eyes, the fair Miss Sloane would cause a dead man to sit up and take notice.

And the way she'd read that ticker tape, with such confidence and skill, had almost knocked him on his ass. He hadn't met a woman that quick with numbers since Fannie Reid, owner of the most successful bordello in Five Points.

"I'm sorry, you said no?" Her blond brows pinched, and he had the ridiculous urge to smooth his thumb over the tiny creases that dared mar her immaculate forehead. "Why?"

He forced his gaze to hers. "I said no for two reasons. First, I have no interest in owning an investment firm. And second, while it seems you have a knack for speculating, I cannot see how this is a good idea. I wish you luck, however."

Her shoulders went rigid, and he knew he'd offended her. "I have more than a 'knack.' Why do you think I will not succeed?"

How could he explain it to her, that talent only got one so far in business? More important were cunning, a lack of scruples, and an ever-ready supply of favors you could call upon at a moment's notice. This woman was far too well-bred to play in the street with the other vermin.

"The world you think to involve yourself in is a cutthroat, nasty business. I cannot believe you have the stomach for it."

Her lips thinned into a white line. "And how do you know what, precisely, I have the stomach for?"

She hadn't backed down, so perhaps Miss Sloane was stronger than she appeared. Still, she had no idea what awaited her if she continued along this insane path. Bribes. Lying. Cheating . . . Christ, he'd bought off two politicians already today—and the day was only half over. No woman, especially one whose family could be traced to the Dutch patroons of New Amsterdam, should swim in those filthy waters.

"I don't, not really," he admitted. "But I have a strong suspicion."

"A suspicion based on how I look. On my last name."

It was not a question, but Emmett felt he owed her the truth. "Yes. Life in Washington Square will not have prepared you for—"

Anger bloomed on her cheeks, her pristine skin turning a dull red. "You have no idea of my life or what I'm prepared to do. I know as much about stocks as any man. Women shouldn't be forced to put up with . . . with . . ."

She trailed off, and Emmett couldn't drag his eyes away. Furious, she was downright breathtaking. Emmett's body began to take notice, but the last thing he needed was a bit of stiff in his trousers. With an effort, he returned to the conversation. "With?"

"With men like *you!* You are just as closed-minded as my brother."

Emmett frowned. God knew he wanted nothing in

common with Will Sloane. Emmett hated her brother with everything he had, which was quite considerable.

He studied the determined set of Miss Sloane's shoulders. The resolute gleam in her steady gaze. "Why?" he finally asked.

"Why, what?"

"Why do you want to do this? You have to know it won't be easy. You'll likely be shunned by high society once word gets out. And who will serve as your clients?"

"They won't shun me, not if I've proven myself. Which is why I need a prominent name on the door, one that people will accept at first. As for my clients, they'll likely be mostly women at the outset. Shopgirls, teachers, widows, society women. And ladies with . . . other sources of income."

"Prostitutes, you mean." God Almighty, her brother would lose his snobbish, blue-blooded mind if he knew. Emmett was growing to like this girl.

She flushed, but did not dodge, answering, "Yes, those as well. But a successful businessman as the face of the company will encourage other men to invest their money. I just need help getting started, really. My gender won't matter when the company returns a profit."

He admired her conviction, but wondered at the reason behind it. Were the Sloanes in some sort of financial trouble? Why else would she be here, so anxious to prove herself, instead of doing this on her own? The idea had Emmett nearly salivating; he'd had his eye on Sloane's Northeast Railroad Company for a long time. Owning the railroad that transported his steel across the country would almost double Emmett's profits.

And bringing the stick-up-his-ass Sloane down while

helping his sister engage in something scandalous? Nearly irresistible.

Yet something held him back, like his strange reaction to her presence. His gut told him to run the other way from this woman—and he always trusted his gut.

"I like your determination," he admitted. "But—"

"Wait!" she blurted. "I have an idea. Let's make a wager. You give me an amount of money, and, if I cannot double it on the exchange within three months, then you're off the hook."

Before he thought better of it, he asked, "How much?"

She shrugged. "You may decide. Five thousand, perhaps?"

He admired her spirit, so he played along. "Too low. Make it ten."

"Fine. And when I double it, I'll take the twenty thousand and another fifty to start my business."

"Our business," he corrected. "And you only get three weeks. Not three months." No use making it easy on her.

Her jaw dropped. "Three weeks! I cannot possibly—"

"Then we have nothing else to discuss." He stood and walked around his desk. "Good day, Miss Sloane."

"Fine! Three weeks from today."

He suppressed a smirk. She would need to learn better negotiation skills for certain. He shoved his hands in his pockets. "Tell me something."

"Yes?"

"What's in it for me?"

"Well, money, of course."

"I've got plenty of money. You'll have to do better than that."

This caught her off guard, and she started chewing her lip. "I . . . There's nothing other than altruism and money in it for you, I'm afraid."

"One unappealing and the other completely unnecessary. What else?" He moved toward her, relieved to see she didn't back away from him like other women had in the past. When he reached the edge of his desk, he leaned on the heavy wood and crossed his feet. "For example, what happens if you fail? I'm out ten thousand dollars."

"I don't have the money to pay you back, at least not yet." She paused, then brightened. "But I can repay you in Northeast stock. From my trust."

"I can purchase common stock anytime I choose."

"This is preferred stock. My father started the company only a few years before he died, and he put some in a trust for me. I'm certain I have enough stock to sign over to you, should I fail. Which I won't."

Emmett swore he could hear his heart beating in his ears. Northeast hadn't put preferred stock on the market in eight years. Owning some not only promised a higher dividend return on the company's earnings, but such stock could possibly allow him voting rights. Will Sloane would shit himself when he found out—not that Emmett would tell any of this to Elizabeth.

"Why not wait until your twenty-fifth birthday, then, to start your company?"

"Because I am tired of waiting. Another four years is intolerable."

Something about her answer felt off; Emmett would swear on it. The woman stood to inherit a large trust in a few years, so why not wait? More evidence all was not well in the house of Sloane.

Damn, he'd enjoyed this visit, probably more than he should have. He liked her; it surprised him how much.

The two of them had little in common—his upbringing in the filth of Five Points could not be more different than her privileged youth—but she had spirit, an unwavering desire to succeed, much as he had when first starting out.

A shame their paths wouldn't cross again. No chance she would win the wager, not in such a short period of time. Which meant her brother would never learn of this visit. Unless . . .

"You present a tempting offer, Miss Sloane. Now, would you like to hear my counteroffer?"

"A counteroffer?"

"Yes, something I want from you in exchange."

She clasped her hands, almost as if bracing herself. "And what might that be, Mr. Cavanaugh?"

"I want you to have dinner with me."

"Dinner?" Rounded gray eyes quickly narrowed suspiciously. The woman had no idea how to conceal an emotion. Really, the jackals on Wall Street would swallow her whole. "When?"

"Friday, at Delmonico's."

"I couldn't possibly do that. What would . . ."

When she didn't finish, he said, "Yes, what would they say? Knickerbocker's finest, dining with the likes of me. Could the city handle such a scandal?"

"You are mocking me."

"I do no such thing, Miss Sloane. I want to have dinner with you. Are you brave enough, or should you like to check with your brother first?"

That had the desired result. She threw back her shoulders, determined to prove she was one of the modern, independent women who answered to no one. Emmett could only imagine the conversations in the Sloane household. She must drive her brother daft. Yet another reason to like her.

"Fine. Which Delmonico's?"

"Twenty-Sixth Street, of course," he replied smoothly.

"Of course," she repeated, her tone sardonic. He knew why she would be unhappy. The location ensured that all of New York society would see them together. The news would race to Sloane's ears before dessert had been cleared. "In the main dining room, I assume."

He inclined his head. "Indeed. Shall I write the bank check? Do we have a deal?"

She swallowed, her eyes uncertain, and he was filled with a sudden desperation for her to say yes. Clearly from a desire to bedevil Sloane—not the anticipation of watching her full, delectable mouth as she ate.

Finally, she jerked her head. "We have a deal."

Elation and relief bubbled inside Lizzie as she left the Cavanaugh mansion. She had actually done it. A signed bank check now rested in her small bag, the first step to her new future. She hadn't convinced him to fund her company outright, of course, but it was a start.

She had no doubt in her ability to win the bet, even if he'd cut the time of the wager to almost nothing. She could do this—no, she *must* do this. Not because of the Sloane name or legacy, or even for her and Will's comfort, but for the hundreds of servants and Northeast Railroad employees who depended on the Sloanes for their livelihoods. Two members of their household staff had already been let go, and Lizzie would do all in her power to prevent any more dismissals—even if it meant sharing dinner with Emmett Cavanaugh.

Her brougham remained where she had left it, on Seventy-Fifth Street where prying eyes might be less likely to see it. At her approach, her driver, Brookfield, moved to open the door. "You've got guests, miss."

"Guests?"

Brookfield colored slightly. "I apologize. I didn't see them sneak in, miss, and by the time I noticed, they wouldn't leave." He opened the door, and two young girls stared out from the carriage depths. They both had pretty, dark hair done up in ringlets and wore matching yellow dresses. The two almost looked like twins, but Lizzie could tell that one girl was slightly older. She guessed they were no more than twelve or thirteen.

"Hello," she said, climbing inside and sliding onto the empty bench.

Both girls grinned. "You're pretty," one of them said.

"Very pretty. I love your dress," the other girl said, gesturing to Lizzie's outfit. It was one of Lizzie's favorite day dresses, a French silk of blue stripes paired with a pointed basque trimmed with lace. The skirt had two deep ruffles and pannier drapery. She had wanted to look her best when meeting Cavanaugh.

"Thank you. I am curious who you are, though."

"We're Emmett's half sisters. I'm Kathleen," the older-looking one said. "But everyone calls me Katie."

"I'm Claire. May I touch your hat?"

Cavanaugh's . . . half sisters? Lizzie quickly recovered from her shock and leaned forward, bending her head toward the girl. "Yes, of course. That's an ostrich feather. What do you think?"

"It's so soft," the girl whispered. "Thank you."

"You're welcome. I like it, too." Lizzie straightened. "So how old are you, Katie and Claire?"

"I'm thirteen. Claire's fourteen months younger than me."

"Oh," Lizzie said. "That must be nice, having a sister so close to your own age."

While Lizzie appreciated her older brother, she'd always wished for a sister. Borrowing clothes, sharing stories, discussing young men . . . A sister would have been a friend and confidante to help ease the lonely years of adolescence. Will had done so much for her, but his responsibilities at the company and finishing his schooling hadn't left much time for his younger sister.

"It is, especially since Mama died when I was born," Claire said.

Lizzie's chest tightened. She knew all too well the hole a mother's absence left in a little girl's heart. "I'm sorry. My mother died when I was young as well."

Both girls gazed at her with solemn understanding. "Do you remember her?" Katie asked.

"Very little, I'm afraid." Lizzie had been four when Caroline Sloane died in childbirth, along with the baby. She could recall brushing her mother's long, blond hair at night. The ghosts of a few other brief moments existed— a kind word or a kiss on the forehead—but never as many as she'd wished. Will had provided Lizzie with most of the memories, often telling her stories of her parents. Did Emmett do the same for his half sisters?

Lizzie refocused on the young girls. "I'm sure your mother loved you both very much."

Katie smiled. "Brendan tells us about her all the time."

"Brendan?"

"Our other half brother," Katie said. "We all had the same father. Emmett's the oldest, then Brendan, then us. Emmett and Brendan's mother died, too. Before our father married our mother."

"We spend a lot of time with Brendan. Emmett's usually too busy for us." Claire swung her booted feet, her legs too short to reach the carriage floor. "He works all the time."

Lizzie could well imagine, considering Will's hectic schedule. Empires did not run themselves. "How long have you lived with your brothers?"

"I was almost three. Claire had just turned one."

So Emmett, then only a young man himself, had taken in the small girls and assumed responsibility for them. What had happened to their father?

"Where do you live?" Claire asked Lizzie. "We used to live near Union Square, but Emmett had this big house built a few years ago, and we came to stay here. This house is so gigamtic. It has seventy-eight rooms."

"*Gigantic,*" Lizzie corrected. A short conversation with these two little girls had provided more information about Cavanaugh than a year's worth of newspapers. "That is very big. It must be fun, though, having all that space. I live on Washington Square with my brother."

Katie's eyes went big. "The park there used to be a graveyard. Do you have ghosts? We've always wanted to see a ghost."

"I haven't seen any ghosts, but I've never really searched for one. Perhaps you'd like to visit sometime and we could go ghost hunting."

Both girls grinned, their expressions hopeful. "Truly?" Katie asked. "Do you mean it, Miss Sloane?"

"Absolutely," she said, and realized she meant it. A ghost-hunting excursion with two adorable young girls sounded like fun. Perhaps she could convince her friend Edith to join them. "I'll speak with your brother about it. By the way, do you girls have a governess? If so, I imagine she's looking for you."

"Yes. But we snuck out," the older girl said.

"She thinks we're practicing our music. I play piano,

and Katie plays the clarinet." Claire mimicked piano keys with her fingers.

"Won't she be worried if she discovers you missing?"

Katie lifted a shoulder. "Probably, but we had to come down to see what you looked like."

"Ladies never call on Emmett," Claire elaborated, fingering the satin bow on her dress.

"Well, not ladies like you," Katie said, and they both giggled.

"Girls," Lizzie admonished, though she tried not to laugh. "Your brother's private life is his own business. You should not know what sort of ladies he sees."

Katie rolled her eyes. "Everyone knows Emmett only sees actresses. We read the gossip columns every day. Brendan says it's because—"

The door was flung open, and the imposing figure of Emmett Cavanaugh came into view. With a fierce frown directed at his younger half sisters, he crossed his arms. A tense silence descended, and Katie and Claire shrank into the velvet seats. "Girls, get back inside," he finally said, his words tiny white clouds in the frigid air.

"But Emmett—" Katie started until her brother's hard voice interrupted.

"Now, Katie."

"Does this mean you won't give us a swimming lesson this afternoon?" Claire asked. "Please don't take away our lesson, Emmett."

Lizzie's mouth nearly fell open. Cavanaugh was teaching his sisters how to swim?

He held up a finger and pointed at his sisters. "If you do as Mrs. Thomas says and do not escape her again today, we'll still have a lesson. Deal?"

"Deal!" the girls said quickly. Then they murmured

polite responses to Lizzie and scurried out of the carriage. "Good-bye, girls," Lizzie called as they descended.

They disappeared behind his broad back, yet Cavanaugh kept his cool, flat gaze riveted on Lizzie. "I apologize for my sisters."

"I didn't mind. They were curious about me." She couldn't resist adding, "They said ladies never call on you."

A cold wind blew at that moment, ruffling his dark hair and suit coat. He didn't move, just stood tall and broad like an impenetrable force of nature. One too strong to ever bend or break. She shivered.

"That is because most ladies know better." Without giving her a chance to respond, he stepped back. "Until Friday, Miss Sloane."

Chapter Two

⚜

Riches are desirable, but many a one who has had money at his command has been entirely unable to find ingress to good society.

—American Etiquette and Rules of Politeness, 1883

On Friday evening, Lizzie entered Delmonico's at eight o'clock, as per Cavanaugh's terse instructions delivered yesterday. Charlie Delmonico met her at the door and greeted her warmly.

"Miss Sloane." The young man beamed. "Welcome back."

"Hello, Charlie. I am having dinner with—"

"Mr. Cavanaugh, yes," he said. "Everything has been prepared, and Mr. Cavanaugh has arrived. I will escort you to your table."

Lizzie nodded, trying to calm the nerves fluttering in her stomach. *It's merely dinner,* she told herself. Though she still couldn't figure out why Cavanaugh wanted to dine with her. What did he hope to gain?

Something told her he never did anything without a purpose.

Lizzie had spent the past three days with her nose

buried in stock reports, plotting a strategy on how to double Cavanaugh's money. She needed more time, but there was no chance Cavanaugh would extend their bet. The man was reputed to be as malleable as granite, and she suspected she'd have an easier time moving Grand Central Depot to Weehawken than getting him to change his mind.

Charlie led her deeper into the familiar dining room, a space designed to appeal to the most sophisticated New Yorkers. Dark mahogany furniture gleamed in the soft light of crystal chandeliers, the ceiling decorated with impressive frescoes worthy of an Italian master. Tall windows framed the swaying trees and yellow gas lamps of Madison Square, a view unlike any other in the city.

In the center of the room, a man rose to his feet and Lizzie's heart began to race. She'd forgotten the impact of Emmett Cavanaugh, the sheer impressiveness of his towering frame and handsome face. His wide shoulders were framed in the newest style, that of a black tailless dinner jacket. A white single-breasted vest stretched over his immense chest, while his white bow tie and shirt collar contrasted with his tan skin. This was not a man who lived for ponies and pleasure, idling at his club while the world awaited his whim. Here was a man unafraid of hard work, who snatched what he wanted and forged it with his own bare hands. She admired that. Even envied him, a little.

Her eyes locked with Cavanaugh's obsidian gaze. He never glanced away, just watched her with an unreadable intensity that sucked all the air from the room. She nearly stumbled, but somehow remained on her feet as they arrived at the most coveted table, one in the center of the room next to the elaborate marble fountain. Where everyone would see them.

"Miss Sloane," Cavanaugh greeted and moved to pull

out her chair. Did she detect a bit of relief on his face? She couldn't be sure, but that hint of vulnerability made him more . . . human. If he ever smiled she might faint dead away.

"Mr. Cavanaugh."

She lowered and arranged herself on the seat, careful not to crush her bustle, as he pushed her chair toward the table.

"I didn't think you'd come." He signaled to a waiter hovering nearby.

She liked his deep voice. It was huskier than Will's, each word pronounced with authoritative precision.

"Why wouldn't I? I said I'd have dinner with you. I keep my promises."

"Surprising for a Sloane," he muttered, so softly she was certain he hadn't meant for her to hear.

"What does that—"

"Champagne, miss?" A waiter holding an expensive bottle appeared, and Lizzie had to bite off her questions as their glasses were filled.

When they were alone, Cavanaugh lifted his flute. "To possibilities." The words, combined with his fierce expression, caused her mouth to dry out. Was he speaking of their business venture?

She raised her glass. "To possibilities." She took a hasty sip, focusing on the far wall instead of him.

"I hope you don't mind," he said. "I've gone ahead and ordered our meal. I thought it would save time."

"I suppose that makes sense, but what would you have done if I'd stayed home?"

"Eaten alone, most likely. Did you consider not coming?"

"Of course not." A lie. She'd considered backing out at least a dozen times over the last few days.

The side of his mouth hitched, a simple gesture that softened his hard features, making him even more striking. "If you plan to join the world of business, Miss Sloane, you must learn to lie."

The suggestion bothered her. First, he was surprised she'd kept her word to dine with him this evening. Now he was encouraging her to lie. Was he so cynical, then? "You might believe that to be true, but I prefer to practice honesty in all things."

"Is that so?" When she nodded, he leaned in and lowered his voice. "Did you tell your brother you were meeting me tonight? Or Rutlidge, for that matter?"

"As it happens, Will has been away this week, and I have not seen Mr. Rutlidge."

"And all forms of communication at your disposal are . . ." He waved his hand, as if searching for the right word. "Broken?"

Her cheeks grew warm, and irritation swept through her. "Why did you want to have dinner with me, Mr. Cavanaugh? What do you hope to gain?"

"Companionship?"

"Because you are lacking in feminine attention?" She finished her champagne and placed the glass on the table. A waiter instantly materialized to refill it. "I find that hard to believe."

Had that sounded like a compliment? She nearly winced. Champagne tended to loosen her tongue, unfortunately.

He tilted his head, studied her. "And here I thought you'd be too busy reading the stock reports to pay attention to the gossip columns."

"I don't read them. The gossip columns, I mean. But one does hear rumors."

"Rumors are often untrue—whether it's on the exchange or in print."

"So you're not seeing that actress, Mrs. Rose?"

His face slackened, mouth parting slightly, but he quickly recovered. "I'm obviously at a disadvantage. It seems you know quite a bit about me, but I know nothing about you. Other than your family and your interest in the stock exchange, of course."

"What would you like to know?"

"Are you going to marry Henry Rutlidge?"

She took a deep breath and reached for her champagne. It was crisp and sweet on her tongue, the bubbly liquid giving her courage. "There are many who think I should."

"Yes, but what do you think, Miss Sloane?" His eyes, nearly black in the soft light, gave nothing away, no hint as to what he was thinking.

She shifted in her seat. "I'll need a lot more champagne before I answer that question."

The first course arrived, a plate of fresh Blue Point oysters. After everything was arranged, the waiter asked, "Will there be anything else at the moment?"

Cavanaugh held her gaze. "Yes. We'll need another bottle of champagne."

Emmett threw back more of the sickeningly sweet drink and tried to rein in his lustful thoughts. Sitting across from Elizabeth Sloane had evolved into the worst kind of torture. She wasn't even the type of woman he preferred; he liked earthy, raw, lusty women who gave as good as they got. But watching her eat oysters, then lick the salty flavor from her plump lips, was so innocently erotic that he couldn't tear his eyes away.

Foolish, the idea to sit in the main room. He'd thought the more people who witnessed them together, the better. But now he wished they were alone.

*Where you would . . . what? You'll never have her,
Cavanaugh.*

She wore dark green velvet this evening, the cut high
on her neck to contrast with the beautiful pale gold of her
hair. They drew stares from all across the room—patrons
no doubt curious about why the two were dining together.
The golden beauty and the guttersnipe. Let them talk;
word would reach Sloane's ears faster that way. Emmett
nearly grinned. What he wouldn't give to see her brother's
face upon learning the news.

Everyone came out ahead in this plan. Sloane would be
annoyed, Emmett would relish annoying him, and Miss
Sloane gained a chance to start her investment firm. Not
to mention, Emmett would learn more about the financial
stability of Northeast Railroad. There was no drawback,
unless one counted his perplexing physical reaction to her
presence. He hadn't expected to feel anything for her, but
every time he saw her gray eyes twinkle, every time she
smiled at him, it was like a club to the gut.

He just needed to try harder to ignore his body's response. There had been an attraction to various unsuitable
ladies over the years, and he'd successfully fought it. This
one should be no different.

He forked an oyster into his mouth, enjoying the slick,
briny taste as it slid down his throat. When he went to
wipe his mouth, he noticed her gaze transfixed on his lips,
a flush staining her cheeks. Good Christ, was that . . . for
him? His body tightened, pulse pounding in his groin. The
room could have been on fire for all he knew because
everything had ceased to exist. Everything except her.

She broke the contact first, lowering her head to stare
at her plate, and Emmett gulped the rest of his drink, desperate to cool himself down. What was this woman doing
to him?

She cleared her throat. "Is it true you bought the steel mill where you once worked?"

Finally, a topic that would squash any interest in him. His past was not normally up for discussion, but she needed to hear it, obviously. "Yes, I did. Does that shock you?"

"No." She delicately dabbed at her mouth with a linen napkin. "I find it fascinating. Will you tell me the whole story? No doubt there's more to it than what I've heard."

Fascinating? "I'm not certain this is suitable dinner conversation."

She cocked her head. "Would you rather discuss the weather? Or perhaps the latest fashions on the Ladies' Mile?"

"God, no," he murmured. "I was twelve when I left for Pittsburgh."

"And you grew up downtown?"

"Yes." He clamped his jaw shut. That portion of his life was closed off for good, no matter who asked.

"And you found work in a mill. What was it like?"

He thought for a moment. "Grueling. Twelve-hour shifts, seven days a week. No breaks or even time to eat. What I remember most is the sweat. You've never imagined anything like the heat inside a steel mill. I lost twenty pounds in the first three months I worked there, which is quite a bit on a paper-thin twelve-year-old boy." All day long the sweat had run down his arms, his legs, and collected in his boots. Emmett hated to feel that way now, with perspiration clinging to his clothes and skin.

"How did you come to purchase it, then?"

"I was injured, and the company gave me a small settlement, which I successfully invested a few times over. Came to New York, started playing the market. In four years, I had enough to buy the mill."

"And East Coast Steel was born."

The tone of her voice, it sounded like admiration . . . when it should have been revulsion. She'd romanticized something truly awful and hideous in his past. If she had any idea of the things he'd done in his life, the things he'd seen . . .

The waiter arrived with more food, this time a baked salmon with dill sauce. Emmett pretended to attend to his dinner while his thoughts churned.

Elizabeth Sloane thoroughly confused him. Why wasn't she uncomfortable dining with him? At the very least, she should have taken stock of the room to see who would be spreading gossip tomorrow. But she hadn't assessed their fellow diners once that he'd noticed. Instead, she'd stared at his lips and peppered him with questions on his past. What the hell was happening here?

He never misjudged people. The ability to read others, to know what they were thinking, had made him a millionaire many, many times over. He knew what investors needed to hear in order to hand over their money. Or what workers needed to hear in order to avoid labor strikes. So why couldn't he figure out one high-society princess?

He searched for an impersonal topic. "Would you care to discuss your progress on our wager? I'm curious as to how you're doing after a few days."

"I haven't invested the money yet. I have been working on a plan."

"Stocks take time to mature, so that must mean you're hoping to capitalize on a one-day swing." He whistled. "You are either very confident or very foolish."

"Time will tell." She threw him an enigmatic smile and picked up a bite of salmon. He watched, mesmerized, as she slipped the piece in her mouth and then her pink tongue emerged to clean the dill sauce from the corner of her lips. His groin became heavy, his trousers growing tight. *Jesus, Mary, and Joseph.* Did she have any idea the eroticism of such a gesture?

"What's the largest amount of money you've made on the exchange in one day?" she asked, thankfully distracting him.

"Almost five hundred thousand. But that was in the panic of '73."

Her eyes grew wide. "That's impressive. You must know quite a bit about stocks."

"I do."

"What was the injury?"

Emmett frowned. "Pardon?"

"The injury in the mill, the one that prompted the settlement. What was it?"

"So curious," he murmured. "Are you certain you aren't aspiring to be another Nellie Bly?"

She gave him a chagrined smile. "I suppose that's a polite way of telling me it's none of my business."

Better she find out now, to erase any misconceptions she had about him. He propped his elbows on the chair rest, steepled his fingers. "I was burned. Chains holding a steel pipe overhead broke because the pipe hadn't been given time to properly cool. When it fell, the pipe landed on my back."

Her eyes rounded, filled with sympathy. Before she could say anything, he continued, "You see, I was rushing the other men. My shift was nearly over, and there was a brothel less than a mile from the mill. I was eager to get back to the girl I'd had a few nights before. So I convinced the other men that the chains would hold, to hurry up and move the pipe. And when the chains broke, two men died."

She stiffened, the sympathy in her expression now a memory, yet he had no intention of stopping. He lifted his flute and swirled the contents. "The union, assuming the company's equipment to blame, fought to get me a small settlement. I took that money. I took it and never said a word about how the accident came to be, that it was my fault, because I wanted out of that steel mill more than I wanted my next breath."

He could still feel it sometimes, the sweat. Woke up at night drenched in it. No, he had absolutely no regrets about getting out of the steel mill or the things he'd done since.

After downing the rest of his champagne, he placed his glass on the table with a thump. "Do not try and make me into something I'm not, Miss Sloane."

Her throat worked before she croaked, "And what is that, Mr. Cavanaugh? What exactly am I making you out to be?"

He leaned in and held her startled gaze. "Nice."

An awkward silence stretched, and the sounds of the dining room swirled around them. Lizzie concentrated on her food and tried to get Cavanaugh's warning out of her head. No doubt he'd been trying to scare her with his story, but the opposite had occurred. There were many layers to the man, all of them fascinatingly complex. He was flawed, just like the rest of the mortals on earth, but it was the flaws she wanted to unwrap and study like the stock tables she loved.

And that worried her. Her purpose was not to examine all the various facets of Emmett Cavanaugh, but to save her family's finances.

Her gaze bounced around the room as she tried to regain control of her emotions. Near the windows she spotted two older women who happened to be terrible gossips, their bold stares fixed on Cavanaugh as they whispered to one another. Both wore clear looks of disapproval, and Lizzie grew annoyed on his behalf. He'd done nothing untoward tonight to deserve their criticism.

Then the ladies looked at her, and she could read the judgment from across the room. *Is that Elizabeth Sloane? Why on earth is she dining with him? Notice how she isn't even paying him attention, how uncomfortable she appears.*

She straightened her spine. She didn't want anyone feeling sorry for her or believing she was here against her will. True, he hadn't given her much choice in the matter, but no one need know that. Moreover, Cavanaugh had been a perfectly respectable dinner companion.

She did what came naturally, from years of training by governesses and deportment tutors: she pasted a smile on her face and launched into conversation. "You have a brother, I understand."

That question seemed to snap Cavanaugh out of his thoughts. He relaxed in his chair, his mouth curving. "Yes, I do. Brendan. He's a doctor."

"I can see you're fond of him."

"I am. He's annoyingly smart. Works himself to the bone nearly every day, practicing in the roughest parts the city."

"He must find it rewarding," she offered.

"I suppose, though I keep reminding him he needn't work. Save himself the aggravation."

"He could, but some people prefer to work."

"I suspect you fall into that category as well." He tapped his fingers on the edge of the table, his gaze shrewd. "Why stocks?"

She shrugged. "I like the excitement, the risk involved. And I've always had a head for numbers. In fact, my best memories are of my father reading the stock tables to me during breakfast."

"How old were you when he died?"

"Seven." A familiar ache welled up in her chest. "I remember not believing it, that he was truly gone. Even when I saw his body, I kept waiting for him to get up and tell me it was a big joke. I'm afraid I was a handful for poor Will."

For some reason, that made Cavanaugh's lips twitch. "I can only imagine. You're smarter than other women, probably were even back then."

She inhaled sharply, drawing the unexpected compliment deep inside her, to where uncertainty and self-doubt thrived. No one had ever called her smart—no one other than her brother, though he used the word as a way of discouraging her ambitions. Will tended to say things such as, "*You're too smart to go into business,*" and, "*Let a husband appreciate your intelligence with money.*"

It meant something that Cavanaugh thought her smart.

She picked up the full glass of cold champagne, tried not to let him see how he was affecting her. "I don't know that I'm so clever. Perhaps just more reckless."

"Recklessness is never a bad thing." Something about his tone, the way the low, husky words rumbled from his chest caused her body to heat. Was he flirting with her? No, she must be misreading him. He preferred actresses, as everyone knew.

She tried to return them to safer waters. "In business, Mr. Cavanaugh?"

"In everything. But there's a difference between recklessness and stupidity." He placed his fork and knife down carefully on his gold-rimmed plate. "And I think it's safe for you to call me Emmett, at least during dinner."

"That would hardly be proper."

Cavanaugh said nothing, merely reached one large hand toward his delicate champagne glass. His skin looked rough and tanned, with fine brown hairs on the knuckles. Strong, capable hands that were different from any she'd seen. She wondered what they would feel like, if they would be gentle.

"Do you remember," he said, "what happened when you Knickerbockers were determined to keep the new monied-types out of the Academy of Music?" He took a sip and leaned back in his chair. "Alva rallied everyone who'd ever been shut out, myself included, and raised the money to build the Metropolitan Opera House. And now what's happened to your precious Academy? It's become a vaudeville house."

"And your point?"

"My point, Miss Sloane, is that your rules don't stand a chance, no matter how fervently Mrs. Caroline Schermerhorn Astor wills it to be so. Money always wins, and too many of us undesirables have it now."

Lizzie bristled, resenting that he lumped her in with the rest of the old families so desperate to retain the status quo. "They are not my rules. I was never in favor of keeping the Vanderbilts out of the Academy, not that I had anything to do with it considering I was *fifteen* at the time. The world is changing, and if you think I'm not eager for it, then you don't know me at all."

His eyes glittered, and he pressed his lips together, as if amused but desperate not to show it. "Is it so hard to admit I'm right?"

"Fine. Emmett," she snapped quietly.

He let out a short noise, and she suspected it might be

a laugh, albeit a rusty one. Sort of like the hinges on a door long gone unopened.

"You wanted me to make a fool of myself." She swallowed the rest of her champagne, and her head swam. How many times had her glass been refilled?

"No," he said. "I wanted to point out the absurdity of continuing to call me Mr. Cavanaugh." His face softened, and her chest expanded with giddiness. Goodness, he was attractive. Little wonder why actresses fell at his feet.

"I have another question for you." He leaned in and lowered his voice. "Why hide behind a man's name when you start your investment firm? You're a Sloane. I'd think you could do anything you pleased and no one would deny you a thing."

The comment nearly caused her to chuckle bitterly. He'd be surprised how much she was denied, because of both her station and her gender. Even if women were welcome on Wall Street, none of them would be from the old families of New York society. Young unmarried ladies of Lizzie's set could never do what they pleased. Nevertheless, this venture could not fail—the future of the Sloanes hinged on it—so if employing subterfuge for a short time helped her succeed, she would not hesitate.

"Women with my background are not supposed to work. We're bred to support a husband and run a household. It's exactly as you first assumed, that my life has not prepared me for more than parties and dress fittings. But I need to do more—I *can* do more. Society will come to accept it, after I've proven myself."

"So the investors will believe the advice you're dishing out is from me?"

"Not quite," she said. "They merely need to believe you're invested in the financial success of the firm. That I have your ear. I'll do the rest."

A shadow fell over their table. "Hello, Lizzie."

Lizzie drew back swiftly and found Henry Rutlidge standing unsteadily at her side. His eyes were rimmed red, and his slick, brown hair was mussed. Not to mention, he reeked of spirits. Was he inebriated? "Mr. Rutlidge. You know Mr. Cavanaugh, I assume."

"Evening, Cavanaugh." Henry gave a jaunty salute.

Emmett's lip curled. "Rutlidge."

"Here I was at the Fifth Avenue Hotel," Henry slurred, "having drinks, when my friends and I decided to pop over here for dinner. Could hardly believe it when I heard you were here, too—and with Cavanaugh, no less. I said, 'I've got to go and save Lizzie from that bouncer!'" He turned to Emmett. "No offense intended, Cavanaugh."

Emmett downed the remaining champagne in his glass. "Oh, no offense taken."

Lizzie frowned at both the insult from Henry and the barely restrained loathing from Emmett. This could be very bad, indeed. "I am fine," she told Henry quietly. "I do not need rescuing. Mr. Cavanaugh and I are merely having dinner. Perhaps you should go home, Henry."

He suddenly clutched the table. "Whoa. The room has started to spin. Do you feel it, Lizzie?"

"You're *drunk*, Rutlidge," Emmett enunciated slowly. "No one feels it but you."

"Come on, Cavanaugh. You're no stranger to the drink." Henry leaned close to Lizzie and spoke in a stage whisper. "He lived in the Old Brewery for a time, I heard. Ran with a gang. A regular b'hoy, he was."

"That would be a feat, considering the Methodists took over the building a few years before I was born," Emmett said dryly. "But I'm certain I could remember a trick or two from my days downtown, if you're interested in following me outside."

Oh, for heaven's sake. The last thing they needed was a brawl in the middle of the Delmonico's dining room. "Mr. Cavanaugh, thank you for dinner. I think it would be best if I saw Mr. Rutlidge home."

Emmett's jaw clenched, and Lizzie pleaded with her eyes for him to understand. She had known Henry forever, yet she'd never seen him like this. Who knew how many more insults he would lob at Emmett before things took a disastrous turn?

Emmett signaled a waiter. "I'll take you both in my carriage."

"No, that is unnecessary," she rushed out. "I am perfectly capable of getting him into a hack."

"Nevertheless, it would be my pleasure, Miss Sloane." She opened her mouth to refuse, but his cold, dark gaze stopped her flat. His tone brooked no argument as he said, "And I insist."

Chapter Three

Men will seek the essential principles, but all the nicety and elegance of polished manners must and do come through woman.

—American Etiquette and Rules of Politeness, 1883

Henry lapsed into unconsciousness on the ride home, thankfully preventing any further interaction between the two men, and Lizzie breathed a sigh of relief. Noting Emmett's rigid jaw, she deduced he was still quite angry—not that she could blame him. Henry's appearance and drunken, rude comments had upset her as well. For some reason, Henry had been determined to insult Emmett into a reaction, which made no sense.

This new side of Henry worried her. He was usually so jovial and sweet. Of course, she'd never seen him inebriated before.

Since Henry was sprawled on one side of the opulent carriage, Emmett and Lizzie had been forced to sit next to one another on the other side. With his huge shoulders and long limbs, Emmett took up a good amount of space. She tried to put distance between them, but there was no place to go.

He stared out the small window, more remote, more untouchable than before. An incredible gulf had risen between them, and she found herself strangely eager to breach the distance.

"I'm sorry our evening was cut short," she said.

"Are you?"

"Of course. I wouldn't say the words if I didn't mean them."

When he turned, his expression revealed nothing. His emotions were completely under control, and she couldn't read him. "Are you truly considering marrying that imbecile?"

"He is not an imbecile. And I have never seen him intoxicated before. He's not a habitual drinker."

"Oh, yes," Emmett remarked with a disbelieving roll of his eyes. "No doubt this was a celebration of some kind. There's always one to be had for men like him."

She cast a glance at Henry's sleeping form. He looked so boyish and young, like the Henry she remembered while growing up. "He's not a bad sort."

"Undoubtedly—until the liquor kicks in. Elizabeth and Henry," Emmett drawled dramatically, as if on the stage. "You should marry him. You'd be the darlings of New York society."

"That's a terrible reason to marry someone." The only reason to marry was for love, in Lizzie's opinion. And as fond as she was of Henry, she didn't love him. That information, however, was none of Emmett Cavanaugh's business.

"I can't think of one better, actually."

"You're a cynic, then," she returned.

"Indeed, I am. Among other things."

"Such as?" He didn't answer, just stared down at her. So she elbowed him in the ribs. "Come, now. I'll trade you my faults for yours."

Even in the low light she could see his mouth quirk. "Did you just jab at me with your elbow, Miss Sloane?"

She did it again. "No." He jerked in surprise, and she had to bite her lip to keep from giggling.

His focus settled on her mouth, where her bottom lip was currently caught between her teeth. "Have dinner with me again," he said in the rough, husky tone that caused her stomach to flutter.

"Why?"

"To conclude the wager. We'll either toast your success or drown your sorrows."

"Oh, I won't fail."

"Is arrogance one of your faults, then?"

"Says the man who believes only men to have the stomach for—what did you call it?—this 'cutthroat, nasty business,'" she retorted.

"I'm beginning to see why Rutlidge drinks," Emmett said dryly.

She elbowed him again, more seriously this time. "Take that back. Henry and I are merely friends."

"Miss Sloane, if you nudge me once more, I fear there will be consequences."

Lizzie didn't believe a word of it. His dark eyes were twinkling, and he looked on the verge of actually smiling. Heaven help her if he actually laughed.

"What sort of consequences?" she blurted before she thought better of it. She was goading him, pushing, without considering what might happen. Yet she couldn't seem to stop herself.

At that moment, their eyes locked, and all the available air left the carriage. Shadows played across the planes of his handsome face, highlighting the small delectable dent on the tip of his chin. A buzz of sensation broke out over her skin, and she could not look away. His lips were full when he wasn't scowling or frowning, and she wondered how they would feel on hers. She'd kissed only two men in her life, Henry being one of them, but no kiss had caused her to lose her head, not like the novels promised would happen when a man embraced you.

Something told her Emmett was different, that this man could cause a woman to lose her head. So did that scare her . . . or tempt her beyond reason?

He leaned in, ever so slowly, and she held her breath, remaining perfectly still. They were so close she could see the hint of stubble on his jaw, while a faint trace of wool and cigar smoke teased her nose. *Please, kiss me. Just once, so I'll know.*

Suddenly, the wheels hit a bump in the road, jostling the carriage, and Henry snorted loudly. Emmett and Lizzie both jerked apart, the moment broken.

While he turned to the window, Lizzie tried to calm her racing heart. Entertaining feelings for this man was a considerably bad idea. She barely knew him. And he was too . . . forceful. She wanted someone who was understanding and peaceful. Easygoing. Who would give her room to breathe. Heaven knew, a man with Emmett Cavanaugh's reputation, he would be a locomotive that crushed anything in his path.

The carriage slowed as they arrived in Gramercy Park. Lizzie reached across to gently pat Henry's cheek. Her friend didn't stir, not even when Emmett opened the door. "Henry, wake up. You're home."

"Allow me." Emmett stood outside the carriage. He leaned in, grabbed Henry's ankle with one large hand, and pulled hard. Henry slid to the carriage floor with a bone-jarring thud, and Emmett continued to drag him toward the door. Bending, he threw Henry over his shoulder like a sack of flour.

Mouth agape, Lizzie scurried after them. Emmett's driver, a stocky, muscle-bound man, opened the wrought-iron gate to the stairs, and Emmett climbed them easily, as if he weren't lugging a large man over his shoulder. He pounded on the front door, the wood rattling with the force of the blows.

The Rutlidges' butler, Price, came to the door. The servant did not seem all that surprised to have an unconscious Henry on the doorstep. "Come in, please," Price told Emmett.

Lizzie followed Emmett inside, and they continued to the small receiving room Henry's mother used for close friends. "Put him there, if you please." Price motioned to a sofa.

Emmett dumped Henry on the furniture with no ceremony. He straightened and looked at Lizzie, a silent question in his eyes.

"I will rouse the cook for some coffee," Price told the room and disappeared.

Emmett's dark stare remained on Lizzie. She thought back to the moment in the carriage, when he'd nearly kissed her. Oh, how she'd wanted it, even though she knew it was madness. Reckless and running counter to everything she'd been brought up to believe, that kissing men you hardly knew was insanity. A sure way to ruin her future. She'd kissed Henry only twice, and they'd known each other all their lives.

This . . . attraction to Emmett Cavanaugh was dangerous. And getting in a carriage with Emmett now, alone, would only mean more temptation.

"I should stay and make certain he is all right," she said quietly.

"Of course." Emmett dipped his chin, his expression a mask of civility. "Then I bid you good night."

His long legs carried him out of the room swiftly. "Emmett," she called, and he stopped on the threshold. "Thank you for dinner."

"You are welcome," he returned over his shoulder.

He disappeared and soon the front door closed, allowing Lizzie to draw her first deep breath of the evening.

"Ah, you've returned."

Emmett handed his top hat and walking stick to his butler and glanced up in the direction of the voice. His brother, Brendan, came limping down the stairs, leaning heavily on the railing to keep the weight off his left leg.

Five years younger than Emmett, Brendan had been run over by a wagon as a boy. Emmett had been up to no good with the Popes at all hours, avoiding a father who drank too much and liked to use his fists. With no one to care for him, six-year-old Brendan had gone out to steal food one afternoon, slipped, and gotten caught under a passing wagon. Lucky to be alive, they said at the time . . . but not so lucky as to retain full use of both legs.

Though Brendan was now a doctor—a graduate of the Harvard Medical School—the ache in Emmett's chest, the crushing guilt over his brother's affliction, never let up. It had been Emmett's job to protect Brendan, and he'd failed. Their mother had disappeared shortly after, ending up dead four years later in San Francisco—not that Emmett blamed her for leaving. Patrick Cavanaugh had been one cruel bastard.

From that day forward, Emmett had vowed to do

anything—beg, cheat, or steal, if necessary—to get his brother out of Five Points. That resolve had only magnified when Emmett's two half sisters were born. His three siblings would not suffer harm or go hungry, not while Emmett had breath left in his body.

Brendan reached the bottom of the stairs, a smile on his face. "Destroy any companies today?" he asked, his voice teasing.

"Just two," Emmett answered with all seriousness.

"God, you're telling the truth. I'm glad I'll never have to go up against you. Except in billiards, of course. Can I tempt you into a game?"

"Mr. Cavanaugh." Colin James, Emmett's secretary, strode swiftly down the hallway. Twenty-four and smart as a whip, Colin remained a permanent fixture in the mansion, residing in one of the guest suites, since Emmett tended to work round-the-clock. "I have your messages, sir."

Emmett took the cables and slips of paper and flipped through them. Nothing that couldn't wait. "Tomorrow," he told Colin, "I want you to find someone who can get us the Northeast Railroad P&L statements. No matter what you have to pay. I have a feeling the company might be ripe for the pickings. But that's enough for tonight. We'll pick up in the morning."

"Very good, sir." With a broad smile, Colin raced up the main stairs like a man possessed.

"He's sweet on some shopgirl over at Lord and Taylor," Brendan murmured, watching Colin depart. "I think he's taking her out dancing tonight. I offered to show him some steps, but . . ."

Brendan chuckled, amused, but Emmett could see no cause for levity. When he closed his eyes, he could still see his brother's small, broken body on the bed. "Brendan . . ."

"It was a jest, Em." Brendan slapped Emmett's shoulder. "You're too serious. Come on. Let's play for a bit."

Emmett could sense his brother would not relent, so they made their way to the billiard room, one of Emmett's favorite places in the house. No expense had been spared here. A five-light gasolier illuminated the huge rococo-inspired billiard table, a one-of-a-kind piece complete with an intricately carved walnut base and green baize-covered slate surface. The mosaic-tiled floor—imported from a palace in Italy—had been reinforced just to hold the massive table. The walls were papered red with gold accents, and the furniture held a Far Eastern flare. Brendan often called the room the "opium den."

"How were your patients today?" Emmett asked his brother.

"Sick." Brendan leaned against a stick, a cut-crystal glass full of whiskey cradled in his hand. "I poured you some gin."

Emmett murmured his thanks as he went to select a stick. Out of the corner of his eye, he saw Kelly stride in. Kelly was Emmett's driver and guard, as well as the only person Emmett fully trusted—and that was only because the two of them had grown up in Five Points together. They'd fought and scraped their way out of one of the worst hellholes on earth, and there wasn't anything one wouldn't do for the other.

"Where were you tonight?" Brendan asked Emmett. "Off with your Mrs. Rose?"

"Gettin' into trouble, is what he was doing," Kelly answered. "With one Miss Elizabeth Sloane."

Brendan whistled. "Elizabeth Sloane? That's a new one. Not your usual type of woman, is it, Em?"

Emmett didn't answer, and Kelly prompted, "Well, go on. Tell him, then."

"It's business," Emmett said, selecting his stick and testing its weight. "I'm backing her company."

"Over dinner." Kelly poured a glass of fresh orange juice and sat. Kelly never drank alcohol, not since they had left Five Points. Emmett just glared at him.

"Dinner!" Brendan exclaimed. "Well, that is surprising."

Emmett finished arranging the balls on the table and lifted the rack. "You break."

Brendan stepped to the table, lined up, and jammed his cue forward. A loud smack, and the balls careened around the felt. Two went in, one striped and one solid. Brendan claimed stripes and moved in for another shot. He made one, missed the next.

Emmett approached as Brendan returned to his drink and the earlier conversation. "So why is taking Elizabeth Sloane to dinner going to cause trouble?"

"I suspect her brother'll have a thing or two to say about Bishop's dinner tonight," Kelly said. "Considering pissing the brother off was the motive for takin' her out in the first place."

Kelly was the only person Emmett allowed to use his old childhood nickname, Bishop. Kelly used the name out of habit, but Emmett was not proud of the way he'd earned it. He ignored them and concentrated on sinking the solid-colored balls.

"But Emmett would never do that. He'd never use some innocent woman out of spite. Would you, Em?"

Emmett couldn't even look at Kelly, who knew exactly what Emmett was capable of, so he kept his gaze focused on the table as he put away a second ball.

"You aren't sweet on her, are you?"

Emmett stopped to scowl at his brother. "Don't be

ridiculous. Even if I was, which I'm not, it would be a waste of time."

Brendan and Kelly exchanged a brief glance that set Emmett's teeth on edge. "Because she's a step above? A girl with Elizabeth Sloane's money and pedigree can choose whomever she wants, I think," Brendan said. "And I'm coming to like the idea of having her as my sister-in-law."

"No one has even mentioned marriage, Bren. Besides, you don't even know her," Emmett growled, and thrust his cue forward, smacking two balls and missing the pocket.

Brendan sauntered forward for his turn. "Don't need to know her. What matters is her social standing. Have you thought about what happens in three years when Katie wants to have her coming out? Or the next year when Claire follows suit? That's not a lot of time, Emmett. How are you going to get society to accept them?"

"I don't give a damn if society accepts them or not," Emmett snapped, and reached for his gin. "And I have a hefty dowry that says they will."

Kelly muttered, "Tell that to Alva Vanderbilt."

Poised over the table for a shot, Brendan paused and straightened. "Kelly's right. Money can't buy acceptance, not with these people. And you should care whether Katie and Claire are shunned or not. Because you want them to make good marriages, to men who will take care of them like"—he waved his hand to sweep the room—"this. Or do you want them on the Lower East Side, stealing and grasping to put food on the table?"

The idea of his half sisters struggling for one second had Emmett's chest tightening into a fist. He well remembered the uncertainty, the hunger, and the anger of everyday life in the slums. "They are both heiresses in their own right. Just as you never need work, should you come to your senses."

"I know, and we all appreciate your generosity. But like it or not, their husbands will control whatever money Katie and Claire possess. What happens if they fall in love with the wrong man, instead of selecting one you've approved? The papers are full of men who've lost their fortunes."

"You gotta give it to Harvard," Kelly said, using his nickname for Brendan. "He's makin' a lot of sense. Elizabeth Sloane gives you a way into Mrs. Astor's circle."

Emmett had never cared about Caroline Astor or her precious "circle." Business was what mattered. He'd always been friendly enough with the men of high society, friendly enough to launch several interests with them over the years. That was the way of it. Emmett bothered himself with the financial gain, never the social side of things. He damn well wouldn't start now.

"I'd never give my blessing for any union between one of the girls and some goddamn fool bent on spending her money. And even if I did, I'd take a brickbat to him before I let her money be pissed away."

"Which Claire or Katie would appreciate, no doubt." Brendan shot Emmett an amused look. "You'd best prepare yourself, Em. They read the society pages every day. Every. Day. They're already planning the guest list."

Emmett didn't want to think of debuts and marriages. The girls were too young, for God's sake. He could still remember them toddling around his first house over off Union Square.

But Brendan was right, damn it. Emmett hadn't considered the future. His intention had been to learn something at dinner, some insight into Sloane's financial stability, but he'd been so blinded by Elizabeth that he'd forgotten even that.

He downed the rest of his gin. "Why don't you marry Elizabeth Sloane, then? Or another one like her?"

"Sure. All women hope for a lame doctor still mooching off his older brother. I'll have a wife by breakfast."

Emmett narrowed his eyes on his brother. Brendan was smarter than all of them put together. After his injury, he'd been housebound, where he had spent all his time reading. But Emmett knew better than to argue; stubborn pride ran in their blood.

Just as he knew there would be no society wife. Not now. Not ever.

"Get back to the game, Brendan. I've got work to do."

The door to Emmett's study opened, and Kelly poked his head in. "Sloane's just pulled up. You wanna see him?"

Satisfaction surged through Emmett. Fourteen hours. It had taken only fourteen hours for the news of the dinner to reach Will Sloane's ears and prompt a visit. Not bad, considering Sloane had been in Boston yesterday.

"Oh, yes," Emmett told his longtime friend. "I definitely want to see him. Colin, take a walk."

Emmett's secretary nodded and rose from his desk to disappear into the depths of the massive house. Emmett went back to his reports, though he didn't see them.

He'd hardly slept last night, thinking of Elizabeth's face in the carriage. He knew when a woman wanted to be kissed. When her eyes turned dreamy and she moistened her lips. When she stared at a man like her next breath depended on his mouth meeting hers. Elizabeth Sloane, of the Washington Square Sloanes, had looked at him in precisely that manner—even after learning what he'd done at the steel mill. Unbelievable. It made no sense.

Christ, how he wanted her. Craved her with the same unrelenting drive that had burned in his gut to get out of the slums. Out of the steel mill. The same determination that had him up at dawn each morning to amass more wealth, ensuring his family never experienced poverty again.

If he'd given in to his baser instincts, God knows what might have happened. He'd never kissed a Knickerbocker. Did they use tongues? No doubt she would have slapped him. Hell, if he were in her shoes, he'd slap him, too.

In the end, what he desired made no difference. He would ignore the attraction between them as he'd ignored countless other women who thought of him as a prize to be won. Emmett knew precisely what he was, and there was no prize underneath the expensive tailoring and pleasing face.

The door swung open, and Kelly came through. "Mr. William Sloane," he announced properly, as if he were a butler and not a former bare-knuckled boxer.

Sloane stormed inside. Emmett had never seen the man so disheveled. His blond hair, normally slicked to perfection, was a mess, and he still wore his evening clothes from the night before. His expression thunderous, he took a threatening step toward Emmett. "My sister? Have you no goddamned scruples, Cavanaugh?"

Kelly swiftly inserted himself between Sloane and the desk, an impenetrable wall Sloane would never topple.

Sloane kept his furious gaze pinned on Emmett. "Call off your guard dog, you thug, and face me like a man."

Kelly snuck a glance over his shoulder, and Emmett jerked his chin. Kelly withdrew, leaving the room and closing the door softly, though Emmett knew his friend wouldn't go far.

Emmett leaned back. "Would you care to sit down?"

"No. What I'd like to do is punch you in the face."

Emmett suppressed a smile. "You could try, Sloane, but I wouldn't advise it."

"Yes, we all know you're no stranger to violence. Do you think I haven't learned about your past? Why they called you the Bishop—"

Emmett shot to his feet, slapped his palms on his desk. "Careful. You's best be very careful about what you're sayin' next." He heard the slip in his speech, the guttural tone and pronunciation of his youth thanks to the rage now burning inside him. He forced himself to take a deep breath, to calm down. He needed to face Sloane as an equal.

"Or else what?" Sloane shot back, nostrils flaring. "If you think I am afraid of you or your ruffian friend out there, you are dead wrong."

"Is that so?"

"Did you . . . touch her?"

Emmett lowered into his chair and folded his hands. He hadn't touched her, but Elizabeth's beautiful face floated through his mind, her skin flushed and pouty lips glistening in the low light of the carriage. Oh, he'd been dying to touch her. Still hungered for it, even this morning. Not that he could have her. But a man's cock did not possess the ability to reason, sadly.

"Is that what you're worked up about? Worried I've tainted your precious blue Dutch blood?"

Sloane closed his eyes as if in pain, his chest heaving. "If you touch her, I will kill you with my bare hands. I may not have grown up on the streets with the Popes, but I will see it done. Do you understand me?"

"So violent. You are full of surprises, Sloane," Emmett said sardonically.

"You are deliberately toying with her, attempting to ruin her reputation because of some petty desire for revenge against me. All because I backed out of one deal a few months ago. Christ!" Sloane threw up his hands. "Are you really that insane?"

Emmett pictured Elizabeth's molten-gray eyes, how they turned to liquid silver in the gaslight. Now he wished he *had* kissed her, just so he could throw that fact in Sloane's face.

"I know it might be tough for you to believe, Sloane, but not everything is about you. Perhaps I truly like your sister."

Sloane's lips thinned, and he spat, "You're incapable of feelings. You have no heart. No conscience. No morals. But make no mistake: I will hold you accountable if her reputation suffers. She will not be cast into a disreputable light because you hope to shame my family."

Emmett flicked open the silver-guilloche enamel cigar box on his desk and withdrew one of the special H. Upmanns he imported from Havana. Using the platinum cutter, he snipped the end. "Your sister came to see me. Was I supposed to turn her away? Is that how you fancy Knickerbockers learned to treat ladies?"

Sloane gripped the back of a chair, his brow lowered. "My sister paid a call on you? Here? What did she want?"

"A dinner companion?"

"No. She has Rutlidge for that, and any other number of men who are . . ."

"Better suited?" Emmett struck a match and lit the end of the cigar. He drew the smoke into his mouth, savored the sharp nutty flavor, and blew it out. "Come, say what you really mean, Sloane."

"Yes, better suited than you, Cavanaugh." Sloane pointed a finger at Emmett. "I'll use everything I have to bring you down, if need be. She's my only family left, and I mean to see her settled with someone who will take care of her and respect her. Not a man who cavorts around town with any woman who's had a two-bit part in a burlesque show."

Emmett sighed and took another drag off his cigar. This conversation had turned tedious. "You could use everything you have—and borrow even more—and that wouldn't touch me. And you know it." Cigar clamped between his teeth, he rose and slipped his hands in his trouser pockets. "You've made your point, Sloane. Now stop annoying me, and take your privileged ass back downtown."

Sloane fumed, his eyes narrowed to slits. "Is it any wonder why they don't accept you? Why you were unable to buy your way into the Academy of Music or the Union Club. Why you are never invited to the exclusive parties. There are some things your money cannot buy. My sister happens to be one of those things. Stay the hell away from her."

Sloane spun on his heel and flung open the study door with such force that it bounced against the wall. Kelly appeared, and Sloane brushed by him, slamming into the driver's shoulder. Squat and sturdy with a physique like steel, Kelly didn't even budge, and Sloane stormed off.

"He seemed a might pissed off. Guess we won't be toastin' your nuptials any time soon." Kelly closed the door and strolled in. He slid into a chair and put his feet up on Emmett's desk.

Emmett rolled the cigar in his fingertips and exhaled a mouthful of smoke. "I'm not worried about Sloane."

"You can see where he's comin' from, though. You got sisters. You know how you'd feel if someone was playin' one of 'em, Bish."

"I'm not playing her."

Kelly raised one eyebrow. He didn't even need to say it, that's how well they knew one another.

"Fine. But I'll do what I damn well please, whether Sloane approves or not."

"Is that what this is about, getting a jab at Sloane? And before you try to think of a lie, boy-o, allow me to remind you that I seen the two a' yous together last night."

Nothing had happened. Emmett could state this as fact, but Kelly wouldn't care. Kelly would only bring up the fact that Miss Sloane was a far cry above the women with whom Emmett normally dallied. As if Emmett weren't painfully aware of that already. "Since when have I ever asked you to weigh in on my private life?"

"Since never . . . and that's never stopped me before. Best be careful. You might get more than you bargained for with this one."

Chapter Four

There are no purely good manners in the absence of correct tastes.

—American Etiquette and Rules of Politeness, 1883

A knock sounded on her dressing room door, and Lizzie barely had time to hide her stock tables and notes before her brother burst in.

"Will!" she said, pulling the lace curtain of her dressing table closed. "You've returned."

Her brother had a strange light in his eye as he bent to kiss her cheek. "Hello, Lizzie. I apologize for barging in, but I need to speak with you."

He shifted away, and she felt a stab of alarm. He looked terrible. And had that been whiskey she smelled on his breath? Why were all the men in her life suddenly drinking heavily?

"Is there something the matter?"

Will leaned against the wall near her dressing table, folded his arms. His stern expression reminded her of the day he'd caught her replacing her tutor's books with stock tables. "It is my understanding," he began, "that you paid a call to Emmett Cavanaugh this week."

Oh. So this was about the dinner. In her worry over Will's discovering her stock research, she'd forgotten. "Yes, I did."

He waited for her to elaborate, and when she didn't, he prompted, "May I ask why you would risk your reputation in such a reckless manner?"

"Curiosity," she lied. "He is one of your friends, after all."

"*Friends?*" Will's lip curled slightly. "Why on earth would you believe that?"

So Will did not like Cavanaugh. Lizzie hadn't expected that. "You have dinner with him and those other two men every month."

"How could you possibly know about those meetings?"

She snorted. "Like I'd tell you." No need getting their driver fired. But she'd learned ages ago of the monthly dinners at the Knickerbocker Club between Emmett Cavanaugh, Calvin Cabot, Theodore Harper, and her brother.

Will lifted a hand to rub his eyes.

"Will, you look tired. Perhaps you should—"

"Lizzie, please. Those meetings . . . You shouldn't know of them. No one should know of them. They are for business only. Do you understand?"

Business. Sloane business, which meant they were his concern and not hers. A familiar ache flared in her stomach. *Have parties, Lizzie. Go to the opera. Leave the serious matters to me.*

"I haven't told anyone, if that's your worry. Though I do not understand why the meetings need to be kept secret."

"Because they must. Why did you agree to dinner with him?"

The more time that passed, the more secrets Will kept from her. He traveled constantly, rarely telling her where, not to mention his evasion about their financial well-being.

The business was his first concern—not her, the only family he had left.

Well, she had secrets of her own.

"Because he asked."

"You make it sound as if you are desperate for companionship. What about Rutledge? Have you considered how your cavorting with Cavanaugh will affect your relationship with—"

"Henry and I are friends, Will. Nothing more. I know you want me married and off your hands, but Henry is not the man for me."

"Lizzie, you're twenty-one. If I wanted you married off it would have happened years ago. Nevertheless, you can't wait forever. Rutledge is a good match. I like him, and I think he cares for you."

For the life of her, she couldn't picture Henry's face. All she could see was Emmett Cavanaugh's dark, piercing eyes in the carriage last evening. He'd almost kissed her, his hot stare never leaving her mouth. What would it have felt like? She bet the kiss would have been rough and wild, just like the man himself. She suppressed a shiver.

"Maybe I do not want to marry at all."

Will gave her a compassionate half smile. "You're just being stubborn. Of course you want to marry. One of us has to ensure the next generation of Sloanes."

"That's your responsibility, since my children won't be Sloanes. And I don't see why I need to marry." She cocked her head. "Does this have anything to do with the paintings and stocks you sold—"

"No," he cut her off. "I want you settled because I'm gone half the time, and I worry about you in this big place by yourself. And if something happened to me . . ." He sighed and dragged a hand through his hair. "I need to know you're taken care of. Mother and Father would have wanted that for you."

The mention of their parents hung heavily between them, a reminder of the grief they shared as siblings. Will had assumed so much at a young age after their father's death fourteen years ago. Lizzie hated to add to it. "I'll think on it," she hedged.

"That's a girl." He came over, pulled her to her feet, and wrapped her in a hug. "I want you to be happy, Lizzie."

"Then give me the money to start my brokerage firm."

He backed away and threw his hands up. "That again! You cannot go to work, like some low-class shopgirl. You're a Sloane, for God's sake. Think of your reputation. What would everyone say?"

"Will, I know the business is in trouble." Her brother flinched, but she continued. "There are things you aren't telling me. Please, let me help. I can—"

"Absolutely not." He pushed back the sides of his coat, shoved his hands in his pockets. "We've talked about this. Everything is fine. There's absolutely nothing for you to worry about. Let it go, Lizzie."

He was lying. She knew it in her bones. Yet each time she presented him with proof, he had an explanation ready.

Never mind him. The Sloanes would not go broke, not if Lizzie could do anything about it. She had been speculating in her head for years. Now she would take that ability and invest on a much larger scale for others, retaining a nice percentage for her efforts.

"Now," Will continued as he strode toward the door, "I've sent a note to Rutledge asking him to join us for dinner tonight. Being seen together will help put this god-awful Cavanaugh business behind you."

She thought briefly about refusing, since Will had no

business confirming dinner plans without checking with her first, but instead she blurted, "Why do you dislike Mr. Cavanaugh?"

Will stopped and turned, his expression hard. "He's the worst sort of man. Selfish and cold. If you knew some of the things he'd done in order to get ahead . . ." Will shook his head. "And the parade of women . . . Dear God. Stay away from him. I do not want you anywhere near Emmett Cavanaugh."

He opened her door. "I can only be thankful you two ate in the main dining room. If he'd taken you to a private dining suite, I would've had to kill him." Will closed the door, and his footsteps echoed down the hall.

Lizzie drummed her fingers on the table. She was more determined than ever to win her bet with Cavanaugh. Winning meant starting her own firm, and when she began turning a profit, she could help Will keep Northeast Railroad afloat as well as assume some of the household expenses. And with Cavanaugh as her backer, other investors would soon follow, she was sure of it.

Reaching beneath her dressing table, she withdrew her notes. She needed a plan for investing Emmett's money. Less than three weeks was hardly enough time to double a large sum. A heavy dose of luck would be crucial.

And she could not afford to fail.

A few days later, as fierce early January winds pummeled Wall Street, Lizzie watched as a young, auburn-haired man exited the restaurant located in the Mills Building. The man was Robbie, one of the traders Will used on the exchange. Lizzie planned to convince Robbie to make her trades as well.

Pulling her coat tighter, she hurried after him. "Robbie?"

He spun around and placed his hat on his head. "Yes?"

"I am Miss Sloane, William Sloane's sister." She thrust out her hand, which he shook reluctantly. "May we sit in my brougham and speak?"

"I suppose. Is Mr. Sloane there?" He glanced hopefully to the carriage waiting at the curb.

"Not today. I would just like a moment of your time." Without giving him a chance to refuse, she linked her arm with his and began pulling him toward the busy street.

Once they were settled, she said, "My brother has been quite pleased with your firm, and I'm wondering if you would be willing to assist me with a small matter."

"A small matter?"

"Yes, you see I have a large sum of money that I need to invest on the exchange. I know you usually deal with my brother, but I'm hopeful that you will be amenable to dealing with me as well."

"You need me to place an order for you?"

"Yes. Obviously, I cannot do it myself."

He scratched his square jaw, his gaze wary. "Why not go through your brother, if you don't mind my asking? Wall Street's no place for a proper lady, miss."

The tips of her ears warmed, and she fought her anger, struggling to remain calm. "Are you unwilling to take my money, merely because I am a woman?"

"Taking money from a woman isn't a problem for me, Miss Sloane. I just don't want to do nothing to upset your brother."

She could understand his concern, as Will had recently fired his previous investment firm. But Lizzie had no intention of letting Will learn of this transaction—at least not yet. "Let me worry about my brother."

He tapped his fingers on his knees. "So how much do you have to play with?"

"Ten thousand."

"That's a nice chunk of greenbacks. I'm thinking one of the oil companies like Pacific Coast. They've been making steady gains. Your brother—"

"Pardon me, but I don't have time for steady gains. I need to double this money in less than three weeks."

"Less than three weeks!" He jerked back, mouth agape. "You need a miracle, Miss Sloane."

"I was thinking a short sale. Remember the Regional Telegraph rumor in November?"

He chuckled. "Of course. I pocketed almost a thousand dollars off that one."

"I can imagine. Must have been a wild day on the floor." She would have given anything to be there. Single-day stock swings of that nature were rare and a thing of beauty—as long as you weren't on the losing end.

"It was." He stared at her a beat. "I'm not certain I can guarantee a large return in a short amount of time. I'll do my best, though."

"I'd like you to hold off investing it for now. Just until we see an opportunity for a large gain." She withdrew the check out of her small purse. "Here is the money."

He accepted the paper and tucked it into his inner coat pocket. "So I'm just to hold on to this for now?"

"Yes. I'll be in touch soon."

"I assume you'll be asking your brother's advice on where to invest it."

The implication was clear: no woman could possibly be savvy enough to understand stocks. Lizzie longed to set Robbie straight, to tell him she likely knew as much as he did, if not more. But he would learn of her skills in due time, provided he did not balk at dealing with her.

So, for now, she would play the game. "Yes, of course," she lied. "I plan to speak with him at my first opportunity."

* * *

As he did the first Thursday of every month, Emmett Cavanaugh entered an alley off Thirty-Second Street and stepped into the busy kitchens of the Knickerbocker Club. The four men always met here, on neutral territory, where the risk of discovery was low. Not his preferred location—the blue-blooded club had once refused his membership application—but the other three had agreed on it, so Emmett went along.

Hardly mattered where they met, as long as they continued their little cabal. This was how business ran—serious business, anyway. The men here tonight were the visionaries, with enough power and money to shape the future. And Emmett aimed to see those plans shaped to his benefit, which was the reason he never missed a meeting. Who knew what would be set in motion if he didn't show up to protect his interests?

The waiters and cooks ignored him as he strode along the white tiled floor, the staff too well-trained to gawk—not that Emmett would have cared either way. Once up the service stairs, he continued to the big private dining suite at the end of the hall. A waiter in a black coat and white shirt opened the paneled door for him without a word. Emmett handed over his stick, hat, and coat.

Harper had already arrived. "Cavanaugh," the man said, rising to shake Emmett's hand. A financial genius, Theodore Harper was a force to be reckoned with on the exchange. His New American Bank was one of the most powerful in the world, a backer to many of Emmett's ventures.

"Evening, Harper," Emmett said as the two of them re-laxed into seats around the large, linen-covered dining table. A waiter slipped a glass onto the table in front of

Emmett, his preferred drink of chilled gin, a hint of vermouth, and a twist of orange rind. A long way from the days in Ragpicker's Row, Emmett thought, when straight gin had been like mother's milk.

Emmett sipped the spirits, enjoying the burn of juniper and citrus as it slid down his throat. "Where are Sloane and Cabot?"

"Cabot was coming into Grand Central from out west somewhere," Harper said, referring to Calvin Cabot, the publisher of three of the country's most powerful newspapers. Harper swirled a tumbler of bourbon whiskey. "But he cabled that he'd be here. I have no idea why Sloane's late. He's usually early."

Perhaps Sloane wasn't coming. The man had been furious when he stormed into Emmett's house on Saturday morning. Emmett nearly smiled at the memory. Sloane could be a sanctimonious prick, and Emmett had been on the receiving end of Sloane's scorn more times than he could count. He'd be damned before he gave up an opportunity to annoy the elitist bastard.

"How's Mrs. Harper?" Emmett asked. Harper had met a young woman by chance on a train to St. Louis recently and quickly married her. Emmett happened to be very fond of the young but levelheaded woman.

Harper's rare grin emerged. "Wonderful, thank you. Still keeping me on my toes. She wants to go back to work at the perfume counter after the baby's born." He shook his head. "I may have to buy out Hoyt's and close the damn store just to keep her home."

Emmett chuckled. "Might not be a bad investment in either case. I've been looking to buy into a department store."

The door opened just then, and a perfectly polished William Sloane strode in. Harper came to his feet and shook Sloane's hand. Emmett remained seated, downing more gin, and if the slight bothered Sloane he gave no hint of it. Neither man acknowledged the other.

A waiter delivered a glass of red wine to Sloane's side as Sloane leaned toward the candle on the table to light a cigar. "Cabot coming?"

"Yes, he said he would be here," Harper said, then looked between Emmett and Sloane. "Are you two not speaking to one another?"

Emmett said nothing, and Sloane blew out a long, thin stream of smoke. "Don't be ridiculous."

The door bounced open, and the tall form of a perpetually harried Calvin Cabot appeared. "Sorry I'm late," he rushed out.

"We were just about to get started," Emmett told him, rising as handshakes were traded.

"Good." Cabot dropped into a seat, and a large tumbler of lager arrived by his right hand. "Sloane, I'm told you've got a real problem with the union in West Virginia again." There had been a large-scale railroad strike in the area a little more than ten years ago, and word had it the workers were mobilizing once more.

"I know. I'm headed there tomorrow." Sloane reached into his pocket and withdrew a sheet of paper. "Here's what I'd like you to print."

Cabot pocketed the piece without glancing at the contents. "Fine. Before we begin"—he lifted his glass for a long draught—"I heard Cavanaugh had dinner with your sister, Sloane . . ."

"I'd like to get down to business," Sloane snapped. "Some of us have places to be."

Cabot exchanged a look with Harper. Tension permeated the room like sweat at a dance hall. "Sure, if that's the way you want to play it. Who wants to go first?"

As the talks progressed, demands were thrown about and concessions granted. Emmett agreed to Cabot's request for cheap building materials out in San Francisco and Harper's desire to drive the stock down on a chemical company. When they got to Sloane, he turned to address Emmett for the first time that night. "I've decided not to go in on the Ninety-Sixth Street pier and waterfront property."

Harper and Cabot stilled, and the temperature in the room plummeted.

"You can't back out," Emmett said, his tone chilly. "We agreed on that ages ago, and they're breaking ground in less than three weeks."

"Well, now I'm un-agreeing."

"This is the second deal you've backed out on since August," Emmett noted, his voice low and hard. "I think you owe me an explanation. If this is about what happened the other—"

"I don't have to explain myself to you," Sloane said, stamping out his cigar in a crystal dish. "The reasons why are none of your goddamn business."

Emmett seethed, his hands curling into fists. This deal had been eighteen months in the making . . . and Sloane just backed out on a fucking whim? Or worse, as retribution for Emmett's having dinner with his sister?

Of course the pier project was expensive. If Sloane was experiencing financial difficulties, that could explain his need to pull out. Emmett's mood lifted considerably. "Far be it from me to stand in your way, then. After all, we are here to help one another."

Emmett then launched into what he needed from each man: Cabot's help in uncovering information against a politician; Harper's backing in a resort project on the Jersey shore; Sloane's influence with city hall to get permits approved cheaply.

With agreements all around, handshakes were then exchanged. Sloane hurried out, wasting no time in departing, but Cabot and Harper both hung back, apparently trying to judge Emmett's mood.

"You took Sloane's news on the pier well." Harper finished his drink, setting the tumbler down. "I was about to start taking bets on who would swing first."

"No contest." Cabot shook his head. "Cavanaugh would rip Sloane limb from limb."

Emmett knew they thought of him as a thug, one step above the filthy gutter he'd been born in. The reputation followed him wherever he went, especially since Emmett hadn't done much to disprove it. Why would he, when the notoriety served his purposes so nicely? Very few were stupid enough to cross him.

Sure, fifteen years ago this might've been settled in an alley with fists. But those days were behind him now. Mostly.

"Elizabeth Sloane." Cabot whistled. "I had no idea you ran in those circles, Cavanaugh."

"I don't," Emmett said. "And I have my reasons for not challenging Sloane on the pier."

"Yeah, like a second dinner with his sister." Cabot snickered and elbowed Harper.

Emmett just smiled enigmatically. Let them think what they wanted while he dug a bit deeper into the Sloane finances. The reasons would become clear soon enough.

The outside of the Metropolitan Opera House, called "the Yellow Brick Brewery" by some, was wretchedly ugly. The design of the palazzo-style façade fell far short of the beautiful Italian Renaissance buildings on which it had been based. Instead of honoring the classic European buildings, the Opera House resembled a factory at its corner of Broadway and Thirty-Ninth Street.

The inside, however, was glorious, unlike anything else in New York. Light and sunny, the interior swam with ivory and gold accents around a stage that seemed larger than any in the world. Paintings covered the ceilings, and life-sized statues of the eight Muses adorned the proscenium.

From her well-positioned private box in the lower tier, also called the "Diamond Horseshoe," Lizzie peered at the Friday night opera crowd in the gaslight. There were many familiar faces, including Edith Rutlidge, who sat four boxes away with her parents.

Emmett Cavanaugh had been one of the initial investors in the Opera House, yet she'd never seen him at a performance here. Still, a small part of her had hoped he would appear at tonight's staging of Wagner's *Siegfried*. Lizzie herself attended only because Will had insisted, saying they needed to maintain appearances after "that disastrous dinner with Cavanaugh."

Lizzie disagreed. She had fond memories of last week's dinner. Emmett was a fascinating man, certainly more interesting than the thick-jowled, heavily mustached society types surrounding her. He'd been given nothing in life, yet had taken everything. What drove such a complicated man?

Then there was the moment where he'd almost kissed her, his gaze intent and predatory inside the carriage. No other man had ever looked at her in such a way, like she was a banquet and he hadn't eaten in years. Though it may be shameless of her to admit it, she wished he had followed through on that kiss. Wished that he'd held her close and pressed his lips to hers. Slipped his tongue inside her mouth. . . .

Heat slid through her veins, warming her all over, and she used her ostrich-feather fan to cool her skin. The movement caught her brother's attention. He leaned over, a blond brow raised in question.

"Are you ill?".

No, I am lusting after a man you hate, apparently.

"I need some air," she whispered, and then rose. He started to get up as well, but she patted his shoulder. "Please, sit. I'll visit the ladies' dressing room for a few minutes." Lizzie lifted the skirts of her ivory satin opera gown and departed, passing the other gentlemen Will had invited this evening. Business acquaintances, he'd told her. Hardly surprising, since that was all her brother cared about.

She passed through the small salon at the back of their box and then into the corridor. Behind the tier were dressing rooms for the ladies and smoking rooms for the men. Lizzie traveled to the nearest dressing room, intent on pressing a cool cloth to her neck.

When she entered, there were three middle-aged women inside, busily chatting with one another. Lizzie recognized them as the wives of men who had recently built their fortunes—one with a telegraph company, one in shipping, and the other with a mine somewhere out West.

She nodded in greeting and continued to a small dressing table, where she requested a cool cloth from the maid hovering nearby. As Lizzie waited, she stripped off her gloves. The tight quarters made it impossible to avoid overhearing the ongoing conversation, not that the women put forth any effort whatsoever to keep quiet.

". . . and I told him that we don't own china fancy enough to serve Mrs. Astor." That was Mrs. Connors, whose husband was the president of Gotham Telegraph.

"Which Mrs. Astor?" the miner's wife asked.

"Don't be ridiculous," the third woman snapped. "Waldorf's wife hardly has the same social weight as Caroline Astor. But why would you need to serve her? I thought her husband called to see Mr. Connors."

"Yes, he did. Snuck in, too," Mrs. Connors said as Lizzie accepted a cool cloth from the maid. "Didn't want to make too much of a stir, he said. Can you imagine, Backhouse not making a stir? The man never leaves his yacht, so of course I was shocked to see him. But now that he has called at our home, surely convincing him to bring his wife to visit shall not prove difficult."

Lizzie wanted to snort. Etiquette demanded the lady of higher social rank pay a call first, yet Caroline Astor did not pay many calls. As the reigning matriarch of New York society, she hardly needed to. She had a large circle of friends, one that did not include new-monied types or divorcées.

"So what did Astor want with your husband?" one of the women asked.

"I haven't a clue. He met with Mr. Connors and one of the Gotham lawyers. They were sequestered in the study for hours."

Lizzie blinked, the cloth in her hand forgotten. Why would Mr. Astor sneak around to see the president of Gotham Telegraph and his lawyer? Gotham was incredibly profitable; their stock had split twice in the last fourteen months. Connors had started the family-run company two decades ago, just as the telegraph boom hit. He had two sons who would, according to reports, step up when Connors no longer wanted to oversee the company.

So what had been the purpose of the visit? No rumors of a sale had circulated, but if traders even suspected Astor was considering investing in—or buying out—

Gotham, the stock would climb, perhaps enough to double Emmett's money.

All Lizzie needed was the right moment, a few hours for the stock to jump in price, when she could buy and sell quickly. The rumor didn't necessarily need to be true, either. Wall Street traded in innuendo and suspicion. If she could purchase a large chunk of the Gotham stock before any rumors of a sale began, then she would stand to make a huge profit.

"Whatever they met over, it certainly put Mr. Connors in a jubilant mood," his wife said. "He told me to start booking my spring trip to Paris, and said he'll finally be able to come with me this year. I tell you, that man hasn't vacationed with me since our honeymoon."

Things began adding up in Lizzie's brain. Connors must be selling Gotham to Mr. Astor—and sitting on something wasn't Mr. Astor's style. He'd rather focus on horse races and yachting than on business, so she assumed the deal would be announced soon. If she could buy enough shares next week, then a well-positioned word in the right ear could spread like fire over the exchange. When the price of Gotham stock rose high enough, she could sell and win Emmett's ridiculous bet. Excitement bubbled through her, a swell of anticipation that had her leg bouncing.

"Lizzie! Are you ill?" Edith Rutlidge appeared, her silver beaded gown rustling as she approached.

Edith was twenty, unmarried, and Lizzie's closest friend. The two had met as small girls in Newport, though Lizzie could never give an exact date. It seemed the Sloanes had always been acquainted with the Rutlidges. Thanks to her close friendship with Edith, speculation began during Lizzie's debut, linking her to their oldest son, Henry—speculation Lizzie had done her best to extinguish at every turn.

"I saw you get up," Edith said, frowning. "I was worried."

Lizzie came to her feet, unable to hide a grin. "I am quite well."

Edith cocked her head, her gaze assessing. "Are you certain? You are acting very strangely lately."

"Strangely, how?"

"Staying home more often than not. Refusing callers. Dinners with nouveau riche."

Lizzie choked, then coughed to cover the sound. "It was one dinner. In full view of the other patrons, no less. Hardly anything worth noting."

"Are you joking? It's all anyone's been talking about this week. Rumor has it your brother went to Cavanaugh's house and punched him."

Lizzie's shoulders jerked, her body rocking back in surprise. Will wouldn't have done that . . . would he? He'd looked terrible that morning, with his hair askew and eyes rimmed red, but Will rarely grew angry or raised his voice. She couldn't imagine him doing anything so uncivilized. "You know Will would never do that."

"That's what I told everyone. Your brother is the stuffiest man I've ever met. It's as if he was born with a stick up . . . well, you know where."

Though Lizzie adored her brother, not even she could argue that point. "Let's get back, shall we?" she said. "I don't want to miss the last act." Threading her arm through Edith's, she led them toward the exit.

As they passed the small group of women still chatting inside the dressing room, Lizzie stopped. "Excuse me, Mrs. Connors?"

The older woman looked up. "Hello, Miss Sloane. Miss Rutlidge."

"I wanted to say thank you," Lizzie told her.

Confusion marred Mrs. Connors's weathered face, and she clutched her long strand of pearls. "Whatever for?"

"For coming to the opera tonight." The comment would make no sense to anyone other than Lizzie . . . but few people ever understood her anyway. What were three more? "And I would be honored if you and Mr. Connors would join my brother and me for dinner one evening. Perhaps I could invite Mrs. Astor as well, to introduce you."

Mrs. Connors appeared shocked, but rushed out, "How kind of you to offer, Miss Sloane. I would quite enjoy that."

"As would I. I'll speak to my brother and call on you soon. Good evening, ladies."

As they walked to the boxes, Edith murmured, "I didn't know you were so fond of Mr. and Mrs. Connors."

"After tonight, I am their biggest champion."

Chapter Five

The man who never gives cause for offense is the true man.

—American Etiquette and Rules of Politeness, 1883

The front door swung open, and Graham, Emmett's butler, stepped into view. "Welcome back, sir." A footman dashed by on his way to collect the bags from the hack as Emmett came up the walk. "I trust you had a pleasant trip."

Emmett had spent the past few days in Pittsburgh. The expansion project on his largest mill had lagged this winter, construction not happening nearly as fast as it should—and Emmett soon learned why. The foreman had accepted a bribe from a Pittsburgh city official in order to stall, which he'd admitted after some creative coercion on Emmett's part. Then Emmett had tracked down said corrupt official, who quickly came around to Emmett's way of thinking. Dangling out of a fourth-story window tended to do that to a man.

"*Pleasant* is not the word I would use, Graham." Emmett crossed the threshold and came inside the entryway. He handed over his derby and stick, then shrugged out of his coat. "Have Rogers bring a fresh shirt to my office," he told the butler, and started down the hall.

"Very good, sir. Mr. Colin is waiting for you."

When Emmett traveled short distances, he preferred to do so alone, which meant Colin remained behind to deal with matters in Emmett's absence. The young man was efficient and direct, two qualities Emmett respected in an employee.

His secretary waited inside the study, a stack of cables in his hands. "I have at least ten items that need your immediate attention," Colin said without preamble.

Emmett held out his right hand, and Colin obediently placed the stack of messages in Emmett's palm. Emmett was flipping through them, reading and prioritizing, when Rogers, his valet, appeared with a fresh shirt.

Emmett slipped out of his coat, placed it on the back of a chair, and continued reading through the cables. "Colin, any success with getting those Northeast P&Ls?"

"Is that blood on your silk vest again?" Rogers asked sharply as he removed Emmett's gold pocket watch and chain.

"No lectures, Rogers. If you can't get it out, then just purchase a new one, for hell's sake."

Frowning disapprovingly, the valet busied himself with collecting the soiled clothing.

"No, sir," Colin responded to Emmett's earlier question. "I am still working on getting those for you."

"Work harder," Emmett told him. "Or let's hire a Pinkerton to see it done."

Colin nodded just as Brendan sauntered inside. "Welcome back, Em," his brother said. "We expected you this morning. Did you run into trouble leaving Pittsburgh?"

"I didn't realize you were so anxious to see me. But yes, there was a delay on the track. Cows, I believe."

Brendan dropped into a chair and propped his cane against the edge of the desk. "Then I fear you have an even longer night ahead of you. Mrs. Rose called from the theater this morning to confirm you're still taking her to dinner tonight."

Fresh shirt in place, Emmett held out his wrist so Rogers could affix cuff links. "Dinner? Did I make dinner plans for this evening?"

Colin appeared equally perplexed. "No, sir. I don't show any dinner on your schedule tonight."

Brendan held up his hands. "I'm merely the messenger. She said it was very important you meet her at Sherry's at nine."

"Fine." He hadn't seen Mae in three weeks, and perhaps a night in her bed would finally erase the memory of Elizabeth Sloane. Mae preferred to dine at Sherry's, which was fast becoming the most popular restaurant in town. A small space at Thirty-Eighth Street and Sixth Avenue, they had decent food and spectacular service. Louis Sherry went to great lengths to accommodate his customers' requests, and Mae loved the attention.

"Send her flowers and tell her I'll be there," he told Colin and pulled up his suspenders. Rogers slipped a green patterned vest over Emmett's shoulders and came around to do the buttons.

"No need," Brendan said easily. "I already confirmed for you."

Emmett started to tell Brendan to mind his own damn business, but he was suddenly reminded of something. Today was Tuesday, the last day of the bet. Emmett reached for his pocket watch and then remembered he was changing clothes. "What time is it, Colin?"

"Just after four."

Trading had closed an hour ago. Had she succeeded?

The two of them had planned to dine together this evening. At least, he'd asked Elizabeth to meet him again, and she had agreed. It was entirely probable, however, that she'd forgotten.

He shouldn't see her. It was a fool's errand. She wasn't the type of woman he preferred. Actresses, whores, singers . . . those he could handle. Women up for a good fuck, who never wanted anything serious.

Elizabeth Sloane screamed *serious*. She was not the type to bounce between the sheets and then go along her merry way. Christ, he'd probably scare her the first time he whipped his cock out—never mind his scarred back.

"Colin, send a cable to Miss Elizabeth Sloane on Washington Square. 'Unable to meet you tonight. Cable your results tomorrow. Yours, etcetera, etcetera.'" His secretary nodded, furiously writing on his pad.

"I'll send it," Brendan said, rising smoothly to his feet with the help of his cane. "You both have a lot to catch up on, and I have nothing else to do." He plucked the paper from Colin's hands.

"You are uncharacteristically helpful today." Emmett scrutinized his brother. "Did something happen that I should know about?"

"Nope. Just trying to earn my keep around here."

Rogers held up a brown frock coat, and Emmett waved him away. "No need for that. I'll be up to bathe and change for dinner around seven thirty." He rolled his shoulders, relieved to feel marginally human again.

Just as he was about to sit, Katie and Claire exploded into the room in a blur of churning legs and petticoats. "Emmett!" they called as they charged his desk. "You're back!"

He grinned and thrust his hands into his trouser pockets. "Hello, girls. I see you've slipped Mrs. Thomas again."

"We had to see if you brought us anything," Katie said, now shifting impatiently in front of him. "Did you?"

"We want candy!" Claire announced at her sister's side. "You promised us candy."

"Yes, I did. But only if you were very good for Mrs. Thomas."

"We were!" both of them said loudly.

He began to slowly pull his hands out of his trouser pockets, the girls' eyes growing wider by the second. "I went to a new place this time, the Clark Company. They make something called"—he withdrew his hands and opened his fists—"the Clark Bar." The candy was wrapped in a dull red package with the name in yellow letters. "I think you'll like them."

"I'm sorry, sir," said a winded voice by the door. Mrs. Thomas, the governess, gripped the doorframe, her hair askew from chasing after the girls. "They promised me they would wait until dinner."

Emmett lifted his arms—and the candy—out of the girls' reach. "Katie. Claire. Did you lie to Mrs. Thomas?"

Katie avoided his eyes, and Claire's lip began to quiver. "We couldn't wait," she whined. "Don't take our candy away!"

"You may have the candy, but you both will do one extra hour of music lessons for lying. Do we have a deal?"

"Deal!" they both shouted, and he handed over the candy. The girls scooped up the red packages and darted out into the corridor.

"You are such an easy mark," Brendan said with a chuckle.

"Don't you have somewhere to be?" Emmett snapped at his brother. "Saving lives, perhaps?"

Brendan raised his hands in surrender. "I'll leave you to it. Have fun tonight."

Lizzie tapped her fingers on the linen-covered tabletop, unable to sit still. She had arrived at Sherry's early, too excited to wait. Even her trepidation over dining in a small private suite could not dim her joy.

She'd succeeded. She'd won Cavanaugh's wager, doubled his money, and would soon be starting her own brokerage firm. Her chest seemed ready to burst with sheer happiness.

Filled with giddiness, she'd placed a call to Emmett this morning to confirm their dinner. She wanted to deliver the news in person. Emmett had been unavailable, but his brother, Brendan, had been very helpful.

"Oh, yes," Brendan had said over the line. *"Emmett told me himself that he plans on meeting you at nine o'clock, Miss Sloane. Said he's looking forward to it."*

Apparently Emmett had arranged for the private dining room as well. What did that gesture mean? Heaven knew she'd contemplated the near-kiss in the carriage a hundred times since that night, wondered over what it would feel like to have his mouth on hers. And now they would spend the evening here, together, all alone. Her brother would be furious, of course, but Lizzie didn't care about her reputation. Nothing could ruin this evening for her.

The red velvet curtain swept aside, and Emmett strode in. He drew up short, almost as if surprised, but then continued toward her. Lizzie sucked in a breath. He looked huge in his black evening clothes, larger than life. Chiseled jaw, stark cheekbones, long eyelashes, and the bedeviling dip in his chin . . . Her skin grew hot, her stomach jumping. The man was hazardous to female kind.

Lizzie stood and smoothed her violet silk Worth evening gown. She tried to contain her wide smile, her face aching with the effort. It would be silly, but she had the strangest desire to run and throw herself into his arms, to share the euphoria exploding within her.

"Miss Sloane."

"Mr. Cavanaugh."

He clasped his hands behind his back then studied her, his obsidian gaze dark and intense. "Your eyes are dancing. Can I assume you've good news?"

The grin broke free, and she clapped her gloved hands. "I did it! As of yesterday, your investment stands at twenty-two thousand, twenty-nine dollars and sixty-three cents!"

"And a day early. I am impressed, Elizabeth." The lines of his rugged face softened, making him impossibly handsome. "This is cause for a celebration."

He strode back to the curtain and spoke to a waiter in the hall. She resumed her seat and busied herself with peeling off her purple gloves. Emmett returned and took his place, the setting dangerously close to hers. In fact, along with the candles, the entire atmosphere screamed *intimate*.

She did not care. Tonight was for gaiety. Worries were for tomorrow.

"You must tell me how you did it," he said, shifting toward her. A strong thigh slid close to her knee, and Lizzie felt her mouth go dry.

Thankfully, the waiter arrived and began pouring champagne, allowing Lizzie a chance to compose herself. Emmett affected her in the strangest way.

When they were alone again, he plucked a full glass off the table, handed it to her, then lifted his own in a toast. "To partnership."

Lizzie beamed. Hard to believe she would soon own her brokerage firm—well, half own. Regardless, she would have the opportunity to use her gifts in a practical sense, not merely as an exercise by herself. Financial security was close at hand. "To partnership."

They drank, and then Emmett said, "Will you tell me how?"

"Gotham Telegraph."

His eyes widened. "The rumored sale to Astor. Impressive. No one saw that coming."

"I know. I was in the right place to overhear a relevant piece of information."

"Is that so?"

"Yes. Sometimes women share innocent things from their home life that can be used to gauge a company's stock value."

He studied her, stared with such fierce concentration, that she nearly squirmed. She couldn't guess what he was thinking. Just as she was about to ask, he said quietly, "You are entirely unexpected, Elizabeth."

From his flat tone and serious expression, she couldn't comprehend his meaning. "Is that good or bad?"

"I haven't decided yet."

The moment stretched, their gazes locked, and her breath came faster, the air suddenly in short supply. Their faces were so close she could see every one of the dark lashes framing his eyes, the hint of whiskers along his jaw. She sensed a strange tension emanating from him, a barely leashed energy that filled the room.

A waiter returned, this time with the first course, and

she reached for her champagne, downing it. Oysters again, she noted in an effort to focus on something other than the inscrutable man next to her. The plates were arranged, and Emmett murmured something to the waiter, who promised to return momentarily.

The next few moments were dedicated to the food. Lizzie enjoyed the oysters and tried not to dwell on Emmett's nearness, or the way their arms nearly brushed with each movement. *More champagne should help*, she thought and reached for her flute.

"Have you considered where you will set up an office?" he asked.

Surprised, she put down her glass. She hadn't yet contemplated the practicalities, like an office or hiring a staff. Winning the bet had consumed her thoughts. No doubt her brother had space to spare in the Northeast Railroad offices, but she couldn't fathom having Will a few feet away each day. He would interfere, try to take over.

"No, I haven't. Silly, I suppose, but I've been so focused on the wager. I'll need to lease an office near the exchange."

"I have plenty of available space in my new building on Beaver Street."

"Oh, I don't know—"

"I insist. At least until you start to turn a profit and can afford to lease a space on your own. The building is completely outfitted with all the latest conveniences."

The waiter appeared, placed a crystal glass of clear liquid near Emmett's right hand, and departed. Lizzie watched as Emmett took a long sip.

"Is that water?" She nodded toward his glass.

The side of his mouth kicked up. "No, it's gin."

"May I taste it?"

"Have you ever had gin? I'm betting they don't serve it at any of your fancy parties."

"Perhaps that's why fancy parties are so ridiculously boring." She held out her hand. "Please, Emmett. I had the impression we were celebrating."

She stared him down, even when he frowned fiercely. For some strange reason, she wanted to know more about him, to learn as much about Emmett Cavanaugh as she could.

"And we are. Here." He placed his glass in her hand. "By all means, see how the common folk drink."

The crystal cool in her palm, Lizzie lifted the spirits to her mouth. The smell was strong and flowery. Potent. She put her lips on the rim. There was something thrilling about putting her mouth where his had just been, and the sleepy, intense way he stared at her intimated he might be thinking the same.

Emboldened, she took a healthy sip and swallowed. The cold liquid burned down her throat, a river of fire scorching everything in its path to her stomach, robbing her of the ability to breathe.

A large hand thumped her back, and the glass disappeared from her grip. "Breathe, Elizabeth," his deep voice commanded, and she gasped. Her lungs desperately dragged in air, as a shiver worked its way down her body.

"My God," she wheezed. "How can you stand that?"

"I'm used to it." He put the crystal to his beautiful lips and, drink suddenly forgotten, her thoughts returned to kissing. The burn in her stomach spread to ignite other parts as she watched him swallow, the strong cords of his tanned throat working above his white shirt collar. The divot in his chin dipped and bobbed, mesmerizing her like a snake in a charmer's basket.

"You should stop staring at me like that."

"Like what?" She propped her elbow on the table and put her chin in her hand, leaning toward him.

"Like you want me to kiss you."

The gin must've conspired with the champagne to take hold of her tongue, because she blurted, "And you don't want to kiss me?"

"Wrong." His eyes blazed as he brushed his bare thumb gently over the seam of her lips. "I would give everything I own for the privilege. But there would be no going back."

Lizzie's skin came alive, itching and crawling with restlessness at his light touch. The fervent pounding of her heart behind whalebone and cotton echoed in every pore and cell, so loud she was certain he could hear. He stared at her mouth, rough pad of his thumb continuing to trace her lips.

He broke away first and reached for his glass, and she was pleased to see his hand shake slightly. He was so cool, so composed except for that slight tremor in his hand. Could he be pushed? Could she break a bit of the heavy-plated armor he seemed to surround himself with?

"Everything you own? I'm told it's considerable."

His mouth quirked, and he took another sip. "It is."

"Then I am flattered."

"You shouldn't be." He set the crystal down with a thump. "You should stay away from men like me."

She lifted a shoulder. "I'm not certain that's possible. I've never been very good at doing what I am told."

Was she flirting with him? Yet another surprise when it came to Elizabeth Sloane.

It had been a shock to find her here tonight. Clearly, Brendan had a lot to answer for. Emmett's brother was the only explanation for Elizabeth's presence in the private dining room. But as annoyed as Emmett was over Brendan's interference, he was also strangely relieved. He hadn't wanted to see Mae. No, the woman he desired was right here in front of him.

He reached for his gin in a desperate attempt to cool his growing desire. Elizabeth was beautiful, yes. And intelligent. That had been unexpected, the quick wit. Most women of her ilk only concerned themselves with parties and gossip. Elizabeth was different, and he'd always been drawn to uniqueness, things that stood out.

Yet she was like a package too pretty to open. Someone too fragile and pure for a man like him, a man who'd fucked more nameless women than ones he could recount.

So why was he lusting after her like a lad? He knew better. This could go nowhere beneficial.

"How was Pittsburgh?" she asked.

He frowned, certain he hadn't mentioned his trip tonight. "How did you know I was in Pittsburgh?"

"Your brother told me, when I called." She wiped her immaculate mouth with the linen napkin. "He seems very nice."

Nice was not how Emmett would have described Brendan at the moment. "His patients certainly think so. And my trip was . . . productive."

"I've never been to Pittsburgh. Will goes, though."

"You might like it. Have you ever traveled west?"

"No, though I've always wanted to see San Francisco. With the hills and the water, it's supposed to be beautiful," she said, and her eyes turned soft and dreamy, like silver clouds. Holy hell, he couldn't look away as lust flared to life deep in his gut. A man could drown in that swirling gray mist, and he wondered how that color would change when she was aroused.

Forcing his gaze to his plate, he swallowed and tried to bring his body under control. "I was there last year. I didn't have much time for taking in the sights, however. In fact, I hardly left my hotel and the construction site."

"Oh, Emmett. That's a terrible shame." Her hand suddenly clasped his left forearm where it lay on the table. They both froze, though likely for different reasons. He blinked, transfixed at the sight of her bare, slim fingers on his black evening coat, the heat of her body seeping through the thin cloth to reach his skin.

A flush crept over her face as she realized what she'd done, and he wondered how much of her brazenness had to do with the champagne she'd consumed. Not that he cared. He liked her hand there, touching him. Liked it a lot. So he held still, waiting. The fire reflected in her gaze, the wide-eyed wonder at whatever this was between them, sent a white-hot jolt through his blood, straight to his balls.

He watched her throat work, and she started to pull back. "I apologize."

His other hand caught her small wrist, holding her in place. "Don't. I like your hand there."

"We shouldn't."

"When have the rules ever stopped you, Elizabeth?"

"More often than you'd believe, most likely," she whispered before dropping her focus to his mouth. She licked her lips, and Emmett lost the battle.

"Liar," he murmured, and closed the distance between them.

He knew he should stop, or at least go gently, but the instant his lips touched hers, it was as if a dam burst free inside him. Desire kicked hard in his groin, and he could not control his reaction to the very first taste of her. Sweet. And pure. Like rain that washed the dirt and grime from your body after a long day in the sticky heat.

More, his mind whispered.

He cupped her jaw, his rough fingers spread wide over delicate, creamy skin, and he sealed his mouth tighter to hers. Soft and lush, her lips contained the heady hint of champagne and the gin he never should've allowed. The combination should have served as a reminder of how different they were, of the gulf that separated them, but he found it intoxicating. A strange mix of two things that did not belong together, yet were undeniably delectable.

Oh sweet Christ, she was kissing him back.

Instinct swiftly took over. He parted her lips with his tongue and delved inside. Tasted the warm, wet recesses of her mouth. Her tongue welcomed his with bold strokes. She was not shy, and her eagerness acted as a lit match to dry kindling, burning him alive from the inside. The soft pants of her breath, the feel of her slick tongue sliding along his . . . He thrust deeper, wanting to sink into that velvety richness, to let her lusciousness envelop him.

A small hand clutched his shoulder, holding on. Pulling him closer. Euphoria flooded his veins, and more blood rushed to his cock. He nipped her plump bottom lip, needing to mark her, needing to sink his teeth into her perfect skin.

She gasped and rejoined their mouths, immediately opening for him, her tongue every bit as impatient as his. He felt feverish, an all-consuming heat enveloping his entire body. God, what he wouldn't give to raise her skirts, lift her on the table, and push inside. No one would know. He'd told the waiters to leave the food and not return until he called. Anything could—and usually did—happen in these private dining rooms.

With a tug of his foot, he brought her chair closer, then placed a hand on her waist. She was small, so tiny compared to his giant hand—not that it stopped him from touching her. He needed to feel her, to memorize every inch of her.

He paused as the enormity of what was transpiring swept through him. Not only was he treating her inappropriately, they were in a semipublic place. Why in the hell had he started this?

Breaking free, he sucked in air. She stared at him with glazed, sleepy eyes, the wonder on her face nearly causing him to kiss her all over again. The urge to make her tremble, to hear her shout his name, just about brought him to his knees.

"I'm sorry," he said quickly. "I shouldn't 'a took advantage of you."

She blinked a few times, and he realized he'd slipped into his old speech patterns. Shit. He cleared his throat and started to ease away.

With one hand still on his shoulder, she prevented his retreat. Her gaze dropped to his chin. Delicate fingers slowly touched the indentation there. The Devil's mark, his father had called it. Elizabeth traced the dimpled skin, fascinated. "I have been wondering what this feels like," she whispered.

What the hell? She'd been thinking about his chin?

Her fingers slid over his jaw and up along his sideburns, brushing his ears. "Don't stop just yet. Kiss me again."

"Why?"

"Because you're right. The rules haven't ever stopped me. Please, Emmett."

He lunged, took her face in his hands, and found her mouth. Just one more kiss, then he would stop. One more taste of her before he never saw her again. She mewled, a needy sound deep in her throat, and he heard himself growl in response. Her tongue met his, and the jolt of pleasure from that simple motion streaked through his groin. He was harder than iron, his cock begging to be released from behind his clothing.

She squirmed, and he pulled her closer, until her corseted breasts were brushing his chest. His hand traveled south, intent on—

"*Goddamn it!* Get your hands off her, Cavanaugh."

Chapter Six

*When you are compelled to differ from others you
should be controlled by reason and moderation.*

—American Etiquette and Rules of Politeness, 1883

Elizabeth squeaked, jumped back, and Emmett turned in
time to see Will Sloane's fist—just before it collided with
his left eye. His head snapped back with the force of the
blow, rocking the chair. Elizabeth shouted and grabbed
her brother's arm, while Emmett shot to his feet. His
vision blurred, but it wasn't the first time he'd caught an
unexpected punch. Far from it—and no matter what, he
always picked himself up to fight back.

Sloane's face was purple with rage, his chest heaving,
but Emmett paid him no mind. Elizabeth had gone the
color of snow in an effort to restrain her brother. "Step
back, Elizabeth, before you get hurt," he ordered.

"And you dare to call her by her Christian name!"
Sloane lunged again and caught Emmett off balance, the
two of them crashing onto the dining table. Food, china,
and glass rained onto the floor. Sloane got in another
punch, this time at Emmett's midsection, before Emmett
landed a few choice blows of his own. Sloane attempted

to wrap his fingers around Emmett's throat, so Emmett grabbed the man's arms as they wrestled on the floor, battling to gain the upper hand.

And then the fight ended. Strong arms lifted Sloane straight off the floor.

"About time," Emmett grumbled as he staggered to his feet. Kelly just grinned, his beefy arms easily restraining a struggling Will Sloane.

The stark lines of Sloane's face were etched in fury as he tried to break Kelly's hold. "Release me, you imbecile."

Louis Sherry flew through the curtain, his eyes huge as he absorbed the destruction. "Gentlemen, is there a problem with your meal?"

The awareness of an audience seemed to pull Sloane together. He stilled, nostrils flared, but otherwise appeared calm. Kelly glanced at Emmett, a question in his eyes.

Emmett jerked his chin, and Sloane was released.

"You idiots!" Elizabeth marched forward. "You both could have been hurt." Even angry, she was perfection. The woman exuded sophistication and polish, so beautiful she put even the most ostentatious decoration to shame. And here Emmett had been brawling on the floor, like the hoodlum he was.

Well, better she see his true self now. That would quell any tenderness arising from their earlier kiss.

"Lizzie, go wait in my carriage." Sloane's hard gaze drilled into Emmett as he spoke. "I want to have a word with Cavanaugh."

"No," she shot back. "Will, you cannot send me out of the room like some recalcitrant child. I won't have you hurting each other—"

"I want to talk to him."

She stuck out her chin. "So talk. I'm not leaving."

"*Lizzie, get in the goddamned carriage!*" Sloane roared.

Before Emmett knew what he was doing, he'd grabbed Sloane by the throat. "Watch your mouth," he snarled in his most menacing voice, his face inches from Sloane's.

Lips pressed in a tight line, Sloane didn't back down. They squared off, neither budging, for a long moment. Emmett had to give him credit; Sloane was either incredibly brave or incredibly stupid. Not that the prick would have lasted a minute in Emmett's old neighborhood.

Finally, the other man sneered and shoved Emmett's hand to the side. He turned to his sister and draped an arm around her shoulders, leading her to the exit. Sloane was saying something to her, but the hushed tone was too soft for Emmett to overhear.

Emmett promised to pay for the damage and waved Louis Sherry away. Now that Sloane's initial fury had been spent, Emmett had a good idea of what was coming next—and they did not require an audience for this particular conversation.

"Want me to stay, Bish?" Kelly asked him quietly. "Make sure he don't give you another sidewinder?"

Emmett shook out his throbbing hand. He'd gotten in a few good shots, considering he'd been taken off guard. Hopefully Sloane's jaw would hurt like ever-living fuck tomorrow. "No, that's not necessary. Just wait in the hall."

Elizabeth was now agitated, whispering rapidly to her brother, with Sloane shaking his head in disagreement. The woman had fire in her. She might have the face of an angel, but her spine was pure steel. Emmett liked that about her. A lot.

He'd glimpsed that heat earlier when he'd kissed her. It had nearly blown his goddamned head off. How had a Knickerbocker learned to kiss like a chorus girl?

The exchange hadn't been what he'd expected, not in the least. He'd been prepared to go slow, thaw her out.

Break down all the elaborate barriers protecting her from men like him. But there hadn't been ice to crack or high walls to scale. Instead, she'd burned hot and bright, a live electric charge in his arms. A jolt of current that reached the long-dead places inside him.

Hard to say whether he wanted to run toward that feeling or far, far away.

Kelly elbowed him in the ribs. "You know what he's gonna say, right? You're not gonna have a choice this time."

"There's always a choice," Emmett muttered, gingerly touching the tender skin around his left eye. He'd have a hell of a shiner tomorrow. "Go away, Kelly."

Chuckling, Kelly disappeared through the curtain. Elizabeth and her brother seemed to come to some sort of agreement, because she was nodding. Sloane took a step back, and Elizabeth lifted her chin. "Thank you for dinner, Mr. Cavanaugh," she said from across the room.

"My pleasure, Miss Sloane."

With one last glance at her brother, she swept out of the room in a rustle of silk. That left just Emmett and Sloane for a conversation neither wanted to have.

Emmett located a chair in the debris of the room. He withdrew a cigar from his inside pocket and had just snipped the end when Sloane righted a second chair. Apparently, Mr. Washington Square was prepared to be civilized.

"Do you have another?" Sloane asked, dropping heavily into the seat.

Clamping the unlit cigar between his teeth, Emmett fished a second out of his pocket, along with his cutter. Sloane thanked him and took the items. Emmett found a candle on a sideboard, lit his own cigar, and held the flame out to Sloane.

Once Sloane's cigar was burning, the two of them

leaned back and puffed. The silence stretched as the room filled with pungent smoke. Emmett could well understand Sloane's fury, but he'd be damned if he'd apologize for what had happened in this room tonight.

"You're going to have to marry her," Sloane finally said.

"Not a chance in hell—and don't pretend you think it's a fine idea."

"It's a terrible idea, but I have no choice. She will be ruined by morning. Someone sent me a note, telling me you both were here. It's not as if it's a secret."

"That's hardly my problem."

"I'm afraid it is. No decent man will have her, and she'll be steeped in scandal the rest of her life. I won't have it, Cavanaugh. You will do right by her."

Emmett didn't like the guilt that twisted and tightened in his belly. "Or?"

"Or I withdraw from our pact. I'll join Carnegie and Morgan. Spend the rest of my life bringing you low. Are you ready to lose everything? Because I swear that's what it'll come to. You, your brother, your two sisters . . . Nothing will be left when I'm through."

"You think you could do that?" Emmett scoffed.

"If it comes to that, yes, I do. I'll start by forcing Cabot and Harper to choose sides. They won't stand by you, not after they learn you brought Lizzie to a private dining room to ruin her."

Emmett expected no loyalty from anyone—one of the lasting effects of his upbringing—but he wasn't worried about Sloane. Or Cabot and Harper, for that matter. They could try but they'd never ruin him.

And little good it would do now to share how the private dining room had come to pass.

"Your sisters are what age, now?" Sloane casually

smoothed his dark trousers. Emmett said nothing, just clenched his jaw, while Sloane continued. "The oldest is thirteen, I believe. Not long before you'll be suffering through dress fittings in Paris for their debuts. How do you think society will receive them if you decide to walk away from Lizzie tonight?"

Impotent fury whipped through Emmett, settling at the base of his neck. Sloane had latched onto the one area where Emmett had no leverage. The one deal he couldn't buy his way into, the one arm he couldn't twist. And how could he possibly explain to Claire and Katie that their futures had been destroyed by his stupidity? He'd been backed into a fucking corner, and he didn't like it. Not one bit.

"In case you're unclear on the answer, allow me to assure you that I will personally call on every house of consequence between Eightieth Street and Battery Park to ensure the Cavanaugh girls are never accepted. Anywhere."

"This feels a lot like blackmail."

"That's because it *is* blackmail." Sloane let that statement linger. "And your reticence makes it seem as if my sister is unacceptable or repugnant," he said, his voice laced with anger. "We both know that's not the case, nor is it how you feel. I saw you two together, remember. You'd be damned lucky to have her."

Lucky was not the word bouncing around in Emmett's head right now—and he wasn't backed into a corner just yet. "If I do consider marriage, what are you offering in terms of a dowry?"

He could almost hear Sloane grinding his teeth together. "I'm not giving you a goddamned dime."

"I want Northeast stock." Sloane opened his mouth to argue, and Emmett added, "Twenty-five thousand shares."

Sloane threw his head back and laughed. "You have unbelievable nerve. No way in hell I'd give you that. Only board members have that much."

Emmett blew out a long, thin cloud of white smoke. "If you don't agree to the stock, I won't tell you where to find Cabot tonight. Which means you'll never get news of the engagement in the morning paper. Word of this dinner will be up and down Fifth Avenue before noon."

Sloane let out a creative curse that surprised even Emmett. "Ten thousand shares," the other man ground out. "Now are we done, you greedy bastard?"

"Fifteen thousand and we're done—not that Elizabeth will ever agree."

Sloane puffed on his cigar. "Wrong. She has no choice in the matter. Not after tonight."

Lizzie huddled in Will's carriage, humiliation burning her alive.

Her brother had just witnessed her kissing Emmett. Passionately kissing, in fact. She'd practically been draped in the man's lap when Will burst into the room. Positively mortifying.

And the two men had fought, nearly destroyed the room. Had she ever seen Will so livid?

She hated disappointing her brother, the person who'd always protected and cared for her. Had cheered her up as a child. Took her to Newport for her birthday each year. And tonight had witnessed her acting shamefully with Emmett Cavanaugh.

Her lips swollen, she could almost feel Emmett's mouth still on hers. The kiss had been intense. Mind-numbing. The steel magnate might appear cold and remote, a man

made of stone, but that façade had cracked during those
few moments. His breath had been hot, his touch brand-
ing her through layers of clothing, while his warm and
seductive tongue slid into her mouth. She'd fallen under
his spell completely—at which point her brother had
stormed in.

How could she have been so stupid? Bad enough she'd
dined with Emmett in a private room. Kissing him was a
hundred times worse. And no chance it could be kept
secret, not with a brawl erupting. She should have walked
out the second she realized they would not be dining on
the main floor.

She glanced at the front of Sherry's, through the large
windows to where tables of gaily dressed patrons enjoyed
their evening. Lizzie recognized a few of them, and wondered if news had already spread about her and Emmett.

Let me talk to him, Lizzie, Will had said as he ushered
her out of the private dining room. *Trust me to fix this.*

What had he meant, "fix" it? What were the two men
discussing up there?

A group of people spilled out of the entrance and onto
the walk. Then Will emerged directly behind them, his
face grim as he dodged the revelers and hurried toward the
waiting carriage.

He hauled himself up and slammed the door, and the
carriage set off toward Fifth Avenue.

Lizzie didn't know what to say, but she had to say
something. "I'm sorry, Will."

"I should be apologizing to you. If I'd been around
more . . ." He shook his head. "I should have insisted you
marry ages ago. Then this never would have happened."

"You act as if people care what I do. He and I have
dined together before, and it didn't even make the papers."

"Because I called in favors to kill the story," Will said tersely. "That's why it was never printed, Lizzie."

She blinked. "I . . . I had no idea."

"I know. That's the way I wanted it. I've tried to protect you to the best of my ability, but I cannot do it this time. Someone sent me a note tonight, telling me you both were here. Word will get out about tonight's dinner, no matter what I do. There's only one way to stop this scandal."

A cold knot of dread settled in her stomach. Surely he didn't mean . . . *that.* She tried to joke in order to lighten the tension, hoping she was wrong. "You're going to have Cavanaugh killed?"

Her brother's mouth flattened. "If I could, believe me, I would."

"So that means . . ."

Will said nothing, letting the silence provide his answer. A ball of fear gathered steam inside her, the terror growing to engulf her like a giant cloud. "You wouldn't."

"There is no choice. You will be ruined, Lizzie. *Ruined.* It'll be worse than being a divorcée, and you know how those women are treated. Do you want to leave New York and live abroad, in shame, for the rest of your life, like that Hayes girl a few years ago?"

Agatha Hayes had been an acquaintance of Lizzie's, an unmarried debutante who'd been rumored to be carrying on an affair with her coachman. Society had turned on Agatha quickly, and her parents had no choice but to squire her off to Rome. Lizzie didn't want to move to Rome . . . but she didn't want to marry Emmett Cavanaugh either.

"Living abroad wouldn't be so terrible," she hedged.

Will let out a disbelieving sound. "If that is the way you feel, then why did you refuse that viscount sniffing around for a bride last year?" She didn't answer, and he continued,

"Let me ask you, do you make a habit of going to dinner with single men, unaccompanied, and kissing them?"

"No!" Her spine straightened. "Absolutely not!"

"So I can only assume that you"—he grimaced—"feel something for Emmett Cavanaugh. Most marriages of our station are started with much less. Hell, you might even end up being the one woman who can break through to find out if the man has any feelings."

"This is madness." A hysterical giggle burned in her throat, and she rubbed her forehead with gloved fingers. This could not be happening.

"This is reality," Will snapped. "Our world has very strict rules, and you cannot thumb your nose at them. You've seen such a small part of life outside ours, Lizzie, but it can be terribly harsh, especially for women. I will not have you struggle or suffer. You'll marry Cavanaugh, and that will be the end of it."

The word "marry" echoed ominously in the enclosed space of the carriage. She did not want to marry Emmett Cavanaugh. She hardly knew him for one thing. He could be a philanderer. Abusive. An opium addict. Or any other manner of horrible and cruel traits undesirable in a husband.

Also, she had sworn to marry only for love. To have a man so besotted with her that he never strayed, never even glanced at another woman. Like the stories of her mother and father, the ones Will used to tell her late at night when she was too scared to sleep.

And though he caused her knees to go weak, a man like Emmett Cavanaugh would only bring heartache.

"What if I say no?"

Will heaved out a sigh. "Then we suffer the consequences. But Cavanaugh wants to marry you, Lizzie. Said so himself. Give him a chance to convince you."

"Mr. Cavanaugh wants to marry me?" She couldn't believe it. He did not seem the marrying sort.

"Yes. Asked for your hand and everything. He's not my first choice—far from it—but I believe he'll make you happy. I've already agreed. It's done."

"Will! How could you agree without even talking to me first?"

"Because I am your guardian and, like it or not, I have the right to make these decisions for you."

"But . . ."

She couldn't even finish it. Having the choice taken away, not being able to decide her own fate, angered Lizzie more than anything else.

You decided your own fate when you baited Emmett into kissing you tonight.

No, that wasn't fair. She'd never expected things to go this far. Hadn't thought anyone would discover them. She certainly had never considered a marriage would result. All she'd wanted was to open her own investment firm, she thought, rubbing her throbbing temples.

"Lizzie, your reputation is all you have. If you lose it, no one will even look you in the eye, let alone speak to you. You'll cease to exist to those in our circle."

Sweet mercy, her brother was right. Any chance of luring the wealthy society matrons and respectable widows to invest with her would disappear if word of tonight's episode got out. A lump settled in her throat. Why had she been so stupid?

Perhaps she could talk Emmett out of an actual wedding. They could enjoy a long engagement and then call off the wedding before the ceremony. That made more sense. All they had to do was wait for the scandal to settle. Then they could cancel the wedding and go their separate ways, reputations intact.

A fine plan, she reasoned.

"I can see your thoughts turning," Will said, her brother's shrewd gaze too knowing. "Give over, Lizzie. It's done."

Wrong. This was far from done. But she bit her lip and kept her ideas to herself. Just like always.

The announcement appeared in the paper the following morning.

Dressed in a pale china-blue morning gown, Lizzie stirred her morning coffee, her mind swirling faster than the cream in her Limoges porcelain cup. This was her brother's doing, she knew it. She hadn't a clue how Will had managed the feat, but news of the impending nuptials graced the front page, shouting her misery to the world in stark black-and-white.

ELIZABETH SLOANE TO MARRY
"PRINCE OF STEEL" CAVANAUGH!

KNICKERBOCKER PRINCESS
THROWS OVER RUTLIDGE HEIR!

BROTHER WILLIAM SLOANE
"THRILLED" AT THE MATCH!

Lizzie rubbed her brow. Hadn't the idea only been discussed last night? She had hoped to find a way out of the situation before word became public. Today's paper certainly changed that. Not only would stopping the marriage prove more difficult, the news that she'd broken things off with Henry painted her like some man-hopping hussy.

And "thrilled at the match"? Will had hardly spoken to her on the ride home from Sherry's, depositing her at the front door before disappearing into his home office, clearly eager to begin ruining her life.

Just then, her brother walked into the breakfast room. Tall and confident, his blond hair was perfectly oiled, his dress immaculate. How could he appear so put together on a disastrous morning such as this?

"Good morning," he said casually.

Lizzie tapped anxious fingers on the table while he pulled out a chair and sat down. A servant rushed over with coffee.

"Excellent. You've seen it." He gestured to the paper. "I suppose you'll be besieged by callers today."

Oh, dear heavens, she'd forgotten. Lizzie pinched the bridge of her nose. No doubt the ladies of New York society were ordering the wheels of their coupés greased at this very moment. She would have to face them, if not today then soon.

"Why did this need to appear in the morning's paper? Can't I even have a moment to let the idea settle?"

Will turned to the footman by the wall. "Paul, give us a moment." The servant withdrew, shutting the door behind him, and her brother leaned forward, his expression clouding. "This had to appear this morning because you chose to meet Cavanaugh in a private dining room, Lizzie. Someone knew about your dinner, someone who sent me there to find you. This is me, protecting you." He stabbed a finger at the newspaper. "I had to rouse the publisher out of a . . . quite unsavory place last night just to have the page reset."

Bitter, ugly feelings expanded in her chest until she could hardly contain them. It was all happening too fast. No one was listening to her, or taking into account what she wanted. This was not how she had imagined her engagement. "Maybe I am tired of your protecting me!" she snapped. "You never include me in decisions, at least not anymore. You do whatever you please, telling no one, and damn the consequences!"

His eyes rounded. "Did you just swear in our breakfast room?"

"Yes, I did. If ever a day required swearing, this is it. Maybe I'll never stop! Damn, damn, *damn*."

A muscle jumped in Will's jaw. "I won't apologize for this. Not for any of it. I've done my best, but you've brought all this on yourself. You're Cavanaugh's problem now." Will rose, gulped his coffee, and set his cup in the saucer with a snap. "And I wish him luck."

Lizzie watched Will go, resisting the urge to call after him. She hated fighting with her brother, but she refused to roll over and allow others to decide her fate. *There has to be a way out of this,* she thought with another calculating glance at the paper.

Not long after, a noise in the hall caught her attention. She had just finished her breakfast when Edith Rutlidge strode into the breakfast room with Frederic, their butler, hot on her heels.

"I cannot believe it!" Edith declared at the same time that Frederic apologized for not announcing their guest.

"It's fine, Frederic. Edith, please sit."

Edith sat while the footman arranged a clean place setting in front of her. When finished, he wisely quit the room.

Edith's eyes were wild and disbelieving. "You're getting *married?* To Emmett Cavanaugh? I . . . I'm speechless, Lizzie."

Well, not exactly speechless, but Lizzie refrained from pointing that out. "We are engaged, yes," she hedged.

Edith's gaze dipped to Lizzie's finger. "Then where is your ring?"

Oh. Lizzie hadn't thought of that. She twisted her hands together, hiding her bare fingers. "It was only just decided last evening, which is why I didn't tell you."

"The other night, that's who dropped you and Henry off at the house. It was Cavanaugh, wasn't it?"

"Yes."

Edith slumped in the chair, her face as unhappy as Lizzie had ever seen. Guilt wormed its way under Lizzie's ribs to clench her heart. She didn't like hurting Edith's feelings, but she was not ready to discuss the true nature of her engagement to Emmett Cavanaugh.

"I didn't even know you two were acquainted. He's so . . ."

Large? Handsome? Intense? There were a hundred ways to finish that sentence, but they were not here to discuss Cavanaugh's strengths and weaknesses. "Edith, I realize this is a shock. The whole business caught me by surprise as well."

Edith studied Lizzie's face. "Caught you by surprise, in a good way? What I mean is, did he sweep you off your feet?"

Lizzie swallowed the rest of her coffee, which had turned cold. "In a manner of speaking."

"You're not telling me much. I'm supposed to be your closest friend. Henry is hurt by this," she said, gesturing to the paper. "You should have seen his face this morning. And you cannot even tell me how Cavanaugh convinced you to marry him?"

"You are my closest friend, and I'm sorry for not being forthcoming. I'm still . . . reeling."

"Do you love him?"

That question nearly made Lizzie laugh, but she restrained herself. Love him? She barely knew him. "Hard to say. It's all been so sudden."

Edith huffed. "You have maintained for years you'll never marry except for love. And now you're saying you are not in love with your betrothed? This makes no sense."

"You need to take my word for it," Lizzie said sharply. She did not want to argue with her friend, but Edith needed to stop peppering her with so many questions.

Frederic appeared, a silver salver in hand. One lone card rested on the surface, and Lizzie picked it up. When she saw the name, her stomach fell. Why was he paying her a call?

"What? Who is it?" Edith reached over to pluck the card out of Lizzie's fingers before Lizzie could stop her. "Oh, my heavens."

Lizzie wanted to run upstairs and draw the covers over her head. Instead, she told Frederic, "Show him to the front receiving room, please."

"I'm coming with you," Edith declared. "I want to meet him."

"No, absolutely not," Lizzie said emphatically.

A determined set to her chin, Edith shot out of her chair and rushed from the breakfast room. Realizing what was happening, Lizzie hurried toward the front of the house. Her friend was faster, however, and by the time Lizzie arrived, Edith was boldly introducing herself to Emmett.

In a wool morning suit of light gray and white stripes, he appeared tall, sturdy, and impossibly handsome. If he was bothered by the news in today's paper, Lizzie couldn't tell from the way he politely greeted Edith.

"Good morning," Lizzie said.

Emmett glanced up, his dark eyes slowly traveling the length of her before settling on her face. That intense scrutiny made her shiver, despite her best intentions to remain unaffected by him.

"Good morning, Miss Sloane. My apologies for the early call. I hadn't expected you to be entertaining."

"That's my fault," Edith said. "I couldn't help but come downtown as soon as I read the paper. It came as quite a surprise."

To everyone, Lizzie longed to add. She wanted to rip open the door and scream into Washington Square Park, *I have no intention of marrying him.*

Emmett gave Edith an inscrutable look. "To me as well, Miss Rutledge," he admitted. "But a pleasant surprise, indeed."

Edith's expression softened, as if the statement had been a declaration of undying love. "Oh, you have no idea how relieved I am to hear you say that. When I saw the announcement this morning, I feared the worst."

"And what would the worst be?" he asked her.

"Lizzie has sworn to marry only for love—"

"Edith! That's enough. Mr. Cavanaugh is very busy, and we wouldn't want to delay him."

Emmett cleared his throat. "I won't stay long. I wondered if we might have a word in private, Miss Sloane?"

"Oh," Edith said, glancing between Lizzie and Emmett. Calls were required to be chaperoned, though Lizzie certainly wouldn't have worried over propriety if she had been alone. Edith's presence complicated matters.

"Excuse us, Edith. I'll speak with Mr. Cavanaugh in the hall." She turned and led the way out of the room.

Chapter Seven

———❦———

Couples should know each other thoroughly before they become engaged.

—American Etiquette and Rules of Politeness, 1883

Emmett followed Elizabeth into the hall. Obviously he'd broken some absurd social rule by asking to speak with her alone, if the horrified look on the Rutlidge girl's face had been any indication. Not that Emmett cared about the ridiculous rules, especially not after the previous evening.

Elizabeth stepped further along the corridor. The house, he couldn't help notice, was decorated with the tasteful elegance one would expect from a family such as the Sloanes. No garish colors or gold leaf. Old, subtle paintings. Worn, expensive carpets. It was the kind of home that reminded you how long the occupants had been here, how well rooted their wealth.

But was that wealth only for show? That was what Emmett meant to find out. One way or another, Will Sloane would pay dearly for his part in all this.

Elizabeth stopped and faced him, her expression wary. She had dark smudges under her eyes, as if she'd had a terrible night's sleep. He could relate. He'd hardly closed his eyes.

Reaching into his pocket, he withdrew a robin's egg–blue box that was tied with a white ribbon. "Here." He presented the box to her, and she accepted it hesitantly.

"What is it?" She untied the bow and lifted the lid to reveal the smaller box within. She flipped the top open and then gasped. "Oh my."

The way her gaze lit up, gray eyes sparking fire, caused a heady jolt of lust to streak throughout his body. He wanted to stoke that fire, watch her burn beneath him. Whatever else was between them, he could not help but notice her, react to her. He'd relived that kiss a hundred times, wondered how much more passion he could coax from this proper young woman.

Since she hadn't made a move to touch the ring, he took the box from her. "I thought you might need this today."

He reached for her hand and slipped the band on her small finger. A perfect fit, yet uncertainty gnawed at him as she remained silent. Did she not like it? He'd been led to believe that diamonds were the fashionable stone these days, at least that's what Charles Tiffany had said last night when the man reopened his store so Emmett could pick out a ring. His choice, an antique setting containing a four-carat, emerald-cut yellow stone, spoke to his betrothed's refined taste, he'd thought. But perhaps it was too gaudy—

"Emmett, this is . . . It's too much. You shouldn't have."

His stomach sank. Of course he'd bungled this. He started to take the band off her finger. "I'll exchange it, then. You may pick out whatever you want."

Elizabeth curled her fingers protectively, surprising him. "No, I love the ring. There's no need to exchange it for something else. I just . . . I can't believe you thought of this."

"Why wouldn't I buy you an engagement ring?" As soon as he said the words, he knew the answer. Elizabeth didn't consider them engaged. No doubt she'd been trying to think of a way out since they left Sherry's last evening.

Not that Emmett hadn't been trying to come up with an escape plan himself, but any way he looked at the situation, the two of them had to marry. He'd not allow his sisters to be ruined before they even debuted, period. They deserved the very best, and no matter the personal cost to himself, Emmett meant to ensure they had every advantage in life. He was marrying Elizabeth, and his sisters would be fully accepted into New York society.

And the retribution he planned for Elizabeth's brother was no one's business but his own.

"Emmett," Elizabeth said, "I don't want you to think me ungrateful, but perhaps we should discuss this supposed marriage."

"There is no 'supposed' marriage, Elizabeth. This is real. Do you want me to hire someone to see to the details, or would you rather take care of the planning?"

Her jaw fell open. "The planning? Hire someone? We hardly know one another. You can't seriously be considering going through with this."

As if he had a choice. Indeed, Will Sloane would pay dearly for blackmailing Emmett to go through with the ceremony, no matter how long Emmett's revenge took. Getting his hands on a large chunk of Northeast stock took a bit of the sting out, but Emmett would make sure Sloane regretted this.

His fiancée, for her part, couldn't sound more horrified if she tried. That shouldn't surprise him, but it did. After all, she was the one who'd asked him to kiss her. Had she been slumming? Wouldn't be the first time a high-society woman had thrown herself at him. Though the other night was the first time he'd taken up the offer.

As he'd done his whole life, he buried his emotions deep. He stepped back, putting distance between them. "I am prepared to marry you," he said flatly. "If you want to break it off and suffer the repercussions, that is your decision. But I won't be the one to go back on my word."

Her eyes narrowed. "Go back on your word? Your word to whom, exactly?"

Emmett could have bitten his tongue. Sloane had wanted Elizabeth to believe the marriage was real, that Emmett desired the match. *Make it look convincing, Cavanaugh. If she suspects you're lying, she'll never go through with it. And your sisters will suffer the consequences.* "That's an expression. All I mean is that I am going forward with this marriage."

She blinked, her brows flattening. "Why?"

"Does that matter?"

"Yes. You know nothing about me."

She knew even less about him—and Emmett meant to see it stayed that way. But he'd be damned if he'd try and convince her of something neither of them wanted. "Talk to your brother. If this wedding is called off, I won't be the one responsible. Grace Church has been booked for February twenty-second."

"But that's merely a month away!"

"You are welcome to bow out, Elizabeth." Emmett strode toward the entry, collected his hat and walking stick, and continued directly out the door. Before he closed the heavy wood behind him, he heard Edith Rutlidge say, "You have a lot of explaining to do, Lizzie."

* * *

On Saturday afternoon, Lizzie found herself sitting in a brougham next to her fiancé. Emmett had written to ask if she cared to go for a drive, and she had agreed. Perhaps this way she could find out why he was determined to go through with this marriage. Her reasons were more obvious, as protection against scandal, but Emmett's baffled her.

The brougham turned south on Broadway. "Wait, you said we were going for a drive in Central Park."

Emmett's lips twisted. "No, I said I wanted to take you for a drive. You assumed I meant Central Park."

Yes, she had assumed as much. All betrothed couples of a certain status were expected to participate in the obligatory afternoon brougham and landau procession at Fifty-Ninth and Fifth. But then, Emmett Cavanaugh did nothing according to expectation. And thank goodness for that.

"Then where are we going?"

"A surprise."

He appeared so pleased with himself, the devilish twinkle in his eye causing her heart to pound. Though it had only been a few days since his visit, she'd forgotten about his magnetism. The way her body was *aware* of him at all times. The cramped space in the small vehicle seemed to shrink in his presence, the air growing thinner to make her dizzy.

In a month she would be this man's *wife*. The idea boggled her mind. She hardly knew him. Was he truly prepared to marry her?

"How are the wedding plans progressing?" he asked, as if he could read her thoughts.

She sighed. "Exhausting. I had no idea there were so many details."

"You are welcome to hire whomever you need in order

to see everything done. Have the bills sent to me. There's no reason to run yourself ragged, Elizabeth."

"Thank you, but I'll manage. Since you insisted on taking over the reception, I don't have much to organize."

"All the same, please do not hesitate to cable if there is anything I or Colin can help with."

They rode in silence as they crossed Houston then Canal, and continued on. When they passed St. Paul's, she asked, "Are we going to the Battery?"

"No," he said, but didn't elaborate.

Finally they turned onto Beaver Street. Lizzie studied the buildings out the window. "Didn't you say you had an office building here?"

"Yes, I did." Just then the wheels slowed before a new five-story limestone-and-brick office building, one with *EAST COAST STEEL* carved into the elaborate archway over the door.

The Romanesque revival structure encompassed almost half the block. Rows and rows of windows stretched into the sky, so high that one could probably see Brooklyn from the top floor. Thick columns, heavy arches, and intricate carvings turned the building into a work of art.

"Come with me." Emmett descended and assisted her to the ground.

She lifted her skirts and walked with him through the large wooden door. A list hung on the wall, the offices and businesses contained within. Excitement hummed in her veins. Would one of these be hers?

"It's not there yet, if that's what you are wondering," Emmett said behind her.

"What's not here?"

"Your company name." He gestured to the black-and-white letters. "I wasn't sure what you planned on calling the investment firm." He pointed to the listing for *Cavanaugh* with an office on the third floor. "This is you."

"Oh, Emmett." She clutched his arm and grinned. "Really? My own office?"

His eyes dropped to her mouth, and he blinked a few times. "Yes," he told her gruffly. "I told you the space is yours for as long as you like."

She bounced on the toes of her half boots. "May I see it?"

"Of course. This way."

Giddiness surged through her, and she had to clamp her lips together to keep from peppering him with questions as they took the elevator up two floors. When they stepped out, he took her arm. "You are at the end of the hall."

Each door they passed had the company name written in big, white block letters on the glass. "Will I have my name on the door as well?"

"Yes. Just as soon as you tell me your company's name."

She'd been so focused on the wedding plans that she hadn't thought on what to call her investment firm. Best to use her name, because using *Cavanaugh* seemed strange . . . but then she wouldn't be a Sloane for much longer.

Emmett stopped at the last door. Reaching into his vest pocket, he withdrew a key and held it out in his huge palm. "Would you like the honor?"

She snatched the key and fit the metal end into the lock with a trembling hand. The tumbler caught and disengaged, and she turned the ornate brass knob to open the panel. A tiny waiting area appeared, another door behind it.

"This is for your secretary," Emmett said, and strode farther inside. "Now come and see the rest of it."

Hurrying forward, she threw wide the door. An airy,

well-lit space, the office had a row of windows along one side. The plaster walls had not yet been painted, and wires stuck out from where holes had been fashioned. The wood floor was beautiful, finished to a glossy shine, and a very impressive six-arm gasolier hung from the ceiling. A small pot-bellied stove rested in the corner, ready to keep the room's occupants warm.

The space wasn't perfect. It needed quite a bit of work. Furniture, paint, equipment . . . but she loved every raw inch. "Oh, Emmett." She turned in a circle to take everything in. "This is . . ."

"Not very dashing, I know. But the wiring's in for your gas, electricity, and telephone. I had them refinish the floors in pine. I wanted to leave the aesthetics to you, the furniture and the paint. But if you don't like it—"

He was nervous, she realized. Couldn't he tell how much she adored it? "No, I love it. I'm . . . I can't believe the office is really mine to use."

His shoulders visibly relaxed. "Good. There was another space on the second floor, but without as many windows."

She crossed to see the view. Beaver Street stretched out below, with Delmonico's at the corner of the next block. This would be her base as she advised clients, studied the stock reports, read the ticker tape . . . as she built a life for herself. The possibilities nearly made her giddy. "Where is your office?"

"Two flights up," he said, coming up alongside to lean against the window frame. "East Coast Steel has the entire top two floors. Perhaps we can ride to work together in the mornings."

Just hearing the words aloud sent a warm sizzle down her spine. Would she really be sharing a home with this man? The idea sounded insane . . . yet strangely appealing.

No one had affected her so deeply in such a short amount of time, not like Emmett. He was different from the other men, the bon vivants who spent time at parties and clubs, with no aspiration other than to waste their family's money.

While Emmett might not have as much polish or shine, he had depth of character. A solid foundation, just like the surrounding empty space. And with a bit of attention and care, who knew what might happen?

"I would like that," she said softly, referring to his comment about traveling to work together. "You won't mind a wife who works?"

He frowned, the cleft in his chin deepening. "I am not your brother or one of those other high-minded society fools. If you want to work, I'll not stand in your way. I'll support you, whatever you decide."

Relief nearly weakened her knees. Though he'd encouraged her, a small part of her had worried he would try to curtail her attempts to run her own company. It was one thing to partner with a business associate's sister. Quite another matter when that woman was your wife. Not all husbands would be so accommodating—at least not husbands in her social circle.

And with that, the answer seemed clear. "What about the Sloane and Cavanaugh Investment Company?"

His mouth hitched into a half smile that curled her toes. Heavens, he was a handsome man. "I think I like Cavanaugh and Cavanaugh better."

"But I'm not a Cavanaugh yet," she teased.

"You will be. In a month, Miss Sloane." Something in his dark gaze sparked, and a resulting heat rippled along her spine. As if someone had drawn in her corset, she suddenly could not take a deep breath. Was he thinking about kissing her again? Because she was most *definitely* thinking about kissing him again.

The moment stretched, their eyes locked, with the air coming in shorter and shorter supply. His fingers rose to gently tuck an errant strand of hair behind her ear. "Four weeks," he repeated, this time in a low, husky register that slid under her skin to settle in the marrow of her bones. She leaned in, seeking more, but Emmett took a hasty step back.

Embarrassed, Lizzie turned to the window. What was it about this man that tempted her, caused her to act so recklessly? Clearly he was not as eager for her . . . though there had been something in his tone just now. Some edge of restraint and frustration. Or had that been her imagination?

He cleared his throat. "I should return you home. It will grow dark soon."

She nodded, and he led her to the door. With one last hopeful look over her shoulder, Lizzie began to think that things might not turn out as badly as she had feared.

He'd nearly kissed her. Again.

As Emmett and Elizabeth rode back to Washington Square, he tried not to stare at her. Damned difficult, when he considered how appealing he found her—and not just her looks, either.

Though he'd never seen a more beautiful creature, there was much more to this woman than just her appearance. Her wit. Her intelligence. Her daring. She surprised him at every turn—and that should scare him shitless. He was not a man who enjoyed surprises.

Growing up on the streets of Five Points, every day had been unpredictable. Rival gangs, corrupt coppers, fights in the street . . . and at home. He'd never known what to expect there, whether his father would be drunk and his mother cowering in fear. Even finding food had been an undertaking, and some days there'd been none at all.

So when he'd started earning enough, he had fought to ensure there were no more surprises. He had assumed responsibility for his siblings. Acquired the best of everything. Trusted no one. Stuck to actresses because they were dependably single-minded, more concerned with their careers and his name than with monopolizing his time.

No, only the privileged liked surprises. When you lived in the gutter, a surprise could very well kill you. So why couldn't he get this woman off his mind?

"When do you think the office will be completed?" she asked, gaining his attention.

"Soon. I am having a private water closet installed for you. The materials will be delivered sometime in the next week. In the meantime, you should make all the cosmetic decisions with regards to the furniture and the paint colors."

"It also needs a private space, one where ladies may visit discreetly, preferably with an entrance off the hall. Women may not feel comfortable discussing finances in the main office where anyone can overhear."

He hadn't considered that. "Fine. I'll see it done."

"Thank you. Have you owned the building a long time?"

"I bought the land little more than a year ago. I tore down the existing buildings and had this one constructed. They finished about two months ago."

"And where were your offices before that?"

"Not far, on Broadway. But a smaller space."

"What did my brother say to you the night he found us at Sherry's?"

Emmett blinked at the change in topic, his brain rapidly searching for an answer. He couldn't tell her the truth, of course, yet he hated lying to her. She deserved to know the depths her brother had sunk to in order to ensure this wedding, but Emmett couldn't say anything. Revealing Sloane's blackmail would destroy Claire and Katie's future.

Lies had never been a problem for him before, not until Elizabeth Sloane. The more he saw her, the harder the struggle to keep the truth buried. Moments ago, in her new office, her clear, slate-colored eyes had gazed up at him with such trust and hope . . . which only contrasted with the ugliness surrounding so much of his life. This woman deserved better.

He brushed imaginary lint off the arm of his overcoat. "He was angry. Understandably so."

"Was there more fighting, then, after I left?"

"No. We argued, but in a civilized manner."

She seemed to turn that over in her mind, worrying her bottom lip between her teeth. "You don't like my brother, do you?"

At least he could give her honesty there. "No, I don't."

"Why not? Everyone else does."

Of course they did. Who wouldn't love the Golden Boy, who'd been given everything on a polished silver platter? Emmett couldn't wait to see Sloane brought low.

"Your brother worries over appearances, what the other notables will think, whereas I could not care less about the opinions of others."

"But you meet with him, and the others, every month. At the Knickerbocker Club."

"That is business, not friendship."

She shook her head, gaze fixed squarely ahead. "I don't know how you men do it. I could never go into business with someone I did not like."

"Not true. You were prepared to go into business with me, and we hadn't even met."

"Yes, but I thought you were a friend of my brother's. Which at least spoke somewhat to your character."

"What, that I have terrible taste in friends?" he said dryly.

She bumped her shoulder against his. "Be serious, Emmett."

God, he loved hearing his name on her lips. "I am always serious. You should know that by now."

"Hardly," she said with a huff. "My knowledge of you is appallingly scant."

True, yet she would be surprised by how much of himself he'd revealed. Elizabeth knew more than any other woman of his acquaintance, certainly. Maintaining a distance had been easy with the rest, but Elizabeth had slid under his skin. Burrowed deep into his tissues, so that the mere thought of her caused his cock to harden. "Men are uncomplicated creatures, and you are a bright woman. I have no doubt you'll figure us all out in no time."

He heard her sharp intake of breath, and he frowned. "What did I say?" Had he offended her somehow?

"No one has ever called me bright before," she said, and his shoulders relaxed.

"Not even your brother?" She shook her head, and Emmett said, "Then he is a bigger fool than I thought."

Elizabeth's head swung sharply, her stare locking with his. Emotion swirled in the gray mist of her pupils. "Thank you," she said.

Warmth slid through his belly, a reminder of the desire that had simmered all day in her presence. The urge to kiss her resurfaced, stronger than ever. He considered leaning forward, touching his mouth to hers, drinking her in and teasing her until she gasped for breath. However, kissing her would not help her decide to call off the wedding, which was the only foreseeable way out of the mess her brother had created.

He shifted to the window and collected himself. Today had been a colossal mistake. In spending time with her, he'd only unearthed more guilt he did not need and failed in providing her with reasons to break the engagement. Not to mention driven himself half-crazy with desire. Why had he thought bringing her to Beaver Street a good idea?

Admit it, he told himself. *You wished to see her again.* Christ, he was an idiot.

They rode in silence for the remainder of the journey, the awkwardness as thick as coal dust. As a distraction, he concentrated on everything he needed to do today, the hundreds of tasks awaiting him in his office. Important tasks that did not include one blond, silver-eyed former debutante.

When they arrived in Washington Square, he helped her down from the brougham. Kelly remained in the driver's seat, attending to the horses and thankfully quiet. The Sloane butler opened the door as they came up the steps, and so Emmett turned to bid her a polite good-bye.

"A moment, Frederic," Elizabeth said to the butler, and Emmett's stomach sank. He'd hoped to escape without delay.

The butler disappeared behind the closed door to give them privacy, and she tilted her head. "I enjoyed today very much. Thank you."

"You're welcome."

She waited, not speaking, studying him, and he asked, "Was there anything else, Miss Sloane?"

"You once told me that you are not a nice man, but I think you're wrong. You're willing to marry me, and I don't truly understand why, but I am very grateful for all that you've undertaken for me."

The tip of his tongue burned with the need to tell her the truth, to set her straight about both himself and the reason he was marrying her. By sheer force of will, however, he kept his mouth closed. With a dip of his chin in acknowledgment, he reached to rap on the front door. The panel swung open immediately, the butler emerging, and Emmett wasted no time. He spun on his heel and hurried to the walk, intent on climbing back in his carriage and getting the hell away from Washington Square.

There would be no more outings, he swore. No rides. No visits. No plump, berry-colored lips parted in breathless anticipation. The next time he saw her, if she did not call off the wedding first, would be at the altar of Grace Church.

Chapter Eight

❦

Be sure you do not spend your money just for the sake of showing how liberal you can be.

—American Etiquette and Rules of Politeness, 1883

An unbelievably large crowd had gathered inside Grace Church on a cold Wednesday in late February for the wedding. *Her* wedding.

A hysterical laugh burned in Lizzie's throat, and she struggled to suppress it. Dressed in an eight-thousand-dollar wedding gown, she waited with her brother at the back of the church, the enormity of the moment nearly causing her to turn and run.

Four weeks had passed without a word from Emmett, her soon-to-be husband. During the whirlwind of planning and dress fittings, Lizzie hadn't allowed herself to dwell on his notable absence. But standing here, on the verge of pledging her troth to the man until death do they part, she couldn't help but wonder what he'd been doing in that time. What had been so pressing to keep him away? To prevent him from writing to her?

And she was *marrying* him. For mercy's sake, how could she walk down the aisle?

She thought of her investment firm, of her office on Beaver Street. The one dream she'd had for years. If she didn't go through with the wedding, she'd never succeed. If she were shrouded in scandal, failure would be guaranteed. Will had been right; she might not like society's rules, but she could not change them, not now.

Remember the man who took you to see your office, she told herself. Emmett had been kind and solicitous on that trip. Respectful. Excited to show her the space he was readying for her. The fragile hope she'd clung to since then resurfaced, allowing her to take a deep breath. Perhaps this marriage would flourish in the end.

Edith appeared at Lizzie's side. "You look beautiful," her friend said, and squeezed Lizzie's arm. "Are you certain you want to go through with this?"

Lizzie shook out her gloved hands, trying to rid herself of the nerves. "Yes," she said, though she didn't necessarily believe it. If there were another way out of this mess, she would've figured it out by now.

"Well, I will stand by you no matter what you decide," Edith whispered seriously. "I still don't believe you want this marriage."

"I have no choice. The deed is very nearly done."

"It's not over until after the wedding night," Edith said pointedly, then stepped back to her place in line as the maid of honor.

The mention of the wedding night sent panic through every part of Lizzie's body. She put a hand to her middle, took deep breaths, and willed her stomach to calm.

"Everything is going to be fine." Will placed a large hand on the small of her back, steadying her. "Remember, Sloanes aren't quitters."

She stared at her brother, so handsome in his gray morning coat and matching trousers. She needed his strength and reassurance, just as she had when she was a little girl. "Will, I don't know if I can do this."

He grabbed her hand, his expression calm. "Lizzie, you have no choice. It's done. All you need to do is walk to the front of the church and repeat your vows."

"I hardly know him."

"You'll be fine. Cavanaugh takes his responsibilities seriously. He'll take care of you, as he's done with his brother and two younger sisters."

"I don't want to be a responsibility," she said, her voice rising. *I want him to love me,* she thought, even though such a thing would likely never happen. She might as well hope to be given a seat on the stock exchange.

"You know what I mean. He won't hurt you; I swear it. But you may always come to me, Lizzie. I'm here for you. No matter what happens with Cavanaugh, I'll support you in whatever you need."

The organ music swelled, robbing her of the ability to answer. The bridesmaids and ushers started down the aisle. She closed her eyes and dragged in as much air as her corset allowed. The time had arrived.

She felt Will's arms go around her in a tight hug. "Lizzie, you're the smartest, bravest woman I know," he said softly in her ear. "It's been my honor and privilege to see you grow up, to watch you evolve into the woman you've become. And I'm sorry that our parents are not here to see it as well. They would be just as proud of you as I am right now. I love you, runt."

Tears welled, and she concentrated on not ruining Will's perfectly starched white shirt. She couldn't answer, so she hugged him back.

Will spoke to someone nearby, then said to her, "They're waiting for us."

Exhaling, she pulled away from her brother and smoothed her cream satin gown. Trimmed simply with Duchesse-point lace, the gown was low on her neck with elbow-length sleeves. The train, sewn with hundreds upon hundreds of tiny pearls and edged with orange blossoms, opened to a jaw-dropping ninety inches. Lizzie had argued the garment too extravagant, but Will had insisted, saying, "Appearances must be maintained."

He'd also instructed Lord & Taylor to spare no expense on her trousseau. Some of the lingerie had made her blush. To actually wear those pieces? Mortifying.

"It'll work out," Will said quietly. He fluffed her tulle veil that was attached to a wreath of natural orange blossoms. "You shall see, Lizzie."

Palms gone damp inside her gloves, she clutched her bouquet of white roses and lilies of the valley, and concentrated on not tripping as they started down the aisle. Familiar, curious gazes followed her path. Friends and acquaintances she'd known all her life, each one likely wondering why she was marrying Emmett Cavanaugh today. Not that she knew the answer.

A man stepped forward, and Lizzie's lungs seized, robbing her of breath. *Emmett.* A dove-colored tailcoat covered his broad shoulders, while a stark, white tie graced his throat. His hair had been oiled, highlighting his chiseled features, and his near-black stare focused only on her. Her stomach fluttered, his intense concentration both disarming and flattering. How could he, in a crowd of hundreds, make her feel like the only woman on earth?

He did not look hesitant or unhappy. He looked . . . proud. Confident. As if he had no misgivings whatsoever about what was taking place. But then, he usually appeared as such, like the world bowed to his whims, not the other way around.

Did he expect the same obedience from her?

He came down the few steps to meet her. Lizzie's panic flared once more, and her feet faltered. Will held steadfast, clutching her hand where it rested on his arm, to ensure she didn't fall on her face.

They stopped at the base of the stairs where Will bent to kiss her cheek. He uncurled her fingers from his forearm, and presented her to Emmett. She waited for some reaction, some hint as to what Emmett was thinking as he led her up the steps, but he'd become unreadable.

"Relax," Emmett said for her ears alone. "You aren't being led to the gallows."

She stiffened but, before she knew it, they were kneeling on the small bench, and the rector began speaking. The ceremony was short and to the point, though Lizzie would never remember it in the years to come. All she could think about was the large, enigmatic man at her side. Why was he doing this? Where had he been the last few weeks?

When they finished reciting the words binding them together, Lizzie was too numb to worry about what followed. So when Emmett lifted her veil, leaned in, and kissed her, she had no defenses in place. This was no mere brush of the lips, either. His mouth lingered on hers, warm and deliberate, the kiss embarrassingly thorough. Lizzie wasn't fooled; this was a show of possession in front of New York society. A way to prove they were truly married.

He finally pulled back, and she caught the burning fervor in his eyes, one she hadn't seen since the dinner at Sherry's. Before he turned her to the crowd, he put his lips near her ear. "You're mine."

* * *

From across the ballroom, Emmett watched as his new wife wobbled slightly. Her cheeks were flushed, eyes overly bright. All the signs were there, he thought, drumming his fingers on the table. He was certainly no teetotaler, but he did not wish for a drunken bride.

Not today. Not when he had plans for her later.

He signaled a waiter. "Please see that Mrs. Cavanaugh is not served any more champagne," he said quietly. The waiter nodded and disappeared into the crowd to carry out the master of house's order.

Over three-hundred guests had crammed into Emmett's home for the reception, and no expense had been spared. The house was decorated completely in white, from the thousands of white roses on every surface to the white satin chair backs. White Limoges china and crystal goblets flown in from France. There were complicated ice sculptures and even a champagne fountain. Delmonico's had provided the eight-course dinner as well as the six-tiered white wedding cake.

Emmett had planned the reception himself, hiring a small army to see it done. Sloane had offered to contribute, but Emmett refused. This day reflected on him as much as the Sloanes, perhaps more so, and he'd wanted all of New York to choke on how far this Five Points thug had risen. Besides, there were other, more public ways of driving Sloane to the poorhouse than a wedding reception.

Like stripping Northeast Railroad out of Sloane's hands.

Emmett's gaze returned to his wife. Definitely drunk. For the last hour, she'd circulated through the guests, hardly taking the time to eat, let alone speak to her husband. He'd kept his eyes on her, though. That's how he knew when she began weaving on her feet.

"You keep staring at her like that, she's likely to go up in flames," his brother murmured at his side.

Emmett frowned pointedly at Brendan. "Don't think I've forgotten your part in this."

Brendan lifted his hands, palms out. "How was I to know someone would send her brother to discover the two of you? I thought one harmless dinner—"

"In a private dining room set up for me and my mistress. Indeed, how could anything go wrong?" Emmett swallowed the rest of his drink, slammed the empty tumbler back on the table.

Brendan chuckled. "You still compromised her, dear brother."

Yes, Emmett had kissed her. That hardly seemed enough to warrant marriage. "Well, you've gotten your wish. Claire and Katie's coming out is all but guaranteed. Is there anything else I can do for you, *dear brother?*"

"Yes, you can collect your bride and start your honeymoon."

Honeymoon. A sizzle slid over Emmett's skin, the heat working its way to his balls. He'd have Elizabeth all to himself for two weeks. She might appear reserved and proper, a buttoned-up blue blood, but that exterior melted away when he kissed her. She became a live electric wire in his hands, a shock of raw passion unlike any he'd ever experienced. And he meant to have every bit of that passion.

"These were a nice touch, by the way." Brendan lifted the expensive Cuban cigar wrapped in a one-hundred-dollar bill. Each male guest had received one, while every woman at the reception had received a gold-and-emerald Tiffany bracelet. Lavish, but a necessary statement.

Emmett might not have been born with a silver spoon in his mouth, but he could buy and sell these Knickerbockers ten times over.

He noticed Elizabeth sway once more. "I think I'll fetch Mrs. Cavanaugh."

Brendan slapped Emmett's shoulder. "See you in two weeks. And congratulations, Emmett. She's a smart, funny, and attractive woman. I think you've met your match in her."

Though he didn't need it, Emmett was glad of Brendan's approval, since they would all be living together when Emmett and Elizabeth returned from Newport. Emmett rose and left the ballroom for the adjoining hall, where he found Kelly lurking around the corner.

"Are we ready to depart?" Emmett asked.

"Sure thing, Bish. Just tell me when. But I figured you'd want to hang around your fancy guests some more."

"No, I'd like to get going before dusk."

Kelly's lips twitched. "Anxious for tonight, are you?"

"Go to hell," he said, though the words lacked heat. Kelly was right, and no use arguing it. "I'll inform Elizabeth that we're leaving."

"I'll pull the carriage around." Kelly pushed off the wall and started for the back of the house.

Emmett pivoted—only to discover Will Sloane directly behind him, a deep scowl on the other man's face. Emmett folded his arms across his chest. "I wondered when you'd find me, Sloane."

Sloane stalked forward, shifting around the corner where they wouldn't be overheard. "I'll be checking on her, ensuring she's happy. And if you don't make her happy, there will be hell to pay, Cavanaugh."

Emmett would have laughed, if he hadn't been so disgusted at the hypocrisy. He couldn't wait to bury this man.

He stepped closer and snarled, "Spare me your sack of shit. If you were concerned at all with her happiness, you wouldn't have forced this marriage. You wouldn't have blackmailed me by threatening to ruin my sisters unless I married yours."

"You left me no goddamn choice," Sloane fired back, not backing down. "You attacked her in a private dining salon with half of New York society one floor below."

Emmett threw his head back and gave a disbelieving laugh. "*I* attacked *her*? Is that what you've told yourself in order to sleep at night? Your sister practically begged me to kiss her."

Sloane's entire body went rigid. "You bastard. Do not even imply that she is not pure."

"I don't give a damn whether she's pure or not," Emmett said with a malevolent smile. "But I do intend on finding out the answer tonight."

Sloane's nostrils flared, and he closed his eyes briefly. "You are crude and disgusting, Cavanaugh." He shoved his hands in his trouser pockets, possibly to keep from hitting Emmett. "You don't deserve her."

No argument there, Emmett thought. The differences between him and his new wife were glaringly apparent to everyone. The two of them had, however, stood before man and God today to pledge until death do they part, so Sloane could shove his opinion up his own ass.

"I might not deserve her, but I have her, Sloane. And there's not a damn thing you can do about it." Brushing past the other man, Emmett stalked to the ballroom. The time had come to retrieve his bride and get the hell out of here.

* * *

Lizzie could no longer feel her toes. Whether the numbness resulted from the champagne or her tight wedding shoes, she could not say.

The entire day had been surreal. First the wedding, then the ride uptown with Emmett—who had been unnaturally subdued after the ceremony—to this extravagant reception that paraded both the wealth and power of Emmett Cavanaugh.

Her *husband*.

She had married him. The idea hadn't yet sunk in, but one glance at her wedding gown confirmed the event had transpired. What happened now? Lizzie hardly knew what to say, how to act. What did he expect from her? No one had prepared her for the wedding day, let alone the wedding *night*. Women of her class never talked about what happened in the bedroom. She had a vague understanding, but the hot, intense stare Emmett leveled at her as she moved about the ballroom made her even more nervous. The best course of action had seemed to avoid him.

"Hello, Mrs. Cavanaugh."

A handsome man and a young red-haired woman suddenly stood in front of her. She searched her muzzy brain for a name. "Mr. Harper. And Mrs. Harper. Thank you both so much for coming." Mr. Harper was one of Emmett and Will's business acquaintances and the owner of the New American Bank. He'd recently married himself, having met Mrs. Harper on a train. The two were a strikingly adorable couple.

Mrs. Harper boldly grabbed Lizzie's hand, pumped it a few times. "I know we met in the receiving line, Mrs. Cavanaugh, but that wasn't anything substantial. Certainly not enough to get a feel for a person. I told Ted that we must have you and Mr. Cavanaugh over for dinner soon. I can't believe he decided to get married—and to someone from such an impressive family!"

She paused for a breath, and her husband smiled at her indulgently. He must be used to the way his wife talked, as if she had to get everything out as quickly as possible. "What Mrs. Harper means," he said, "is that we're very happy for the both of you. From what I've seen today, I think you will bring some much needed joy to Emmett's world."

Lizzie certainly hoped so. Before she could answer, Mrs. Harper blurted, "And that kiss at the church!" She fanned herself. "Oh, my. I thought half the ladies in attendance would faint."

Heat engulfed Lizzie. Embarrassment aside, she decided she liked Mrs. Harper. Hard to hate a woman who said exactly what she was thinking, with no filter of any kind. Mrs. Harper reminded Lizzie of Edith. "Thank you both for the kind words. I would love to come to dinner."

"Oh, excellent." Mrs. Harper beamed. "Maybe you'd call one afternoon, as well? Ted's house is so big, and I'm not used to having that much space. I lived in a boardinghouse before I married him. Did you know that?"

"No," Lizzie answered honestly. "I didn't."

"Come visit me, and I'll tell you the entire story," Mrs. Harper said.

"I'd like that," Lizzie said. "And please, call me Lizzie."

Mrs. Harper blinked a few times, and Lizzie thought the woman might cry. "Thank you. And you must call me Clara."

"It was lovely to meet you, Clara, Mr. Harper. I do hope you enjoy the rest of the afternoon."

"Before we go," Mr. Harper said, "Emmett has told me

of your new venture. If you ever need help or credit, please don't hesitate to contact me at the bank."

The offer was unexpected and extremely generous. Moreover, he hadn't belittled or discouraged her. "Thank you, Mr. Harper. I just may do that."

The couple said their good-byes and moved back into the crowd. As Lizzie turned, she glimpsed Emmett rising from their table and striding toward the exit. His long-legged, confident gait ate up the ground beneath him. Heads turned as he passed—remarkable when one considered the room was stuffed with dignitaries, industrialists, and the crème of society—and she wondered if they saw what she did: Power. Intelligence. Unrelenting drive. Combining these qualities with his all-too handsome face, she could hardly stand to look away.

Then she noticed someone else headed in the same direction, and her stomach knotted. *Will*. And the expression on her brother's face did not bode well. Was he following Emmett?

Lizzie hurried after her brother, intent on discovering the problem and possibly preventing a brawl. Her dress hindered her a bit, and by the time she stepped into the corridor, she heard two angry male voices.

". . . and if you don't make her happy, there will be hell to pay, Cavanaugh."

Lizzie nearly smiled. Will had always been protective of her, oftentimes too much so. She opened her mouth to intervene, but her husband's furious words stopped her cold.

"Spare me your sack of shit. If you were concerned at all with her happiness, you wouldn't have forced this marriage. You wouldn't have blackmailed me by threatening to ruin my sisters unless I married yours."

Lizzie jerked as if the words were blows. *Blackmailed*. Will had . . . blackmailed Emmett into marrying her? By

threatening Emmett's sweet, young half sisters? She
pressed a fist to her middle, surprise and shock nearly
doubling her over.

He hadn't wanted to marry me. Will had lied. This was
all a *lie*.

Oh, God. She was such a *fool*. Will had claimed Emmett
wanted to marry her, and Emmett had shown up with the
ring, saying this was a real marriage. How could she have
believed either of them?

She could not breathe, her corset digging painfully into
her ribs. There wasn't . . . enough air. She put a hand to the
wall to keep from falling over.

"You left me no goddamn choice," Will was saying.
"You attacked her in a private dining salon with half of
New York society one floor below you."

Emmett laughed, though the sound came off as cold
to Lizzie's ears. "*I* attacked *her*? Is that what you've told
yourself in order to sleep at night? Your sister practically
begged me to kiss her."

Her mouth fell open in silent horror. Had he truly
said . . . To her brother? Humiliation scorched her insides, and bile burned the back of her throat. She had to
escape. Pivoting, she had no choice but to return to the
ballroom. Where hundreds of people were celebrating a
marriage that was a sham. A hoax.

A complete fraud.

The brilliance of the white ballroom nearly blinded her,
an atmosphere that had seemed romantic only moments
ago. The idea of Emmett's laboring over every detail, ensuring the day would be perfect for her, had comforted her
earlier. Obviously she'd been deluding herself. This had
nothing to do with her.

Guests smiled at her as she passed, murmured their
congratulations. People she recognized, all familiar faces

from the world in which she had lived her entire life. *I'll only marry for love*, she'd sworn. *Do not marry because you're forced to, because society expects it.*

Failure had never tasted so bitter.

Grabbing a glass of champagne off a passing tray, she downed the sweet bubbly in one swallow. Unfortunately, the bitterness remained. Pressure built behind her eyes, but she fought the tears. No good would come of crying. The deed was done; they were married. She'd wanted the money to open an investment firm, and she had succeeded. Unless . . .

Had Emmett lied about that as well?

No, he hadn't lied about wanting to marry her, she recalled. *I am prepared to marry you,* he'd said. Told her he would not go back on his *word*. It had been Will who had proclaimed that Emmett wanted to marry her, not Emmett. If only she had known of Will's machinations, the level her brother had lowered himself to, she would have called off the wedding.

Too late, she thought. And New York had the strictest divorce laws in the country. Acquiring one would be impossible. An annulment, however, would be much easier.

And really, why wouldn't Emmett agree? He hadn't wanted to marry her. With an annulment, it would be as if the marriage had never taken place. Will certainly couldn't quibble over that. She would save her reputation, and Emmett's sisters would be protected. An annulment meant they could both walk away, forgetting the whole thing.

Resolved, she straightened her shoulders. Yes, an annulment was the answer. But would he still back her investment firm? He'd promised, but all would be lost if he reneged. She'd be right back where she had started.

"Lizzie!" Edith Rutlidge arrived with two other girls at her side. "There you are. Come, we want to show your dress to Lucinda Van Cortland. She's marrying an English duke in the fall, and I told her that your dress had considerable dash, and she had to see it up close."

Lizzie nodded woodenly as another waiter passed by with a tray of champagne. She stopped him, ready to swap out her empty glass for a fresh one, but the waiter started to pull the tray out of her reach. She was quicker, however, and had a full glass before he could get away. Was there some unwritten rule about how much champagne a bride could imbibe on her wedding day?

If so, Lizzie planned to break that particular one.

"I know you're cold, Mrs. Cavanaugh, but please, try and remain still," her maid said, tediously unfastening the long row of buttons on Lizzie's wedding gown.

Lizzie was having trouble remaining still, but the reason had nothing to do with her temperature. She was drunk, so drunk that the remaining time at the reception had proved bearable. She'd been able to smile and laugh, as any bride should on her wedding day, despite the hurt and anger inside her chest.

And when her husband had cornered her with instructions to change for their journey, she'd managed to nod instead of shouting at him like a Bowery hot corn girl.

"There," Pauline said. "Let's get it off, then."

"Are you accompanying me on the honeymoon?" she asked her maid as they worked the luxurious gown over Lizzie's head.

"I am, ma'am. Your husband asked me himself. Newport will be mighty cold this time of year."

Newport? Strange that he'd informed Pauline of their

plans, but not Lizzie. Didn't he even care to consult with her, to ascertain her wishes on their honeymoon?

But then, why would he, when he'd never wanted to marry her in the first place?

Once she was dressed in a smart traveling ensemble there was no reason to stay behind. Still, she dawdled. "Did you pack the blue gown, the one with the—"

The adjoining door burst open, and her husband strode in. He'd changed into a striped dark blue coat and matching trousers. Lizzie blinked, struck by his handsomeness. Then she remembered his words from the hall: *Your sister practically begged me to kiss her.*

All the loathing and fury she'd been suppressing rose to the surface, causing her to snap, "Don't you knock?"

Calm as could be, Emmett turned to Pauline. "That will be all. Go and ready yourself for the journey."

"Of course, Mr. Cavanaugh." With a curtsy, she hurried from the room.

Lizzie ignored him, instead busying herself with putting on her gloves. It proved a difficult task, considering the champagne in her system.

Heavy footfalls signaled his approach, and then the tips of his black shoes appeared in her vision. He took her wrist, and long fingers began to slide the tiny pearl buttons of her glove through the matching holes. Her breath picked up, his nearness surrounding her, causing her head to swim. He was gentle, treating her as if she were fragile and precious. She wasn't fooled. This was still the crude man from the hall who'd discussed bedding her with her brother.

When he finished with both gloves, a large hand lifted her chin. His eyes were hard, glittering with an emotion she couldn't decipher. "I never need knock, wife. You'll do well to remember that."

Champagne and heartache made her brave. She jerked away from his touch. "I am not one of your actresses. I'm your wife, and if you confuse the two, I'll do more than lock my door."

His lips twisted in amusement, lines bracketing the sides of his mouth. "If you think I could ever confuse you for one of those women, you're drunker than I thought."

"I am not drunk," she snapped. "And it wasn't as if you were abstaining at the reception. I saw you down more than one glass of gin."

"Watching me, were you?"

She gritted her teeth. "Hardly. I think we both know where this ridiculous marriage stands."

Fury flashed before he could hide it. But the satisfaction didn't last because his cool, impenetrable mask soon slipped back into place. "Let's go." He stalked to the door and yanked it open. "The train's waiting."

They descended the pink marble staircase in silence. The guests were still enjoying the reception, the revelry of the ballroom a dull hum throughout the giant house. What was Emmett's hurry to leave? Not that Lizzie minded. She'd had enough of pretending to be a blushing bride. Moreover, the sooner they arrived in Newport, the sooner she could discuss the annulment with him.

When they reached the front entry, Katie, Claire, and Brendan stood at the door, while Graham, the butler, waited with their coats. The girls looked nervous, their fingers twisting in the ribbons on their fancy dresses made especially for the wedding. Brendan leaned down and whispered something to them. Katie stepped forward first and gave a proper curtsy. "Welcome to the family, Elizabeth."

Claire glanced up at Brendan, who nodded. Emmett's littlest sister also curtsied. "We are glad you married our brother," she said in careful, measured words. Brendan had obviously been coaching them.

Lizzie's throat closed, her heart melting. No matter how she felt about the eldest Cavanaugh, she could not resist these two adorable girls. She went to hug Katie. "Thank you, Katie. I hope we'll become good friends." Then she hugged Claire. "Thank you, my dear."

"May I touch your collar?" Claire asked.

"Of course," Lizzie answered, and the girl ran her small hand over the fur on Lizzie's jacket lapel.

"It's so soft," Claire marveled. "I have a coat that feels just like that. Emmett bought it for me."

Emmett stepped forward. "That's enough. Give Elizabeth room to breathe," he said gently. "Girls, come here." He drew his half sisters aside and dropped to one knee. He held their hands and spoke softly to them, too low for Lizzie to overhear.

They nodded and smiled, and he hugged them both, wrapping his big arms around their tiny bodies.

"He does that every time he travels," Brendan said quietly at her side. "He reassures them that, no matter what, he'll always come back."

She didn't want to care, but curiosity won out. "Why?"

"Because everyone's always left him."

While she struggled with that revelation, Brendan took her coat from Graham and held it out for her. Lizzie slid her arms inside, and he drew the garment over her shoulders. "Give him a chance," Brendan murmured. "He's not nearly as hard as people assume him to be."

A host of comments came to mind, mostly all the reasons she did not want to give Emmett a chance. Brendan seemed to sense her reticence, so he leaned in and kissed her cheek. "Welcome to the family, Elizabeth."

"Please," she told him, "call me Lizzie." She liked Brendan. He'd been perfectly polite and charming since she'd met him at the reception today. Decidedly different from the dark and brooding man she'd married.

Brendan grinned. "All right, Lizzie."

Emmett slid into his heavy woolen coat and then offered his arm to Lizzie. "Shall we, Mrs. Cavanaugh?"

The name shocked her, as it had each time she'd heard it since the wedding. Thankfully, she would not be Mrs. Cavanaugh for long.

Chapter Nine

~~~

Husband and wife should remember that they have taken each other "for better or for worse."

—American Etiquette and Rules of Politeness, 1883

Elizabeth was certainly doing a damn fine job of pretending he didn't exist, Emmett thought as they waited in his private Pullman car. Was his new wife planning to ignore him for the entire journey to Rhode Island, or merely the beginning?

He tried not to stare at her trim waist or lush curves. Tried and failed. Her traveling costume hugged her frame, and the vision left Emmett simmering in anticipation. He hadn't looked forward to the wedding, but the wedding night had definitely inspired some creative fantasies over the past weeks.

"Drink?" he asked her, standing at the small bar positioned at one end of the car.

"Yes, please," she said, continuing her pattern of one- and two-word answers since leaving the house.

He poured a glass of water and brought it to where she sat, her posture perfectly rigid. "Thank you," she said, and took the glass from his hand. Their fingers, now both gloveless, brushed, and the slight contact made him edgy. Christ, how he desired this woman.

"Water?" she remarked coolly.

Cradling a crystal goblet full of wine in his hand, Emmett lowered himself down next to her. He stretched his arm along the back of the sofa. "I think you've had enough champagne, don't you?"

She reached to set the glass on the side table. Then she folded her hands in her lap and stared out the window.

He waited for her to speak. When she didn't, he asked, "Are you planning to ignore me for two weeks, then?"

Her head swiveled toward him. "I am not ignoring you. I merely have nothing to say."

"That is a surprise," he murmured, and then chuckled at the glare she leveled at him. "You must admit, you are not shy about sharing your opinions."

"If you are intimating that I am some harpy—"

"Of course not. Though time will tell on that, I suppose. We've only been married a few hours."

She pressed her lips together, tiny creases forming around the edges. "And what sort of husband do *you* plan to be, Emmett? A faithful one?"

He hadn't even thought about it, to be honest, but the way she sneered the last question, as if he couldn't possibly remain faithful, rankled. "Are you saying you'll satisfy all my needs, Elizabeth?"

Her porcelain cheeks bloomed a pretty pink, and something that felt a lot like longing wound its way through his guts. This incredibly lovely woman—his wife—was more beautiful than he deserved, certainly.

"You know that's not what I meant. We know absolutely nothing about one another."

Wrong, he wanted to tell her. He knew of her intelligence, her determination. Her kindness, not only from seeing her with his sisters but from watching her speak to the guests today, ensuring each one felt welcomed. She also had a playful sense of humor and a tendency to bite her lower lip. And he knew how well she kissed.

He also knew that he was dying to have her, to possess her in every way. The thought caused his groin to grow heavy, so he put sleeping with her firmly out of his mind. He did not want their first time together to be on a train.

A door in the rear of the car opened, and Kelly leaned in. "We're hitched and everything's loaded. You need anything?"

Emmett shook his head. "No. Thank you, Kelly."

The door closed, and Emmett noticed Elizabeth staring at it, her brow lowered in confusion. Perhaps this was a good time to address her earlier complaint. "What would you like to know?"

Her gaze flew to his. "About Kelly?"

He lifted a shoulder and took a sip of his wine. "About anything. We have to pass the journey somehow."

"How do you know him?"

"We grew up together in Five Points. Kelly was . . . an enforcer of sorts in the group we ran with."

"And what was your role?"

"No. That's not something I discuss. Ever."

"But how—"

He held up a hand. "Ask me about anything else, Elizabeth. I won't answer questions about my childhood."

She tapped her fingernails on the edge of the sofa. She'd removed her gloves when they first entered the car, revealing her slim, graceful fingers and smooth, white skin. He imagined those hands on him later, teasing and stroking, and he began to harden. Damn it.

The train lurched as the wheels started turning. Elizabeth fell toward him, and he caught her shoulder with his free hand. When she reached out to stabilize herself, her palm landed on his thigh, face dangerously close to his. If he shifted forward a few inches, he could kiss her.

Neither one of them moved, eyes locked, and he waited to see what she would do. The warmth of her hand burned through the fabric covering his leg. Then her fingers shifted ever so slightly on his thigh, as if testing the feel of him, and Emmett stopped breathing as more blood rushed to his groin. He would give everything he owned if she would slide those digits a mere six inches higher.

A few more hours, he told himself.

She suddenly dropped her gaze and retreated, righting herself. "I apologize."

Emmett took a healthy swallow of wine, glad to have a moment to regain his composure. He hadn't been this worked up over a woman since his first visit to a brothel at the age of twelve.

After a moment, she said, "So I can ask you anything?"

"Yes, as long as it's nothing to do with Five Points."

"Do you still plan to back my brokerage firm?"

He frowned. "Why wouldn't I? You won the wager." She looked vastly relieved by that statement. Had she thought he would renege on their deal? While he might be many things, most of them unpleasant, he was a man of his word.

"I wasn't sure you would still . . ."

"Still, what? Live up to my agreements?"

She didn't answer, and his lip curled in annoyance. Before he could tell her how wrong she was about that, she asked, "Did you send the note to my brother? The one that caused him to discover us at Sherry's?"

"No," he bit out, jerking in surprise. "Why in God's name would I have done that?"

"Well, *someone* did. And it was convenient, wouldn't

you say, that Will arrived just when things . . . appeared the worst?"

"And you believe I would orchestrate that? Do you honestly think so little of me?"

Her frigid gray gaze met his, her lips compressed into a thin, disapproving line. An answer all unto itself, really. *Fuck me.* Anger lit him up, like coal shoved into a blast furnace. What did he need to do in order to prove himself to this woman? Would she always presume the worst?

He shot to his feet, determined to get away before he did or said something he regretted.

"Where are you going?"

"Outside," he snapped, stalking toward the door. "It's a hell of a lot warmer out there."

Founded in the middle of the seventeenth century, Newport, Rhode Island, had been best known for its colonial architecture until William Shepard Wetmore constructed the giant Chateau-sur-Mer cottage on Bellevue Avenue. New York society took notice and swiftly turned the tiny town into *the* place for the summer.

Lizzie had been traveling to Newport all her life. The Sloanes owned a fourteen-room, Gothic-style "cottage" on Wellington Avenue, used exclusively for the eight weeks of the summer social season. She loved it here; from lazy afternoons at Easton's Beach to ambling along the Cliff Walk, the seaside town had always been her favorite place to visit.

But winter cast the surroundings in a much different light, she thought as the carriage ambled toward the center of town. Austere. Forbidding. A description that applied to the man sitting across from her as well.

Emmett had not returned to his car during the remainder

of their journey. And since disembarking, he'd hardly spoken, seemingly content to watch the landscape roll by. The fading light played across his profile, highlighting the rigid jaw and strong cheekbones.

Your sister practically begged me to kiss her.

Mercy, she could nearly die recalling those mortifying words, mostly because they were true. She'd prefer her brother didn't know of her wantonness, however. Unlikely she'd ever forgive Emmett for revealing it, either. One thing she knew for certain, she would never, ever beg Emmett Cavanaugh for another dratted thing.

The carriage turned off Bellevue and rolled toward the water. Soon a three-story, white Italianate-style mansion came into view, the property set back on a sweeping lawn. There were large windows with black shutters and a porch that ran along the entire south side. A wide staircase curved up to the front entrance, and she counted five—no, six chimneys. The house seemed to go on for miles.

"I remember this one," she said. "I've never been inside. Hasn't it been empty for the last two years?"

"Three," Emmett answered. "I acquired Oceancrest last month as part of a business deal. The man who built it five years ago died unexpectedly. The interior has not been re-modeled, but it's been cleaned and aired out. I had a small amount of furniture delivered as well. You should, of course, feel free to redecorate as you wish."

She should correct him, take the opportunity to explain she had no intentions of redecorating anything since the two of them would soon procure an annulment, but she held off. Better to have the conversation inside, once they both settled in and where the driver would not overhear.

The interior was even more impressive than the exterior. Two massive chandeliers hung over the two-story entryway, which had to be at least forty, perhaps fifty feet high, all carved, white marble. Archways flanked by Doric columns had been cut out to lead deeper into the house, including one over the dramatic sweeping staircase. Designed like an Italian palazzo, the open-air second floor overlooked the great hall from surrounding balconies.

But there was hardly time to gawk. An army of servants had lined up to greet the new master and mistress of the house, and so she came forward. Emmett surprised her, warmly greeting each staff member and talking at length, smiling broadly, and she attempted to do the same.

After he thanked and dismissed them all, he turned to her. "Would you like a tour?"

"No. I'm exhausted. I'll wait until tomorrow to explore." *Alone*.

He inclined his head and led her up the stairs. The maze of corridors astounded her, but her husband navigated them easily. Finally they stopped at a door, and he turned the latch, motioning her inside. The bedroom was elaborate, even more so than her new room in Emmett's Fifth Avenue home. Pale green walls accented by stark white crown molding, with three elegantly curtained Palladian windows that faced out to an expansive back lawn. She recognized the furniture as Louis XVI and wondered how Emmett had managed to accomplish all this—buying, updating, and furnishing—in one month.

"Thank you," she told him sincerely. He might not have wanted to marry her, but he had moved mountains between the reception and this house. Not to mention her new office on Beaver Street. So why had he done it all, when he'd been blackmailed into marrying her? His actions made no sense.

He seemed taken aback by her gratitude. "My pleasure," he said. "You have three closets. The panels are flush to the wall." He pushed on the plaster, which unlatched a clever door. "You can store all the clothes you need here—"

"Emmett, wait," she blurted before he could explain anything further. The thoughtfulness, the care, was too much. If she hadn't overheard the conversation between Emmett and her brother, she'd likely be a puddle at the man's feet.

But she had heard the truth, and there was no erasing it from her memory.

He thrust his hands in his trouser pockets. "Yes?"

"I—I wanted to talk about this evening. About later."

"From the way you are blushing, I assume you mean the wedding night." He stared at her, calm as could be, while Lizzie wished for the ground to open up and let her disappear.

Still, she had to forge ahead. Sloanes were not quitters. "Yes. I do not wish to have one. A wedding night, that is."

"You do not want a wedding night?" She nodded, and he continued, "Are you, by chance, hoping to rush that particular event, or to postpone it indefinitely?"

"Postpone. Indefinitely."

His brows lowered menacingly, the divot in his chin deepening with his frown. "Dare I ask why? We are married, after all."

"I plan to petition for an annulment once we return to New York."

Emmett threw his head back and let out a bark of laughter. "You've got to be joking."

Lizzie drew up taller, determined to face him down, no matter his reaction. "I happen to be serious."

"An annulment? On what goddamned grounds?" he said, his voice rising. "I can assure you, not a soul will buy impotence."

"Consent obtained by force."

He stared at her, his eyes dark and hard, the walls closing in as the moment stretched. A muscle in his jaw twitched. "So you plan," he said, his tone laced with menace, "to say in a court of law that you were forced to marry me."

"Yes. I will say my brother forced me."

No relief crossed his face. Instead, he snarled, "Do you have any idea how that makes me look?"

"Emmett, I know the true circumstances behind our wedding." The anger drained from his expression, leaving him looking confused, so she told him the rest. "I overheard your argument with my brother today. I know he blackmailed you into marrying me."

Emmett spun to the window, his outline as still as that of a statue. When he spoke, his gaze remained on the view. "I regret that you overheard that conversation, Elizabeth. I would have preferred you never learn of my arrangement with your brother. However, I am prepared to live up to my responsibility toward you."

There was that word again, *responsibility*. She did not want to be a chore, something in his life to be borne. To be dealt with, like a sore tooth. She wanted passion. Love. To be needed more than his next breath.

And his response was even more proof of the mistake they had made today. She would not back down.

"When you've had a chance to think on the idea, I'm sure you'll come round to my way of thinking," she said. "With an annulment, it's as if the marriage never happened."

"We stood in front of God and four hundred people. Pledged ourselves until death do us part. And you think everyone will just *forget*?" He turned and put his hands on his hips. "Is that how it works in Knickerbocker society, where it means nothing to go back on your word?"

She rubbed her temples. What did any of that mean when the rest of their lives were at stake? They would make each other miserable until they *died.* Was that really what he wanted?

He drew close, stopping mere inches from her. "Is the idea of marriage to me so abhorrent that you would lie and embarrass us both to get out of it?"

She craned her neck to see his face, a face now etched with disgust and fury. The question confused her, when he hadn't wanted to marry her in the first place. What answer could she possibly give? And really, masculine pride aside, he would come to realize she was right. So she said nothing.

In the silence, his expression changed from a mix of disbelief and vulnerability to the indifference to which she'd grown accustomed. "I wondered what was wrong at the reception, why you were avoiding me. And convenient that you waited to tell me of this until after we'd arrived here, and not when we were in New York. Tell me, had the house been completed, full of fancy furnishings, would you still be asking for the annulment? Or perhaps the location doesn't meet your blue-blooded standards?"

Anger rushed through her, strangling her insides. "You think this is about your wealth, or what you can buy me?"

"Everything is about wealth, Elizabeth. Anyone who tells you otherwise is either a liar or very rich."

"I don't want your money. I never wanted anything—" *But you,* she'd almost said. Pride held her back, however. No sense in arming him with that information for his next argument with Will.

"Never wanted anything to do with me," he finished incorrectly, then gave a hollow laugh. A lump had formed in her throat, and she couldn't bring herself to correct him, even though she knew he was hurt. *He didn't want to marry you,* she told herself. *He'll eventually thank you for releasing him from the marriage.*

"So I was good enough when you wanted your precious investment firm, but I'm not good enough for your bed." She hated the words, hated the implication, but did not speak. In the end, what did it matter what he believed?

His jaw like granite, he stalked toward the door. "An annulment sounds like a fine plan, Mrs. Cavanaugh. God knows my cock would fall off if I stuck it inside you, you're so damn cold. Don't worry, I'll have no trouble finding a woman who wants me to fuck her every way I know how."

He stopped with his hand on the knob. Looking over his shoulder, he said darkly, "And I know plenty of ways how."

Emmett tossed the angel figurine into the air and swung the short drapery rod he'd taken down from the window. Wood met porcelain to cause an unholy crash all over the empty ballroom. He grabbed the gin bottle at his feet and took another swig, wondered when the alcohol would kick in. Whole damn bottle was nearly gone.

The rabbit figurine was next. Toss. Swing. A satisfying burst of tiny bunny fragments rained down on him. He'd already cut his face twice, and his hands had scratches all along the exposed skin. Not that he noticed. He felt nothing. Absolutely nothing.

"That's all of 'em. At least the ones I could find," Kelly said as he dropped a few more figurines on the side table Emmett had dragged to the center of the room. "Are you ready to tell me what happened?"

"No. Feel like pitching?"

"Not particularly. You do know you're bleedin'?"

Yes, Emmett knew it. And couldn't find enough energy to care. "I need another bottle of gin." He held the bottle to his lips and took several long pulls.

Kelly's eyes went wide as Emmett swallowed. "I wouldn't recommend that."

"No one asked you," Emmett responded when he got his breath back. Then he exchanged the bottle for a figurine, stepped away, and let her rip.

"Your swing's improved since those days on Mulberry Bend." Kelly brushed porcelain dust off his shoulders. "So I guess you're not having dinner with your wife."

Emmett said nothing. The fact that he was in his shirtsleeves, in the ballroom, swinging at ceramic bric-a-brac seemed enough of an answer. Trouble was, the smashing wasn't making him feel better. The center of his chest still felt as if it had been hollowed out with a dull spoon. A familiar feeling, one he hadn't felt in a long time. But one he never forgot.

She doesn't want you. So what? Not like it's a surprise.

The room spun as he reached for another figurine, and he stumbled. Kelly's hand landed on his shoulder, steadying him. "Whoa there, Bish. Careful."

Emmett straightened and snatched a tiny bowl. Moving into the room, he tossed and swung. The bowl smashed on the floor. Emmett stared intently at the broken pieces. How had he missed?

"All right, that's enough," Kelly said as he removed the stick from Emmett's hands. "Let's sit down and tell Uncle Kelly all about it."

"Don't coddle me," Emmett growled. "I'm not a child. Wasn't a child even when I was a child."

"Yeah, I know. You were full of piss even then."

Kelly led him to a chair. Lucky for Emmett, he nabbed

the gin bottle before Kelly did. "How many bottles before I pass out?"

"Usually three," Kelly answered as he dragged another chair over. "But you're hell on wheels the next day."

Who gave a fuck about tomorrow? Emmett took a long drink. "I'm a bastard. Yelled at my wife. Cursed at her, even. Used words I doubt she's ever heard in her privileged life."

Kelly sat, his big, hulking frame almost ridiculous in the fancy furniture. "So did you have a reason for cursin', or did you just want to shock her?"

"Both, I think." He rubbed the back of his neck. "She plans to get an annulment once we return."

Kelly winced. "On what grounds?"

"Coercion."

"Christ."

"'xactly." Emmett poured more gin down his throat. The liquid burned a path to his stomach. "Overheard her brother and me arguin' at the reception, when we talked about the blackmail."

Kelly winced again, which made Emmett feel a hundred times worse. "Can't imagine she appreciated that."

"No, she did not. What a goddamn disaster."

"You don't plan to give up, do you?"

Emmett frowned at his friend. "Not a matter of givin' up. This ain't a business deal. The woman hates everything about me."

"Not true. I saw the way she was lookin' at you. When you wasn't paying attention, of course. It's the same way all of 'em look at ya, like they're dyin' to get you between the sheets."

Emmett was shaking his head before Kelly finished. "You're insane. Elizabeth don't feel that way 'bout me." God, if only she did.

"Then why'd she let you kiss her at Sherry's?"

"Same reason any of those society women throw not-so-veiled invitations my way. Slumming."

Kelly thought about that while Emmett busied himself with drinking. "I still say you could convince her, if you wanted," the other man said.

Convince her? Emmett didn't want a wife he had to convince or cajole into bedding him. If he'd had any idea she planned to get an annulment, he wouldn't have shown up at the church this morning. Fuck Will Sloane and his threats.

"Hardly matters when one woman's just as good as 'nother," Emmett replied. His tongue was starting to thicken with drink. Good.

"If you believe that, then why'd you cut Mae loose?"

Yes, the beautiful Mrs. Rose. He'd broken it off with her as soon as the engagement had been announced, much to her disappointment. He tried to bring to mind her lush curves and dark, exotic looks . . . but all he could see were gray eyes and blond hair. Damn it.

"Doesn't matter. I'll find another. Actresses love me."

"They love your deep pockets," Kelly muttered.

"At least they're honest." The two sat in companionable silence for a few moments, while Emmett finished the rest of the bottle.

"What do you plan to do about the annulment?" Kelly finally asked.

Emmett rose, swayed a bit, and got his balance. He picked up a ceramic figurine off the table and threw it as hard as he could against the far wall. It shattered in a cloud of porcelain. "Nothin'. That's what I plan to do."

"Ain't like you. Never seen you beat before, not even when One-eyed Jackson and his boys found you alone in that alley."

Emmett's lips twisted at the memory. "Three weeks it took me to recover."

"And I'll never forget when you returned the favor, the sight of those three kneeling at your feet, beggin' the Bishop for mercy."

He dragged a hand through his hair. "It's not the same. And this isn't Five Points."

"Indeed, it ain't," Kelly said. "Sometimes, I think it's worse. At least there, we never gave up. There was a time you wouldn't have let a little thing like 'no' stop you from taking what you wanted."

"You don't understand, you stubborn shit-sack." Emmett snatched another small bowl and hurled it against the wall. Then another. Two weeks he would be trapped here. Fourteen nights of wanting something he'd never have. There wasn't enough alcohol or knickknacks in the world to keep him from going crazy. But he wouldn't scurry back to New York to expose his failure, where everyone would discover it had only taken a day—*not even one fucking day*—for his marriage to be revealed for what it really was: a sham.

"Cable Colin. I want him here first thing tomorrow morning. Tell him to bring as much work as he can carry."

Kelly sighed. "Does that mean . . ."

"What it means," Emmett snarled as he reached for another figurine, "is that the goddamn honeymoon is over."

Chapter Ten

~~~~~~~~~

Every young lady or gentleman should cultivate a love for society—not as an end, but as a means.

—American Etiquette and Rules of Politeness, 1883

Over the next four days, the atmosphere in the house grew colder than the brisk winter winds now blowing in off the Atlantic Ocean. Lizzie closed her eyes, enjoying the sting against her cheeks, as she stood on the back lawn, facing the water.

She'd hardly seen Emmett since the exchange in his bedroom, when she'd announced her plan for an annulment. Instead, he spent all his time in the office with the door firmly closed. She had passed him on the main stairs once, and they had shared an incredibly awkward breakfast with his secretary, Colin, who'd appeared ready to flee at a moment's notice. Emmett's flat, dark eyes had barely spared her a glance, his attention firmly on either his food or his secretary. It was as if she had ceased to exist to him.

She tried not to be hurt. After all, she'd asked for the annulment. Wasn't this distance for the best, especially since her brother had blackmailed him into the wedding?

So why, then, did his final statement the other night leave her chest aching?

I'll have no trouble finding a woman who wants me to fuck her every way I know how. And I know plenty of ways how.

Lizzie sighed and buried deeper into her cloak, kicking a pebble on the garden path with her boot. She had no hold over him, though they were married. If he wanted another woman, why should she care?

"Lizzie!"

She spun toward the house and discovered Edith Rutlidge racing down the back lawn, a wide smile on her friend's face.

"Edith!" Lizzie grinned, experiencing her first true burst of happiness since the wedding day. She ran toward her friend and embraced her fiercely. "I cannot believe you are here."

"It's terribly rude, isn't it? I hope I am not interrupting your honeymoon. I just thought I would pay an afternoon call to check up on you."

Lizzie took Edith's arm and guided them toward the dormant gardens. "You are not interrupting. I am always happy to see you. But what are you doing in Newport?"

"Father had business here, and I begged him to let me come along. I thought I might be able to see you, make sure you'd recovered."

"Recovered from what?"

"The wedding night, silly," Edith said with a laugh. When Lizzie didn't join in, Edith's gaze narrowed. "Oh, no. Tell me what that man did to you—"

"Calm down. Emmett didn't do anything." Nothing Lizzie wanted to make public knowledge, anyhow. Her long exhale emerged as a white cloud. "And I don't want to talk about him."

"I knew you shouldn't have married him. It was too soon, Lizzie. Henry was right."

"Henry? What did Henry say?" Edith's brother hadn't spoken to Lizzie since the engagement announcement, nor had he attended the wedding.

The two women started down an arbor framed with vine-covered trellises on all sides. It would be stunning come springtime. Too bad Lizzie would never see the blooms.

"That you rushed into the marriage, yet no one can figure out why. Everyone is speculating on the reason you met him in that private dining room. I've heard everything from you are carrying his child to hypnotism."

"Both of those are ridiculous." *I met him because I wanted to. He's unlike anyone else in New York.* Of course she couldn't say that, not if she planned to argue coercion in a court of law. "You needn't worry. Everything will be fine."

"I know you," Edith said. "You're up to something. But I also know you won't tell me until you're ready."

Lizzie did chuckle at that. "Yes, and yes. So be patient and try not to worry."

"Well, we should get you inside. Your lips are blue, and you're shivering."

Lizzie stopped to take in the huge stone structure. Oceancrest had one of the best views in Newport, right on the cliffs overlooking the ocean. The house was beautiful, a marvel of engineering and convenience. Water closets with hot and cold running water in every bedroom. Speaker phones to connect with the servants. There was an indoor fountain under the main stairs, for heaven's sake.

To Lizzie, however, the home held no warmth, no joy. It was a brittle, sterile shell of unhappiness.

"I don't want to go back in. Not just yet."

"Then I'm taking you with me, to Poplar House," Edith

said, referring to her family's cottage here. "Come, spend the day with us and have dinner there."

The offer of company, of laughing and forgetting for a while, appealed more than Lizzie wanted to admit. Being alone here day after day, with hardly anything to do and only the servants for company, was starting to take a toll on her. But how would she explain her husband's absence?

"I shouldn't. Your family will inevitably ask questions. What would I say?"

"That Emmett is working—which, I'm assuming, is the truth."

Lizzie's shoulders relaxed. "Fine. But you won't mention anything to your family, will you?"

Edith turned an invisible key in front of her lips. "I won't say a word."

Emmett struck a match and lit another cigar, his third in the last two hours. He'd been sitting here, in the salon off the main entry, drinking and smoking while waiting for his wife to return. The clock had struck twelve some time ago, and he began to fear she might not come home at all.

In which case, he would ride to the Rutlidge house and smash down every single door until he found her.

One more hour. He'd give her that much before he assumed the worst.

Earlier, when Edith Rutlidge had arrived, he'd thought nothing of the visit, not even when the two women departed. Then Elizabeth hadn't returned for dinner, and Emmett had grown concerned. Not that the two of them had planned to dine together, of course—any pretense of a honeymoon had ended on that first day—but a nagging suspicion told him there was more at play. And, sure enough, he'd learned that Henry Rutledge had arrived in Newport as well.

Coincidence? Not on Emmett's fucking life.

So he'd sent the staff to bed and positioned himself by the door to wait, his anger mounting with each chime of the mantel clock.

Would she really just leave him without a word?

Yes, a voice inside his head answered. *The real question is why she'd bother to stay.*

God knew she'd be better off with Rutledge, but until the annulment went through, Emmett would stop at nothing to prevent his wife from hopping into bed with another man.

The faint sound of carriage wheels caught his attention. He stamped out his cigar in the crystal dish at his side while trying to rein in his fury.

When the front door opened, his wife's silhouette appeared in the darkness. She crept in like a thief in the night, taking care to softly close the heavy wood behind her.

"Enjoy your evening?"

She jerked at the sound of his voice and put a hand to her chest. "Emmett? Heavens, you scared me."

He reached over and turned up the lamp at his elbow. A soft glow illuminated the salon—along with the guilt on his wife's face.

A savage calm rushed through his blood, settling in his muscles to tighten them, as he watched her approach. He made no effort to stand.

"What are you doing?" She removed her gloves and then unpinned her hat. "Why are you waiting down here?"

"Did you have a nice visit with the Rutledges?"

"How did you . . ." She lifted her chin and whipped off

her cloak. "Yes, I did. It was nice to have someone to talk to again."

A dark chuckle escaped his lips, and he slid out of his chair. "Why, Elizabeth, I had no idea you were lonely." He stepped toward her, jealousy and righteous indignation propelling him forward. "If only you'd mentioned it earlier, I would have been more than willing to entertain you."

He advanced, and her eyes grew wide. She began backing away from him. Good. *Run, little rabbit, because when I catch you . . .*

"Emmett, stop." Alarm flickered over her flawless features, and she held up her hands as if to ward him off. "I went for tea and stayed for dinner. That's all. Whatever else you're imagining—"

"And Rutlidge? Was your former beau there as well?"

Her back hit the wall, and she gave a little squeak of surprise. "Henry? He is in Newport, but—"

Emmett pressed in until he loomed over her, one hand braced on the wall above her head. "Did you cry on his shoulder, tell him of your misery?"

Elizabeth's brows flattened. "Absolutely not. I would never do something so disloyal, no matter where things stood between us."

That surprised him, but the words did nothing to lessen his outrage. "Did he take you to his bed, wife? Did you allow him to slide between your creamy, soft, well-bred—"

Her hand shot up—to crack across his cheek, no doubt—but Emmett was faster. He snatched her wrist and pinned her hand against the wall, fitting his body tightly to hers. "You do not want to do that," he told her in a low voice.

Her chest rose and fell swiftly, her skin flushed. She was so lovely, damn her. Despite everything, he felt his cock respond, hardening between them. She lifted her face to meet his eyes, her plump lips parted, and he struggled to keep from kissing her.

"I would never be unfaithful, annulment or not. If you knew me at all, you would never question me. Now let me go." She struggled, but he held tight. He would have answers, by God.

"Do you expect me to believe you stayed there, well after midnight, talking? Do you think me that stupid?"

Her gaze flicked to his mouth, now hovering near hers. The air around them grew heavy and thick, like standing in front of a blast furnace. He could feel the sweet warmth of her rapid breath, could see the color staining her creamy skin. "I do not care what you believe," she whispered, licking her lips. "I am telling the truth."

He wasn't sure what to believe when it came to this woman. No one had ever put him so firmly off balance. Was she lying?

With her curves melding so perfectly into his body, he lost the ability to care. All he could focus on was the feel of her, the smell of her, the temptation of her full lips. . . .

Before he could talk himself out of it, he dipped his head and sealed his mouth to hers. He'd last kissed her in the church, but this was nothing like that modest exchange. This was possession and anger. A kiss of raw desperation. He needed her complete surrender.

He didn't tease or coax a response from her like a Knickerbocker gentleman. Instead, he thrust his tongue past her teeth without warning. She opened for him eagerly, and he drove deep, tasted her relentlessly. Her tongue matched him stroke for stroke as they devoured one another, and soon he was drowning, falling, unable to break away from her luscious mouth.

When she whimpered in the back of her throat, he

released his grip on her wrist so he could touch her. His hands skimmed over her curves, threaded through her hair, dragged her closer. . . .

Her small hand came up to rest on his shirtfront, fingers shifting—but not to push him away. Instead, she seemed to be exploring the planes of his chest. Angling his head, he gentled the kiss, trying to get nearer. He longed to seduce her, to hear that whimper from her throat once more . . . to worship her and remove the memory of every other man.

She was his *wife*. And he'd dreamed of having her far too often in the past few weeks. Had stroked his cock to the image nearly every morning, the ritual far from satisfying. What he needed was the real thing, this woman right here, the one grinding her hips into his thigh. His erection throbbed against her corset-covered abdomen, and he wanted nothing more than to lift her legs around his hips, throw up her skirts, and slide into her wetness.

Then he remembered. *The annulment.* He broke off from her mouth and stumbled back. Panting, he tried to catch his breath. She was beautifully disheveled from his hands, her lips rosy and swollen. Had Rutledge witnessed the same thing earlier tonight?

Anger at his own stupidity flooded his veins, so much that he shook with it. "If you plan to entertain a lover while awaiting your annulment, you'd best think again. I'll not allow that to happen."

She pushed a lock of hair off her forehead. "Why should you care about infidelity? You certainly do not plan to remain faithful, considering what you said the other night."

Realization dawned. It had bothered her, him calling her cold and promising to fuck other women. "Merely say the word, Elizabeth. I'll carry you upstairs and show you things Henry Rutlidge wouldn't ever dare to try."

She drew in a shuddering breath. "You know why that is impossible."

Yes, he did. How could he forget when she threw it in his face at every turn? He ground his teeth together, his thoughts spinning. Perhaps this situation needed less emotion and more strategy on his part. She obviously responded to him physically, as he did to her. So what was the harm in enjoying themselves for the short period of time they'd be married? "We wouldn't be the first couple to lie about consummation."

She lifted her chin. "I cannot lie about that. I won't lie about it."

"Yet you'll lie about being coerced."

"Because that happens to be true! We were both coerced."

"Bull. No one twisted your arm to meet me for dinner. No one forced you to kiss me. I even tried to stop you, and what did you say?" He paused, then repeated, "'*I've never been very good at doing what I am told.*' And two minutes ago, I could've had my hand up your skirts. So stop playing the goddamned martyr, Elizabeth."

Her mouth flattened into an unhappy line as she pushed away from the wall. "Are you always this crude and hurtful?"

A dry, brittle laugh escaped him. "Well, I sure as hell didn't get to where I am by being polite and nice. But you shouldn't worry," he said, turning toward the hall. "You won't have to put up with me much longer."

Graham opened the front door to the Cavanaugh mansion, his demeanor polite and professional. If the servant was surprised to see the master and mistress of the house a full ten days sooner than expected, he gave no hint. "Good afternoon, sir. Madam. Welcome home."

It was the day after their explosive encounter in Newport. Before she'd even had breakfast, Emmett had demanded they return to the city. Though Lizzie didn't care to be ordered around by an overbearing husband, she had been anxious to return to New York. So she'd hurried to assist Pauline with the packing, ready to put this disastrous honeymoon behind her.

Emmett dropped her arm the instant they crossed the threshold. "I'll be in my office. Send Colin along when he arrives." Without removing his long black overcoat, her husband strode through the entrance hall and into the depths of the mansion.

"Your things, madam," Graham said gently, and Lizzie realized she'd been staring at the corridor long after Emmett disappeared.

"Thank you, Graham." She removed her gloves and began to unbutton her heavy coat.

"Did I hear—?"

Lizzie looked up and saw Brendan, Emmett's brother, at the top of the steps. His wide eyes met hers, his frown visible from across the expanse of the impressive entry-way.

Brendan started down the steps, leaning heavily on the rail due to his leg. Lizzie wondered what had caused the injury, and whether it was recent. He was a handsome man, affable and intelligent. Dedicated to helping the lives of others. So different from his brother, who could be so cold and distant. *Except when he's kissing you.*

"Hello, Lizzie." Brendan reached the bottom step as Lizzie finished handing her things to Graham. Lines creased his forehead. "You've returned early."

"Yes."

"Thank you, Graham," Brendan said, excusing the butler. When they were alone, Brendan asked, "What happened?"

She lifted a shoulder. "We were both anxious to return home. Newport is dreadfully boring in the winter."

His shrewd gaze narrowed. "Boring? Your honeymoon was boring?" He sighed and shook his head. "That would be amusing if I wasn't so fond of you both. What did he do?"

"Nothing. I promise."

"Well, that explains why you were bored," he said dryly, and she chuckled despite herself.

"Brendan, you shouldn't worry. Things are . . . complicated between us." Did he know about the blackmail? Very likely, she supposed. Nevertheless, she didn't want to discuss the annulment. The world would learn of the separation in due time.

His frown deepened. "I grew worried when he summoned Colin to join the two of you. And now, I can see it's even worse than I feared."

"No, it's—"

"You'll give him a chance, won't you? I know he can be . . . intense. He's always been that way, and he tends to work too much. But he's loyal, Lizzie, and smart. He—"

She held up her hand. "Please, stop. I know you love him and you want him to be happy. But we need to work this out on our own."

"Of course," Brendan said, dragging a hand through his light brown hair. "Forgive me."

"I'll forgive you if you agree to give me a tour of this monstrosity."

He grinned. "You're trying to distract me, but I happen to love giving tours. So the answer is yes." He held out his arm, which Lizzie accepted.

They went slowly to allow for Brendan's limp. "Why

do you not use a cane?" she asked him when they finished a tour of the third floor.

"You sound like Emmett," he groused, holding onto the rail as they came down the stairs. "And I do when I leave the house. But it's a nuisance inside."

"Does it pain you? I have no idea how recently you were injured."

"Oh, this happened ages ago. I was six."

Her chest tightened. Lord, he'd been only a small boy. "I am sorry. It's none of my business, really."

"We're family now, Lizzie. There are no secrets, especially about my injury. I was run over by a wagon." She let out a small gasp, and he threw her a rueful half smile. "I'd been out stealing food, so some would say I got what I deserved."

A six-year-old, out stealing food? Where had his parents been? Or Emmett, for that matter? An uncomfortable lump settled in her throat. "I hardly think a serious injury suitable punishment for a young boy trying to keep from starving."

They reached the bottom of the staircase. She took his arm once more, and he said, "I survived. Perhaps if my medical care had been better . . ." He sighed. "But without my injury, who knows what would have happened to me."

"What do you mean?"

"My father was not a nice man, Lizzie. He liked to drink, and when he did, he turned violent. He would hit anything and anyone who caught his notice. Mostly Emmett, until he was old enough to join the Popes. Then it was my mother."

Mostly Emmett. Lizzie's stomach clenched at those words. This tale was breaking her heart, and she feared she hadn't yet heard the worst.

"When I was injured, I had to stay in bed, and so my

father stopped noticing me. I'd rest and read whatever I could get my hands on. Emmett used to bring me books, though I have no idea where he got them. I learned everything I could from those books. I never would have made it to Columbia, let alone medical school, if it hadn't been for my injury. Instead, I likely would have joined the Popes as well."

"And what of your mother? What happened to her?"

"She left once I came home from the hospital. I think the injury was too much for her, you know, the guilt. And my father was an outright bastard. I don't blame her for leaving. She ran off to California, we were told. Died a few years later."

Because everyone's always left him. Lizzie recalled Brendan's words before the honeymoon. *And that's exactly what you're planning to do,* she reminded herself. Rubbing her brow, she swallowed the regret. What choice did she have? Yes, she enjoyed his kisses, but staying married to Emmett was pure madness. Her pride would not allow her to acquire a husband through blackmail.

"Come on," Brendan said. "Let's go all the way down, and I'll show you the indoor pool."

The March winds were particularly fierce along Fifth Avenue on Thursday evening as Emmett traveled to his monthly meeting with Cabot, Sloane, and Harper. He flexed his fingers and wondered how he'd get through the night without punching Sloane for manipulating him into this farce of a marriage.

Emmett hadn't seen his wife since returning from Newport. More often than not, he slept in his office on Beaver Street. The distance made things easier. She certainly didn't want him around, and Emmett had no intention of begging for her attentions.

Kelly kept pace at Emmett's side. His friend wasn't happy that Emmett had decided to walk to the Knickerbocker Club after dining at the Fifth Avenue Hotel. But Emmett needed the bracing cold right now, to be outside, moving around. Not sitting in a damn carriage.

"You goin' home tonight, or back down to the office?" Kelly asked him.

"Office."

"Spendin' a lot of time away from home, aren't you, Bish?"

"I was just there this afternoon to bathe and change."

"Yeah, and you spent five minutes with Brendan and fifteen minutes with your sisters. Don't you think—"

"Whatever you are prepared to say, stop right there." Emmett had seen his family, checked in on their welfare. For his wife, he'd left a perfunctory note. Her office would be finished next week, after which she could move in and start her investment firm. After all, wasn't that what she wanted from him?

No doubt annulment proceedings would shortly follow.

"Anything else on Sloane's finances?" Kelly asked. "Does it look like he's hurting for cash?"

"We haven't been able to find out. He's guarding things closely, but it doesn't seem as if he's flush. Some assets have been liquidated and a few of the household staff let go, but we don't know anything concrete." They dodged a carriage and started across the street. "There must be a problem, though. Why else would Elizabeth have gone to such lengths to secure funding?"

"You could just ask her, you know."

Emmett frowned at that. Leave it to a boxer to dance

around and then come back to his real purpose. "Yes, I could. But hiring an investigator is so much more fun."

Kelly snorted. "You've always been too stubborn for your own good."

"Add it to my list of faults, then. No doubt you've got a running total of them somewhere."

"'Course I do. Count's up to three hundred and fifty-seven."

Emmett muttered a very descriptive curse at his friend, who only chuckled in response, and turned into an alley. He left Kelly at the back door and traveled through the club's kitchen to the inner stairs. He'd purposely arrived late to avoid any idle talk. Business was what mattered in this world, something he wouldn't let himself ever forget.

When he stepped into the room, three pairs of wide eyes tracked him to the table. "Good evening," he said, and took his usual chair between Cabot and Harper. He avoided looking in Sloane's direction.

"Evening, Cavanaugh. We weren't expecting to see you tonight," Harper started.

"Aren't you supposed to be on your honeymoon?" Cabot said with all the subtlety of a blunt hammer.

"I came back early." Emmett's usual glass of cold gin appeared before the waiter departed.

"What do you mean, you came back early?" Sloane leaned forward, his voice low and angry. "What the hell have you done to my sister?"

Chapter Eleven

Before we enter society we should subdue our gloomy moods.

—American Etiquette and Rules of Politeness, 1883

Emmett kept his expression deceptively calm as he faced his brother-in-law. "My *wife* is no concern of yours, not any longer."

Something flashed in Sloane's eyes. "Wrong. Lizzie will always be my concern. What did you do to her?"

Not nearly everything I'd hoped. "She's fine, Sloane. I had work to finish. And Elizabeth is anxious to get started on her investment firm."

"Her *what?*" Sloane bellowed, his fair skin turning a deep red. "Do not tell me you're allowing her to go through with that insane idea. Her reputation will be destroyed."

Savage satisfaction flooded Emmett's veins. He gave Sloane a cold smile. "Not only am I allowing her to go through with it, I'm financing the whole venture. And I'm designing an office for her in my building near the exchange."

Cabot let out a low whistle, but Emmett kept his eyes

locked on Sloane, who appeared almost apoplectic. "You . . . you are financing it? She is a Sloane, by God. You are going to turn her into a laughingstock."

"She is not a Sloane, not any longer. She is a Cavanaugh." At least for now—and he'd bring this goddamn city to its knees before he allowed anyone to laugh at her. "And you're wrong. They'll be lining up around the block to hire her."

"You have no idea what you're talking about. She'll be ostracized. No woman can run a successful firm like that."

"Woodhull and her sister did it a few years back," Harper put in.

"Until their mother blackmailed the Commodore and he withdrew his backing." Cabot cracked a grin. "God, what a great story."

"Exactly," Sloane exclaimed, pointing at Cabot. "Both women were trollops and flimflammers, not of Lizzie's social caliber at all. No decent woman should go into business for herself."

"Your sister will be the first, then." Emmett lifted his gin and took a large swallow. "Prepare yourself, Sloane. If I were you, I would support her."

Sloane pinched the bridge of his nose. "This is terrible timing for me. And you're enjoying the hell out of this."

"Yes, I am," Emmett said without hesitation. Sloane had no idea of the trouble Emmett planned to rain down on him. The investment firm was merely the start of Emmett's efforts to get even with her brother. "Not to mention that your sister won a wager with me. I won't go back on my word."

"You have no idea what you're starting, Cavanaugh," Sloane said. "You'll regret this. Mark my words."

Emmett couldn't argue with that. With Elizabeth already

plotting an annulment, he had nothing but regrets. Not that he'd admit as much to Sloane.

Instead, he leaned back and lifted his glass in a toast. "I know exactly what I'm starting, Sloane, and I mean to finish it, too."

Mood blacker than coal, Emmett stomped down the back stairs of the club. The meeting had concluded quickly, each man wasting no time negotiating demands once Sloane had finished his tirade. Unfortunately, the satisfaction Emmett had experienced over Sloane's reaction hadn't lasted long. The darkness rooted in his chest since Newport persisted, an ache he began to fear might be permanent.

He stepped out of the kitchens and into the alley. Before he could reach the walk, a voice slid out of the gloom, stopping him.

"Cavanaugh."

Emmett twisted to find Henry Rutlidge loitering amongst the refuse. "Slumming, Rutlidge? I wouldn't think you'd risk dirtying your shoes."

"Whereas you're completely comfortable, no doubt. God knows you are no stranger to squalor."

The damned fool. Did Rutlidge honestly think reminders of Emmett's past would prove hurtful? Those wounds had long healed over. Nothing this spoiled prick could ever say would damage Emmett. "You know what else I'm familiar with? The noises my wife gives when—"

"You bastard." Rutlidge advanced, his eyes flashing fire. "How dare you discuss a lady in such a manner!"

Emmett wanted to laugh. The boy was so transparent. "Give over, Rutlidge. You can't fight me with either your fists or your money, and I've already married her. You've lost, no matter what you tried in Newport."

Confusion flickered over Rutlidge's features before he masked it, which confirmed Elizabeth's claims that nothing had happened between them on the honeymoon. A flicker of guilt worked through Emmett, but he squashed it. He'd deal with an apology when the time came.

"Yes, let's discuss Newport," Rutlidge said. "Like how your trip was cut short. Lizzie must've come to her senses and realized the kind of man she married."

The barb cut deeper than Emmett would have thought, becoming a sharp ache in his gut even as he maintained a cool mask of indifference. "The reason behind her actions no longer concerns you, nor do mine. You'd best forget about her and return to your parties and spending your father's money."

Rutlidge's lip curled into a sneer as he leaned in. "I'll find a way, Cavanaugh. No matter how long it takes or what I need to do. I'll win her—"

"Bish, everything tip-top back there?" Kelly appeared a few feet away, a hulking menace in the near darkness.

"Perfectly fine," Emmett replied, and started for the mouth of the alley. "Nothing here but the vermin, anyway."

"I still think the desk should rest on the other wall," Edith said as they surveyed the furniture in Lizzie's new office. "You'll turn as pink as a berry in the sun."

"That is what the curtains are for," Lizzie reminded her. "And I think the desk should stay where it is." While she appreciated her friend's help, it was obvious Edith did not fully understand Lizzie's desire to go into business. There had been a litany of doubt and contradicting opinions today from the other woman.

"Fine, but don't say I didn't warn you when you sprout freckles. When will you open for business?"

"Monday," Lizzie said, a wide grin splitting her face. "I hired a secretary this morning."

"You did? What is she like?"

Lizzie recalled the interview with Miss Grayson and how efficient the young woman had seemed. "She's young but smart. She has office experience and appears quite capable. I think I'm going to like her."

"Well, I hope you can trust her. You'll be dealing with a lot of money, Lizzie."

"Yes, hopefully I will. I plan to cable her references before I leave for the day, so you may rest easy."

Edith twisted the locket she wore around her neck. "I am worried about you. What happens if you fail?"

"I won't fail. You know how long I've been doing this on paper. It's time I use this ability for something other than a way to pass the time between balls and masquerades." Not to mention for rescuing her family's finances. "I'll be fine. Everyone will believe this is my husband's firm, not mine."

"I hope so, for your sake. In the meantime, we shouldn't tell anyone of your involvement."

The comment bothered Lizzie, yet she knew Edith was right. Lizzie needed to establish herself before revealing her skills to society. Still, it sounded as if Edith was embarrassed of her. Before she could question her friend, the office door opened and her brother appeared, his tall form wrapped in a long black overcoat.

"Will," Lizzie said in surprise. "What are you doing here?" On weekdays, he never left the Northeast Railroad offices before nightfall—and often stayed later. She had long given up sharing dinners with him back in Washington

Square, with the only meal they regularly ate together being breakfast.

He removed his derby and closed the door. "Hello, Lizzie. Miss Rutlidge."

Edith held out her hand and Will bowed over it, then he leaned in to kiss Lizzie's cheek. "Miss Rutlidge, may I have a moment alone with my sister?"

Edith nodded. "Of course, but only if you agree to call me Edith. We've known each other for years, after all."

"It still wouldn't be—"

"Proper," Edith finished dryly. "Yes, I know. Lizzie, I'll take a walk around the building. When I come back, we'll decide where to hang your pictures."

"Thank you, Edith." Her friend departed, and the sound of the latch echoed in the cavernous space. Silently, Will tugged off his gloves and shrugged out of his overcoat. He carefully placed the items over a chair.

"Will, you're scaring me."

He heaved a sigh and gestured to the room. "I cannot believe this. I cannot believe you are doing this against my wishes. We've discussed this, Lizzie."

She had no idea how he'd learned of her office, but that hardly mattered now. She drew herself up. "No, you told me what you wanted and ignored everything I said. I repeatedly mentioned how badly I wanted to run my own investment firm, and you wouldn't listen."

"I did listen!" He dragged a hand through his flattened hair. "This is a terrible idea. You have no idea how it will make you appear. Do you care nothing for your name?"

The nerve of him. Heat raced through her blood, and she folded her arms across her chest. "I assume by that, you mean the Sloane name. Odd, I'm no longer a Sloane, thanks to you."

"Believe me, runt, if there had been any other way . . ."

Not even the use of her childhood nickname could stem the rising tide of her anger. "There were other ways to sort the situation without resorting to blackmail!"

"How did you . . . ?" He grimaced, and regret swam in gray eyes so like her own. "I knew he would walk away otherwise, and you wouldn't marry him unless you believed it was real." He hung his head and rubbed his eyes. "What was I supposed to do, Lizzie?"

"Not manipulate everyone to get what you want. You should have let Emmett and I figure it out. Now it's too late."

Something in her voice must have caught his attention because his head snapped up. "What happened? What has he done to you? Did he hurt—"

"Will, calm down. He hasn't hurt me." Not physically, anyway. Her heart was another matter altogether. "We just don't . . . know one another. It hasn't been easy."

That seemed to mollify her brother. His shoulders relaxed. "Well, you cannot divorce him, so you'll need to make the best of it. You won't be the first married couple to live separate lives."

Yes, she wanted to say, *but I never wanted such a cold arrangement for my own marriage.*

"I realize that. And he has agreed to give me the capital to start my investment firm. As well, he'll serve as my backer. So it's not all doom and gloom." *Especially since the marriage will soon be annulled.*

"You're too practical for doom and gloom," he said, a half smile lifting the edges of his mouth. "It's one of the qualities I like best about you."

"Thank you, but you are not forgiven."

"I didn't expect I would be," he said with a chuckle, then sobered. "If you're bound and determined to do this, you should know I cannot hire you to trade for Northeast."

"Why not? I could help—"

He held up a hand to stop her. "I'm working on some new deals. Perhaps when things are settled, if you're still in business."

"Oh, what faith from my only brother," she drawled. "You don't think I can do it, do you? I've been speculating on paper for years, and I always come out ahead. Why shouldn't I do it for clients?"

"Because it's common, Lizzie. You don't see any of the other girls of the smart set going into business."

"I don't care what anyone else is doing. I never have, Will. It's you who cares, not me."

"You need to care. I've done everything to protect you up until now, but I cannot do anything more. Cavanaugh has money, but he does not have a place in society. Be careful you do not lose yours, because you won't be able to win it back."

"I'm not worried over my social standing. But if it eases your mind, Emmett and I agreed to let him be the face of the business, at least up front. Still, should everyone discover my secret, I won't cry if the invitations dry up."

"Say that now, but what of Emmett's half sisters? As of this moment, you are their only hope for a successful debut within the bosom of New York society."

She clenched her jaw. He was right, of course. Katie and Claire made no secret of how much they looked forward to their debuts, with all the pomp and circumstance that accompanied the tradition. And Lizzie wanted that experience for them. Even after her marriage was annulled Lizzie had planned to help them—which she couldn't do if she lost her social standing. "I hate when you are reasonable."

He smiled and walked over, his arms enfolding her in

a tight hug. "I know. Some days I feel like the last sane man in New York. And if I cannot talk you out of this foolish venture, just promise me you'll keep this small and respectable. Let people assume it's Cavanaugh's."

"If I agree, do you promise not to blackmail anyone else?"

He waited a beat. "I won't blackmail *you*. . . ."

She pulled back and patted his cheek. "Then please stop telling me how to run my business, dear brother, and I won't tell you how to run yours."

A few days later, Lizzie bounded out of bed before dawn and rang for Pauline. Too much excitement had prevented her from sleeping well last night, so she might as well get dressed. Today, she would officially start her own investment firm—well, Emmett's firm, if one wanted to be precise.

The stock exchange would open at ten o'clock. While she couldn't be on the trading floor, she would be nearby, monitoring the action from her ticker tape. She had two clients—Emmett and Edith Rutledge—and she planned on luring several more over the coming weeks.

In addition, traveling to Beaver Street would get her out of the house. Her husband's rooms were deathly quiet; she knew he hadn't come home last night. Again. She tried not to think about where he was spending his evenings—or, more important, with whom. His absence hurt too much, despite the fact she'd been the one to insist on the distance in the first place.

This was for the best. Other than the ridiculous physical attraction, they had nothing. And just because a man could kiss you stupid was no reason to stay with him. The scandal had been weathered, the trouble had passed. No damage would be done, and the two of them could part ways before they made each other miserable.

Emmett Cavanaugh wants to marry you, Lizzie. Said so himself.

What a lie.

She was brushing her hair when Pauline came in. "Good morning, madam. You're up early today."

"I apologize for the hour, but I couldn't sleep. I'm quite anxious to get to my new office today."

Pauline brought in a lilac day dress and undergarments from the dressing room. "But madam, there's snow on the ground."

Snow? It had rained yesterday, though the winds had been strong. Lizzie went to the window and looked out onto the gardens behind the mansion. Even in the dim light, a thin blanket of white could be seen, with more snow still falling. "Once it warms up, I'm certain the snow will stop. There were near summer temperatures on Saturday, for heaven's sake."

"Shall I come along with you?"

Lizzie discarded her wrapper on the bed. "No, that's not necessary. I'll have the coachman take me downtown. Maybe I'll even ride the elevated home tonight."

Pauline snorted as she helped Lizzie into a clean chemise and drawers. "Good thing your brother isn't around to hear that. I'm thinking he'd have a fit, madam."

"You are probably right, but I hardly care about his opinion." Though Will had apologized, she was still angry with him. Blackmailing Emmett, lying to her . . . What sort of man had her brother become?

"I think several petticoats today to keep you warm, madam. I don't like the look of that sky."

By the time they'd finished with her clothing and hair,

the sun had risen. Lizzie ordered the carriage and then made her way down the stairs.

Breakfast in the Cavanaugh mansion rivaled anything Lizzie had ever seen. Each day, food covered nearly every available surface of the breakfast room, with offerings of fruit, breads and rolls of all kinds, eggs prepared three ways, two types of sausage, butter, crepes, blintzes, along with coffee and tea. The chef had been hired away from La Maison Dorée in Paris, and he was most definitely worth whatever exorbitant amount Emmett paid him.

Lizzie asked a footman to have two muffins wrapped for her ride downtown. While she waited, she poured coffee into a delicate porcelain cup.

"Good morning, dear sister-in-law." Brendan limped in, his hair slightly damp.

"Good morning, handsome brother-in-law," she said in return. "Are you off on your morning rounds?"

He reached for the coffee urn and shook his head. "No, not today. I'm afraid the snow will keep me home." He gestured to his leg. "I slip easily in bad weather. What about you? Are you headed downtown?"

"Yes," she grinned. Brendan knew all about her office. He'd even stopped by last week to see the new furniture. "I cannot wait. My firm is going to trounce all the rest—just you wait."

"I do not doubt it. Emmett never backs a loser. He'd have never given you the funds if he didn't think you would make him money."

There was a note in Brendan's voice, something there she couldn't put her finger on. "You don't think that's wise of him?"

Brendan sipped his coffee, replaced the cup in the saucer. "Not everything worthwhile can be measured in terms of dollars. Money is not everything, Lizzie, but I fear my brother often doesn't see the value in anything else."

Following his line of thinking, she asked, "Like a wife?"

"I'm sorry. Your relationship is none of my business. I just . . . I'm aware Emmett has not been sleeping here."

"I don't want to discuss your brother. Things are—"

"Complicated, I know." Brendan sighed, a rueful twist to his lips. "I wish you had seen his face when you first appeared at the end of the aisle. You were focused on the crowd, but I saw my brother's reaction. He didn't take his eyes off you, not for a second. The awe and reverence, Lizzie . . . I've never seen anything like it, not with Emmett. Like he was about to receive a gift he'd waited on his entire life. He cares, Lizzie. People think he doesn't, but he's learned to hide it better than the rest of us."

Lizzie didn't know what to make of that statement. "He only married me because of the scandal." *Because my brother threatened your sisters.* "He had no choice in the matter."

Brendan huffed a laugh. "No one can make my brother do anything against his will, Lizzie. Countless have tried and failed. Trust me, Emmett definitely wanted to marry you."

Emmett blinked awake. Damn, morning had already broken. He closed his eyes and willed himself to sleep. Discomfort prevented any rest, however, and he was forced to move and stretch. Working until all hours and then sleeping on a small sofa was hell on a man's back.

Nevertheless, better to remain at the office. No temptations. No distractions. No sounds from his wife's bedchamber that had him fighting the urge to see her or touch her. Taste her. He'd relived that soul-stripping kiss from Newport a hundred times, driving himself nearly mad with lust each time. How far would things have progressed if he hadn't pulled away? Or would she have remembered her precious annulment?

Coerced, his balls. The woman had nearly crawled into his lap at Sherry's, and then she'd ridden his thigh in Newport. Was she so stubborn that she couldn't admit to the attraction? Most marriages were started with a lot less. He sighed and vowed to put her out of his mind.

Sitting up, he rubbed a hand across the stubble covering his jaw. He needed a shave. Since Kelly had insisted on going home last night, Emmett would have to wield the razor himself.

Fortunately, the coal stove in the corner still pumped out sufficient heat. His personal office encompassed almost half of the top floor and had all the modern conveniences, including a water closet with running hot and cold water. There was even a dressing room—a small storage room Kelly had commandeered two weeks ago when it became apparent that Emmett would be here more often than not.

Emmett peeled himself off the sofa and added more coal to the stove. Then he stumbled to the water closet. When he emerged thirty minutes later—washed, shaved, and wearing clean clothes—he felt marginally human again. The overly bright office windows caught his attention, and he noticed white flakes cascading past the panes. How long had it been snowing?

He looked out onto Beaver Street. Hell's bells. Tall mounds had already accumulated, the winds blowing the snow against buildings and wooden poles. Two carriages slowly rolled through, and a few brave souls trudged forward on the walks, hats clutched firmly against the bracing March breeze.

Immediately, he went to his telephone and asked to be

connected to the house. Under no circumstances should Kelly or Brendan attempt to come downtown. When Emmett was put through, Brendan was on the line.

Static crackled, and then he heard Brendan say, "I hope you are inside somewhere warm."

"I'm at the office. Keep everyone home today, will you, on account of the weather?"

"Sure. And you'll keep Lizzie there, with you?"

A sickening feeling blossomed in Emmett's gut. He gripped the edge of the telephone box. "Elizabeth left home?"

"Yes. To come down to her office. She left some time ago, before the roads became impossible to traverse. You haven't seen her?"

Chapter Twelve

Talk as little of yourself as possible, or of the business or profession in which you are engaged.

—American Etiquette and Rules of Politeness, 1883

Emmett flew down the building's steps, fear piercing his chest like a hot poker. Dark thoughts of Elizabeth stranded and half-frozen in an overturned carriage flitted through his mind. Why had Graham allowed her to leave in a storm such as this? Emmett would be having words with his butler at his very first opportunity.

He yanked open her inner office door and almost fell to his knees in relief. Elizabeth stood in front of the windows, her willowy frame clad in a perfectly styled lilac shirtwaist and matching skirt. She was here. Oh, thank Christ.

She spun around at the sound, hand clutching her throat. "*Emmett.* You scared the life out of me."

"What in the hell are you doing?" he shouted, anger and annoyance replacing anything else he'd been feeling.

One blond brow rose. "And a good day to you as well, husband." She returned her gaze to the window, dismissing him, and Emmett exhaled.

He thrust his hands on his hips and tried to get control of his rioting emotions. "I apologize. I did not realize you had gone out in this weather until I spoke with Brendan. I was concerned."

"As you can see, I am perfectly fine."

Yes, he had definitely noticed. He walked to the windows, which held the same view as his, only closer to the ground. "Why in God's name would you travel all the way down here on a day like today?"

"Because the snow wasn't nearly this considerable when I set out. I never dreamed it would come down this hard."

They both watched through the glass as the flakes continued to stream down. It was like nothing Emmett had ever seen.

"What time did you leave ho—the house?" He'd almost said "home," but it wasn't truly her home. Merely a temporary residence until she walked out.

"A few minutes past dawn. I wonder if the coachman returned safely," she murmured.

"I can find out, if you wish." He propped a shoulder against the cold panes. "Why haven't you set a fire?"

"There's no coal. I hadn't thought to have some brought up before now."

Guilt clogged his throat. He should have seen to that. "Come up to my office, then, to stay warm."

She flicked him an apprehensive glance. "I'm fine. The radiators are still hot. As soon as it lets up I'm leaving."

"The hell you are," he said sharply. "Not with these winds. It's too dangerous. The lines will start coming down soon enough. And what happens if you get stuck somewhere?"

"Well, I cannot stay here. Maybe I'll walk over to the Astor House—"

"Which is where every other pad-shover, trader, and broker will already be camped out. It will be chaotic and unsafe. You are not leaving this building, Elizabeth."

"You don't have the right to order me about," she bit out, her shoulders growing tight. "If I want to leave, that's my own choice."

"I absolutely have the right to order you about—a legal right as well as a moral one. You are not staying in this cold office or leaving the building until this blows over."

She stared him down, resentment brightening the silver depths of her eyes. "And if I refuse?"

He leaned forward, saying in a deliberately calm, slow manner, "Then I'll throw you over my shoulder and carry you up two flights of stairs."

Sighing, she faced the windows once more, as if hoping to see the sun burst through the layer of white. "Is anyone else in the building?"

Emmett hadn't thought of anyone other than her, but he would need to ascertain whether the building was empty. Nevertheless, was altruism Elizabeth's concern? Somehow he doubted it. "Afraid to be alone with me?"

She swallowed and chaffed her arms. "Absolutely not." But her voice rang hollow, and he saw the words for a lie. Did she hate him so much that not even self-preservation could force her to his side? If he hadn't sought her out, would she have stayed here, stubbornly freezing, instead of coming to him?

A familiar bleakness rose up within him, the darkness that stemmed from rejection. Before Elizabeth, he hadn't experienced the feeling in years. But his wife never failed to serve as a reminder of all the ways he was unacceptable.

Drawing on an icy reserve infinitely more bitter than the winds now whipping along Wall Street, Emmett said, "Up to my office, Elizabeth. Now."

* * *

As they climbed the stairs, Lizzie had finally resigned herself to spending a few hours in Emmett's office when the electric lights cut out. The surroundings plunged into darkness, and a sliver of panic prickled along her neck. Reaching out, she fumbled for his hand, unsure if he'd rebuff her, but desperate for reassurance of some kind.

"Here." He threaded their fingers together tightly. "Stay with me." He guided her up the remaining steps and along a short distance, then opened a door. Comforting heat greeted her, while the white sky shone through a long row of windows to illuminate the spacious interior. He quickly let go of her hand.

She drew closer to the coal stove while taking stock of the thoroughly masculine space. There were dark-paneled walls, bookcases, and an oversized wooden desk. One side of the room held a sitting area, complete with a dark brown sofa and plush leather chairs. She could well imagine him here, overseeing his empire.

The heady scent of cigar smoke, gin, and shaving lotion hung in the air, and a tiny thrill worked its way down her spine. The last time she'd inhaled that particular combination had been during that mind-numbing kiss in Newport.

Afraid to be alone with me?

Oh, yes. Most definitely yes.

Her husband disappeared into a small antechamber and returned with three lamps, which he placed on the desk. He lit one and then returned to the other room. When he came out, he'd donned his hat and overcoat, the latter causing his normally wide shoulders to appear even wider.

"Where are you going?" she asked uneasily. "I thought you said it was too dangerous."

"I need to check the building, to ensure no one freezes inside here during the storm. Then I'll find us some food and more coal."

"You can't go outside in this. Not right now. At least wait—"

He held up a hand. "There's no way of telling how long this storm will last. What if we are trapped here overnight? Think, Elizabeth. We need to be prepared."

Overnight? Just the two of them? Panic forced her to her feet. "Then I shall come with you."

"No." Grabbing the lamp, he strode to the door. "I'll be back as soon as I am able."

Even with all the uncertainty between them, she would go mad if she had to wait here alone. She had to do something. "Then I'll check the building. At least allow me to do that."

She could see the surprise in his opaque gaze, yet he remained unswayed. "No," he said. "It won't take me long. Your floor is the only one with tenants at present. And if someone is here to seek shelter . . . Desperation can make people aggressive. I know what it's like—" He pressed his lips together and shook his head fiercely. He started for the door.

"You know what it's like to what?"

"Forget it. I need to go, before the storm gets worse."

What had he been about to say? That he knew what it was like to be stranded during a storm?

She did not appreciate being left behind, so she tried one more time. "Perhaps all this is unnecessary. Do you truly believe we'll be stuck here overnight?"

His brow furrowed as he took in the scene outside. "I have no idea. But I won't risk your well-being by doing something foolish like trying to get back uptown. We'll

wait the storm out here." He strode to the door, his heavy
treads continuing down the hall toward the stairs.

Lizzie exhaled, frustrated at both the storm and being
unable to help. She glanced about her husband's working
space and wondered what to do until he returned. The
room was neat, the only clutter some papers strewn about
his massive desk. She had a strong urge to peek at his
things to see what she could learn about him. She knew
next to nothing about Emmett, the mysterious and brooding man she'd married—other than that he'd been blackmailed into marrying her. Perhaps if she did it quickly and
carefully . . .

Of course she wouldn't. She had no right to pry into his
private affairs, even if he was her husband for a short time.
And knowing him makes it harder to leave him.

She rubbed her temples. No use thinking on that now.
They needed to get through this storm first.

In the water closet, she took care of her needs. The lux-
uriousness of the decor—gleaming gold fixtures, thick
marble counters, patterned Italian tile—did not surprise
her. Emmett seemed to surround himself with comfort
wherever possible. She noted his shaving supplies, which
appeared recently used. Had he been here all night? She
assumed he'd been sleeping at a mistress's house, or perhaps a hotel. Why would he rather stay here?

Pushing those questions out of her mind, she wandered
back to the main room. The powerful storm raged on the
other side of the glass, snow pelting the windows with
ferocity. It had been sheer folly to think she could travel
in this. What would she have done if Emmett hadn't found
her? He'd been frantic when he'd come into her office.
Had he been worried about her?

No one was outside now, every sane and reasonable

person having already sought shelter. But Emmett was out there. What if he became hurt, or trapped in the snow?

Uneasiness forced her away from the windows. He would return. The man was a force of nature in his own right, and she doubted anything could best him, not even this storm. Nevertheless, he would be freezing when he came inside. She stoked the fire and then struggled to drag both of the large armchairs directly in front of the blaze. Next she readied a large glass of brandy from the selection of bottles on the sideboard.

Thirty minutes after she settled in one of the chairs with a book, the door flew open. Emmett, hatless and covered in snow, stepped into the room, his massive chest heaving with exertion. In his right hand were two water buckets packed with snow. His other hand held a brimming coal scuttle. A large satchel was strapped across his chest, two thick woolen blankets wrapped around his neck. Lizzie jumped up from her chair and rushed forward to help him.

"Move back," he said, and stepped in. Setting all three buckets down, he hung there, bent at the waist, trying to catch his breath.

"Here. Let me have these," she said, and unwound the blankets from his neck. She tossed them on the floor and then lifted the strap of the satchel up and over his head, past his shoulder. Laden with supplies and wet from the snow, the leather pack was absurdly heavy. She dropped the bag to the floor and turned to him.

A shiver racked his body as he straightened. His teeth chattered, and icy clumps clung to his damp brown hair. Without thinking, she reached for the buttons of his overcoat. "We need to get you out of these wet things or you'll catch your death." Fingers flying, she opened the garment and then pushed the cloth over his wide shoulders, letting it fall to the floor.

Emmett stood perfectly still as she removed his frock coat. She attempted to remain brisk and efficient, and not dwell on the hard strength of him so apparent even through his clothing, but her movements slowed when she went to work on his vest. He loomed over her, blocking out everything else, his chest steadily compressing under her fingertips. Tingles broke out along her skin, a delicious and electric warmth spreading in her belly. She could feel the weight of his stare, but dared not look up at him.

The vest slipped over his shoulders and arms to land atop the other pieces on the carpet. He said nothing as she pushed down his suspenders and unknotted his black necktie. When she plucked out the studs to his shirt collar, he swallowed, his Adam's apple bobbing. The small movement fascinated her. Was he equally affected by her?

Fingers trembling, she started on his shirt, popping the single row of buttons. As each loosened, the crisply starched fabric parted, and she could see the plain white undergarment he wore next to his skin. Lower her hands went, over his breastbone and abdomen, until she ran out of buttons. He bent slightly to help her pull the shirt off, which she let flutter to the floor.

When he straightened, her knees actually wobbled. The tight combination clung to his imposing torso, outlining an impressive bulge of muscles. Many men supposedly wore corsets to pull in their waists, but Emmett obviously didn't need one. There was no extra flesh on him, none that she could see.

Forcing herself to keep going, she reached for the waistband of his striped black trousers—only to have his fingers snatch her wrists. "I'll do the rest," he said brusquely, before walking away.

* * *

Every time Emmett thought he knew his wife, she surprised him.

Now alone in the makeshift dressing room, he removed his remaining garments and wondered how far Elizabeth would have gone in stripping him. His trousers? His underclothes? Christ, he'd grown hard the instant she'd unbuttoned his coat. The rest had been unimaginable torture.

Though she'd started in a businesslike manner, her movements had soon slowed. Turned seductive. And all he'd been able to think of were her small, delicate hands wrapped around his shaft, stroking him from root to tip. Her fingers tugging and pulling, bringing him off with that fierce determination she so often exhibited . . .

He bit back a groan and willed his erection to soften. What was it about his wife that made her unlike any woman he'd ever met? She was beautiful, yes. But that alone would never tie him up in knots. He wished he could figure out the appeal so that he could ignore it and move beyond this strange attraction to her. A damned nuisance, especially when the woman wanted him about as much as a bout of typhoid fever.

But that didn't explain why her hands had trembled when she'd unbuttoned his shirt.

He quickly changed into dry clothing. The brutal weather showed no signs of abating, and he doubted they would be leaving the building any time soon. Even traveling the few blocks he'd managed had not been easy. He wasn't sure how Elizabeth would take that news, but she had little choice in the matter. In another hour or so, snowdrifts would completely cover the outer door of the building.

When he returned to the office, he found her at the windows, where she was bathed in the light streaming in from outside. Her pale hair looked like spun gold. A gilded angel, beautiful yet untouchable. He shook his head at that fanciful idea and headed for the stove. He saw that she'd unpacked all the supplies he'd managed to acquire, and had set his wet clothing by the heat to dry.

He dropped into a chair before the fire, exhausted, and he heard Elizabeth come toward him in a cloud of rustling silk. A glass of brandy emerged before his eyes.

"Here, drink this," she said softly.

He accepted the crystal gratefully and finished the spirits in two swallows. The liquor burned his throat and belly, a pleasant distraction from the heat he felt in other parts of his body.

She lowered into the other chair, bottle of brandy in her hand. "More?"

He nodded, and she refilled the crystal tumbler. He took a more reasonable sip this time and then held the glass out to her. "You should have some as well, before I tell you what I learned."

Gray eyes widened. "Was it so terrible?"

"Worse," he replied truthfully, and her hand snaked out to grasp the brandy. She swallowed some, coughed, and then exhaled.

"The drifts are piling higher than the doorways. And even if we could get out, the roads and walkways are impossible. We're stuck here until it stops snowing and I can dig us out."

Shock lined her face before she lifted the heavy crystal back to her lips for a longer drink. "How long do you think that will be?"

"No way of telling. But we won't starve or die of thirst. We have plenty of coal. As long as we remain indoors, we'll be fine."

"Where did you find the food and supplies?"

"A rum-hole four blocks over. Everyone else is shut up tight." And the amount the owner had charged him was pure robbery, but Emmett hadn't quibbled. He'd pay any amount to keep Elizabeth as comfortable as possible.

She handed him back the tumbler, which he accepted, and then settled deeper into her chair. "Good thing you have lots of books."

"Yes, but we have to conserve the lamp oil as best we can. I might have some candles about, but I can't be sure. Once it gets dark, we should try to keep to the light of the stove."

"Oh dear," he heard her mutter before she rubbed her brow.

Yes, he was of the same mind—but not because he didn't want to spend time with her. Quite the opposite. He wanted to spend a lot of time with her, alone. Without clothing. Just being so near her was hell on his overactive imagination.

"Where is Kelly?" she asked.

"He returned home last night. Said he wanted to get the horses out of the rain, but I think he's tired of sleeping on the cot in the dressing room."

"Does he ever leave your side?"

"Rarely. Not since his wife died, anyway."

"Kelly was married?"

"Yes, for a little over a year. She died of consumption."

"Oh, that's terrible."

"It was, yes. She worked in a factory, sewing buttons, in Hell's Kitchen. They lived in the roughest part of the Tenderloin district, despite the fact that I offered to rent him an apartment in a better part of town." Emmett shook his head, remembering Kelly's stubbornness over not taking Emmett's money in those days. Granted, there hadn't been as much of it, but he'd always been glad to share whatever he had with Kelly. The man had certainly saved Emmett on more than one occasion.

"What did Kelly do? Did he work for you?"

Emmett shook his head. "He wouldn't. Was too proud. So he used to fight for money."

"Fight, as in boxing?"

"Yes. In alleys. It can be lucrative, if you win."

"And if you lose?"

"You can be killed. But Kelly never lost. He's the best boxer I've ever seen."

Tilting her head, she studied him. "Did you ever fight?"

"Only when I had to. But not like Kelly, in organized fights. Mine were more survival than anything else."

"Why don't you ever talk about your boyhood?"

He lifted a shoulder. "Not much I can say in polite company. Why would you want to hear about it, anyway?"

"Because I'm curious about it. About you, how you grew up."

"Let's just say it was a far cry from how I imagine your upbringing, with a big house in a fancy neighborhood. Servants. Plenty of food and heat. Parents who worshipped the ground beneath your feet and never—" He snapped his jaw shut to stem the tide of words rushing out of his mouth.

"Parents who never what?" she asked gently, her brow furrowed in concern. When he didn't answer, she said, "Come now, there's little else to occupy our time. We might as well talk to one another."

He wanted to laugh at the absurdity of the idea. The two of them had been ignoring each other since Newport. Even if they were stuck together for however long the storm lasted, he had no intention of confessing all his deep, dark secrets. No, those were buried for good.

"You don't like talking, do you?" she asked, interrupting his thoughts.

Though he didn't plan them, the words tumbled out of his mouth naturally. "Seems when I'm with you, there are other things I like to do more."

Lizzie sucked in a breath, both shocked and suddenly aroused by his words, not to mention the wicked light in his near-black irises. She wasn't precisely sure to what things he referred, but just recalling the way he'd embraced her in Newport, pressing her into the wall, had her skin prickling with excitement.

Not that she wanted to kiss him again. Kissing led to cravings and longings. Yearnings. All things she needed to avoid.

She cleared her throat. "Are you attempting to distract me?"

"It's possible. Is it working, Mrs. Cavanaugh?"

The name generally irritated her, but hearing it in his low, husky rasp turned her blood thick and slow, like warm honey. Her husband was a hundred times more potent than the brandy she'd imbibed. "No, but I'll stop pestering you about your past." *For now.* "What are you working on?" She gestured to his desk, artfully covered in papers.

He finished his brandy and rose. "You might be able to help me, actually. Come," he said, and held out his hand.

She slid her fingers into his palm, ignoring the jolt that coursed through her system at the contact. He pulled out the enormous desk chair and gestured for her to sit. Once she was comfortable, he shuffled some of the papers on the surface and withdrew a thick stack. He placed those, as well as a ledger, in front of her.

"This is a company I am thinking of acquiring. As I do

with any company I might purchase, I obtained a copy of their books—"

"How?" she asked. To do so would be nearly impossible, unless the company wanted to be sold, which she doubted was the case in this circumstance.

The side of his mouth hitched. "I have my methods. How I got the books is immaterial; what they say is another matter." He tapped his fingers on the ledger. "I suspected a weakness, so I had Colin work up the stock transactions going back for the last two years. He said there are a number of inconsistencies, but I haven't yet had the time to sort them out. Perhaps you can see if everything's aboveboard?"

"I'd be happy to," she said, nearly bouncing in the chair. Not only was this a chance to use her skills, this endeavor would keep her mind off his wickedly powerful presence. "May I have some blank paper and something to write with?"

Emmett reached into a drawer and produced the items. "I'll leave you to it, then." He picked up what appeared to be a contract and went to sit by the fire.

Lizzie delved into the numbers, comparing and studying. Time passed, but she hardly noticed. It didn't take long to arrive at the same conclusion her husband had, that something wasn't quite right. But the error was well hidden, deep in the stock transactions. Her brain buzzed with the compulsion to find the solution, to make sense of what she could feel in her gut.

Emmett placed a lamp at her elbow, and she was surprised to see that dusk had fallen. Snow still pelted the ground, giant flakes falling fast and furious past the windows, as the storm showed no signs of abating. "I thought you said we should conserve the oil," she told him as he strode back to his chair.

He shrugged. "You seem to be making progress. We'll survive if we run out."

Back at her task, she began adding up her findings. Not long after, the answer hit her. "I found it!" She smacked the ledger. "I found what's wrong."

His head lifted. "Did you? Allow me to see."

When he arrived at her side, she started explaining. "I added up the stock sold over the last three years, and compared that to the amounts recorded." Her hand accidentally brushed his as she pointed at the ledger, yet she stuck to the task at hand, ignoring the giddy rush she received from the innocent contact. "The company has sold more stock than they're actually worth."

"To water down the stock price?"

"I can't say for certain why, but they definitely sold more shares than they should have."

"That is remarkable," he said, his lips curving into a satisfied smile. "You have no idea how much work you've saved me. This information is very valuable. Very valuable, indeed." He rubbed his jaw, lost in thought, as he stared at the ledger.

She grew hot under his praise. "My pleasure." Excitement thrummed through her body from the discovery. "I feel as though we should celebrate."

"I agree. And I can definitely assist in that endeavor. How does champagne and dinner sound?"

"Champagne? Do you have an icebox somewhere I cannot see?"

"Just you wait," he told her before he disappeared into his dressing room. He returned a few seconds later with a bottle of Moët and continued toward the window. In a blink, he unlocked the latch, lifted the sash, and placed the bottle in the snow that had collected on the stone ledge outside. Quickly, he lowered the window.

"Clever," she said as he brushed snow from his sleeves. "You are surprisingly resourceful for a steel tycoon."

"Thank you. If I'd known this would impress you, I would have conjured up a blizzard weeks ago."

No doubt he probably could, if he so wished. The man seemed unstoppable. "Well, I haven't yet had this dinner you promised, so I'll reserve judgment."

He smiled, a real, genuine grin, revealing two dimples that would have knocked her down had she been on her feet. "You are a tough woman. I would hate to negotiate against you. I don't think you'd give an inch."

"Not to you," she threw back. "You're a locomotive, rolling over everything in your path to get your way."

"Because I have to be." He leaned against the window. "I learned very early that no one gives you a damned thing in this world."

She remembered the story he'd told her, about working in the steel mill, and knew he meant that. And while she admired his single-minded focus and drive, she didn't want to be a casualty, either.

"But," he continued as he rubbed his jaw, "I do try to weigh the advantages and disadvantages to a situation. It's merely that, once I decide I want something, nothing will stop me from having it." His dark gaze held hers, the intensity of his stare setting her insides aflame.

Was he talking about her? Or were they talking about business?

She rose and smoothed the fabric of her dress while avoiding his eyes. "Perhaps we should eat. I wouldn't want the champagne to freeze."

Chapter Thirteen

If the young women of the present day possessed a sufficient force of character, their influence would be greater.

—American Etiquette and Rules of Politeness, 1883

Something had shifted between them. Emmett could feel the change, a truce of some kind. Elizabeth smiled at him often, the mood decidedly lighthearted—and he hadn't even poured the champagne.

He set out their provisions of salami, cheese, and bread on a blanket he'd spread over the carpet. Night had fallen, and the snow continued outside, but the room was comfortable. He popped the cork on the bottle and filled both of their glasses.

Indeed, this was a celebration—though his wife would hardly agree if she knew the stock transactions she'd just evaluated belonged to Northeast Railroad. Turned out her brother had been selling too many shares of the company's stock. While this wasn't entirely unheard of—Fisk and Gould had watered down the Erie Railroad stock to keep the company out of Vanderbilt's hands—it was fraudulent.

The shares would be worth absolutely nothing, no matter what the investors had paid for them.

So how would Emmett use this information against Sloane?

The water closet door opened, and Elizabeth emerged. "I removed my bustle. All things considered, I thought I should be comfortable."

He closed his eyes briefly. The idea of her removing clothing, even something so innocuous as a horsehair bustle, was embarrassingly tantalizing. "Of course. I agree wholeheartedly."

She turned to show her profile. "It ruins the line of my dress."

He gestured to the empty room. "I think formalities can be bent in these desperate times. Of course I am happy to loan you some of my clothing, if you'd rather."

She snorted and came toward him. "Not even in desperate times, I think. Oh, that looks delicious. I am starving."

"Come, sit." He held out his hand and helped her down to the floor. "It's not much, but—"

"Emmett, it's wonderful." Her gray eyes sparkled in the firelight, gratitude shining up at him. "Thank you. For everything. If it weren't for you, I'd be downstairs, freezing and hungry."

No, you wouldn't, he wanted to tell her. Nothing would have prevented him from reaching her today. Not snow or wind, or even ice. He would have found a way to get to her. But he couldn't imagine admitting that aloud, so he merely said, "You are welcome."

The next several minutes were spent attacking the food and the champagne. They ate in companionable silence, reminding him of the first time he'd taken her to dinner.

"Why are you smiling?" she asked him.

"I was just thinking we get along remarkably well when food is involved. It's the other times . . ."

"Do you plan to carry a hunk of cheese in your pocket every time you wish to speak with me?"

A brief noise escaped his throat, the sound rusty and hoarse.

"Was that a laugh?" She peered at him with exaggerated seriousness. "Oh, I cannot believe it. I actually made you laugh."

"Do not get ahead of yourself. I didn't exactly guffaw."

"Still, I shall treasure it always. The time I made the perpetually serious Emmett Cavanaugh laugh."

He shook his head at her foolishness. "I'm not always serious. Just ask Kelly or Brendan."

"Is that so? Your sisters say they hardly ever see you, that all your time is spent working."

True. He didn't spend enough time with them, but they were surrounded with tutors and governesses, learning how to be proper young ladies, as they should, befitting the status that Emmett's wealth gave them. Claire and Katie would not scrounge and grasp for a husband when the time came. "And your point is?"

"Perhaps you need a bit more fun in your life." She popped a piece of cheese in her mouth and chewed.

He leaned down and cut another small piece of cheese. Lifting it between his thumb and forefinger, he held the morsel in front of her lips. The teasing light in her gray gaze faded, only to be replaced by a dark curiosity that never failed to make him hard. Her lips parted on a breathy sigh, acquiescing, and he slipped the bite of cheese inside. "Perhaps you and I have a difference of opinion on what constitutes fun. Shall I show you my version?"

Bold as brass, she closed her lush mouth around the tips of his fingers. Her lips were soft and smooth against his rough skin, and he wanted nothing more than to feel them on other parts of his body. She held his stare, not shy in the least, and a fierce hunger that had nothing to do with food swept through him.

How could an innocent woman be so brazen? How could a sheltered heiress be so intelligent? How could one woman force him to feel things that none other had even dared?

He slid his hand over her jaw. "You are unlike any woman I've ever met," he said quietly.

Her eyes fell, and she drew back. Reluctantly, he let her go and watched as she reached for her glass. Her hand trembled, and satisfaction tore through him. He'd unnerved her. Good.

He plucked his own glass off the rug and decided to ease his conscience a bit. "I owe you an apology."

"For?"

"What I said in Newport. I was deliberately crude and cruel. I know it doesn't absolve me of what I said, but I didn't care for the idea of you and Henry together."

"Henry and I are not together. We never were."

"I realized as much, and I'm sorry."

She blinked a few times, her mouth working before she said, "Thank you." She sipped more champagne. "Why actresses?"

He was growing used to her knack for abrupt changes in topic. "Why not actresses? They're beautiful and talented. Self-sufficient."

"So you want a woman who will leave you alone?"

"At times. Or I merely want to spend the evening with a pretty woman. I buy them whatever they want, and their names appear in the newspaper. Both parties benefit from the arrangement." He finished his drink then reached to refill both their glasses.

"That sounds . . . cold."

He flashed her a leer. "I promise you, it is not."

She threw her head back and laughed, a rich, joyful sound that stole through his entire body. "You are shameless. How did I never suspect it?"

Probably for the same reason he'd come to realize countless things about her over the past few hours. Like how she tapped her foot when she was concentrating. Or how her hair shined like wheat in the lamplight. "Because we hardly know one another. Isn't that what you once said, when you were trying to finagle out of the wedding?"

Pink bloomed on her cheeks as she reached for the bread. "And it was true."

"But no longer?"

She opened her mouth to take a bite and anticipation slid through his gut, tightening his muscles. Is this what he'd become, a man desperate for the mere sight of a woman's tongue? Then the pink flesh emerged to lick her lips in an innocent-yet-provocative gesture, and Emmett nearly groaned.

At that moment, a decision settled over him with steely resolve. Annulment be damned.

He would seduce his wife in this room before the storm ended. Let her worry over that ridiculous annulment. He no longer cared.

"I am developing an . . . understanding that I did not have before." She cradled her glass of champagne, clutching the flute in front of her chest like a talisman.

Too late, he wanted to tell her. The devil would not be dissuaded, not tonight.

Tonight, she was his.

* * *

Lizzie strongly suspected her husband intended to seduce her.

He'd inched closer and closer on the rug, his long limbs and brawny shoulders entirely too distracting. His dark gaze followed her every movement, tracking her like a hunter on the African plains. He seemed especially fascinated by her mouth and lips while she ate. Heat lurked in his eyes—heat, and a promise.

Perhaps the fault of the champagne, but she was coming to like the idea. Quite a bit.

Selecting another small piece of cheese, she slowly placed the morsel in her mouth. Emmett watched intently, saying nothing. All masculine grace, he was reclined back on an elbow, one knee propped up. A thrill skated down her spine, a heady rush of something wicked and mysterious, as she waited to see what he would do.

"My brother likes you," Emmett said casually. "Claire and Katie, as well. They said you promised to take them ice skating."

"I did." She smiled. The girls were curious about her, constantly peppering her with questions about her life, her clothes, the people she knew. Had she been to the Patriarchs' Ball? What had it been like to debut? How many marriage proposals had she received? Lizzie didn't mind. She could talk to the two adorable girls for hours. They were clearly starved for a female presence in their lives. "You should come as well."

He glanced away, a muscle twitching in his jaw. She asked, "Have you ever been skating?"

"No. Never had the time for that sort of nonsense."

"Ice skating is not nonsense. Having fun and spending time with your family is not nonsense." He didn't say anything, so she pushed on his shoulder playfully. "What if I teach you how to skate? I promise I'll only laugh at you once or twice."

"Oh, is that all?" he said dryly. "Let me guess, your brother took you ice skating."

"Yes, he did. Many times, in fact. No, do not roll your eyes, Emmett Cavanaugh. Manipulations and blackmail aside, he was a good older brother."

"So you're saying I'm a terrible older brother?"

"Not at all, but the girls can use more of your time and attention. Beyond dinners and occasional swimming lessons."

"Sounds as if you've been giving them your time and attention recently. I'm grateful, Elizabeth. They can benefit from a woman's perspective, especially one as sophisticated as yours."

"I adore Katie and Claire. You've done a marvelous job in raising them." She picked at a thread on the blanket, unsure of how to broach something during this newfound détente between them.

"But?" he asked, picking up on her struggle.

"You should know the girls have been asking me about you. I do worry the distance between us will upset them."

"What have you told them?"

"That you are busy. That Newport was cold and boring, that I was anxious to start my investment firm."

"All entirely true," he pointed out. "And not all the honeymoon was cold and boring. I seem to recall a very passionate kiss in the salon. In fact, you almost scratched my back with your fingernails while—"

"Emmett!" Her face warm with embarrassment, she shoved at his shoulder once more—but this time he was ready for her. He sat up, caught her wrist, and did not let go.

"I liked it, Elizabeth," he said quietly. "I liked it so much I've nearly driven myself mad with the memory."

Her heart pounded, a steady pulse that seemed to center between her legs. Gently, he slid his hand up her arm and skimmed her throat to bring her closer. "Tell me you don't wonder," he continued, gliding his thumb under her jaw. "Tell me you don't lie awake at night thinking of what it would feel like. What *I* would feel like. How good the two of us could be together."

A denial sprang to mind, one that was a complete lie. Countless hours had been wasted contemplating exactly that—and more. Thoughts of the powerful attraction between them arose at the most inopportune times. Stock tables would swim before her eyes, she would lose track of conversations, and once she'd gotten so turned around in the mansion that a footman had to give her directions to her room.

"We should resist the temptation," she said, her voice thin.

"If I were a better man, I would try. But I am not that man." His gaze dropped to her mouth, where he brushed the rough pad of his thumb along the edges of her lips. Goose bumps erupted down the length of her body in the wake of his tender touch. "I've done many terrible things in my life and will no doubt commit hundreds more. But you are the first woman I've ever met who makes me ache to be worthy."

She drew in a shaky breath. Her resolve to resist was rapidly melting along with her insides, need and desire building at an alarming rate. "Emmett—"

"Let me, Elizabeth. Let me show you." He bent his head slowly and pressed a gentle kiss to the corner of her mouth. She sighed, and he shifted to repeat the gesture to the other side, his lips surprisingly soft for such a large, complicated man.

There was no point in denying that she wanted him, no benefit to running any longer. Lizzie had fought her

physical reaction to Emmett for too long, weighing the
emotional risks against the pleasurable rewards. Something about this man twisted her up, and perhaps he had
been right: No one need know about their intimacies
during the annulment proceedings.

Decision made, she tilted her head, let her lids fall, and
found his mouth with her own. He gave a swift intake of
breath at her surrender just before crushing her to him.
His lips turned insistent, fevered, as they melded to hers,
drawing and teasing until she clung to him.

Large hands traveled over her corseted ribs, and her
breasts swelled. No man had ever touched her this inti-
mately or kissed her with such vigor. Even through layers
of clothing she could feel his touch, as sensitive as if he
slid over her bare skin. Blood rushed through her veins, in
her ears, along her scalp.

He pressed his tongue past the seam of her lips and she
welcomed him, eager to explore the warm, lush recesses
of his mouth. How could a person's tongue be so arousing?
But, oh, it was . . . Lips open, their tongues twined and
danced in a slick, urgent rhythm that stole her breath. He
pulled back to sink his teeth into her bottom lip, causing
the sweetest sting of pleasure and pain. "Such fire inside
you. I am going to enjoy watching you burn, Elizabeth."

He stretched out next to her and kissed her, hard, as
if dying for the taste of her. Their teeth clashed, mouths
attacking one another in desperation. He loomed over her,
bearing down while she strained up, trying to get closer.
The rustle of silk barely permeated her brain before air
washed over her stocking-clad legs. She should be
shocked, but instead nearly moaned in relief. Sensation
gathered in every pore, every cell, creating a restlessness
that demanded relief.

Higher went the layers until they pooled at her waist.

He pushed her thighs apart, then his hand cupped her mound over the cotton drawers. Without even realizing, she rocked her hips into the heel of his palm. The delicious friction sparked more fierce desire up through her belly, along her spine, and she had to break away from his mouth to release a moan.

He dropped his face into her throat. "So hot," he murmured. "So unafraid. God knows why I'm even surprised."

Her hips began moving once again, seeking. Oh, she needed . . . She didn't know what she needed, but everything was building inside her. "Emmett, please," she whispered, her fingers wrapping around his shoulders to pull him closer.

"You have no idea how long I've waited to hear you say those words." His fingers shifted, parting the fabric of her drawers until he reached the feminine heart of her. His touch glided easily through the moisture pooled there. Should there be so much of it?

Embarrassment washed over her, and she turned her head away, even as he traced her entrance. "No, don't hide," he said. "I want to see your face while I pleasure you."

Before she could ask what he planned to do, he dragged his rough finger along the sensitive skin, up to the bud at the top of her cleft. He rolled it, stroking her, and Lizzie's back bowed off the floor, her toes curling. She closed her eyes, unable to focus on anything but what he was doing with his wonderful, marvelous hands. "That's it, my beautiful," he murmured. "Enjoy what I'm doing to you."

His lips nibbled her neck, below her ear, and then he continued to whisper low, husky words of encouragement. How lovely she was, how intelligent, how perfect . . . Lizzie's muscles soon clenched, her body racing higher and higher as he continued to touch her, drive her to the peak. The deep timbre of his voice, his hot breath on her skin, the catch in his breathing every time she moaned . . .

Then he slid a finger inside her, filling her, and excitement built until her body could not contain all the buzzing giddiness—and she exploded in a burst of white-hot energy, a thousand pieces scattering into the air. She dug her nails into the heft of his shoulders, holding on as she convulsed and gasped his name, the incredible sensation overtaking her.

Before she floated down, Emmett positioned himself between her legs, his knees pressing her thighs wide. He shrugged out of his topcoat, threw it aside, and then his fingers flew down his trouser buttons, undoing them, allowing him to reach into his underclothes to withdraw his erection. One hand propped by her shoulder, the other held himself steady as he lined up at the entrance to her passage. Lizzie felt the hard heat of the smooth tip just before he started inside, slowly, until one mighty thrust rendered the proof of her virginity. She sucked in a lungful of air at the uncomfortable stretch, and instinctually tried to twist away from him. Away from this horrible feeling.

"Wait, Elizabeth." Emmett's eyes were closed, his teeth clenched. "Just wait, please. It will get better. I shoudn't 'a taken you so fast, but it'll get better, I swear."

She heard the guttural consonants, the mispronunciation that sounded so unlike his polished, cultured voice. He sounded like his friend, Kelly, and she wondered how long it had taken her husband to lose the traces of Five Points from his speech.

The soreness between her legs began receding. Emmett towered above her, suspended, as he waited for her to adjust. In his shirtsleeves and vest, he looked impossibly large. "Has the pain eased?" he gritted out. "May I keep going?"

"Are you not . . . in?"

He gave a dry rasp of a chuckle. "Almost, sweetheart." He folded himself over her then, coming down onto his elbows, and captured her mouth in a blistering kiss. She could taste his urgency, his need for her, and ribbons of desire unfurled in her groin once again. Her limbs relaxed, and she melted under him. "That's it," he murmured against her mouth, and rocked his hips to press deeper, the broad head of his penis sliding along her innermost flesh. Strange, this invasion . . . but not unwelcome or unpleasant. He did not stop, just kept up a steady advance until their bodies were flush.

When he retreated and snapped his hips forward, the sweet drag of him inside her was unlike anything she'd imagined. They each groaned into the other's mouth. Two more quick thrusts, and she threw her head back with a cry. She'd never guessed, hadn't dreamed their coupling could feel this intensely good.

He levered up over her, supporting himself on powerful arms. She had never seen him so untamed, so out of control. Dark hair fell onto his forehead, sweat beading his brow. The angles of his face were taut, stark in the firelight, the divot in his chin more pronounced. He was breathtakingly handsome.

"I want to be gentle with you, but God help me . . ." He began pumping in earnest, hips churning into her pelvis, rubbing the swollen nubbin of flesh between them. Unable to speak, she held onto his arms, anchoring herself as waves of bliss surged through her limbs. He didn't need to be gentle. She craved this heat, this animalistic response from him, where primitive, raw lust broke free from his ironclad restraint.

"Wrap your legs around my hips. Let me in deeper."

Lizzie did as directed, and then he withdrew, returned,

and hit a spot that made her gasp. Dear God, how did he . . . He did it again, and the storm began building, pleasure gathering where their bodies were joined. His hips pounded into her now, the force driving her across the carpet. Her muscles tightened, her body drawing into herself, clenching, until she snapped, the orgasm rushing over her. She shouted, nails digging into his back, dimly aware of his grunts, the way his hips stuttered.

He stiffened and groaned loudly, the tendons in his throat straining as he spent inside her womb. "Goddammit," she heard him breathe before he collapsed on top of her.

Never had Emmett felt worse.

He had just fucked his wife like an animal in heat. No gentility. No finesse. No tender words—or even a bed. Hadn't properly prepared or stretched her first. He'd taken her virginity on the floor of his damned office, not even bothering to remove her drawers.

Christ.

What must she think of him? He could only imagine how horrified she must be, how appalled. His cock was still hard inside her, pulsing in utter contentment, while Emmett could feel nothing but loathing for the way he'd treated her.

The room was deathly quiet. The only sounds were the flakes hitting the panes of glass outside. This had been a horrible idea. Why hadn't he kept his hands—and everything else—away from her?

Knowing he was probably crushing her, he began to pull away, not meeting her eyes. Calling on years of practice, he hid his emotions, building up an icy indifference where disapproval and disappointment could not touch him. He slid out of the warm clasp of her easily, the skin of his cock so oversensitive that he shivered.

A cloth. He needed to get a cloth and clean her. That was what a normal husband would do, wasn't it? He drew back on his knees, tucked himself back in his combination, and buttoned his trousers. Before he could get up, a small hand wrapped around his forearm.

"Emmett, wait," she said, rising up on her elbows. "What is wrong?"

He blew out a long breath. *You just took your wife's virginity. You're supposed to be reassuring her, you shitsack.* She was spread out on the floor, her blond hair mussed from his fingers, clothing askew. She'd never looked more beautiful. "Nothing is wrong. I want to get a cloth to clean you up."

"You seem unhappy with me."

He shook his head. "Not with you. With myself."

She gave him a hard stare. "Why?"

Instead of answering, he strode to the water closet. He turned on the hot tap and found a clean cloth. The water remained lukewarm, even after a few minutes, which didn't surprise him since the water heater ran on gas. No doubt the poles holding the gas lines had fallen down by now.

He wet the cloth and returned to where Elizabeth lay on the floor. She watched him curiously, as if he were a stock hiccup to reason out. Ignoring her shrewd gaze, he dropped to his haunches by her hip and gently removed her sweat-dampened drawers. A small amount of blood smeared her inner thighs, and he cleaned her as carefully as he could manage with his clumsy hands. When she had been sufficiently tended to, he returned the cloth to the sink. He felt sticky and sweaty, a sensation he intensely hated, but changing his clothes would have to wait. So he washed as best he could.

When he came back, she hadn't moved, so he lowered himself to the carpet and found his drink. "I apologize," he said before finishing the warm champagne in his glass. He nearly gagged, but it was no less than he deserved.

"Apologize for what, exactly?" She sat up and reached for her own glass.

He made a vague gesture to the carpet. "Not doing this properly. Your first time should have been . . . gentler."

Her brows rose dramatically. "Granted, I had no idea what to expect, but that seemed absolutely perfect to me."

"Perfect? You must be joking. On a floor. Nearly fully clothed. I can only imagine what you are thinking of me."

"Actually, I am thinking," she said with a small twist of her lips, "that I want you to do that again."

He blinked at her even as some of the tension left his shoulders. "What?"

"Did you not enjoy it?" Uncertainty deepened the lines of her face. "I thought that you . . ."

"I had an orgasm, yes. But there was never a question of whether I would enjoy sleeping with you."

Even more lines appeared, and her gray eyes turned troubled. "Because every woman is the same?"

Jesus, he was mangling this. Rubbing the back of his neck, he said, "No. You are different from every other woman I've ever met. I've wanted you naked since the moment you read that ticker tape in my office."

"You have?" A broad grin broke out on her face. She hitched her skirts, rolled onto her knees, then shuffled forward until she reached him. "I didn't understand my reaction the first time I saw you," she was saying as she began to unbutton his vest. "You were entirely too hand-some."

"You weren't afraid of me? Afraid of my size?"

She cocked her head and studied him. "Absolutely not.

I was afraid of what you made me feel. After all, I didn't even know you. Why should I have such an immediate, visceral reaction to the sight of you?"

That admission struck him squarely in the chest. Tossing the crystal aside, he wrapped his arms around her waist and dragged her on top of him, falling to the floor at the same time as he took her mouth. He ravaged her, kissed her with everything he could not express, cupping her buttock with one hand while the other buried in her silky hair. She held nothing back, her tongue meeting his, the two of them struggling for dominance in this pleasurable game.

He was hard and heavy already, a feat he hadn't expected so soon after spending, but Elizabeth affected him like none other. Still, he would do this properly.

Forcing himself away from her sinfully tempting mouth, he kissed her jaw. "I want to see every inch of you." He palmed her small, round breast over her clothing, pleased when she arched into his hand. "May I undress you?"

He held his breath while awaiting her answer. If she refused, he very well might beg.

She nodded and slid off him. He rose and offered her a hand, aiding her to her feet. The row of buttons on her lilac shirtwaist beckoned, tiny buttons much too delicate for his large, anxious fingers. His mistresses had always worn garments factoring for a man's impatience. Undressing his wife would no doubt be a test of his fortitude.

He began forcing the buttons through the holes. Anticipation churned in his gut, his skin tight and hot, and he considering rending the fabric. If they were at home, he wouldn't hesitate, but he did not want to ruin her one available garment during the storm.

The release of each button revealed further glimpses of

her underthings. Silk and lace covered unblemished, creamy skin. He traced his fingers over the hard edges of her collarbones, watched her shiver. He didn't stop, but forced himself to slow down. The first time he removed her clothing, the first time he saw her entirely naked needed to be forged into his memory forever.

Buttons undone, he pushed the sides open and over her shoulders, revealing a white cotton corset cover fashioned with bows and more buttons. Sweat broke out on the back of his neck as he unwrapped her, and when he reached her pale pink corset, she was breathing fast, the motion forcing up the small mounds of her breasts. Ever lovin' hell, the woman was perfection.

"So lovely," he murmured before bending his head to place reverent kisses along the edge of the heavy fabric. She clutched at him, and the proof of her desire lit a match to the fever inside his blood. He had to have more of her, had to taste her. He held the weight of her corseted breast, plumped the soft flesh to expose it, then he rained kisses over the creamy slopes. After a long moment, he pulled back to drag in air, his cock aching, harder than it had ever been. Christ, the threads of his control were unraveling quickly, and she was still more than half dressed.

He stepped behind her, appreciated the curve of her delicate shoulders. At her waist he found the ties of her outer skirt, pulled the loops free. The ruffled petticoat came next, dropping to the floor on top of the skirt. He ran his fingers along her spine, over the lacings of her corset, enjoyed the gasp she gave as a result. Grasping her hand, he helped her step out of the skirts, moved them to the side with his foot.

He spun her around and found her wide eyes burning with a myriad of emotions. Desire, excitement, curiosity, embarrassment . . . She held nothing back from him, and he wanted to pay her back in kind. "You are the most magnificent woman I've ever seen."

The smile she gave him tightened his chest with something entirely unfamiliar. Something unexpected.

Something he must ignore.

This was not forever; she still planned to leave him. Freedom could be attained with one creative lie to the judge regarding consummation. And why wouldn't she, this high-bred girl from wealth and privilege, one who could have her choice of worthy men?

Nevertheless, Emmett had her now. And he meant to have his fill of her.

His hands popped open the fastenings of her corset, exposing her bit by bit. The heavy piece fell to the ground with a thump. Unable to resist, he stroked her small breast over her chemise. Soft and round. He plucked at the hard nipple, then pinched, and her head fell back with a moan. With deft hands, he undid the bow and buttons, lifted the garment over her head. Her skin gleamed in the firelight, her breasts high and perfect, with dusky areolas that surrounded pink nipples just begging for his mouth.

Bending, he drew a nipple between his lips, onto his tongue, and sucked. She exhaled sharply, her fingers weaving through his hair to grasp his head. He repeated the motion, then bathed her nipple with his tongue, circling, alternating with suction, until her knees gave out.

He caught her easily and lowered her to the carpet. She gazed up at him from under long lashes. "I had no idea," she breathed.

"You still don't," he said, before giving the same attention to the other breast. She was writhing beneath him by the time he removed her stockings. He took a moment to appreciate the view. Long, smooth legs. Downy blond curls. Tapered waist and gorgeous breasts. "My God, but you are a vision."

"Emmett." She reached for him.

"Wait. There's something I must do first." Shifting lower, he positioned himself between her legs. His fingers parted the folds until he reached the plush, slick center of her. Moisture pooled there, so much that his mouth watered. He wanted to devour her, to bury his face in her cleft for days and never come out. The tip of his finger traced her entrance. She would be sore from their earlier encounter, so he would need to restrain his own lust this time. But he could pleasure her.

"Lie back, Elizabeth. Let me taste you on my tongue."

Chapter Fourteen

Always hand a chair for a lady, and perform any little service she may seem to require.

—American Etiquette and Rules of Politeness, 1883

Panic stole through her. Did he mean to kiss her *there?*

Before Lizzie had a chance to contemplate all the reasons she found that embarrassing, he dragged his tongue along the seam between her legs, lapping at her, and fire sizzled in every nerve ending. He repeated the action once more, and she nearly crawled out of her skin at the exquisite, sharp pleasure. Then his attention turned to the hard bud at the top of her sex, and she thought she'd lose her mind.

He was relentless, the intensity like nothing she'd imagined. His lips and tongue kept up the steady friction until she couldn't hold back any longer. The world reduced to that one spot and how he was mastering it so thoroughly. When he sealed his mouth around the nub and sucked—she went over the edge, the crest fierce and undeniable, her legs shaking against his shoulders, her cries echoing in the big room. She shouted freely in this private world, safe from the storm, safe from the rest of the city. Safe from the reality that was their marriage. Here, nothing mattered but the pleasure, and the bliss continued on and on as he worked her. Finally, she grew sensitive and jerked away from his wicked mouth.

His lips met her inner thigh and he kissed her sweetly, almost as if expressing gratitude. Silly, when she was the one who should be grateful.

He moved to her side, propped up on an elbow, and stretched out. A large, rough hand traveled over her hip, swept across her stomach and ribs, glided between her breasts. Surprisingly, he was as out of breath as she.

"Did you enjoy that?" His eyes tracked the path of his hand.

"There are no words," she answered honestly. "Why did I not know?"

"Because you haven't been naked with me before." The arrogance in his voice made her smile.

"Is that so? Allow me to guess: you are the only man in the world with such superlative bedroom skills?"

"Yes, of course. Do not ever consider otherwise."

She laughed. "You can be quite charming when you want. But I do wonder why I am the only person without clothing in this room."

He traced a path around her nipple with a fingertip. "You will be sore."

"But I'm not sore now," she said, and dragged the flat of her foot over the soft wool covering his calf. He was back to his tightly controlled, enigmatic self, and she much preferred the man who lost his mind with need for her. The one who couldn't hold back.

She should be nervous, she supposed, since she lay naked on a rug with a man she hardly knew, but she couldn't manage it. His dark eyes remained focused on her body, as if he had a hard time believing she were real.

As if he had to keep a hand on her to prove they were both truly here. And a muscle jumped in his jaw, a sign of struggle that she relished.

He'd lost his vest and necktie at some point and was now in his shirtsleeves, collar, and trousers. Unbelievably, he still had on shoes. Rising up, she reached to unlace his square-toed low boots that were the height of fashion. She slipped each one off his foot, tossing it to the carpet. "Elizabeth," he said, part warning, part something else that caused her to tingle in newly discovered places.

"Yes, Emmett?" she asked innocently as she shoved his black silk socks down. First one, then the other.

He swallowed hard, his stare fixed on her backside, which she'd unwittingly positioned toward him. Good. She scooted a bit, not turning, so she could unbutton his trousers. The fastenings came undone easily, the striped wool parting in her hands.

"You are playing with fire." His voice, low and rough, sent a thrill through her.

"Not yet, but I soon will be, I hope." Shifting, she lowered his suspenders. He rolled onto his back, lifted his hips off the floor, and pushed his trousers down, continuing until he kicked them off. "Now the shirt," she told him.

In a flash, he dispensed with his shirt collar and shirt, leaving him in a thin, white combination. The tight, one-piece undergarment left little to the imagination. The fabric clung to him, showing off every ripple, every ridge, every bulge. Indeed, *every* bulge. Her heart skipped in her chest at the sheer masculine beauty of him. The seams struggled to contain his massive shoulders, and dark hair peeked out from the top edge under his collarbone. Her fingers itched to touch and explore, to learn the man underneath.

"Well?"

Her gaze snapped to his face. "Well, what?"

"You seemed to enjoy giving the orders. I was merely awaiting more direction."

A surge of feminine power coursed through her. "And would you do anything I ask?"

He slipped his hand under his head, causing his bicep muscle to pop. "Unless it involves going outside, yes. Unequivocally."

"Then kiss me."

Where had *that* come from? She had no idea where this brazen self-assurance originated, but he must have approved because he lunged up and found her mouth, kissing her deeply. Confidently. As if he knew how much she craved him.

"Not on the floor," he said against her mouth. In one fluid motion, he lifted her and stood, then carried her to the immense sofa, a piece of furniture definitely designed for a man his size. Wide and long, the sofa, covered in soft brown velvet, tickled her bare skin as he laid her down. He followed, giving her his weight in the most intimate and delicious of ways, with his cotton-covered erection hot and urgent against her thigh.

She wrapped her arms around him, and he slid a large thigh between her legs and took her mouth once more. He didn't touch her, merely kissed her until she writhed and clawed beneath him, a mindless mass of blinding desire. Just as she started to beg, his hand drifted between her legs where he expertly stroked the heart of her. Her nails plunged into his shoulders when he pushed a finger inside her warm, wet channel, stretching her, and that digit soon turned into two. He pumped his hand a few times, readying her, and she rocked into the heel of his palm, needing more. Needing everything he could give her.

Needing *him*.

Her fingers flew to the buttons of his combination, tearing at it in her haste. Buttons popped in her desperation to feel his skin against hers, and finally she was able to get the garment open and over his shoulders. He slipped one arm out and then the other, and together they shoved the cloth down his torso, over his hips. Rough, blazing skin touched hers, the soft hair along his belly, chest, and legs dragging on her flesh to make her shiver. His fingers returned to her sex, pleasuring until her eyes nearly rolled up in her head.

She drew back to breathe. "Please, Emmett."

"Touch me," he ordered, gently biting along the column of her throat. "I need to feel your hands on me."

Her fingers found his chest, where she trailed over the taut muscles and stark ridges of his ribs. Learned the contours of his abdomen, the angles of his hip bones. Then she wrapped her hand around the velvety length, lightly grasping the heavy weight of his erection. He gave a sharp intake of breath as she tested the smooth skin, ran her thumb around the plump head.

"Harder," he murmured into her neck. "You won't hurt me." As if to encourage her, he curled his fingers deep inside her and hit a spot that caused her to cry out. She retaliated by tightening her grip on him, stroking roughly. He groaned against her skin.

His hand withdrew, leaving her empty, until he mounted her, fit their hips together, and slowly began entering her. "Tell me if it hurts," he rasped. "I swear, I'll stop."

"I'm fine. Hurry, Emmett."

But he did not hurry. Instead he took his time, as if savoring the experience. He sank inside carefully, demanding surrender, overtaking her, until he'd fully seated himself. She wrapped around his frame, gathering him close as he started to move, pelvis driving, both giving and receiving pleasure. He would not be rushed, long, unfaltering strokes driving her higher, sweat running down his temple, his skin turning damp. Just when she was sure another minute of the exquisite torture would drive her mad, he reached between their bodies and touched her, the pad of his finger causing the pleasure to explode. Her release went on and on, her hands holding him, his name a chant on her lips.

He rose to grip her hips as he sped up, sweaty skin slapping together in the otherwise silent room. Muscles clenching, he threw his head back and shouted, movements stuttering as he poured himself inside her. She marveled at the sheer power and strength of him, the un-restrained masculinity.

He collapsed on top of her. His head dropped into the curve of her throat, while Lizzie's arms came around his neck. They caught their breath, his body still joined with hers. A warm feeling of contentment washed over her, a sense of *rightness*. This was the man, the one she'd imag-ined would cherish her, protect her, yet allow her to chase her own dreams. True, he hadn't wanted to marry her— but that was in the past. They were married now, and perhaps they were far better suited than she could have hoped. As Emmett had said, many couples began with much less. Not everyone had this attraction, this all-consuming desire the two of them shared.

Who said that could not evolve into something more over the years?

The point was, she wanted to try with this man. No one else. No one else had risen so far with so little. Provided for his brother and taken in his half sisters, raised them. And certainly no other man had ever affected her this deeply. Every time she considered the annulment, her chest ached. Leaving would be difficult; lying in a court of law would be impossible.

The only thing left was to give him the truth. "I have changed my mind about the annulment."

Emmett froze, certain he had misunderstood. Before he could question her, however, he had to deal with practicalities. Withdrawing from the warm grip of her passage, he came to his feet and went to fetch another cloth. He heard Elizabeth gasp as he walked away and immediately cursed his forgetfulness. *Shit.*

"Emmett, your back. Dear God." Revulsion? Horror? Pity? He couldn't quite pinpoint what he heard in her voice, but continued on to the washroom.

While waiting for the water to warm up, he cleaned himself off as best he could with the freezing stream from the tap. When he had a cloth ready for Elizabeth, he strode back to the sofa. She had curled up on her side, like a kitten, her gray eyes missing nothing as he traveled the floor. Sitting at her hip, he rolled her until he could gently clean between her legs. The flesh of her sex was red and swollen, and guilt shot through him. He should not have taken her a second time, no matter how much they'd both wanted it.

"Why are you staring at me like that?" she asked.

The pins holding her hair had come loose, her blond locks now falling around her shoulders. He swept a long strand off her smooth forehead. She was so beautiful, so perfect. He'd done nothing in life to deserve having this woman by his side every day, but he'd be damned if he'd give her up now. "I was thinking that you'll be sore tomorrow, and I was regretting that we will have to wait."

Her mouth kicked up at the edges. "I've always been a quick healer."

"Is that so? I guess we'll have to see then, won't we?" He bent to place a quick kiss on her lips. "Let me build up the stove so you stay warm. I don't plan on letting you put clothes on yet."

He returned the cloth to the sink and came out to add more coal to the stove. Elizabeth used the water closet, and he took a moment to appreciate her lithe, naked form as she traversed his office. Unashamed, she winked at him on her way back to the sofa.

Once the fire had been properly stoked, he grabbed the blankets he'd purchased from the tavern and carried them over. He slid in behind her so she'd be closer to the coal stove and covered them both with the heavy wool. She turned toward him on her side, and her head found its way onto his arm, using him as a pillow, while her hand caressed his chest.

"Your back," she said quietly. "Was that the accident you told me about?"

"Yes." Nothing more to say on that subject. The tissue had healed in long, jagged white scars. An ugly reminder of his struggle out of the gutter, not one he cared to think on if he could avoid it.

Elizabeth seemed to understand, nodding. The fact that she was still here, even after learning a tiny portion of his sordid past, seemed an incredible gift. One he intended not to squander.

"So the annulment," he asked. "You've changed your mind?"

"Yes, I have. Unless you think we should still go through with a separation."

"I was against the damned thing in the first place, Elizabeth." He slid his palm over her hip and around to cup her buttock. Squeezed. "I am curious as to what changed your mind, though."

"It wasn't that, in case you were wondering."

"That, meaning my bedding you?"

"Yes. I wanted the annulment because my brother black-mailed you into marrying me. Besides being humiliated, I was convinced we would make each other miserable."

"The humiliation is mine, Elizabeth. I should've known better than to engage in any impropriety with you that night. But I've always struggled with keeping my hands to myself around you."

She tilted her head to kiss his jaw. "And I am glad of it. As you said, many married couples begin with less. I've always wanted a marriage like the one my parents supposedly had, with love and laughter."

Emmett blinked. He knew when faced with insurmountable odds, and this was damn close. Love? Laughter? Jesus, his parents had fought like sailors and hit each other—and that had been on the good days. What did he know of a happy marriage? "Well, I am not sure that's—"

"Don't. Just because you did not have the same growing up doesn't mean you do not deserve it now."

Had he been so transparent? "How are you so certain?"

"Because you are not your father, and I am not your mother. I'm not going to leave, Emmett. I'm going to stick it out, and so are you."

He squeezed her backside once more. "Bossy, aren't you?"

"I can be, yes. But you want a woman who can stand up to you, who isn't afraid of you."

How did she know that when he was only coming to realize it himself? "You are definitely not afraid to shout at me. My ears are still ringing from ten minutes ago when I used my fingers to—"

She pinched his shoulder playfully. "Emmett!"

He kissed her nose, her cheek. She was soft and smelled like lavender combined with their lovemaking, an intoxicating combination. "Laughter, Elizabeth. Don't forget the laughter."

She smiled at him and something tripped in his chest, expanding. He'd never experienced anything so powerful. Then she yawned, and a quick glance at the mantel clock told him it was well after midnight. "Turn around and try to sleep."

She rolled over and pressed her round buttocks into his groin as he covered her from behind. He felt his cock stir and tried to think of the most boring, inane things he could in order to deflate his lust. Transit prices. Upcoming quarterly dividends. What he would do with the information Elizabeth had uncovered about Northeast Railroad. Anything but his wife's luscious, very naked body against him.

"The papers mentioned how you were seeing a . . . woman," she said. "And I know you haven't been sleeping at home. . . ."

Emmett remained silent, and she twisted to shoot him an expectant look. "Well?"

His lips twitched, but she appeared so serious he hated to laugh. "Just ask, Elizabeth."

An elbow dug into his ribs, a sign of her impatience. "Are you still seeing her?"

"No. Not since the engagement was announced, and we hadn't seen each other in the way you're thinking of since before even that." His fingers trailed up her thigh. "And if you elbow me once more, you'll be answering to me, Mrs. Cavanaugh."

She giggled, a sound he was rapidly coming to love. Quiet descended, and he felt himself sliding toward sleep until she asked, "Why do you call me Elizabeth instead of Lizzie, like everyone else?"

Idly, he stroked her hip, and the truth unexpectedly tumbled out of his mouth. "It's a noble name, for a queen. A conqueror. 'Elizabeth' sounds like a woman strong enough to change history, to chart any course she chooses. Anyone could be a Lizzie—but only you could be Elizabeth."

She drew in a shaky breath. "That's . . ." She exhaled, long and slow. "That's the nicest thing anyone's ever said to me."

He pressed his lips to the back of her head. "Go to sleep, Elizabeth."

Unbelievably, the snow continued the next day.

On the storm's second morning, Lizzie sipped some water and looked out at the city she loved, now covered in white. The snowdrifts stretched to the second floor of most buildings, the streets still impossible to traverse. As Emmett had predicted, ice and wind had toppled the telegraph and telephone poles, and the electricity had yet to come back on.

Indeed, with so much wrong, how could she be this happy?

The door to the water closet opened, and she turned to watch her naked, freshly shaved husband emerge. Her breath lodged in her throat. Oh, yes. *This* would be the reason for her jubilant mood.

Impossibly wide shoulders, lean hips, muscles shifting under tanned skin as he moved . . . She would never tire of looking at him. He walked with confidence. Purpose. As if he owned all of New York—which, she supposed, he quite nearly did. The man might have started with nothing in life, but he'd taken all he'd wanted and more, making him both feared and respected.

Today, he'd awoken first, left her sleeping under the blankets on the sofa to begin his morning ritual. She'd missed waking up next to him. Missed feeling all that strength and power under her fingertips.

A knowing smirk on his face, he slipped his arms around her blanketed shoulders and pulled her back into the cradle of his chest. He rested his chin on top of her head as they watched the blur of falling flakes through the windows. "Beautiful," he said softly.

"It is, isn't it? All that white snow."

"Yes, that, too."

She smiled. "Are you charming me again, Mr. Cavanaugh?"

"I only tell the truth, Mrs. Cavanaugh," he replied, and she could see his devilish grin in the reflection of the pane. "And why the blanket? You aren't turning shy, are you?"

"Merely cold," she lied. Nakedness had been easier in the dark, even if Emmett hadn't given her a reason to be self-conscious. She'd never been unclothed with a man before. People of her class never talked about marital relations, but she'd envisioned something civilized, undertaken with the lights firmly off. Lovemaking with Emmett was not anything like that. Raw, earthy, and wild, their encounters were better than any of her youthful daydreams.

"How do you feel?" he asked.

"Well rested. Hungry." Then she added, "Not sore, in case you were wondering."

He huffed a tiny laugh, the great expanse of his chest billowing behind her. "Of course I was wondering. I am a man in the presence of my incredibly appealing wife, after all."

His palms wound under the blanket until he found her

breasts, cupped them. He applied pressure, plumping the soft mounds, and then squeezed her nipples. Desire streaked down her spine, and her head fell back on his shoulder as her lids fluttered shut. Rolling the taut peaks in his fingers, he pressed his now-evident erection into her backside and whispered in her ear, "Shall I pleasure you right here? When anyone stranded in one of these surrounding buildings could be watching?"

She gasped, both shocked and titillated by the idea. Still, there were practical matters to deal with first. She twisted out of his grip. "As soon as I wash up." Gaze firmly averted from his aroused nakedness, she went to the small room at the far end to start her morning preparations.

When she emerged several minutes later, Emmett was busy setting out food for their breakfast. He'd pulled on trousers, but remained bare above the waist, thank goodness. Her husband was a sight to behold.

"I went ahead and set up the food," he said as she approached. "I realize this is a far cry from what you normally have in the morning."

Growing up, she'd enjoyed hot coffee, eggs, ham, buttered rolls, anything she'd wanted for breakfast. The Sloane cook had prepared whatever Lizzie had craved each day. But that luxury paled compared to the simple fare that her husband had braved a storm to retrieve. Would she ever be able to eat salami again without thinking of him? Or recalling the weight of his body as he surged inside her?

He glanced up, his dark eyes studying her. "Are you blushing?"

"Of course not. I'm married. Married women do not blush."

"That experienced, are you?" He smirked. "Would you

care for another wager, this time to see if I can make you blush?"

She pulled the blanket tighter and lowered to the carpet. "Need I remind you who won our last wager?"

"There are two things at which I excel. And they both begin with *f*. The first is finance, and the second is f—"

"Emmett!" Lizzie laughed, her skin flaming.

"—orging steel." His brows rose in exaggerated innocence. "Why, Elizabeth, what did you think I was about to say?"

No chance she would say that particular word. "Fine. You succeeded in embarrassing me."

Though her face was hot, her insides fluttered at his teasing. Who was this playful stranger? Where was the cold, remote man she'd married? She liked this side of Emmett Cavanaugh, a side she guessed not many ever saw.

"And here I thought Knickerbocker ladies didn't know that word." He popped a piece of the cured meat in his mouth and chewed. "You continue to amaze me."

His praise generated more fluttering. There were deep emotions beginning to surface, somewhere in the vicinity of her heart. They unnerved her. Yes, he was her husband, but she'd never experienced this rush of tenderness toward a man before. The sensation caused her to feel both weak and powerful, and she needed time to examine the possibilities. To weigh the benefits and risks for the future. To ensure she was not the only one invested in this marriage.

She reached for the bread, and the two of them ate in silence for a few moments. "Do you believe the snow will keep up?"

"Hard to say." His gaze transferred to the window. "I haven't ever seen a storm like this before. You must be anxious to return home, to a soft bed and warm bath."

"Not at all. I am enjoying myself," she answered honestly, which caused his brows to snap together. Worried she'd given too much away, she added lightly, "Though even a cold bath·would appeal at this point."

"If we run out of coal, that might be easier than you think."

She sat up straighter. "Is that a possibility?"

"Not a chance. Don't worry, the cellar is full of coal. We won't freeze. Though we may have to find more food if the storm goes on any longer than tomorrow."

Though the dancing light in his eyes gave him away, she bumped his hip with her foot, saying haughtily. "Are you implying that I am eating too much? It's rude to comment on a lady's appetite. We are delicate creatures."

"Delicate?" He snorted. "I should have known you were trouble the minute you argued with me in my office over backing your investment firm."

"Which you did not want to do, as I recall."

"Even I have moments of stupidity. Surely you know that by now."

"I am going to make you a lot of money," she said, dusting the crumbs off her hands.

"Us. You are going to make *us* a lot of money. Now, are you finished eating or would you care for more?"

"I am finished. Shall we clean up?"

He reached out and snagged the end of her blanket, slowly pulling the fabric toward him. "Not just yet. I'd like to borrow your blanket first."

The cloth was disappearing from her naked body, so she clutched the edges tighter. "Wait, why do you need it?"

"I don't. I need you, actually. Naked, so that I may taste my favorite part of you for breakfast."

Chapter Fifteen

Be quiet and composed under all circumstances.
—American Etiquette and Rules of Politeness, 1883

Emmett cast a surreptitious glance at his wife across the carriage. Disheveled, wrinkled, and dirty, she'd never appeared more beautiful. Fortune had indeed smiled on him the day she walked into his home. The last few days with her had been as close to heaven as a man like him would ever get—and he'd be damned if he'd ever regret it.

Yesterday, once the snow had stopped, he'd ventured outside and shoveled until his back ached and his calluses sprouted calluses. Fifteen or twenty other men had joined in, citizens determined to get the city back on its feet, to clear enough that the snow removal wagons could get through. While he was working, the sweat had rolled down his back, soaked his shirt and underclothes, and continued to his feet. The sensation, so reminiscent of times he'd rather forget, had caused bile to regularly rise in his throat, which he resolutely pushed down. Elizabeth's safety was what mattered most, not the nightmares of his youth.

Elizabeth. His wife. *Sweet Jesus, Mary, and Joseph.*

She was far more adventurous than he'd even dreamed, amenable to his every suggestion. The memory of her astride his hips this morning, riding him, would stay burned in his brain for a lifetime. Variety in positions had never given him a second thought before, when he'd fucked other women. So without thinking, he'd switched to place Elizabeth on top. Thank Christ, she'd enjoyed the new angle.

He shifted in his seat, adjusting his trousers to hide his burgeoning erection. Each time he had her only worsened his craving. In fact, he was dying to get her up to his bed the instant they arrived home.

The brougham moved slowly through the slick, snow-covered streets, giving them ample time to study the destruction wrought by the storm. Poles had collapsed, bringing wires down with them. Carriages and carts had been stranded, their owners desperately seeking shelter. Horses frozen and stiff in the street. A stalled streetcar nearly blocked Twenty-Third Street and Sixth Avenue. Men were everywhere, some with shovels, some starting fires in the drifts in an attempt to melt the snow, while children scampered about, throwing snow and sliding in their boots. Loaded wagons carted the snow to the river, an arduous task that would take weeks.

"Kelly certainly appeared relieved to find us in one piece this afternoon," Elizabeth said, her gaze trained on the window.

Emmett had been both thankful and annoyed by Kelly's rescue. "No doubt he suspected one of us to have strangled the other after two days of being trapped together."

Her head turned sharply. "Why? What did you tell him about us?"

"The truth. Wasn't like he hadn't already figured it out, based on what happened in Newport."

She contemplated that for a moment, her brow furrowed. "Which company was that, back in your office? The books you had me review?"

He had no plans to tell her of his revenge on her brother, not yet. Not when they'd just built this fragile trust between them. "All in due time, my dear."

"You won't tell me? Even now?"

Especially not now. "It has nothing to do with whether I trust you or not. I am not certain what I will do with the information just yet."

"Are you always so secretive in your business dealings?"

He thought about that. As a boy, he'd learned to keep things to himself. Less risk of being hurt that way. "I don't want you to worry over my plans."

"So what now?"

"Meaning?"

"Are you planning to stay at home? With me?"

There was a note of vulnerability in her voice, revealing how much the answer mattered. He snatched her gloved hand to tug her closer. If not for the cramped space, he'd have dragged her onto his lap. Instead, he had to make do with cupping her cheek. "I do not plan on being anywhere else."

She sighed, her body softening—precisely the way he liked it. He removed his derby, dipped his head, and kissed her, the taste of her filling his mouth. She responded as she always did: eagerly and aggressively. Like she'd been waiting a year for him to kiss her. Did she have any idea how alluring those qualities were in a woman?

Her gloved fingers tunneled through his hair, holding on, and he drove deeper, their tongues desperate for one another. The low whimpers and moans she fed his mouth snaked through his blood to settle in his gut, plumping his cock further. Damn, what he planned to do to this woman when they arrived home.

The wheels had slowed, he noted dimly over the pounding of his heart. He broke off and tried to collect himself before he had to face his family. "You are going to cause me a great deal of embarrassment in front of the girls if we do not stop." He gestured to his lap.

She pressed a shaking hand to her lips, trying to stifle her laughter. "I don't suppose you could keep your overcoat on?"

"Graham would wrestle me for it if I did. But rest assured that I will be dragging you up to my bed as soon as I can manage." He shoved his hat back on his head.

"Before dinner?" she asked with an innocence he did not believe for a second.

"Yes, definitely before dinner. I plan to be under your skirts before the horses have even been stowed."

She chuckled. "I want a bath, so you'll have to wait for that, at the very least."

His gloved fist clenched. He did not want to wait, not one minute longer than necessary. "Take one with me. I have the largest bath in the house. It even has a rain shower."

She seemed to contemplate the idea as the carriage came to a halt. "What will the servants say?"

"Who gives a damn? We're married, Elizabeth. There's nothing improper about tending to your husband's needs during the day."

"Oh, is that what it's called?"

"Sweetheart, I'll tend to your needs any time you ask. All you need do is crook your little finger at me, and I'll be on my knees."

Color bloomed on her cheeks as Kelly opened the

carriage door. *Excellent*. Kelly helped Elizabeth down the small steps and she continued on toward the house.

When Emmett emerged from the carriage, Kelly's eyes were lit with unholy amusement. "The Bishop happily married," his friend murmured. "Never did think I'd live to see the day."

"You might not live the hour, if you don't watch your mouth," Emmett snapped as his feet hit the ground. Kelly's laughter trailed him as Emmett strode up the walk.

Graham opened the door, and Elizabeth sailed through first, Emmett close on her heels. "Good evening, madam," Graham was saying as Emmett came inside.

"Thank you. I am relieved to be home," Elizabeth replied, removing her gloves.

Her use of the word "home" was not lost on Emmett, and his chest tightened with a combination of relief and hope. Was it wrong to be grateful for a storm that had likely killed hundreds of people and caused so much destruction, yet had brought harmony with his wife? He made a note to donate additional funds toward the city's rebuilding efforts, to atone for the selfishness.

"And welcome home, sir." Graham closed the door behind Emmett and began helping Elizabeth with her cloak.

"Graham, a word." Emmett flung his hat and gloves on the side table.

"Yes, sir?" Graham straightened and faced the master of the house squarely.

"In the future, do not allow my wife out of this house in unfavorable weather conditions." He heard Elizabeth sputter, so he added, "I realize Mrs. Cavanaugh can be persuasive and headstrong, but I rely on you to ensure the safety of the house and its occupants. Do not fail me again."

"Understood, sir."

"Emmett," Elizabeth said, "do not blame Graham. He tried to—"

"He should have locked you up, is what he should have done."

Her eyes narrowed to slits. He raised a brow, not bothered in the least. Indeed, her anger only aroused him further.

"You're here. Thank God." Brendan was hurrying down the stairs as best he could, leaning heavily on the rail. "We have been worried sick. Girls!" he called over his shoulder. "Emmett and Lizzie are home."

His brother went to Elizabeth first, just as Claire and Katie emerged on the landing. The two girls flew down the steps, relief evident on their faces. Emmett knelt and held out his arms, one for each of his little sisters.

They crashed into him, their small arms going around his shoulders. "Welcome home," Katie said into his overcoat while Claire cried, "We thought you weren't ever coming back."

He hugged them both. Hard. "I told you, I'll always come back. It took me a little longer than anticipated because of the snow."

"That's what Brendan said, but he and Mr. Kelly were very worried," Katie's muffled voice said.

"Well, everything is fine now. Why don't you both go and welcome Elizabeth home as well?"

The girls nodded, and they all turned to find Elizabeth and Brendan watching closely. Something bright and watery shone in his wife's eyes before she came over to hug his half sisters.

Emmett straightened and went to his brother. Brendan clapped him on the back. "Goddamn, am I glad to see you," his brother said quietly. "I've never been so worried in my life. We couldn't reach you, and had no way to know if Lizzie had found you. I nearly had to tie Kelly down to keep him from starting for Beaver Street during the storm."

"I'm glad you stopped him. He wouldn't have made it past Fiftieth Street." Emmett shrugged out of his coat and handed the heavy garment to Graham. "Now, if you'll excuse us, my wife is exhausted, and I promised her a bath."

Brendan's brow furrowed. "So does that mean . . ." He tipped his chin toward Elizabeth.

"Yes. That is precisely what it means."

"Thank you for coming," Emmett said three days later as he closed the door to his office. It was early, not yet even nine o'clock, and he'd left his very naked, very delectable wife sleeping upstairs to come down for this meeting. A meeting that could not conclude fast enough.

Kelly sprawled in one of the armchairs, while Colin sat at his desk, ready to take notes. Good, they could get started straightaway.

A man rose to shake Emmett's hand. Sheridan was one of the best investigators in New York, having been a Pinkerton for years before leaving and going into business for himself. Emmett used Sheridan for sensitive jobs, where the utmost discretion was required. "Of course, Mr. Cavanaugh. You said it was urgent."

Emmett gestured to the chair. "Please, sit. How are the roads?"

"Clearer up here, sir, but downtown is still a mess."

Unsurprising, since the residents on upper Fifth Avenue had the money to afford crews to dig them out. Those in other parts of Manhattan would have to wait until the city's snow wagons came around or pick up shovels themselves.

Emmett dropped into his seat and folded his hands on his desk. "The reason I asked you here is to discuss a company I have my eye on."

Sheridan nodded. This was familiar territory between them. "Go on."

"They're weak at the moment. They've been watering down the stock, printing and selling more shares than they should. I'm inclined to take this news to the board, rather than the authorities, but I don't want to leave it to chance." He pointed at Sheridan. "Start with the board. Find out who has a weakness we can leverage. If there's nothing we can use, then ferret out those who can be bought. I need at least eight men who are willing to help me. Buying their shares should give me enough for a majority."

"Guess that explains why you just don't want to buy the stock outright, since it's watered down."

"That's one reason. The other is that I need the owner caught by surprise. I don't want him to know until it's too late, when he cannot retaliate or regroup."

Sheridan scribbled in his pad. "Sure. Which company?"

"Northeast Railroad."

The investigator's pencil stalled, the only reaction to the revelation. Not that Emmett cared. Sheridan was paid to carry out Emmett's directives, not offer opinions.

After a beat, Sheridan continued writing. "No problem, sir. I'll get started on this right away."

"Thank you, Sheridan. Our usual rates, plus a bonus if you find me more than eight before the month's out."

Sheridan nodded and took his leave. Emmett stood and stretched, working the stiffness out of his back. Satisfying a wife demanded a lot out of a man, he thought with a

small smile. Had she awoken? He might be able to catch
her bathing, if he hurried.

"Colin, I'm headed up. I'll return shortly, and we can
discuss what needs—"

"She will never forgive you."

That was from Kelly, whose flat, deep voice showered
the room with disapproval. He hadn't moved from his
seat, remaining still as a statue, a familiar, stubborn set to
his chin.

"Colin, take a walk." Emmett's assistant disappeared,
and Emmett resumed his seat. He selected a cigar and
took his time lighting it. Exhaling a mouthful of smoke,
he leaned back and extended his legs. "You wanted to say
something?"

"You don't honestly believe you can ruin her brother,
strip away her family legacy, and not suffer repercussions,
do you?"

"This is business, Kelly. *My* business. My wife does
not get a say in how I run it."

"Business, you say?"

Emmett rolled the cigar between his fingers, studying
the end. "Buying out Northeast would nearly double East
Coast profits, not to mention the income from the railroads. It's a shrewd decision."

"Fuck your shrewd decision," Kelly snapped. "You
are doing this just because you don't like Sloane. You've
always resented him, the way he was raised. Well, boohoo
that you wasn't born on Washington Square, too. You've
married his sister. Ain't that enough revenge?"

"No!" Emmett slapped the desk. "It's not enough goddamned revenge. I want him buried! Stripped of everything
he cares about."

"And what will that do to the woman sleeping in your
bed every night? Do you think she won't be hurt if you

follow through on ruining him? Right or wrong, she loves her brother."

"Yes, but she is my *wife*. She made a choice to love, honor, and obey me—me, not her brother."

Kelly blew out a breath, his jaw tight as he stared at the opposite wall. "I've seen the way she's been lookin' at you since the storm. She loves you, Bishop. Are you willing to throw that away, knowin' you may never get it back?"

Emmett felt himself scowl. Love? The idea seemed ludicrous. Lust, perhaps. That he could believe.

Even if Emmett's taking over Northeast upset her at first, Elizabeth would eventually come to accept it. She knew how business worked, that consolidating and acquiring other companies was necessary to success. If you didn't grow and adapt, your business was soon the one at risk.

"You're a damn fool," Kelly said when the silence stretched. "Guess I'll start moving your things back to Beaver Street." He rose stiffly, flung open the office door, and stomped into the hall.

Kelly was wrong, Emmett thought. Elizabeth would understand. . . . Wouldn't she?

"You're not looking, are you?" Emmett asked for the third time.

"No," Lizzie lied, and lifted the edges of her lids ever so slightly to see her surroundings.

A few moments ago, Emmett had appeared in her dressing room, dismissed Pauline, and picked her up in his arms, the promise of a surprise on his lips. He then instructed her to close her eyes and began traveling through the house. Her husband's size never failed to impress—

even more so when he carried her about as if she weighed nothing at all.

She pressed her face into his throat and breathed him in. Spice, a faint trace of cigar, and soap lingered on his skin, and she couldn't help but to nibble on him. He stuttered, his feet catching. "Witch. Are you trying to hurt us both?"

Stairs came next, and then more walking. "We would get there faster if you would put me down."

"But where's the fun in that?" He pushed open a door, and wet heat hit her nostrils. "Open your eyes," he said, setting her on her feet.

The large, rectangular swimming pool stretched out in front of her, wall sconces burning to cast an otherworldly glow atop the water. The pool, as Brendan had explained weeks ago, was heated underneath, supporting year-round swimming. Important, he'd said, to allow him to keep his injured leg strong, but Lizzie suspected Emmett used the pool as well. How else to explain her husband's physique, more Greek god than steel mogul?

The design of the room had a hedonistic sensibility, with the Corinthian columns, stone, and mosaic tile reminiscent of a decadent Roman bath. The frescoed ceiling above depicted Hades striding from his chariot with a distraught Persephone in his arms. Benches along the wall invited guests to watch the bathers, though she and Emmett were quite alone today.

"The furnace has been on long enough after the storm that the water is warm once again. Come." He drew her forward, skirting the edge of the pool.

"Aren't we swimming?" She did not know how, but the water did look enticing—calm, and crystal clear. Emmett had instructed Katie and Claire on to swim, so was he ready to teach Lizzie, too? She could imagine his hands on her, supporting her, as she floated on the surface. She shivered.

"No, though we can do so later if you wish. I want to show you something else." He crossed through an arched doorway on the left side of the pool, his hand clasped tightly with hers.

"A Turkish bath," she exclaimed once they passed the threshold. The details were exactly as she'd read about, with white and blue mosaic tile, red pallets and pillows, gold accents, and curved doors. A small, clear pool had been carved into the floor, the water replenished by a thin stream pouring out of a lion's mouth on the wall.

"Precisely that," her husband said. "I read that a suda-torium could be beneficial to injuries and sore muscles." He shrugged.

So he'd installed the room for Brendan. Tenderness rolled through her, wrapping like ivy around her heart. She knew from Brendan that Emmett held himself responsible for his younger brother's accident. This must have been Emmett's way of trying to atone. "It's extraordinary."

"I hired the same men who built the Turkish bath on West Twenty-Sixth Street to complete this one. It's authentic, or as close as I could get."

"Brendan didn't show me this room when he gave me a tour of the house," she said as Emmett went to a door.

"Then I am glad to be the one to surprise you. Wait here." He opened the panel and disappeared inside. A few seconds later, he returned. "I started the water heating. We'll have steam in a moment." He threw off his heavy dressing gown and dropped it onto a bench. Next came his shirt, his strong arms unbuttoning the starched white cotton to reveal massive shoulders and muscular arms encased in tight cotton underclothing. No matter how many times she saw him disrobe, the effect was always the same: her breath hitched, and her lower body caught fire.

"Take off your dressing gown," he ordered with a leer.

"I am too busy admiring the view," she said as he stripped off his trousers.

"Are you? Well, when I'm naked, anyone here not yet undressed will be dropped into the cold pool over by the wall."

"You wouldn't dare!"

He quirked a brow that said, *Oh, I think we both know I would,* and Lizzie hurried to untie the sash on her dressing gown, to push the fabric from her shoulders. Standing in her thin chemise, she knew the garment did little to conceal her curves—a fact she was grateful for as Emmett's movements faltered, his eyes growing bright with arousal.

"You'd best hurry," he said huskily as his fingers flew down the buttons of his combination.

Biting her lip in amusement, she furiously worked on the tiny buttons along her bodice. Embarrassment forgotten, her goal was to win, to shed her clothing before he did. When she undid a fair number of buttons, she tugged the hem up and over her head. Hands suddenly caught her while she was blinded by the fabric, crushing her to a taut, naked body.

"Not fast enough, wife," he growled, and bent to throw her across his shoulder. Laughing, Lizzie finished pulling the chemise off and let the cloth fall.

The position allowed her to focus on the most perfect male backside ever created. With not an inch of fat or extra skin, he was a marble statue come to life. She slid her hands along his back, over the rough scars, to cup the high, tight mounds. She was still squeezing and enjoying the shift of muscle beneath the skin when he opened the door to the steam chamber.

A moist cloud of hot air enveloped them instantly. "My drawers! Emmett, they'll be ruined."

He slapped her behind playfully. "Not to worry, I'll peel them off in good time."

Without setting her down, Emmett lowered onto the tiled bench, settling her in his lap. The lush sultriness of the room wrapped around her like a blanket.

"What do you think?" he murmured, leaning in to nuzzle her throat. The heat of him rested under her cloth-covered buttocks, his erection growing by the second.

"I think you like it," she teased, running her palms over the contours of his broad shoulders.

"I certainly do." His palm caressed her bare breast. "You, warm, naked, and slippery, is indeed high on the list of things I like."

He kissed her, his tongue swiftly invading, and he placed her thighs on either side of his hips. Beads of moisture pooled on the surface of their skin, slickening where their bodies made contact. Her breasts met his chest, rough, wet skin and crisp hair teasing the taut points of her nipples while he explored her mouth with exquisite thoroughness.

Gently, he arched her back and dropped his head to her breast, sliding a peak between his lips. He sucked hard, eliciting a gasp from her, the draw of his mouth sending shocks through her core. He laved the puckered bud with his tongue, scraped with his teeth, and allowed no escape from the blissful torment. Her ragged breathing echoed around them, a desperate fever making her writhe in a silent plea, but he continued to torture her with deep pulls and long licks until her insides quivered. Her body tensed, climbing, straining, and she craved more of his touch, wanted him everywhere all at once.

"Emmett, please," she murmured, the sound muffled to her ears as her hips rocked into his groin, seeking relief.

Kisses trailed along the side of her breast, then toward her collarbone. "Yes?"

"I need you. Please, hurry."

His teeth nipped her jaw, and she shivered despite the scorching heat surrounding them. "Where?"

"Everywhere," she rasped, both hating and loving that he was teasing her.

"I'll need specifics, Mrs. Cavanaugh. I'm a man who prefers details."

She knew that to be true. The more direct and bawdy her talk, she'd learned, the more he responded. And since she loved to see him undone, she had become quite brave over the past few days. "Inside me."

"Here?" he asked, his finger tracing her lips, which she parted in order to slide her tongue around the digit. His eyes glazed over, breath expelling in a rush as she tasted him.

"Perhaps later." Her gaze locked with his. "Right now, I want you between my legs."

His chest heaved, and the lines of his face grew taut. Impatient. He guided her over him, her entrance poised directly above his hard length. He reached between them to grip the base of his erection. "Are you wet for me?" he asked, slowly dragging the tip of his penis along her cleft. She threw her head back, biting her lip to keep from crying out. To keep from demanding that he take her.

"Oh, yes, right there," he murmured, and the broad, smooth crown breached her channel slowly, pushing her open and tunneling inside, and she relished the stretch that bordered on pain. Inch by delectable inch, she lowered until her hips met rugged male skin.

His fingers dug into her thighs as she paused to savor the joining, the overwhelmingly full sensation. "Now ride me. Hard."

She obeyed, wasting no time, rising and lowering again and again, her pelvis churning to create the exquisite friction they both needed. Emmett's lids fell, his head propped on the tile as he let her control the pace. The divot in his chin beckoned, so she bent forward to nip it with her teeth. His swift intake of breath caused her to smile.

"The Devil's mark," she whispered, referring to the name he'd once used for the slight imperfection.

"And yet you love it."

"Indeed, I do." *As I love you.* But she held back those final words, kept them close to her heart, and clamped her inner walls around his erection instead.

He growled in response. "God, I love when you do that." She squeezed him once more, and he dragged her close for a long, drugging kiss. "Will you let me try something?"

Her breath stuttered. Thus far, he'd shown her plenty, with each experience better than the last. She had no reason to doubt this would be equally pleasurable, so she nodded.

"Stand up." He helped her off his lap and placed her feet on the tiled floor. He untied her drawers and slid the thin cotton down her legs, lifting one foot and then the other. After folding them, he placed the wet fabric on the tile. "For your knees. I want to take you from behind."

Excitement rushed through her even as she said, "Are you certain?"

"Oh, indeed, I am." Strong hands helped her into position, the tile slick and unforgiving beneath her palms as she bent on hands and knees. She felt exposed in this position, but all complaints flew from her mind when Emmett began working into her passage. "Christ, you are beautiful," he gasped, driving farther inside. He clutched her hips, pulling their bodies together, until he slid home. Lizzie cried out at the fullness, his penetration much deeper this way.

A gentle touch circled her back. "Are you all right?"

She could only nod, the euphoria having stolen her speech. He withdrew, only to return, stroking, pumping, until he hit a spot that made her toes curl. "Oh, my," she exclaimed, and he did it again. "Emmett!"

His thrusts sped up, and her shouts grew louder, until he reached to find the hard nub at the apex of her cleft. The touch pushed her over the peak, her limbs nearly giving out as she convulsed. He soon followed, his hoarse yell bouncing off the tiled walls.

After a moment, he dropped onto the bench, pulling her close. "My God, Elizabeth," he wheezed. "What you do to me . . ."

"I hope it's good," she said, panting into his shoulder.

"So good it scares me." He kissed the top of her head.

Chapter Sixteen

One thing is indispensable to the happiness of married life, and that is confidence in each other.

—American Etiquette and Rules of Politeness, 1883

Lizzie knew something was amiss the moment she stepped into the breakfast room.

With Emmett still dressing upstairs, she had come down alone to breakfast, eager to get a start on her day. She hoped to travel downtown to her office, provided that the streets were finally sufficiently cleared of snow.

Katie, Claire, and Brendan were already seated at the long table, their voices murmuring in hushed conversation.

"Good morning, all," she cheerfully called.

A blur of movement caught her eye before her brother-in-law hastily rose. "Morning, Lizzie."

Katie and Claire tracked her as she approached, their eyes wide and wary. "Good morning, Lizzie," the girls said together.

The footman held out a chair, and Lizzie sat. A strange silence descended as she poured her coffee. "Did I interrupt something?"

"No," Brendan answered instantly. "We were just discussing our day, weren't we, girls?"

"Yes," Katie said. "That's all we were doing. Right, Claire?"

"Yep!" the younger girl said. "We were *not* looking at the newspaper."

Brendan groaned, and Katie covered her mouth in horror. Before Lizzie could address their curious reactions, there was something far more important requiring her attention. "Claire, where did you hear that word?"

"Newspaper?" the girl asked around a mouth full of pastry.

"No. The one I'm referring to is 'yep.'"

"Oh, Kelly says that word. It means yes."

Lizzie made a mental note to discuss the language Kelly used around the girls at her first opportunity. "Claire, a lady should never use coarse language or jargon. She must say what she means, purposely and clearly, in order to be understood. How you speak is a reflection on how you will be perceived by others."

The girl's brows lowered, as she seemed to intently absorb this advice. "Yes, Lizzie."

"Good. Now what was so interesting in the newspaper this morning?"

"Nothing," Brendan answered, with pointed glances at his half sisters. "Same old boring stories."

Lizzie hummed and held out her hand. "Excellent. I love boring old stories. May I?"

Brendan stared at her a moment, and she could see the wheels turning in his brain. Even though they'd only been acquainted a short time, he should have known by now that she would never back down.

Sighing, he withdrew a section of the *New York World*

from under the table. "For the record, no one at this table believes a word of it." He placed the paper in her hand.

Stomach heavy with dread, Lizzie discovered a large cartoon on the page, complete with two unnamed figures she instantly recognized.

A bride stood at the altar, marrying a very Emmett-looking Satan, while the hem of her wedding gown was raised lewdly, well past her ankle. A row of Wall Street bankers lined the wall, their eyes fixed dramatically on the sight of her bare leg. *Open for Business*, the caption read.

Lizzie gasped, her hand flying to her mouth. "Dear heavens." How had the papers even learned of her firm? Before she knew what she was about, she ripped the page out of the paper and crumpled it in her hand. "Emmett mustn't see this," she told Brendan. "And we mustn't tell him, either."

"Emmett mustn't see what?" her husband asked as he strolled into the breakfast room.

Lizzie swiftly put the cartoonless paper on the table, the cartoon itself under her chair. No plausible lie came to her lips, so she glanced at Brendan, pleading with her eyes.

"Oh, nothing," Brendan answered. "Just a news report on the union troubles in Ohio."

"There are no union troubles in Ohio," Emmett remarked, pouring himself coffee. Freshly shaved and dressed in a dark brown morning suit, he was delectable. Lizzie could have eaten him for breakfast. She watched his large hands perform the mundane task of preparing his coffee, and she recalled how those hands had made her feel earlier this morning. A low hum of arousal thrummed through her veins. Perhaps she could convince him to revisit the Turkish bath this evening.

"There aren't? Perhaps it wasn't Ohio, then. Regardless, we didn't want you to worry."

"Bren, you're a terrible liar. Girls, go and find Mrs. Thomas. It's time to start your lessons." For once, the girls did not argue, silently standing and quitting the room. Emmett tapped his fingers on the table, a sign Lizzie recognized as barely controlled impatience. "Now, which one of you wants to give me the truth?"

Lizzie did not want to lie . . . yet the truth was so much worse. Perhaps a slight evasion would pacify him. "It's a silly cartoon. Nothing, really."

Dark eyes pinned her to the spot, and she shivered, thinking about the fierce drive and insatiable will inside her husband. When he focused that same intensity on her in bed, she hadn't a chance of resisting him. In a flash, he could turn her into a begging, quivering pile of lust.

His lips quirked, as if sensing the direction of her thoughts. "Elizabeth?"

She sighed and cleared the prurient thoughts from her brain. "No, Emmett. You do not need to see it."

"I don't?"

"No, you don't."

"I agree, Em. This is one cartoon you don't need to see." Brendan cleared his throat. "For at least a few years."

Emmett plunked his elbow on the table, palm out, and kept his calm gaze on Lizzie, waiting.

"Perhaps we should go swimming first—"

"*Now,*" he growled, and Lizzie withdrew the ball of newsprint from under her chair and dropped it into his palm.

Long fingers smoothed out the paper. He studied the cartoon, then swung around to the footman standing near the door. "Find Kelly. Immediately."

The footman took off at a dead run, and Lizzie said, "Emmett, no. Whatever you're planning—"

"Is my business. I'll handle this my way."

"Oh, God," Brendan murmured, rubbing his brow. "I'm a doctor. You're not supposed to talk about killing people in front of me."

"Yeah, Bish?" Kelly, slightly out of breath, hurried into the breakfast room. "You needed me?"

Emmett held out the newspaper. Kelly came over and let out a long whistle when he saw the cartoon. He exchanged a knowing glance with Emmett. "I'll see to it." He spun around and disappeared.

Calm as could be, Emmett requested poached eggs and sausage from the footman. He reached for the rest of the newspaper and began flipping through it, the pages crackling in the sudden quiet.

Lizzie wanted to strangle him. "Tell me what you are planning."

"Brendan, will you excuse my wife and me for a moment?"

"Of course." Brendan rose and gripped his cane. "I have rounds to make anyway. See you both at dinner."

With a jerk of his chin, Emmett also excused the footman, leaving Lizzie alone with her husband. All sorts of thoughts began swirling in her head. Emmett was incredibly protective, and she could only imagine how angry he was over this. Goodness, he'd nearly choked her brother the night at Sherry's. "What will you do? Are you planning to hurt that cartoonist?"

"Is that what you think I do, go around hurting people if they offend me?"

The innocent tone did not fool her. "Semantics, Emmett. Are you going to have Kelly hurt that cartoonist?"

"Possibly. Would that bother you?"

"Yes!" she exclaimed. "I don't want anyone hurt, even if I'm equally angry. I cannot understand how he even learned of my firm."

"I might have had something to do with that. Calvin Cabot is the publisher of the *New York Mercury* and a few other papers. As you know, he is a friend. I contacted him to propose an interview." He relaxed in his chair, porcelain cup cradled in his hands. "I thought you might want to create a splash in the press for the opening, the way Woodhull and her sister did a few years back."

"You did that without speaking to me first? We decided to keep my involvement a secret, or did you forget?"

"I would have told you when the paper agreed to the story."

"Oh, how reassuring," she drawled. "So Mr. Cabot told someone at a rival paper?"

"Not a chance. He guards secrets better than anyone, a necessity in his business. My guess is that he discussed the idea with a member of the *Mercury* staff, and that person told someone at the *World*. Regardless, everyone involved will pay dearly for the slight, including that cartoonist."

She nearly rolled her eyes. "Emmett, you cannot take on everyone who dares to mock or speak ill of me."

He took a long sip, then replaced the cup in its saucer. "Elizabeth, that is precisely what I swore to do. I promised before God to honor you, and if I have to buy that goddamn newspaper merely to fire this cartoonist, I will. I'll ensure he never picks up another pencil in his life if it makes you rest easier." Leaning in, he drove a finger into the table for emphasis. "I'll gladly take on every paper, every cartoonist—

every single person in this godforsaken city—in order to uphold that promise. Do you understand?"

Her jaw fell open, the breath leaving her lungs in a whoosh. She couldn't speak, couldn't *think* after a declaration such as that, her heart pounding. How was she to react? Her husband was promising retribution, likely physical, and she found it . . . arousing. What was wrong with her?

He hadn't said the words yet, but that certainly sounded like a declaration of love. Still, she was angry he'd revealed details of her firm without telling her first. Had Emmett told Will of her firm as well?

"I understand, but please do not make decisions for me in the future without asking. I was not ready to have this revealed so publicly. This ensures I'll fail before I even get under way."

His expression softened as he regarded her. "My dear, the one thing New York loves more than anything else is a spectacle, so open with as much fanfare as you can stand. You're no coward, and you possess two things society will never comprehend: intelligence and talent. So don't bother hiding. Besides, no one can hurt you—I'll go to any lengths to protect you if they dare try."

Warmth filled her, sank deep into her bones. She loved this man so much that it made her dizzy. Placing her napkin on the table, she rose and took the few steps to his side. She slid her palms over his broad, strong shoulders, the fabric of his frock coat soft and smooth along her skin. She bent until her lips brushed the shell of his ear. "And I promised before God to love and cherish my husband. Would you care to follow me to our bedroom so that I may demonstrate?"

Emmett gained his feet so quickly that his chair teetered. He clasped her hand and began tugging her toward the hall. "If you insist."

* * *

The corner of John Street and Broadway bustled later that brisk March afternoon. Lizzie held the satchel close to her chest as she waited in her coupé, attempting to stay warm while watching the traders hurry in and out of the ground-floor restaurant.

What must it feel like, to stand on the trading floor, power and money flowing through your very hands? Fortunes gained, fortunes lost. It must be a heady rush, indeed. Yet thanks to the men-only policy at the exchange, Lizzie would never know.

Robbie, the man she employed, finally emerged from the building's front door. They hadn't seen each other since before the storm. Instead, she'd cabled him instructions, intimating they were from her brother, but she no doubt owed him an explanation after today's cartoon.

Hurrying along the walk, she raced to catch up with him. "Robbie," she called to his back. "Robbie, please wait!"

He drew to a halt and faced her, his expression wary. He must have seen the cartoon. "Good day, Mrs. Cavanaugh."

"Hello, Robbie. May we speak for a moment?"

He jerked a nod, and soon the two of them were settled inside her small vehicle. She placed her satchel on her lap. "I suppose you've seen this morning's *World*."

"Yes, I did." He said nothing more, his mouth turned into a frown.

She sighed. "I never lied to you, Robbie. When we first met, you assumed my brother would be involved, and I never corrected you."

"Why not tell me the truth?"

"Because I was afraid you wouldn't work with me, that

you wouldn't take me seriously if you knew I was the one providing the orders."

He shook his head. "I have nothing against women who work, Mrs. Cavanaugh. My mother, she holds two jobs since my father was injured a few years back. And from what I've seen in the last few weeks, you likely know more about stocks than most men on the exchange."

"Thank you, Robbie." A little bubble of happiness welled in her chest at the compliment. "I underestimated you, and I am sorry for that. I hope you will forgive me."

His eyes widened a bit, a flush creeping up his neck. "Consider it forgotten, ma'am."

"Excellent. As you are probably now aware, I do plan to open my own brokerage firm. My husband has agreed to back me."

"Well, I'd be honored to keep placing your orders, ma'am, if you like."

"I'd like that very much. I can't say you won't take any ribbing for it, however."

He lifted a shoulder. "I'm not overly concerned about that. I can handle all the ribbing in the world if we're earning money."

"That is certainly my plan. Speaking of, how did we do today? I wasn't watching the ticker." She'd been busy, holed up with her husband in a blissful day of wickedness.

"Here's the tally." Withdrawing a small stack of papers from his satchel, he handed them over. "The gamble on Seneca paid off. You tripled your investment there."

Lizzie smiled, remembering her conversation regarding the textile company with Emmett. She couldn't wait to tell him how much money she had earned them. "Thank you." She tucked the paper into her own satchel and presented him with a list of notes. "Here's a plan for next week."

"If you weren't watching today, suppose you missed what happened to your husband's stock," Robbie said. "It took a wild dip."

She blinked. "It did?" Was Emmett aware? "How low did it fall?"

"I put the numbers in my notes there." Robbie pointed at the satchel where she'd placed his papers. "When the markets opened, there were rumblings about a pending legal investigation. I couldn't get a handle on where the rumor started, but the traders went crazy. Something about corruption charges being filed."

"There's no pending investigation," she said, though she couldn't be sure. Would Emmett have confided in her?

"We both know that rumors don't have to be true to sink a company's stock," Robbie said. "But it all balanced out in the end."

"Did you . . . ?"

"Yes. I followed your direction to the letter. Liquidated some of your other holdings and borrowed from New American Bank to get the rest, as you directed. Congratulations. You now own over one-quarter of the East Coast Steel stock."

The offices for the Northeast Railroad Company resided on Vesey Street, not far from city hall and just north of the exchange. Though the afternoon light was fading, Emmett's anger burned hotter than a hundred suns as he climbed the steps to the second floor. His rage was palpable, a living, swirling beast in his gut, one he hadn't felt this keenly since leaving Five Points.

Sloane was a dead man.

Pristine white lettering adorned the door, heralding the

occupant within. Emmett yanked it open and stepped inside, Kelly right behind him.

Four young men sat at desks, pens in hand, and all eyes turned to the new arrival. There were two inner doors, neither marked. "Where is Sloane?" he growled at the company staff.

Fingers pointed to the far left side of the room, and Emmett shot toward the private office. Turning the knob, he stepped inside to find Sloane conversing with two men, both of whom were well known to Emmett. The mayor, Abram Hewitt, and Richard Croker, the head of Tammany. Christ, Sloane kept terrible company.

Eyes flew to the doorway, where Emmett planted his feet. "A word," he snarled, gaze boring into Sloane's.

Hewitt and Croker rose and donned their derbies, Sloane standing as well. Croker stuck his hand out in Emmett's direction. "Cavanaugh. Heard you married Sloane's sister. My felicitations."

Emmett gave a terse thanks, shook hands with the mayor as well. The power in New York City shifted every few years, and right now these two men were positioned near the apex. Though there were rumblings that Hewitt did not have the support for reelection—not even Croker's. But Emmett tried to stay out of politics as much as one in his position could. Sloane apparently did not feel the same.

Hewitt and Croker departed quickly after, leaving Sloane and Emmett alone. "What the hell is the matter with you?" Sloane snapped, his brows drawn together. "You can't barge into my office and interrupt my meetings."

As always, Sloane was impeccably dressed, not a hair out of place. Emmett's temples throbbed with resentment. "I don't give a shit about your meetings," he said. "I want to know what the hell you think you're doing."

Sloane dropped into his chair and rubbed his eyes. "I am in no mood for your games, Cavanaugh. Get to the damn point."

"My stock."

Sloane's expression did not change, his face an unreadable mask. "And?"

"Care to explain how a rumor of a pending investigation was started, causing East Coast stock to fall so low that one buyer could gain almost a thirty-percent share?"

The side of Sloane's mouth hitched almost imperceptibly, yet Emmett saw it, recognized the satisfaction. Not a trace of surprise. "No. A rumor, you say? A pity I wasn't paying more attention to the market today."

Emmett's hands tightened on the edge of the desk, gripping the wood to keep him from leaping across the desk and squeezing Sloane's throat. "After everything I've done for you, all our deals, even marrying your sister, you have goddamn gall to lie to my face."

"You're calling me a liar?" Sloane's jaw clenched, and Emmett welcomed the anger. If he could throw Sloane off balance, the other man would more readily admit what he'd done.

"Damn straight. Did you really think someone could buy more than a quarter of my stock and I would not move heaven and earth to find out who?"

Sloane stared at Emmett for a long moment. "What difference does it make if it all stays in the family?"

"What in the hell is that supposed to mean?"

"It means I did not purchase your stock." Emmett started to argue, and Sloane held up a hand. "You forget, I am not the only Sloane now active on the exchange— which everyone now knows, thanks to that damn cartoon."

Emmett stiffened, shock stealing his breath. Elizabeth? Why would his wife buy East Coast Steel stock? And with what money? "Are you saying my wife bought that stock?"

"She must have. Who else?"

Sloane could be telling the truth . . . or he might be lying. Emmett couldn't tell. Sloane had only pushed for Emmett's marriage as a way of saving his precious sister. Family always came first—as long as that family was of pure Dutch descent. Sloane made no secret of his dislike for Emmett, how he considered his sister too good for a man raised in the slums. Just how far would Sloane take that hatred?

And would Elizabeth help him?

Dark thoughts, ones of distrust and suspicion, wound their way through Emmett's guts, twining to strangle his chest. His wife had been so attentive, so responsive. Emmett had believed it too good to be true—and perhaps he'd been right. Was she playing him for a fool, all the while plotting behind his back?

Elizabeth is your wife. Why would she want to ruin you?

Because she'd never wanted to marry him in the first place. Because she'd pushed for an annulment, even after the wedding had taken place. Because her interest in him had been purely financial from the start. Perhaps she'd never changed her mind on any of those things.

You never had the slightest hope in hell of holding on to her.

Emmett straightened and drew in a deep breath. He'd certainly faced worse and come out alive. He'd survive this, too. And Will Sloane, of all people, would never witness Emmett's worrying over anything.

"You can be certain I'll ask her, Sloane. Because if I find out the two of you are—" Emmett bit off the words, too furious to voice them.

"Are, what? Conspiring against you?" Sloane threw his

head back and laughed, and the hairs on the back of Emmett's neck stood up. "God, you are delusional."

But no denial followed, Emmett noticed. It wasn't as if the idea of he and Sloane conspiring against one another was far-fetched, considering Emmett had been doing that very thing for weeks. And, unbeknownst to Sloane, Elizabeth had helped Emmett find the railroad company's weakness when she'd reviewed the stock transactions during the storm.

"Jesus, you believe it, don't you?" Sloane was saying. "Why would Lizzie want to hurt your company?"

"She overheard us at the wedding. She's aware of the blackmail."

"She told me. But even if she was still angry over the circumstances of your wedding, she would not hold a grudge or do something so vindictive."

The Elizabeth of the past few days would not, but weren't all women clever actresses? Precisely the reason he'd kept company with ladies of the stage; at least then you *knew* you were being lied to.

But whoever had done this, whoever had purchased the East Coast stock, had snatched it up even before Emmett's own brokers could recover. Almost as if this person had been waiting for this eventuality. As if he or she had been prepared.

Which left Sloane, waiting in the wings, ready to pounce.

"Do not worry," Emmett told the other man. "I will find out what happened. And you better hope to Christ you are not lying about your lack of involvement."

"A threat. How predictable coming from you. Will you send in Kelly to rough me up if I refuse to play nice?" The smug bastard smirked, and Emmett had to restrain himself once again.

Instead, he spun and went for the door. "It's not a threat. And let me leave you with one piece of advice." Hand on the knob, he threw a meaningful glare over his shoulder. "Don't get too comfortable in your chair."

Lizzie awoke with a start. A noise had interrupted her sleep. She waited, hoping to hear it again. Had that come from Emmett's rooms?

When she'd retired for the night, Emmett still had not returned home. According to Graham, Emmett had departed in the afternoon, shortly after her own departure, and had yet to return. So she'd dined with Brendan and the girls and tried not to worry about her husband. He hadn't been away from the house since the storm, instead preferring to work from his home office, but he was an important, busy man. Of course he would need to leave at some point.

That realization had not kept her from missing him, however.

Now wide-awake, she decided to see if Emmett was home. Crawling out from under her satin sheets, she padded on bare feet to the adjoining door. When a knock received no answer, she cracked the panel to look inside. The smell of a lit cigar hit her nose. She peered into the darkness until she found him, a lone, dark figure, unmoving, in a chair by the window. He didn't turn at the sound of her entry, and apprehension blossomed in her belly. "Emmett?" Her feet led her deeper into his bedroom, the carpet soft between her toes. "You're home."

"Yes." He puffed on his cigar, as if in defiance of the social rule that dictated he should extinguish it in her presence.

She waited for him to say more, but he remained focused

on the window. "How long have you been here? I thought
you would have . . ." Heat suffused her cheeks, but she
forced the words out. "I thought you would have come
to me."

"Missing me, were you?" There was something unpleasant in his tone, almost a sneer, and she frowned.

"Is there something wrong?"

The stark lines of his face were shadowed, preventing
her from viewing his eyes clearly. But she could feel the
scrutiny, the cold calculation as he took her measure. It
sent a shiver down her spine. What had happened today?

Oh, his stock. Perhaps he was concerned over the
rumors that had been circulating about an investigation.
"Emmett—"

"I am attempting to think of the best way to ask you,
but I can't come up with anything other than a forthright
approach."

"Ask me what?"

"Did you purchase nearly thirty percent of East Coast
Steel stock today?"

"Yes, I did."

He closed his eyes briefly, as if absorbing the information. "So while you were in my bed, distracting me
with your luscious body, you bought tens of thousands of
dollars' worth of my stock. With what money?"

Distracting him? "I sold all my various other shares,
and I did have some money left from our bet. Also, Mr.
Harper's bank offered me credit, when necessary. Really,
Emmett, what is this about?"

"Why would you buy my stock?"

"To ensure someone else could not." Why did this feel
accusatory, rather than grateful? She crossed her arms
over her chest. "I gave standing orders to Robbie when

you and I married that East Coast Steel should be watched the same way he watches Northeast Railroad stock. If the stock ever were to take a dive, he was to grab as many of the shares as he could before someone else did."

"Robbie. This was your and Robbie's doing? No one else was involved?"

"Who else would be involved, exactly?"

Emmett's expression was a cool mask. He inhaled on his cigar once more, blowing the smoke out slowly. She could hardly look away from his mouth, the full lips of such sin and wicked temptation. The things those lips had done to her body . . .

But there was no warmth now. No teasing smirk. Just cold, flat distrust. "Shouldn't you thank me?" she asked him.

"When someone attempts to buy me out and ruin me, I hardly call that cause for gratitude."

"Ruin you?" Every muscle stiffened, and she rocked back on her heels. "I wasn't trying to ruin you. I *saved* you. Someone started that rumor about the investigation, but it was not me." She could hardly follow, the idea was so insane. God, did he really think her capable of that?

"I went to see your brother today."

He let that statement hang, and so Lizzie asked, "Why?" Then her brain stopped spinning, and she arrived at the answer. *No one else was involved?* He'd asked the question because he believed Will to have played a part, too. That she and her brother had colluded to take over Emmett's company.

"I find it convenient," Emmett continued, "that directly after the storm, after I've finally bedded you, this rumor circulates. Did your brother ask you to keep me occupied? To be willing to do whatever I asked just so I would ignore everything else for one more go between your luscious thighs?"

A weight pressed down on her chest, strangling her, as the recent, tenuous bond between her and Emmett was severed. Destroyed by his mistrust.

Love was like a stock, Lizzie realized. You gambled on its paying off in the long run—but it could just as easily cost you everything.

Tears threatened, but she forced them back. Dragged air into her lungs. "Do you really believe I would participate in such a nefarious plot? That, as your wife, I would try and take your company away from you—whether my brother wanted to or not?"

"As if you could," he threw back, his lip curling. "You should know that could never happen. Tell your brother he'll never gain a majority—and even if he did, the board would never listen to anyone but me."

She stared at him, this complete stranger who happened to be her husband. Precisely why she had never wanted to marry him. Was there to be no faith in one another, no benefit of the doubt? Obviously Emmett had made up his mind, discounted Lizzie's explanation, and condemned her.

The betrayal, this unforgivable accusation, cut deep. Even if he admitted he was wrong, this would always be between them. That he could even consider for an instant she would participate in something so hurtful was intolerable.

Yet even as her heart cracked into pieces, she felt sorry for her husband. To be so hard, so cynical, was to be pitied, in her opinion. Yes, his upbringing had been tragic, but life was not about the past. One had to move forward, into the future, whether one liked it or not. And to always believe the worst of those around you must be exhausting.

"You're wrong, and you'll regret everything you've said tonight," she said, an embarrassing quiver in her voice. "At some point in your life, Emmett, you need to trust someone. To believe that one person might care for you and not want to drag you down. All I know is that person will no longer be me."

Chapter Seventeen

Gentlemen should not address ladies in a flippant manner.

—American Etiquette and Rules of Politeness, 1883

By the time dawn crept over the East River, Emmett had been at his desk, working, for several hours. With cigars and righteous anger as fuel, he had powered through contracts, finance reports, correspondence, newspapers . . . anything he'd put off since the storm.

Never take your attention off the work. He'd forgotten that lesson in the last few days. He would not make the same mistake again.

The door opened, and Kelly strolled in, a china teacup and saucer in his large hands. Emmett ignored him, continuing his letter to the East Coast Steel investors—a reassurance that there was no pending investigation or criminal activity to be concerned over.

Kelly dropped into the chair opposite the desk, sipped his coffee. The silence stretched, and Emmett could feel Kelly's disapproval descending like the steam in the Turkish bath. And little that reminder did to sweeten his mood.

"What?" Emmett finally snapped. "Whatever you need to say, spit it the fuck out."

Colin chose that moment to arrive for work, pushing into the large room. "Come back in fifteen," Emmett shouted. Colin's eyes went wide behind his glasses, and he beat a hasty retreat.

"I guess I don't need to ask how your evening went," Kelly drawled when the door closed. "How long have you been at it? Dawn?"

Emmett didn't answer because Kelly would feel no sympathy. He'd told Emmett to go easy on Elizabeth, to hear her out. Not to leap to conclusions. As far as Emmett was concerned, he'd leapt at the only conclusion that could be reached.

"You were wrong," he told Kelly. "She admitted it."

Kelly's square jaw dropped. "To working with Sloane?"

"No. That she denied. She admitted to buying the stock. Said it was to protect me, to keep someone else from buying it."

"Well, there you are." Kelly nodded as if that explanation tied it all into a neat little bow. "That's hardly a crime. Downright considerate, if you ask me."

"No one did ask you," Emmett shot back. "And I haven't risen to where I am by ignoring my gut—and my gut tells me that she and her brother were working together on this."

"And I think the gin has finally gone to your head, Bish." Kelly tapped his temple with two fingers. "That woman worships you, or at least she did until you screwed up. She never woulda done somethin' like you're thinking."

"Everyone is capable of deceit and cruelty when pushed, Kelly. We, of all people, understand that."

"That may be true, but your wife is different. She's

loyal. And honest. How many women would have kept out of your bed just so they wouldn't have to lie for an annulment?"

"And when that didn't work, look at what happened."

Kelly shook his head. "There's a bigger problem you just don't want to face."

Emmett sighed. "Which is?"

"Someone started that rumor about the pending investigation. And it wasn't Sloane or your wife. So who was it?"

"I think you are mistaken, but I guess time will tell."

The other man sipped his coffee, replaced the cup on the saucer, and set both on Emmett's desk. "So what'll you do to prove her guilty?"

Emmett rubbed his eyes with the heels of his hands. In all the anger and hurt last night, he hadn't gotten this far. Stupidly, he had thought she'd admit the wrongdoing, after which he could throw her out and then divorce her. Christ.

"Have her followed," he said suddenly. "Hire Sheridan. Any time she leaves, I want to know where she goes and who she's meeting with."

Kelly worked his jaw back and forth, a sign he was trying to rein in his temper. "That is the stupidest damn—"

Emmett slapped his hand on the desk, a crack that echoed off the walls. "Do what I say or I'll do it myself— after I kick you out of the goddamned house!"

The two of them stared at one another, locked in a battle of wills. Emmett knew Kelly didn't agree with him, thought better of Elizabeth . . . and Emmett didn't care. The problem would be handled his way—not Kelly's. His muscles tensed, and he gritted out, "See it done, Kelly."

Kelly rose slowly. With exaggerated flair, he bowed. "Of course, your highness." Snapping his heels together, he marched to the door. "Heard her say she's going out to see Edith Rutlidge. Want me to follow?"

Where Henry Rutlidge also happened to reside. That did not take long. No doubt she would cry on her former beau's shoulder while surrounded by her high-society friends.

"Yes," he snarled. "Stay with her this morning, then hire Sheridan this afternoon. And send in Colin—it's past time to get to work."

Lizzie took in the gaily dressed crowd gathered in the elegantly appointed Rutlidge drawing room, a group of people known to her since birth. Familiar surroundings, yet never had she felt more isolated, more apart. To be truthful, she'd never fit in with New York society. The things she wanted were unheard of by women of her set— a career, independence—and the older she grew, the less she cared about hiding her true self.

Tonight's misery, however, had little to do with society's constraints. Lizzie's heart ached, the weight of Emmett's accusations suffusing her with misery. How could he have believed the worst of her?

Because he always did, ever since the moment you met.

No matter how close they'd grown since the storm, Emmett did not trust her. What more could she do? She'd given herself to the man, even admitted she no longer planned to seek an annulment, and what had all that gained her? Certainly not his faith or his love.

Which meant they had nothing.

She dragged in an unsteady breath. Part of her wanted to stay and fight, prove to Emmett he'd been wrong about her, if only to see his face when he learned the truth. After all, he'd come to meet her that night at Sherry's, setting up a private room for them. He'd wanted her then. There had to be part of him that cared for her, that could come to love her someday. Love her as much as she loved him.

The other part of her wanted to throw her wedding ring in his face, walk out, and never look back. Because even if she stayed, how could she ever forgive him?

Edith appeared and linked her arm with Lizzie's. "It's entirely unfair that you can be so beautiful even when heartbroken."

Earlier in the day, Lizzie had confessed the entire sad tale to her friend. Of course Edith had been outraged, ready to take on Emmett herself on Lizzie's behalf. Common sense prevailed, however, and they had decided to drown Lizzie's sorrows with cake instead.

Lizzie attempted a smile. "I apologize. I'm ruining your party."

"Oh, stop. The last thing you need is to be holed up in that giant monstrosity. You need to be surrounded by the people who love you, who understand you."

The implication was clear, that Emmett was not "of their kind," and the idea rankled. Lizzie was tired of hearing what people should and should not do, of being judged inferior merely because their ancestry was different. Under his gruff exterior, Emmett was a good man—a good, misguided, cynical, entirely-in-the-wrong man.

"I'm not certain that's true, but I did not want to disappoint you," she told her friend.

"Don't be absurd, of course it's what you need. Tonight we shall forget about that silly cartoon as well as your husband. Let's have fun instead."

Lizzie sipped her champagne and wished it were that simple. How could she forget a man who'd affected her so deeply, like he'd become a part of her?

Henry, Edith's brother, approached, a crystal tumbler

dangling in one hand. Elegant in his evening dress, he possessed not a hair out of place, though his eyes told another story. Both were rimmed red, as if he'd been drinking steadily. "Good evening, Lizzie."

"Henry," she said with genuine fondness. He'd avoided her in Newport and had refused to attend her wedding. She'd worried tonight would be awkward, so it pleased her that he was making an effort to retain their friendship. "How are you?"

Edith excused herself, and Henry took Lizzie's arm. "Walk with me?" Without waiting on an answer, he led her to the far end of the drawing room. He leaned against the wall and took a large sip of his drink. "You look beautiful."

"Thank you." The Worth cream satin dress had been bought for her never-used trousseau, and Lizzie loved it. Roses fashioned from black seed beads adorned the boned bodice, with more roses on the front of the floor-length skirt. Plain satin gathered at the bustle and draped into a simple train.

"I hear all is not well in Cavanaugh castle."

She stiffened. Had someone told Henry of Lizzie's marital discord? Edith would never dare. "I am not certain I know what you mean."

His mouth hitched. "Come now, Lizzie. I know about his stock. Everyone knows, in fact. Nasty rumor that started the slide, too. What I haven't been able to piece together is who purchased the shares. They were bought up as quickly as they were sold."

Lizzie relaxed, grateful the comment was not a personal one, as well for Robbie's discretion. The young trader had sworn not to reveal information regarding her trades or clients to anyone else. Despite Emmett's somehow learning who had bought his shares, likely no one else would.

She lifted a shoulder and kept her expression clear. "I have no idea, but my husband was not overly worried."

"Not worried? Someone bought a quarter of his company, and he was not worried? He'd be a fool."

Yes, Emmett was a fool—but not over concerns for East Coast Steel. And she did not wish to discuss such a raw topic at this moment. "I couldn't say. If you'll excuse me." She made to move past Henry, and he reached out a hand to stop her.

"Wait, do not leave," he rushed out quietly. "Dash it, Lizzie. I have to speak with you now that I finally have you alone."

She disentangled herself from his grasp. "What is it, Henry?"

He took a bold step closer. "I still want you. I love you, no matter who you are married to."

Lizzie froze at the sheer audacity, the utter inappropriateness. . . . When she didn't immediately move away, Henry blurted, "I can make you happy. It's clear you're miserable. I knew it in Newport, and I'm even more convinced of your unhappiness now. You deserve better than Cavanaugh."

She *was* miserable, but her feelings were no one's concern but her own. That Henry would even broach such a subject—in a semipublic place, no less—caused her to bristle. "My marriage is none of your affair, nor anyone else's. My loyalties lie with my husband. If you thought otherwise, then you were mistaken."

"Do you even care what they are saying about you? About this investment business you're starting?" The words "investment business" were said with the same amount of scorn as one might say "Tenderloin bordello."

"Henry—"

"They say you're becoming common, Lizzie, just a common laborer whose hands are every bit as filthy as her husband's."

Her muscles trembled with shock and outrage, the reaction swift and fierce. Undoubtedly, the words would not bother Emmett, but she rushed to defend him all the same. "Everything my husband has, he achieved through hard work and daring. If you think comparing me to him is offensive, you could not be more wrong."

Henry's mouth twisted, fury and failure turning his boyish visage considerably ugly. "Didn't you notice how Mrs. Van de Berg and the other matrons avoided you tonight? How they turned their backs instead of greeting you?" He gestured across the room to where a group of three older women stood, whispering. Lizzie actually hadn't noticed the slight, her misery clouding her perceptiveness this evening.

"That cartoon has turned you into a joke. They have been gossiping about you and your husband all evening. Wondering how the mighty Sloanes have fallen so far as to let their pride and joy fall into the hands of a coarse barbarian like—"

"Enough," Lizzie hissed, cutting him off. "I won't stand here and allow you to insult me or my husband."

You're no coward, and you possess two things society will never understand: intelligence and talent.

Emmett's remarks bolstered her confidence, and impassioned words poured from her mouth. "I'm tired of caring what people say about me. First they criticized me because I wasn't demure enough during my debut, then they complained I wasn't interested in marriage. I made the unforgivable mistake of not allowing my dresses to sit for a season before I wore them. Oh, and how dare I not shun the Hayes girl as everyone else did? I have garnered censure at every turn, and I am sick of it. I won't live my life for anyone other than myself, not anymore."

Turning away from his bewildered expression, Lizzie set her champagne glass on a side table and marched to the other side of the room. *Might as well deal with this directly.* "Ladies," she greeted in a firm, resolute voice.

Mrs. Van de Berg and the other two ladies spun, surprised at Lizzie's sudden appearance. "Oh, Mrs. Cavanaugh," Mrs. Van de Berg drawled. "How lovely to see you this evening. And where is your husband?" She glanced about dramatically. "Did he escort you?"

If intended to throw her off, the comment failed. Lizzie was prepared for whatever insults these ladies hurled at her. "He did not, as he had other matters to attend to this evening."

The matron nodded sympathetically. "Yes, we have heard of the long hours he keeps. That must be quite tedious for you, a husband obsessed with business—oh, but you're business-minded as well, it seems. Perhaps you two are not as ill-matched as we feared."

A not-so-veiled dig over the circumstances of Emmett's birth, that he did not lead the idle life of a proper gentleman, and of Lizzie's scandalous ambition. But Lizzie had navigated these waters her entire life, and she had no intention of tossing in her oars now. Sloanes weren't quitters, after all.

"Yes, I am starting my own investment firm. I do hope to help less fortunate ladies provide for their elder years. Just imagine if circumstances were slightly different, how trying these times would be for you."

Three mouths compressed into thin, indignant lines at the mention of their advanced age, and Lizzie enjoyed a moment's elation before she continued. "On that note, if any of you decide you'd like to double your pocket money, please come to see me."

With that, she excused herself, a strange euphoria filling her. It was as if a weight had been lifted from her shoulders, one she'd been carrying around for twenty-one years. She would do this. She would launch the investment company in her own name, to hell with the gossips. Why worry over the future when one could speculate on it instead?

She found Edith and pulled her friend aside. "I am sorry, but I cannot stay for dinner." Edith began to protest, so Lizzie leaned in to kiss her cheek. "Happy birthday, darling." She swept from the room, determined but by no means fleeing in shame.

By the time she collected her things, the emotional swing had left her exhausted. She looked forward to a hot soak in her tub. Or, perhaps she'd visit the Turkish bath. Her mind occupied, she descended the steps toward the Cavanaugh carriage—only to have a hand land on her shoulder, startling her.

"Lizzie, wait," Henry said, slightly out of breath as he came up alongside her. "Please, do not go away angry." Taking her elbow, he guided her down the remaining steps. "I needed you to know how I feel."

"Then why didn't you tell me of these feelings ages ago, Henry? Everyone assumed you and I were serious, but you never made your intentions clear. Now that I am married to someone else, I'm to believe you are in love with me?"

"Yes! I *am* in love with you. I have been since the first moment we met."

He sounded sincere, and she could only stare at him. Henry was perfect—handsome, rich, with a background similar to her own—so she should be wildly in love with him. Yet she'd never experienced any feelings stronger than friendship toward him. No rush in her blood or all-consuming desire to be near him, not like with Emmett. Her emotions for Emmett were so strong, so monumental, that she felt her skin could hardly contain them.

"You were never right for me, Henry, and I am not the right woman for you. Somewhere inside, you know that."

They stood by her carriage now, the coachman hanging back a few steps, waiting. "No," Henry said, grasping her forearm to plead his case. "You have always been the right woman for me. I just assumed I had more time. One day I turn around and you're marrying Emmett Cavanaugh. But I know you don't want to be married to that—"

"Stop. Do not finish that sentence."

He sighed and stared across the street at Gramercy Park. "I won't say anything more than this: Think about it, Lizzie. That's all I ask. I will wait for you, no matter how long it takes."

Shadows, dark and depressing, draped the office as Emmett continued to work. He'd shed his coat and vest at some point, leaving him in shirtsleeves and suspenders. His dinner waited, untouched, on the edge of his desk, while a half-empty bottle of gin rested within reach. His eyes, however, remained on the investigator's report that had arrived this afternoon. So far, there were three members of the Northeast Railroad board of directors who, contingent on a sizable bribe, would assist Emmett in taking the company over.

Excellent. He just needed a few more men in his pocket, and then he'd strip the company away from Sloane, giving that pompous bastard exactly what he deserved.

The door to his office opened, yet he didn't look up.

His wife had returned a quarter of an hour earlier, so he knew the identity of his visitor. "Where was she?"

Kelly didn't answer right away, preferring to take a seat across from the desk instead. When the silence stretched, Emmett glanced up to pin his friend with a stare. "Well?"

Kelly scratched his jaw. "She . . . uh, she went to Edith Rutlidge's again, this time dressed for a fancy dinner."

"And?"

"She left early. Seemed a bit rattled. Then Henry Rutlidge followed her to the carriage. I couldn't hear what they was sayin', of course, but I got the impression he was pleading with her."

Anger exploded in a white-hot rush, tensing Emmett's muscles and obliterating rationality. He shot to his feet and started for the door. "Wait!" Kelly called. "She came home. Alone."

Hand on the knob, Emmett paused. That she'd returned did not assuage his anger. Far from it. So she'd gone running to Rutlidge again. Christ on a cross, would they never be rid of that son of a bitch? "How long did Rutlidge talk to her? And did he touch her?"

"A few minutes. Held her arm a bit—"

Fuck. Emmett flew into the hall, racing to the stairs. He had no idea what he would say to Elizabeth, but he would not allow Rutlidge to have her. Not while Emmett had breath left in his lungs. If Rutlidge and Elizabeth thought they could carry on behind Emmett's back, they were sorely mistaken.

He heard Kelly call his name but he paid no attention, taking the stairs two at a time and charging to her dressing room. Not bothering to knock, he threw the door open and stepped inside. Elizabeth's maid gasped, but Emmett ignored her, instead focused on the beautiful, deceitful woman staring down her nose at him despite their clear difference in height.

Blond hair flowed over her shoulders, the locks recently released from whatever complicated coiffure she'd worn earlier, and a silk dressing gown hung from her shoulders. Flashes of bare skin covered in white cotton and lace danced in front of his eyes before she jerked the edges closed, tying the sash tightly. Smudges under her eyes caused her to look tired, and no welcoming light of warmth lit her gray depths as she faced him down. "Thank you, that will be all," she said to the maid, dismissing her.

The door closed, leaving the two of them alone, and a myriad of emotions ran through him. Fear, outrage, jealousy . . . but mostly the insane craving that grabbed hold of his balls every time he was in her presence. She was stunning, even more so undone like this, and he could vividly remember her eagerness, the passion she had exhibited each time he'd taken her. His cock stirred in his trousers, and he resolutely ignored it.

"Yes, Emmett? I'm assuming you had a purpose in barging in here tonight."

"What does he want from you?"

Confusion clouded her expression. "I do not know what you're talking about."

"Oh, don't you?" he sneered. "Henry Rutlidge. Though I can't say I'm surprised you went running to him."

She rolled her eyes. "Yes, I went running to him. That is precisely what I did. Fortunately, my fleeing coincided with Edith's yearly birthday dinner."

A sliver of doubt worked its way down Emmett's spine, but he pressed, wanting some reaction from her. "Convenient he was able to get you alone, press his case. Let me guess, he believes you can do better than a dirty, common lout like me?"

"It hardly matters what Henry believes. If you trusted me in the slightest, we would not be having this conversation. But you don't trust me. You never have, and I'm coming to accept that you never will." She reached for her brush. "Now, get out, Emmett."

Heart pounding, he took a few steps closer. His fingers flexed with the need to touch her soft skin, to cup her plump breasts, to test the wetness of her cleft. . . . Then he noticed the pulse fluttering wildly at the base of her neck, and knew she was not as immune as she pretended. Her response triggered something inside him, an urge to taste her, to have her begging underneath him one more time, a desire so strong that his knees nearly buckled.

He hated this hunger, the insatiable lust that consumed him whenever Elizabeth was near. He was a drunk, willing to do anything for another bottle. Desperate with wanting. But he could not stop the pulsing need, could not prevent his legs from starting forward.

In two long strides, he backed her up to the dressing table. Her palms came up to rest on his chest, both to steady herself and to keep him away, no doubt. In a swift move, he lifted her onto the table, then captured both her wrists, brought them around behind her, and held them easily with one of his own hands.

She struggled a bit, a flush on her cheeks, pupils wide and black. "Let me go," she said through clenched teeth.

"I do not think so," he whispered, skimming his nose over her supple cheek. God, she smelled delicious, like vanilla and soap and stubbornness. "Tell me what he wants, Elizabeth. Tell me why Rutledge followed *my* wife to *my* carriage and dared to put his hands on her."

She gave a sharp intake of breath near his ear. "You're having me followed."

He nipped the edge of her jaw with his teeth, felt her

shiver. He reveled in the reaction, his cock lengthening. "Damn right I'm having you followed."

With his free hand, he lifted the flimsy layers she wore to her waist, then stepped between her thighs, needing to get closer. Her breasts met his shirtfront as he trailed his fingertips along the smooth skin of her inner thigh. He was rigid beneath his underclothes and trousers, his prick clamoring for friction, but he resisted the urge to release himself and drive into her body.

She was panting now, eyelids closed. "You have no right to spy on me."

"The hell I don't." He pressed hot, open-mouthed kisses down the side of her throat, sinking his teeth into the tender spot where neck met shoulder. She arched closer, and he whispered, "You're mine."

"Oh God," she whimpered, her fingers curling into fists behind her back. "Then you must remember that you are mine as well, husband."

He untied her dressing gown and let the edges fall open. The idea of another woman hadn't even crossed his mind. He was too obsessed with the one in front of him. "How could I possibly ever forget?"

He moved lower, using his tongue, teeth, and lips until she was nearly pushing her breast into his mouth. He licked the puckered tip through the cloth until she writhed, and then he wrapped his lips around her nipple and drew the taut flesh into his mouth. Her resulting moan reverberated in his blood, hardening him further.

The need to coat his tongue with her slickness urged him south. He released her wrists and dropped to his knees. Her fingers wound their way into his hair, clutching him tight as he parted her drawers. He could smell her, the womanly musk that signaled her arousal, and then she was bared before him. Glistening, swollen . . . He nearly shot off then and there. Christ, this woman.

He kissed the edges, sucking gently on the plump lips that guarded her entrance, not giving her what he knew she wanted. When she squirmed, trying to get closer, he said, "Tell me. I'll do anything you need, but you must tell me first, Elizabeth."

"Please, Emmett."

"Please, what?"

"Kiss me there."

"Here?" he asked, and pressed his lips to the tendon at the juncture of her thigh. He flicked his eyes to see her watching him, her silver gaze glassy and dark.

Her lips parted, her pink tongue darting forward to wet them. "Inside," she whispered. "Use your tongue."

He was hard and heavy, aching for her, and her words lanced through him like he'd been hit with an electric wire. "Yes," he hissed, before parting her to give long licks with the flat of his tongue. He loved her taste, would never get enough of bringing her to peak with his mouth. The tip of his tongue circled her clitoris before he pulled back to ask, "Who is doing this to you?"

"Emmett," she sighed, her fingers gripping his hair painfully as she threw her head back.

He hummed his approval against her skin, the vibration working its way through her sensitive tissues. She gasped and rocked forward. He decided to reward her and began sucking on her swollen pearl relentlessly. When her cries turned to urgent pleas, he quickly unbuttoned his trousers and pulled his erection out of his underclothes. In a flash, he rose, lined up, and drove into her with one thrust.

So warm and tight. Jesus Christ, she felt utterly perfect surrounding him. He captured her mouth and began to move, his hips working hard and fast, with no finesse whatsoever. The tiny dressing table rocked underneath them, crystal and porcelain tumbling to the floor, but Emmett kept pace, driving them higher.

She kissed him with abandon, every bit as wild as he, and when he felt her walls tighten around his cock, his fingers reached between them and brought her over the edge. She clenched, nails digging into his arms, cries ringing in his ear, and he could not hold back any longer. Pleasure built in his lower back, his legs . . . his fucking *toes*. With a shout, he let go, shuddering as spend erupted from the head of his prick.

Awareness began to creep in when the waves finally stopped. They were wrapped around each other, breathing hard, on a table in her dressing room. What was it about this woman? He didn't trust her, no matter what Kelly and Brendan believed. So why had he just pounced on her like a starving man?

Withdrawing, he began putting himself to rights, resolutely avoiding her gaze. He owed her an apology for taking her like this, but the words would not come. She was his wife—not Rutledge's. "I do not want you seeing him again," he said gruffly. "Is that clear?"

Elizabeth slid off the table and pulled her dressing gown closed. "Do not be ridiculous. He is the brother of my best friend. There is no way to avoid him, Emmett."

"I do not want you alone with him."

"Why?" she asked, genuinely perplexed. Then a bitter laugh escaped her. "Because you don't trust me. Of course, how could I have forgotten?"

He said nothing, just watched as a myriad of emotions traveled over her face. Finally, she asked, "Tell me, how am I supposed to win back your precious trust?"

No answer came to mind, other than that he wanted her to admit what she'd done. It was the only way he could ever be sure. But trust or not, he still wanted her. Ached for her. And he had no intention of allowing another man to lay claim to her.

"For starters, stay the hell away from Henry Rutledge."

Chapter Eighteen

Never ask impertinent questions.

—American Etiquette and Rules of Politeness, 1883

"Good morning, Lizzie," Brendan said as he entered the breakfast room. "I'm pleased to see you looking so well today."

Lizzie ducked her head, avoiding her brother-in-law's assessing gaze. Did everyone know of last night's argument and . . . afterward? "Good morning," she said into her cup, just before taking a long sip of coffee.

Brendan must have noticed her reaction because he held up a hand. "All I know was that Emmett was livid. When he is stomping about the house, it's like a horde of invaders storming the castle gates. He'd never hurt you, but I also know how unforgiving he can be."

That was an understatement. Brendan couldn't have learned of the particulars regarding the East Coast stock purchase, only that Lizzie and Emmett had disagreed over something. And though she'd confided her misery to Edith, complaining to Emmett's brother seemed disloyal. "Yes, he was certainly worked up."

Brendan set a china plate full of food on the linen tablecloth, then lowered carefully into a chair. "Will you stay and have coffee with me?" He nodded toward her empty cup.

She agreed and poured coffee for them both. They made idle conversation for a moment or two before Brendan dismissed the footman hovering nearby. When they were alone, he said, "My brother is making you unhappy, isn't he?"

"Yes, he is." No use pretending.

"I had such high hopes after the storm. I thought . . . well, I thought he'd changed."

"As did I." Thoughts of last evening came back to her, starting with Emmett's anger and accusations. Henry's pleading. The women who had ignored her because she'd dared to use her brain for something more than planning parties. Was Will right? Was she a fool to risk everything she had on this idea?

"Brendan, what will happen if my investment firm causes me to lose my standing in society? Will Katie and Claire be terribly disappointed?"

"Terribly disappointed that you can no longer guarantee their success?"

"Yes."

"Lizzie, there are few guarantees in this life. No one expects you to put aside your happiness for Claire and Katie. Besides, Emmett claims their fat dowries will be enough." Brendan chuckled and picked up his knife and fork. "Though I admit I didn't believe him, which is why I stupidly meddled in your dinner at Sherry's that night."

"What do you mean, meddled?"

An odd look passed over his face. "He never told you?"

"Told me what?"

"No, nothing." He focused hard on his plate and carefully cut into his sausage.

Brendan was a terrible liar. "What didn't Emmett tell me?"

Grimacing, Brendan placed his knife and fork on the plate. "He's going to kill me," he muttered.

"*Brendan.*"

"About that second dinner, the one at Sherry's." She stared at him blankly, and he continued, "About how I tricked him into showing up."

Her ears began to ring, but she forced out, "Tricked him, how?"

"I thought you knew. That I told him he was meeting his mi—" Brendan cleared his throat. "Someone else in that dining room."

"But he asked me to have dinner that night. We had planned to meet."

Brendan winced and said nothing.

Her mind turned this over, and she added up the facts. "He wanted to cancel, but you never passed the message along," she guessed, and Brendan's heavy exhale confirmed it.

She slumped in her seat. Emmett had . . . tried to cancel on her. Instead, he'd planned to meet his mistress for dinner, which was why the room had been set up in such a way. So intimate. For someone else. Embarrassment and misery wedged in her throat. Was anything between them *not* a lie? First the blackmail to marry her, and now this. . . .

"Lizzie, I am sorry. I never meant to hurt you. I thought the association would do Emmett some good. But I never thought that he would try to seduce you there, or that your brother would catch the two of you together."

Lizzie rubbed her forehead. Emmett had been tricked into meeting her. Emmett Cavanaugh and his society wife, a woman from one of the oldest families in New York but naïve enough to believe he'd truly wanted her. Even after she'd learned of the blackmail, that night at Sherry's had always comforted her. The knowledge that he had seduced her, had pursued her.

But he hadn't been pursuing her. He'd been trying to avoid her.

A fist-sized lump settled behind her breastbone. No doubt she'd been a convenient outlet during the storm, a warm, willing body to replace the many mistresses he still entertained.

Pushing away from the table, she rose quickly. She had no idea where she was going, but she had to move, to leave. To get somewhere private where she could try to make sense of everything she'd learned.

"Lizzie, wait!" Brendan clutched her arm. "Please. I know your marriage may have started under less than ideal conditions, but it's clear the two of you have feelings for one another. Do not let what I've told you make you think less of him. He cares for you, I know it."

Lizzie knew no such thing. No wonder Emmett fought her at every turn. She could hardly fault him, considering she served as a reminder of everything he hadn't wished for. Everything he'd been blackmailed into accepting. Ice settled around her heart, a frozen hopelessness gifted by the stark reality of her marriage.

"Do not worry," she told her brother-in-law. "I do not blame you. I blame myself."

While trains were convenient they were also messy and loud. They spewed ash and burning cinders into the air.

The wheels rattled as they churned, the undercarriage jostling and pinging in an unholy racket. Still, they carried you away from places—places in which you'd rather not stay.

Lizzie watched the countryside fly past the train window. She'd needed to escape the house, escape New York, as quickly as possible. The destination hadn't much mattered. This train was headed west, away from a mansion full of distrust and lies, and that was all she cared about. Of course, she could disembark and catch an eastbound train whenever she was ready . . . but would she ever be ready to face Emmett again?

She sighed and settled deeper into the plush velvet bench. Trains were comforting to her, a reminder of her family legacy. Her father and brother had overseen the construction of these cars, these rails. Over the years, she had attended ceremonies for station openings, helped to christen new railcars, even weighed in on carpet and fabric choices for the interiors. Northeast Railroad was in her blood, too.

Today, however, she was not traveling as Mrs. Elizabeth Cavanaugh, née Sloane, in a private Pullman car, as her brother always insisted. She was plain Lizzie, riding with the rest of the passengers, just one lost soul amongst hundreds of strangers. Perhaps the journey could give her the time and space to find herself once more.

"It's almost time for lunch, madam," Pauline said from the other end of the small bench, breaking into Lizzie's reverie. "Shall I go and secure us seats in the dining saloon?"

Food did not sound appealing in the least, but Lizzie knew her maid had been increasingly concerned on the journey over her employer's silence. Not to mention that the poor woman hadn't blinked when Lizzie told her they were leaving for an indefinite amount of time. Therefore, it seemed cruel to refuse small courtesies. "Yes, thank you, Pauline. Did you send the telegram to Miss Grayson, telling her I would be away?"

"Yes, I did. I didn't say when you was to return, however."

The fishing expedition was not lost on Lizzie. "Excellent, thank you. I don't expect it will be long. Just enough time to think, Pauline."

The other woman nodded and rose from the bench, leaving Lizzie to stare out the window. A few minutes later, she felt a presence next to her. "Did you get us seats?" she asked, but received no answer. She glanced over and found a man there—

"Henry!" She straightened, blinking at him. "Good heavens. What are you doing here?"

Removing his derby, Henry Rutlidge slid closer. "I came to find you, of course."

"I don't understand. How did you know I would be here, on this train?"

Reaching out, he clasped her hand. "I know you're running away from him." Lizzie immediately tried to withdraw her hand from his grasp, but Henry held fast. "No, wait," he said, his eyes pleading with her. "Let me come with you. I'll help you. We can return to New York and I will use my influence to expedite your annulment."

"Henry, I hadn't planned anything beyond getting on the train. Please do not force me to make decisions right now."

"Lizzie, in your heart you know what you are doing. You're leaving him. For good. And about time, I might add."

"Stop." She jerked her hand back, and this time he let

her go. "You've made it clear you do not approve of my marriage, but you cannot make assumptions. How can you think to know my mind when I hardly know it myself?"

He shot to his feet. "If that were true, then you would not have left in such a hurry. You would also know when you plan to return. Why do you bother lying to me? You forget how well I know you."

On the contrary, in the past few weeks she'd realized how utterly mismatched the two of them would have been. "You do not know me nearly as well as you think. If you did, you would see why your presence on this train is pure madness, Henry."

"Wrong." He paced as much as one could in the small sitting area of the car. "I've known you since we were children, Lizzie. Cavanaugh's known you for what, three months? You and I are so much alike. We make sense. Cavanaugh is nothing but a lowborn laborer. He's—"

"That's enough," she snapped, then glanced around. Thankfully, the car was not crowded, the other passengers far enough away that they would not overhear. Still, she lowered her voice. "Do not say any more. You sound like an aristocratic snob, Henry. My husband is hardworking and a good man."

The train swayed, and Henry had to reach out to steady himself on a chair. "Do not tell me you actually have feelings for the big ape."

"If you call him another name, I shall switch trains at the next stop—after I throw your baggage into the wilds of Pennsylvania."

"Touching, but you should know that your husband doesn't reciprocate your tender feelings. If he did, then he certainly wouldn't have told me where to find you. How else did I learn which train you had taken?"

Lizzie lost her breath. "He did *what?*"

Henry shrugged. "Even he realizes I am the man you should be married to. So do not think he is at home, pining for you. He's probably trolling the vaudeville houses as we speak, looking for an actress to—"

"Do not say it," she gritted out, though there was every possibility Henry was correct. How could Emmett have thrown Henry at her like this? Only last night, he'd forbidden her to even be alone with the other man. She closed her eyes, hurt and confusion now strangling her insides.

He doesn't want you, Lizzie. He never did.

A terrible pressure built behind her lids, a signal that her emotions were about to crash. She bit her lip, trying to hold back until she could be alone.

Henry shifted closer. "Fine. But you should also know that Cavanaugh's planning to take over your brother's company. I have it on good authority that he's trying to bribe the Northeast board to gain a majority share."

She blinked at Henry. "*What?* Why would Emmett want to take over Will's company?"

"As revenge for forcing the marriage between you, obviously."

Her chest burned, a bitter hurt mixed with fury. Damn Emmett Cavanaugh. She knew he hated Will, but would he really try to take away her family legacy? Granted, there had been some financial difficulty of late—

Oh, heavens. The balance sheets from the storm . . . It had obviously been a railroad company. Had Lizzie been looking at Northeast Railroad's books? If so, then Will had been bilking investors by selling more stock than he should, which meant he could be investigated. Possibly prosecuted for fraud.

Only one person could answer these questions, and he

was not aboard the train. And all this speculation produced nothing but an ache in her temples.

"Henry, you need to stop."

"Fine, but let me ask you: Who is here now? Who has rushed to your side to help you? I have wanted you for years."

"Yet you did nothing. That is not the way I wish to be wanted by my husband."

His expression clouded. She knew he didn't understand, but how could she begin to describe the desperation that overcame her every time Emmett touched her? The need for him was essential, as necessary as air and water.

She didn't prefer to be worshipped from afar while a man bided his time. She would rather be ravished and devoured by a man who took what he wanted, damn the consequences.

"I do want you, Lizzie. I swear it."

"Then why did you leave for Maine instead of attending my birthday party last year? Why did you escort other women to dinner? Or take them sailing?"

"Because I needed to *live* first, before settling down. I was not ready to marry you then."

"But you are now?" she asked with a skeptical tone.

"Yes!" he nearly shouted. "And if my doing those things upset you, why did you not mention them before now?"

"They didn't upset me. I was never jealous, only surprised." Which was true. She'd never cared about what Henry did or who he was with. Not like with Emmett, when the mere thought of him with another woman caused bile to rise in her throat.

Henry frowned, his boyishly handsome face unhappy. "I don't understand why you are arguing with me. Your husband has turned his back on you, but I'm here. I love you and I want to marry you."

Suddenly, all became clear. Everything Henry had ever wanted had been handed to him. He'd never had to work, struggle, or fight for anything. Women, money, friends . . . it was all so easy for him. And he couldn't comprehend why she was denying him what he assumed was his due.

How could she make him understand?

"Henry, you should return to New York. We shall always be friends, but that is all."

His lips thinned in displeasure, and she could see by the stubborn set of his chin that he didn't believe her. "You do not mean that. The travel has obviously overset you, and you're not thinking clearly. I'll let you rest and then see you for dinner."

Taking several strides, he reached the door. Before turning the latch, he shot a look over his shoulder. "I care about you, Lizzie. I only want to see you happy." With that, he disappeared into the vestibule leading to another car.

Emmett paced the length of his bedroom, uncertainty gnawing at his gut as his feet chewed up the distance. Walk, walk, turn, walk. And back again. That damned letter. He couldn't get it out of his head. He'd read the thing so many times, the words were committed to memory.

Emmett,
    I am to leave for a trip today. I am uncertain when
    I will return.

                                Sincerely,
                                Elizabeth

The note was as cold and impersonal as he'd ever seen, but he knew what she meant. Brendan had sworn Emmett was wrong, that she planned to return. But Emmett had been through this before. Another woman, another note . . . and their mother had never returned, either.

Brendan had confessed about his conversation with Elizabeth, that he'd spilled the real reason Emmett had attended the dinner at Sherry's. Guilt weighed heavily on Brendan, and he'd apologized profusely. Yet Emmett could not be angry with his brother. Emmett alone was the reason his wife had left.

Gone. She was *gone.*

Even in all the turmoil since the stock purchase, he had never thought she would up and leave. He'd been angry, yes, but he'd assumed she would stand up to him. Yell at him. Poke and prod him until he relented. He had *wanted* her to prove him wrong. But she hadn't done any of those things, and now she'd walked away.

He had no intention of letting her go, however.

As soon as he'd finished reading her brief letter, he'd started packing. In the meantime, he'd ordered Kelly to Grand Central Depot to discern her destination. That had been over an hour ago. So where in the hell was Kelly with answers?

With the packing now complete, the wait was intolerable. Emmett strode to the bed and closed his small bag. He'd go to the train station and find her train himself.

Just as he reached to open his door, Kelly burst in, out of breath, his cheeks dry and red from the cold.

"About damned time," Emmett snapped, stepping around him and into the corridor. He hurried toward

the stairs, and Kelly fell into step at his side. "What did
you learn?"

"She took the 10:49 Cuyahoga Express."

"That's a Northeast train, isn't it?"

"Yes," Kelly replied as they started down the staircase.
"But there's more." Kelly put a hand on Emmett's shoulder to stop him. Emmett saw the uneasiness on his friend's
face, the trepidation.

"What is it?"

"There was another person on the train."

A moment passed as Emmett tried to understand what
Kelly was saying. Another person, one whose identity
made Kelly uneasy. The pieces fell into place, and Emmett's
free hand clutched at the bannister. Rutledge. *"Son of a
bitch."*

Emmett's teeth ground together, a paltry outlet for the
rage currently coursing through him. She'd run off with
her ex-beau. Jesus Christ. How could he not have seen
this coming? Stupid, so fucking stupid. Emmett wanted to
laugh at the absurdity of it. Here he was, ready to charge
after her and bring her back . . . when she'd left him for
another man.

You didn't really think you could hold on to her, did you?

Emmett shoved his bag into Kelly's arms. "Take that
back to my room." He thumped down the steps, trying to
keep from hitting something.

"Bish, wait up. Where are you going?" Kelly called
from behind. "I'll come with—"

"Leave me alone. I'm going to swim," Emmett snapped.
"I don't need a damn nursemaid."

Several of the footmen and maids visibly shrank from
Emmett as he stomped through the house. No doubt his
face conveyed precisely what he was feeling, that the

tightly held leash on his control was slipping. By the time he stripped down and dove into the heated water of the swimming pool, he could barely breathe. He hadn't felt this way in a long, long time, so vulnerable and raw. So empty.

Cool silence enveloped him as his arms cut through the water, his legs kicking hard. He did this often for exercise, mostly as a way to keep his head clear. The solitude and the quiet helped him think. He had taught himself to swim years ago, as a boy. It had been either that or drown, considering he'd been tossed into the East River by rival gangs one too many times. More proof that he need not rely on anyone else. The only person you could count on was yourself.

When he returned to the end, he noticed his brother's boots planted on the tile. Emmett didn't acknowledge him, just kept going, arms churning and legs pounding. Brendan would try and reason with him, and Emmett felt entirely unreasonable at this moment. There was nothing to say. Nothing he wanted to hear, at least.

So he ignored Brendan and swam until his muscles gave out. When he could no longer lift his arms, he clung to the side of the pool. His lungs bellowed as he struggled for air, and he figured he might as well get it over with. "Well?"

"You've got to go after her."

Emmett made a noise. "The hell I do."

"Don't be a fool." Brendan huffed in annoyance. "You did not see her face this morning, Em. That woman cares about you. She was crushed to learn that you hadn't met her of your own free will."

"Yes, crushed enough to run away with Rutlidge," Emmett muttered.

"That's just it. I don't think she ran away with him. The note she left for the girls said she wanted to take some time for herself—"

"Not that she could tell the girls about Rutlidge." Brendan started to argue, so Emmett held up a hand. "Why would I bother? Give me one good reason to chase her down."

"Because you love her. And because I suspect she loves you, but you're both too stubborn to admit it."

Emmett said nothing, just stared at the far wall. Did he love her?

"At the very least, you must give her a chance to explain. Em, think. For once, pretend this is a company you're thinking about buying—not your wife. She had years to merge with Rutlidge and resisted him. You know her. This is the woman who walked in off the street and asked you to back her investment company. If she had wanted Rutlidge, she would have married him long before now."

That did make some sense, he supposed. Elizabeth was nothing if not resourceful. *Elizabeth sounds like a woman strong enough to change history, to chart any course she chooses.* His own words went through his mind, bringing doubt along with them.

He pushed off from the wall and floated on his back, Hades and Persephone directly above him. He'd always sympathized with Hades, the misunderstood brute who had to resort to trickery to keep a woman. *And wasn't that precisely what you did to Elizabeth by never telling her the truth?*

"Also," Brendan continued, "if she didn't love you, she never would've been so upset over what I said."

Emmett didn't know if that was true or not. Women

were complicated creatures, which was why he'd avoided anything emotional before now.

"I know it's easier to believe the worst in people, Em. Less chance of someone's letting you down that way. But you have to trust her. If she were my wife, I'd be halfway to Ohio by now."

There was that word again, *trust*. Hadn't Elizabeth accused him of the very same thing, of not ever trusting anyone?

"So what would you have me do?" Emmett asked up at Hades. "Chase after her and steal her away from Rutlidge?"

"Well, for starters, get out of the swimming pool, get dressed, and then find a way to stop her train."

"I can accomplish that with one telegram. The question is, why would I bother?"

Brendan stayed quiet for a long minute. When he spoke, his voice cracked with emotion. "We were too young to chase after her, Emmett. Neither of us had the ability to stop her, and then she was gone." Emmett heard him swallow, and a sudden tightness lodged in his own throat as well. "Do not squander this opportunity. There may be no getting it back. Even if you fail, at least you'll have tried. Isn't Lizzie worth the fight?"

Brendan's footsteps faded and Emmett remained in the pool, floating. Was his brother right? Did Elizabeth love him? If so, then why did she leave?

"Harvard's called it, you know."

Kelly's voice rang out from the other end of the room, where he'd clearly been eavesdropping.

"I wondered when you'd show yourself," Emmett said. "You couldn't leave it alone, could you?"

"Did you leave it alone that time I was knifed by the Dead Rabbits? Did you leave it alone when Rebecca died, and I nearly drown in a bottle? Or when I started fightin' again, takin' risks in back alleys?"

Emmett said nothing. He'd done those things for the same reason his friend had followed Emmett down to the pool: because they were family.

"Bish, I know why you keep pushin' her away. You think you ain't worthy of her, that you don't deserve happiness. Do you remember what you said to me when Rebecca died?"

Kelly had nearly been destroyed by his wife's illness and slow demise. When Rebecca had finally died, Emmett had stayed with Kelly for weeks, afraid to leave his friend's side for fear of what Kelly might do.

"I never hid my past from Rebecca. She knew where I came from, what I'd done in Five Points. Said she loved me all the more for my past because I overcame it. But when she died . . ." Kelly's voice trailed off and then he cleared his throat.

"You said it was punishment for your sins," Emmett said gently. "That it was your fault she became ill and died."

"And you told me I was wrong. That my time with Rebecca, no matter how short, was my reward for makin' it out of the slums."

"What's your point?"

Kelly came to stand at the pool's edge and stared down at Emmett. "You hate to admit you're wrong, always have. But your wife is nobody's fool. If you think she doesn't know you, doesn't know the kind of man you are, you're wrong. She knows, and she loves you anyway."

"She doesn't know everything. Not about Five Points."

"Wrong. Brendan has been fillin' her in on a lot of it. She knows more than you think, and she was still willing to put up with you."

Emmett frowned. Brendan had no right to tell Elizabeth any of it, not without discussing it with Emmett first. How much had his brother told her?

"She left because she believes you never wanted her—not because she doesn't want you," Kelly said. "You need to get out of the pool, Emmett. Get dressed and go after your reward before it's too late."

Chapter Nineteen

⌒⌒⌒

*A young lady should be very careful as to the formation
of traveling acquaintances . . .*

—American Etiquette and Rules of Politeness, 1883

"May I join you for breakfast?"

Lizzie glanced up to find a well-dressed Henry Rutlidge by her table. With the dining car near full, it would be rude to refuse, though she truly did not want company. Especially Henry.

Manners won out. "Of course." She gestured to the opposite seat. Henry dropped down, a wide smile on his face.

"Good morning," he said brightly, and then turned to the waiter to order.

She did not feel nearly so chirk this morning. Though she had skipped dinner in an effort to avoid Henry, sleep had not come until the wee hours. Instead she'd lain in her berth and stared out the window, wondering why Emmett had instructed Henry on where to find her. Why hadn't Emmett just been honest with her? And why, despite everything that had happened, did she still miss her husband?

"I thought for certain the train had broken down last night," Henry remarked after the waiter left, interrupting her thoughts.

"Broken down? Why?"

His brow creased. "Didn't you notice how long we stopped in Martinsburg? It was a few hours, at least."

She hadn't noticed. Misery tended to obliterate one's surroundings. "Was there something wrong?"

"No one would tell me. We just stopped and waited. And when the train did finally start up, the wheels creeped over into Ohio."

Now that he mentioned it, the train did seem to be going rather slowly. Lizzie had never traveled this far west, so she had assumed this to be the normal cross-continental pace. But at least they were moving.

"Have you ridden this direction before?" she asked Henry.

"No. The accommodations leave much to be desired, in my opinion. And where is my breakfast?" He glanced over his shoulder, eyeing the length of the car. "Why anyone would choose to travel in a public car is beyond me. It's barbaric."

He was an even bigger snob than her brother. "I don't mind it. I like the anonymity and the sense of adventure."

Henry gazed at her as if she'd advised him to buy high and sell low. "I suppose," he muttered. "But once you've been granted your annulment, we'll be staying in New York."

Her eyes grew wide. That had sounded proprietary, as if Henry had a right to make decisions on her behalf—which he definitely did not.

"Henry—"

The waiter set a china plate in front of Henry along

with a matching cup filled with coffee, cutting off what she'd been about to say. Henry took a bite of food and grimaced. "This is worse than what they attempted to call a dinner last night."

"You may get off the train at any stop. Return back to New York. No one is forcing you to accompany me." No one had even asked, in fact.

"Lizzie." He gave her a patronizing, crooked smile. "I cannot let you face this alone. We're friends. Besides, this journey is not safe for a woman alone, especially not one such as yourself."

"What does that mean, a woman such as myself?"

He scratched his sideburns. "You know, one with your upbringing. With *our* upbringing. This is dangerous for a gentle woman like you."

Gentle? She nearly snorted. If Emmett heard that word used to describe her, he'd laugh. Further proof she and Henry were mismatched. He didn't know her at all if he really believed she was "gentle."

"And that investment firm idea of yours . . . I'm afraid you'll need to put our family first, Lizzie."

"It's more than an 'idea,' and I plan to pursue it, Henry."

A muscle jumped in his jaw, his nostrils flaring, before he forced out, "Of course, my dear."

Though his insincerity was obvious, she dropped the issue and attended to her breakfast. She and Henry had no future together, not one in which he would have any control over her life.

Once breakfast had concluded, they returned to the first-class parlor, where she noticed that the train was pulling into a station. Good. Perhaps she could step out for a bit of fresh air and space from unwanted companions. And most bizarrely, she missed Emmett. Spending time with Henry had only served to remind her how much.

Obviously, she needed to clear her head.

"I think I'll walk around a bit on the platform, Henry. Perhaps we'll see one another this afternoon."

She started for the vestibule, but his hand stopped her. "Wait, Lizzie. I want to talk to you."

"Isn't that what we've been doing all morning?" she asked him pointedly. "I need some air, Henry."

"Please, Lizzie. For me?"

Why was he pushing so hard? She would much rather be alone. Sighing, she resigned herself. Maybe if she heard him out, he'd give her some space. She nodded, and he led her to the sofa, where they both sat on the plush cushions.

"Have you thought any more about what I said yesterday?"

"Which part, exactly?"

"About how I want to marry you." He searched her face before leaning in closer than was proper. "Do you believe me?"

She edged away slightly. "It hardly matters whether I believe you or not, Henry. I think you have made assumptions based on our friendship, assumptions I do not share."

"They are not assumptions. But I realized the reason you doubt me is because I've been too tentative with you. I should have shown you long before now how I felt."

The back of her neck prickled. She didn't care for the strange light in his eyes. "No, that's not why—"

"Of course it is." He reached out to clasp her upper arm in a firm grip. "Let me show you. Let me prove to you how much I want you."

"That's not necessary," she said quickly, trying to pull her arm free and glancing wildly around the car. There was no one else about, no one to help her. The other first-class passengers must be outside on the platform or still in the dining saloon. Where were the porters? "Really, Henry. You do not need to demonstrate—"

Without warning, he jerked her toward him and slammed his mouth down on hers. Surprise rooted her to the spot, frozen, as his lips, cold and determined, moved forcefully on hers. They had kissed once or twice before, but the exchanges had held no passion. No excitement. This time was no different—and she was *married*.

Using all her strength, she pushed him away. "Henry, stop. We should not be doing this. I'm married."

"Your husband is not here," Henry said. "He doesn't want you like I do."

"That does not change the fact that I am married to him. I cannot do this."

"Of course you can." His brows flattened into a disbelieving line. "Let me show you how much I want you."

He leaned in, and she arched away, attempting to scramble to her feet, but he grabbed her shoulders with both hands. He pushed her into the corner of the sofa, blocking her with his body. A sliver of fear worked its way down her spine. How far would Henry go to "prove" his feelings to her?

"You need to let go. This is not right, Henry."

"You're wrong." He bent his head and pressed his face into her throat. "This is exactly right. You need me, Lizzie."

A hand cupped her breast, and she began to struggle in earnest. "Stop, Henry!"

"Shh," he told her. "I'm a very generous lover. Everyone says so. Let's depart here, and I'll find us a hotel room. Allow me to pleasure you. You'll enjoy it, I swear."

She continued to push against him, trying to get up. When that didn't work, her foot connected with his shin. He didn't flinch. "Stop! Let me go. Stop, Henry."

He didn't even acknowledge he'd heard her. Panic seized her, and she did the only thing she could think of: she balled up her fist and landed a swift uppercut to his jaw. His teeth clacked shut, and surprise loosened his grip enough for her to slide away.

She lunged for the vestibule, intent on escape or calling for a porter. Throwing the heavy panel open, she opened her mouth to scream, then promptly closed it.

Emmett Cavanaugh was rushing toward her, his face full of murderous rage.

Emmett's gaze raked his wife, who stood quaking with fear in the doorway, her hair and clothing disheveled. He'd heard her cries as he approached, the panic in her tone causing his blood to run cold. Thank God she appeared unharmed, at least physically.

So Rutlidge would live. Barely.

"Emmett," she breathed, blinking up at him.

"Hello, Elizabeth." He wanted to take her into his arms, crush her to him. Kiss her senseless. Drop to his knees and beg her forgiveness. But he did none of those things, just stared at her instead. Once the surprise wore off, how would she react to his presence?

Emmett suspected Brendan might have been correct. Based on what he had overheard a few minutes ago, Rutlidge was not Elizabeth's lover. So what was he, then?

"What are *you* doing here?" Rutlidge stood in the middle of the first-class parlor, a deep scowl on his face.

"I've come after my *wife*," Emmett said slowly, with a heavy measure of menace he hadn't exuded in years.

Elizabeth stiffened, which he hoped was caused by surprise and not disappointment. Still, he would deal with her after he divested Rutlidge of a limb or two.

Two porters appeared at the opposite end of the car, passengers directly behind them, so Emmett called, "This car is closed for the next fifteen minutes."

"Yes, sir," one of the porters said, before hurrying everyone out of the car.

Grasping his wife's shoulders, Emmett turned her to him. His thumbs lingered to stroke the delicate bones beneath her clothing as he studied her face. Luminous gray eyes shone up at him, and a stab of emotion hit him square in the chest. Damn, he loved this woman. "I have a lot to say to you, but first I need to know, did he hurt you?"

"I'm fine. But what are you—?"

"All in good time, Elizabeth." He took her arm and led her to a chair. "Wait here."

Like a curtain falling into place, all the relief and tenderness inside him was locked firmly away, replaced by cold, hard resolve as he advanced on Rutlidge. The younger man at least had the sense to start backing away once he saw the look Emmett wore. "Did I hear that you were touching my wife against her wishes, Rutlidge?"

The man held up his hands, his face draining of color as he hit the wall. "Listen, Cavanaugh. There was no harm. We were merely talking."

"Even if I hadn't heard her protests with my own ears, I still wouldn't believe you." He wrapped one hand around Rutlidge's throat and squeezed. "Kelly!"

"Yeah, Bish?" Kelly strode into the car, tipped his hat to Elizabeth. "Mrs. Cavanaugh."

"Hello, Kelly," she said with a smile.

"Kelly, take Mrs. Cavanaugh back to my private car."

"Right." He held out his hand. "Come with me, ma'am. I'll get you settled."

Elizabeth shook her head. "Emmett, I think I should stay."

"Absolutely not. Go with Kelly." He shot her a look over his shoulder, gentling his tone. "Please, Elizabeth."

She stared at him for a beat, her expression unreadable. Things were unsettled between them, and he didn't blame her for hesitating. He did, however, need her gone.

"I'm staying. I think you've misunderstood—"

He held up his free hand. "Was he touching you without your permission?"

She bit her bottom lip. "Yes."

"Did you ask him to stop?"

"Now, wait—" Rutlidge started, and Emmett flexed his fingers to cut off the man's air supply.

"Elizabeth?" Emmett said. "Did you ask him to stop?"

She nodded carefully. "I did, but—"

"Then I did not misunderstand. You and I will speak after I'm through with Rutlidge." He jerked his chin at Kelly.

"Come now, Mrs. Cavanaugh. He'll be worryin' if you don't go peacefully." Kelly took her elbow and towed her out of the car and into the vestibule. She appeared concerned, but did not argue further.

When the wooden door clicked closed, Emmett relaxed his fingers to allow Rutlidge to breathe. The other man slumped against the side of the car, air wheezing in and out of his lungs.

Emmett dropped into a seat, brushed a piece of lint from his trousers. "You get one chance to explain yourself, Rutlidge, and it best be good."

"She left you," Rutlidge panted. "Anyone can see you make her miserable. She's headed to California for a migratory divorce."

The news shredded the inside of Emmett's chest with the precision of a straight razor, but he kept his face impassive. Could Rutlidge be lying? "I am still uncertain how that involves *you*."

Rutlidge straightened off the wall, vibrating with anger. "She is too good for you. Everyone says so. I belong with her; I've always belonged with her."

Emmett folded his hands in his lap. "Is that so? Then remind me why she married me and not you?"

"Because her fool brother didn't forbid her to see you as I'd hoped!"

As he'd hoped? "Ah, so you sent Sloane the note, the one telling him Elizabeth and I were dining in the private room at Sherry's."

"Yes! I was trying to get him to intervene, to put a stop to the ridiculous idea of you and Lizzie together."

"And how did that plan work out?" Emmett asked dryly.

"It should have succeeded," Rutlidge snarled. "Lizzie is mine."

Emmett sighed. Rutlidge was nothing but a spoiled, sheltered little prick, hardly even worth Emmett's time. If the man hadn't attacked Elizabeth, Emmett would almost have been tempted to let him go unscathed.

But he had attacked Elizabeth, which was absolutely unforgivable.

"Rutlidge," Emmett started, "do you know why they called me the Bishop back when I ran with the Popes?"

Rutlidge swallowed, but did not cower. He raised his chin. "Why?"

Emmett stood to his full height, hands on his hips to take up as much space as possible. "Because it was my job to decide the punishments that were meted out. Anyone who wronged us, anyone who tried to cheat us or take over our territory, had to kneel before me and plead his case. Then I would give him two choices. After that, I'd ask one question before making my decision."

"Wh-What was the question?" Rutlidge stammered, his eyes big and round.

"Perhaps you should hear your choices first. One is a broken arm because you dared to touch what is mine. The second is a toss off the train because you dared to follow her." Emmett advanced, his hands curling into fists. "Now I'll ask you the question. What punishment do you think you deserve?"

"Neither!" Henry shrieked, backing away with his palms out. "You're insane. You can't do either of those things to me. Don't you know who I am?"

"I know precisely who you are, you snobbish, over-privileged sack of shit." Emmett leaned in and snarled, "She's my goddamned wife, and you have no right to breathe her same air. Choose, Rutlidge. Either I'm breaking your arm or I'm throwing you off this train."

With an unexpected burst of speed, Rutlidge slipped around Emmett and dashed to the door. Emmett turned to give chase and tripped over the leg of an armchair. Damned cramped cars.

He hurried toward the vestibule, intent on grabbing Rutlidge. He ran hard, grateful the car remained empty, his long legs eating up the distance. Rutlidge got into the enclosed vestibule, but Emmett was right behind. Just as Rutlidge opened the door to the next car, Emmett caught up, snatching the man's shirt collar.

Kelly emerged from the other car. "Tried to run, did you?" he said, shaking his head at Rutlidge. "That's a mistake. The Bishop may be big, but he's fast."

Rutlidge struggled. "Let me go!"

Emmett drew his right arm back and let fly with a

powerful hook—and Rutlidge bounced against the side of the small enclosure. "Kelly, tell them I'm ready for the train to start up. Rutlidge is going to decide whether he jumps off now or I throw him off with a broken arm when the wheels start moving."

Rutlidge groaned, holding his cheek, as Kelly hurried back inside the train car. "You can't do that," Rutlidge wheezed. "We're in the middle of nowhere. Some god-forsaken little farmland—"

"Exactly. It'll do you some good to have to figure out how to get back to New York. That is, unless you're killed in the fall."

"You're a thug," Henry spat. "You're nothing more than the filth you were born in. She'll never stay with you."

"That's too bad, because I have no intention of letting her go. She means everything to me."

Rutlidge's lips twisted into a smug smile. "Wrong. Money is everything to you. Everyone knows that. And if I'd been able to take that away, she would have seen it, too."

Emmett blinked. "Jesus. You started the fucking rumor. The one that drove down the East Coast Steel stock."

A gasp sounded behind him. Elizabeth's beautiful, yet surprised face peeked out from the adjoining car. "Henry! How could you do such a thing?"

Chapter Twenty

❦

One of the greatest disciplines of human life is that which teaches us to yield our will to others.

—American Etiquette and Rules of Politeness, 1883

At that moment, the train's whistle, long and shrill, pierced the air, and the wheels jolted forward. Emmett watched as his wife emerged, her eyes shooting fire at Henry Rutlidge. Figured she would not do as told.

Rutlidge tried to plead with her. "I wanted to show you, Lizzie. If he lost his money, you would leave him. Then I'd be able to take care of you."

"I don't care about Emmett's money. His wealth had nothing to do with why I married him. How could you think me so shallow?"

"There has to be a reason you want him instead of me!"

Emmett had often wondered the same thing. He held his breath, waiting to see what Elizabeth would say.

Stature tall and straight, she put her hands on her hips, formidable as a queen. "Because he's a good man, one who has made his own way in this world. One who has ambition and does not begrudge a woman for sharing that same trait. He treats me like an equal, not like a silly little female who should sit at home and do nothing."

The last remaining piece of ice surrounding Emmett's heart cracked and melted. He'd done nothing to deserve this woman, but he'd do everything in his power to keep her happy for the rest of his life.

"Yes, an equal," Rutledge sneered. "Just as he no doubt informed you of his plans to take over Northeast Railroad."

Elizabeth's expression did not change, and Emmett realized this was not a shock to her. *Hell*. How had Rutledge learned that piece of news?

"Yes, he has withheld certain information from me—and he has plenty of explaining and apologizing to do. But he is my husband, Henry."

She hadn't looked at him, and Emmett's gut clenched at the idea that he might lose her for good. He wanted to explain things, tell her how he felt, but he couldn't do that in front of Rutledge.

Still, Emmett had to say something. Bending, he put his lips near her ear. "I have never lied to you. No matter what else you believe, whatever lies this piece of filth has told you, believe that." She dipped her chin in a barely perceptible nod, and the knot inside his chest eased slightly.

The wheels began picking up speed, the vestibule rocking as the train rolled faster along the track. "Don't listen to him, Lizzie!" Rutledge screeched, grasping the wall for support. "He's—"

"About to toss you over the side of the train if you do not shut your trap," Emmett said. "And considering you are the one who sent William Sloane the note that night at Sherry's, I wouldn't say another word about keeping secrets."

"Henry!" she shrieked. "Why would you do something so cruel?"

"Your brother knows the right sort of people with whom to associate. I assumed he would forbid you from seeing Cavanaugh again." Henry dragged a hand down his face. "I had no idea he'd force you to marry so beneath you."

"All this time, I thought you were a friend. But, in truth, you are underhanded and deliberately malicious. It's as if I do not even know you anymore."

"Do not let him"—Rutlidge pointed at Emmett—"poison you against me. I love you, Lizzie. I've always loved you."

"No, you don't. You think you've lost something, but I was never yours to begin with. And I never will be."

Fists curled, Henry took a menacing step toward Emmett, and Elizabeth surprised everyone by putting herself between the two men. "Don't you dare, Henry. Leave my husband alone."

Emmett fought a smile. He hadn't needed protecting . . . ever. And yet his slip of a wife thought to stand up for him, which made him love and respect her all the more.

"You're both disgusting," Rutlidge spat. "I'll see that everyone shuns you, Lizzie. Your invitations will dry—"

"Shut your mouth." White-hot anger shot up Emmett's spine, and he lunged for the other man, intent on ripping off Rutlidge's perfectly styled head.

The other man paled, eyes going wide with fear. He grabbed the outside handle, the one that led to the tracks, and jerked the door open. Wind rushed in as the country-side swept by, the sound nearly deafening in the enclosed space. Rutlidge did not wait. Stepping into the air, he promptly jumped off the moving train.

Emmett reached the edge in time to see Rutlidge hit the ground and roll down an embankment.

Elizabeth peered over Emmett's shoulder. "Will he be hurt?" she shouted.

Emmett yanked the door shut, sealing them in. "I don't care about him any longer. Do you?"

"No, I don't." She stared at him with wary gray eyes. "You're the reason the train stopped last night, so you could catch us. Why did you come after me, Emmett?"

He gave her the honest answer, the one on the tip of his tongue. "I had to. I couldn't let you go."

"Yes, but why? Allow me to guess. You learned Henry was on the train, and you didn't trust me."

Emmett swallowed, unnerved by how close she'd come to the truth. "I trusted you. It was Rutlidge I didn't trust, and with good reason, apparently." Her expression did not change, and he dragged a hand down his face. The time had come to be honest with her.

"It isn't easy for me, trusting in people. Things were so perfect between us after the storm that I couldn't believe it would last. So when I heard about the stock purchase, I assumed you had been fooling me, acting as if you enjoyed being my wife just to catch me off my guard. I'm very sorry, Elizabeth, for all of it. The mistrust, as well as everything I said."

She crossed her arms over her chest, silently staring at the vestibule wall for a long moment. Emmett began to worry she would not accept his apology, that he'd ruined all between them for good. Sweat prickled his brow, and yet he forced himself to remain still, to give her a chance to think.

She finally locked her gaze with his. "Trusting others isn't easy for me, either. My entire life, I've learned to bury my true self, to not reveal too much lest I face the wrath of society. You . . ." She sucked in a shaky breath. "You were the first person who saw all of me and never judged. You made everything I am, everything I want to be seem the most normal thing in the world, even for a woman. But you didn't truly see me, because if you had, you would have known I could never hurt you."

"I saw you," he rasped, emotion lodging in his chest. "I saw a woman unlike any other, one who has looked into the darkest, deepest part of me and somehow managed to find something worthwhile."

Unable to keep from touching her, he closed the distance between them and stroked the softness of her cheek with his fingertips.

"You hurt me, Emmett."

"I know, sweetheart, and I'll never quit apologizing for it." He placed his hands on her shoulders, holding her in place. "I've done many terrible things in my life, Elizabeth. The stains on my soul are vast and permanent. I don't deserve a woman like you—a smart, decent woman with honor and mettle—but I'll be damned if I'll give you up. Whatever I need to do or say, however you need me to change, I'm willing to do it. I just . . . I cannot lose you."

Unshed tears swam in her eyes, and she bit her lip. "Why? You never wanted to marry me. You thought you were meeting your mistress that night at Sherry's. My brother—"

"Did us both a favor."

Her jaw fell open at his statement, and Emmett gave a wry chuckle. "I never thought I'd say it either, believe me. But Sloane could never force me into something against my wishes, Elizabeth, no matter who he threatened. I wanted you, and he knew it. I've wanted you from the very first moment you marched into my office."

"Do you mean that?"

"Every word." She swayed toward him slightly, her shoulders relaxing, and a flare of hope burst in his chest.

Perhaps he was getting through to her. Might as well finish telling her all of it.

Cupping her jaw in his hands, he leaned in to whisper, "Do not leave me. Not now, not ever. I will make this up to you, I swear on my life. I'll prove how much I love you."

She let out a small gasp. "You love me?"

"More than I ever thought possible." Then he kissed her, long and deep, drinking her soft sighs and warm breaths into his mouth. "I'm afraid you're stuck with me."

"That's reassuring, since I love you madly. I'm afraid you're stuck with me as well."

Happiness flooded Emmett's chest, an unfamiliar sense of rightness he'd never experienced before. No one had ever loved him, not in any kind of lasting, real way. His mother had presumably loved him, but had left all the same. And his father . . . Emmett would hardly categorize that as love. The girls and Brendan were his family, his responsibilities, and they would all marry and start their own families one day. Elizabeth, however, belonged to Emmett because she wished to stay.

Which reminded him of Rutlidge's words. "Does this mean you're not going to California to procure a divorce?"

She pulled back, aghast. "Who in the world told you that? I was never going to California to divorce you."

"That lying bastard."

"I assume you mean Henry. Which likely means you didn't tell him what train I was on, did you?"

"He told you that?" Jaw clenched, Emmett started for the vestibule door. God, he wanted to flatten Rutlidge all over again.

Elizabeth put a hand on Emmett's shoulder to stop him. "Calm down. It's obvious Henry lied about that as well." She sighed. "I had no idea he would prove to be so difficult."

"He lost you." Emmett dipped his head and pressed his forehead to hers. "I can hardly blame Rutlidge for lying to get you back. But it'll never happen. You're mine now."

"Does that mean you trust me?"

"Yes, I trust you—and I'm sorrier than you'll ever know that I doubted you. The way I acted . . ." A pang of regret twisted in his gut. "I hope you'll forgive me."

She shifted to kiss him, an all-too-brief press of her lips. "I forgive you. No more doubts, for either of us. And I'm sorry I ran away."

"I don't blame you for running. I never should have suspected you of trying to sabotage my company."

"No, you shouldn't have." She caught the lapels of Emmett's coat in her fists and began dragging him toward the inside door to the train. "And you're going to start making it up to me right now, naked, in the bedroom of your private car."

Washington Square, New York City
Two Weeks Later

Emmett folded his newspaper when he saw his wife emerge from the front door, eager to drink her in from the confines of the enclosed carriage. Jesus, she was beautiful. Three days ago, they had returned from Chicago, where, other than showing Lizzie the Chicago Stock Exchange, he'd had her completely to himself for a week—yet even that had not been enough. He wanted to watch her for hours, learn every twitch, every nuance that crossed her face. She was the sun, air, water—everything essential in his life. And now, the mother of his child.

His chest pulled tight, pride welling up inside him. Thank God she'd shown up on his doorstep, had sold him instead of Cabot or Harper on the idea for her investment company. And he was even more grateful she'd forgiven him after the way he'd mistrusted her. *Look at me now, you miserable bastard,* he said silently to his long-departed father. *You said I'd never amount to anything, that I'd die in the streets of Five Points. And look at how wrong you were.*

Kelly jumped down and opened the door for her, which earned him a grateful smile that had the former bare-knuckled boxer blushing. Emmett could relate; he knew full well the power of that smile.

She slid onto the seat across from him, silk skirts rustling over his trouser legs. He wished they were already home, where he could undress her and touch her soft, creamy skin. Kiss every part of her body. Worship her.

He'd been cautious since learning she was carrying their child. But all three physicians he'd consulted—as well as Brendan—had assured him that intimacy during pregnancy was normal. That he would not harm her or the baby. So perhaps he could pull her in his lap now and—

"Emmett, stop. You must wait until we get home."

His mouth hitched. "How did you know what I was thinking?"

"I recognize that particular look in your eye." She slid the toe of her shoe up along his calf as the carriage started moving. "And I also happen to be thinking the same thing."

He growled in the back of his throat, and she threw her head back and laughed, causing the lace on her small hat to bounce. She enjoyed tormenting him, he'd learned.

Well, he enjoyed tormenting her, too.

"What did your brother say?" Emmett asked as he

picked up her leg and settled it atop his thigh. Then he began plucking at the laces of her half boot.

Her attention on his hands, she didn't answer, so he prompted, "Well?"

"He said yes," she murmured.

Emmett removed her boot and placed it on the seat next to him. Then he clasped her stocking-covered foot in his palms and began to knead the bottom of her foot.

She groaned, her fingers digging into the edge of the velvet seat. He smiled. "Yes to what, my dear?"

"Being a godfather. Good heavens, that feels tremendous."

"And what of the rest?" He moved his fingers to the ball of her foot, the silk stocking smooth and slippery to the touch. "What of the stock?"

"His"—she cleared her throat—"former investment banker was stealing from him. Creating shares and pocketing the money. Will's been strapping himself to buy back the outstanding shares."

"That is unfortunate. But it's what I suspected."

"You did?" she breathed, her chest rising and falling quickly. "Why did you not say anything?"

"Because I wanted to be wrong. I had hoped your perfect brother had decided to turn to a life of crime."

"That's terrible."

"Yes, it is. Indeed, I am a terrible, terrible man." His fingers slid to her toes, pulling on each one to release the tension lodged in the joints. "You should know that by now."

Her brow furrowed, her lips turning into a frown. "I know nothing of the sort. You merely want everyone to think you're terrible."

"Elizabeth, please. If people hear I'm not as cold-hearted as they believe, I'll never successfully negotiate another deal." Shocking, but somehow his wife kept managing to spot a bit of good in him.

"Life is not all about business deals, Emmett. Oh, right there," she groaned when he stroked her instep.

Since his wife was the smartest woman he'd ever met, he was learning not to question her. Through Elizabeth, he'd discovered laughter and love, how to enjoy the small moments—and he looked forward to a lifetime of them.

"You'll be happy to know Will has also hired my investment firm. One more client added to the existing five."

"Congratulations. I told you the article would be a wise idea." The feature on Elizabeth's brokerage firm had been published in the *New York Mercury* yesterday, and she'd been deluged with interest ever since. "So how did you get your precious brother to agree?" Her heel cradled in his palms, Emmett pressed his thumbs over the top of her foot.

She bit her lip, lids fluttering closed as she enjoyed his ministrations. He loved that expression, the one of unbridled pleasure. If he slid his fingers between her legs, no doubt she'd be soaked. His cock grew heavy at the idea. The carriage could not go fast enough.

"I promised to forbid you from doing anything with the information you've gathered against Northeast Railroad."

His fingers stilled. "You'll *forbid* me?"

She peeked through her lashes at him. "Yes. I am officially forbidding you from ruining Will's company."

The air thickened, and a long moment passed while they stared at one another in challenge, heat jumping between them like sparks on a wire. Her boldness had him longing for a bed, where he could have that sass and fire underneath him, surrounding him. With that, he went from semierect to completely hard, and he had to shift to ease the sudden discomfort.

Elizabeth's mouth hitched. "You like when I'm assertive."

Hell yes, he did. He began stroking her ankle, her shin. "To be clear, I never planned to ruin Northeast Railroad. I wanted to take it over and run it."

"You know that would kill my brother."

"I don't think he'd mind very much. There's rumblings he may try his hand at politics."

She sat up straighter, her entire body stiffening. "What? Where did you hear that?"

"My dear, I cannot divulge all my tricks. Where would be the fun in that?"

Relaxing, she settled into the velvet cushions as they continued to roll up Fifth Avenue. "Perhaps when we get home, you'll share one or two. Just to pass the time between deals and negotiations."

His fingers trailed higher up her thigh. "I can think of no better way to spend an afternoon than with you, my lovely and demanding wife. The deals and negotiations can wait."

Keep reading
for a special sneak preview of

BARON,

the next book in the Knickerbocker Club series,
coming in November 2016!

William Sloane did not believe in the ability to commune with the spirit world. Hell, he didn't even believe there *was* a spirit world.

Yet he here sat, inside a ramshackle theater in the Tenderloin district, watching this audacious spectacle. Madam Zolikoff, she called herself. The mystifying medium who could communicate with spirits and perform extraordinary feats. The woman was the worst actress he'd ever seen—and Will had seen plenty.

Eyes closed, she swayed and waved her hands, all while chanting utter nonsense. A man sat across from her, one she'd pulled up onstage, his gaze rapt as Madam Zolikoff attempted to speak to his dead mother. The electric lights overhead flickered, and the audience tittered.

"Ah! I think we are close!" she announced loudly in an appalling Russian accent.

Will nearly rolled his eyes. Was anyone really buying this act?

Shifting in his uncomfortable seat, he glanced around at the meager audience. About twenty men and women, all average-looking, a far cry from the extravagant crowd he usually associated with. No diamond tiaras or swallowtail coats here, just derby hats and plain bonnets. But every pair of eyes was trained on the young woman working the stage.

She was attractive, he supposed, if one preferred liars and cheats, which he most definitely did not. Still, her pale blond hair showed off striking brown eyes. A straight, delicate nose. High cheekbones. Arching brows. Full lips painted a scandalous red.

He liked those lips. Quite a lot, in fact. If he were dead, those lips alone might bring him back.

"I hear her!" A steady rapping sounded, reverberating around the room. An accomplice, no doubt, yet the audience gasped.

"Mr. Fox, your mother is here with us now. What would you like to ask her?"

The man onstage asked simple questions for the next fifteen minutes, with Madam Zolikoff "interpreting" the dead mother's answers. Will absently rubbed his stomach, anger burning over this performance, that she would take advantage of someone's grief in such a profoundly fraudulent way. When Will's own mother had died, he'd fervently wished for something—anything—to bring her back. Nothing had, however, and he'd been left in a cold house with an even colder man.

Madam Zolikoff prattled on, regaining Will's attention. Had this woman no shame? No empathy for the heartbreak that went along with losing a loved one? For the first time tonight, he looked forward to the confrontation with her.

He planned to shut the medium down. Run her out of Manhattan, if necessary, because she was standing in the way of something greater, a different sort of power than he possessed now, but one of equal import. One his bastard father had desperately craved, but fallen short of.

John Bennett, a former New York state senator and current gubernatorial candidate, had asked Will to partner on the ticket as lieutenant governor. It was something Will's father had always wanted, to wield political influence, yet he'd died before his political career could take wings. Now, Will would be the Sloane achieving that goal—and dancing on his father's grave after he and Bennett won.

But John Bennett had a weakness, one by the name of Madam Zolikoff. Seemed the madam had dug her hooks into Bennett, and the candidate would not listen to reason regarding the dangers this presented. But Will wasn't about to allow her to jeopardize Bennett's political career—or his own. They could not afford a scandal six months before the election.

When the performance finally ended, Will didn't bother clapping or stamping his feet like the other patrons. He rose, turned on his heel, and headed straight for the door he'd learned would take him backstage.

No one stopped him. More than a few curious glances were thrown his way, so he tugged his derby lower to obscure his face. He'd run Northeast Railroad for the last thirteen years and came from one of the most prominent families in New York. The name Sloane was as well-known as those such as Astor, Stuyvesant, and Van Rensselaer. Consequently, Will had never shied from public attention, but he'd rather not be recognized here.

For several minutes, he cut through the long hallways in the bowels of the theater. Now at the door to her dressing room, he knocked. A slide of a lock, and then the door opened to reveal a brunette woman in a black shirtwaist and skirt, the same costume she'd worn onstage. Her lips were still painted a deep red. He inclined his head ever so slightly. "Madam Zolikoff."

"Mr. Sloane. I've been expecting you." Her voice was deep and husky, with a sultry tone more suited to a bedroom than a stage. He wondered if it were genuine—or fake like the rest of her. She stepped aside. "Come in, please."

He wasn't surprised she knew his name, but had she noticed him in the audience? Three steps found him inside her dressing room, if one could call a space no bigger than a closet a "room." There wasn't enough square footage to allow for more than the small table and chair already in place. A mirror hung on the wall above the table, and a blond wig rested on a stand atop said table.

She glided around him and lowered into the sole chair, facing away from him, and reached for a cloth. Folding his hands behind his back, he watched in the mirror as she slowly swiped the cloth over her mouth to remove the lip color. She didn't rush, and Will had plenty of time to study her mouth. He highly suspected the display another type of performance, to throw him off balance.

"Is there another name I may call you, other than your stage name?"

"No."

"I feel ridiculous calling you Madam Zolikoff."

"That is your problem, not mine." Finished with her cloth, she dropped the scrap to the table and caught his gaze in the mirror. "We are not friends, Mr. Sloane, so let's not pretend otherwise. I know why you're here."

"Is that so?" He hadn't expected her to be so forthright. In his mind, she'd been meek and frightened, concerned over the unpleasantness a man in his position could bring a woman in her position. But this particular woman seemed neither meek nor frightened. "And why am I here?"

"You want to scare me away from John. Get him away from my evil clutches." She wriggled her fingers menacingly on this last sentence. "How's that?"

"Good. This saves us both time. Now you may agree to never see Bennett again, stop bilking him out of hundreds of dollars, and stay out of his life forever."

"Bilking him?" Her lip curled, drawing Will's attention back to her mouth, damn it. "I've got news for you, mugwump. I've earned every dollar providing services to your friend—and not those kind of services, either. John and I are strictly business."

Will smirked. He'd never met a man and a woman who spent time together with money exchanged who were "strictly business."

"Miss whomever you are, I don't care what kind of lies you're shoveling out there to audiences, but I'm not some rube fresh off the farm. I know what you're about, and all of it stinks."

"Oh, indeed? So what am I about, then?"

"Blackmail. And if he doesn't pay, you'll take whatever personal details you've gleaned about him to the papers and turn him into a laughingstock. I will not let that happen."

She rose and, because of the tight space, this put her close enough that he could see the hazel flecks in her brown eyes. Were those freckles on her nose? "I don't care who you are or what you think of me. If you believe I'm going to let some stuffed, pompous railroad man scare me away from my best client, you are dead wrong."

Ava Jones struggled to contain her smile while the handsome man across from her worked to understand her last sentence.

Yeah, you're catching on, railroad man. I'm not afraid of you.

Everyone in New York knew William Sloane. Obscenely wealthy and from one of the best families, he was mentioned frequently in the papers, both on the financial and the social pages. No doubt men and women bowed to his demands all day, every day. Not her, no way. Ava owed him nothing and did not care about his demands. If not for her desire to get rid of him for good, she would've completely ignored him.

At least she would have *tried* to ignore him. Unfortunately, Mr. Sloane was a man a girl noticed. She'd spotted him in the audience right away. Strong, angular jaw. Pronounced cheekbones highlighting his aristocratic nose. Sandy blond hair swept off his forehead, oiled with precision, and a sharp, unsmiling mouth that challenged a woman to see if she could be the one to loosen him up.

At this distance, the view improved markedly. Piercing eyes that had seemed blue in the theater but were actually gray. He was tall, with an air of confidence suitable for a prince and a near-palpable energy radiating from his frame. Wide shoulders filled out the cut of his fancy coat quite nicely. She'd always been drawn to sturdy, capable shoulders. Something about Atlas bearing the weight of the world appealed to her.

But she'd learned long ago that there was no one to bear the weight of her burdens. Those were hers alone.

"Client?" he scoffed. "Wouldn't 'mark' be a more accurate term?"

Goodness, she was growing to dislike this man. "You assume I am swindling him when I am providing a real service."

"By communing with John's dead relatives? Come now, Madam Zolikoff. We both know that's impossible."

Did he have any idea how lonely John Bennett was?

Whether her clients believed in her powers or not, most needed someone to care about them. A friend with whom to talk. A person to give them hope that there was something beyond this drudgery called life. That was what Madam Zolikoff provided—for a nominal fee, of course.

These performances were another matter. People wanted a spectacle. A unique experience to share with their friends and neighbors. A bit of the fantastic to distract from the fatigue. Not everyone came from a wealthy family and ran a big company as a lark; most people needed a break from their daily trials.

"You speak of things you do not understand," she told him. "When I hear from John that he no longer requires my gift, then I will respectfully back off. But you act as if he's a hophead and I'm providing him with the opium. I am not forcing him to see me."

"What I understand is that you are preying on a wealthy and soon-to-be influential man."

Her muscles tightened, anger building in every inch of her body. "I would never blackmail him—I'm not trying to make trouble. The governor as my client would only help me." Bigger-named clients meant more clients, which equated to more income. All she needed to do was save up enough money to get her two brothers and sister out of the factories. By her calculations, she had only four more months to go if all held steady. Four more months, after adopting the Madam Zolikoff likeness two years ago, and she'd have enough to keep her family safe.

Out of the city. Away from the filth and toils of life in New York. Away from bitter memories. Instead, they'd have clean air and open spaces on a farm upstate. *Freedom.*

Mr. Sloane shook his head and pinched the bridge of his nose with two fingers, which caused Ava to roll her eyes. How could someone so wealthy appear so aggrieved? Did this man not know real problems? The tip of her tongue burned with an offer to take him to the match factory to show him cases of phossy jaw. Had he seen the women with their faces rotting away, jawbones glowing in the dark, all because they'd needed to put food on their table?

Those were hardships. Not the fact that his friend and political partner paid her five dollars a week to read tea leaves and pass on bits of "news" from the great beyond.

"How much will it take?" Mr. Sloane asked her. "How much do you need to walk away?"

Oh, so tempting. Ava could throw out a high number and see if the railroad man would bite. If he did, her siblings could quit their factory jobs. She would have enough to buy that piece of property, and they could all be together. Finally.

But she didn't. First, pride would not allow her. Taking Sloane's money would be akin to admitting she was robbing people, which she did not. Second, she knew better than most that accepting money never came without strings. If you took what was offered, they felt as if they owned you.

And no one owned Ava Jones. Not any longer.

"You don't have enough money to cause me to disappear. But if it makes you feel better, I'll cut you a deal on a séance."

He made a sound in his throat. "That is the last thing I need."

A knock sounded on the door before Gus, one of the assistants, called, "Ava, hurry up. I need the room."

Mr. Sloane's brows jumped, and Ava cursed inwardly, irritated at the small revelation. "Ava," he drawled, as if testing the sound on his tongue. "Pretty. Also, I like your hair better this way, without the wig."

She turned and began shoving her things into her carpetbag, trying to ignore the fluttering in her belly. The compliments were as unexpected as they were unwelcome. "Save the poetry for your Fifth Avenue debutantes, railroad man. You're wasting your time with me." She carefully lowered her wig and wig stand into the bag. Found her bonnet. Then she began shrugging into her coat.

A hand caught the coat and held it up. She slipped her arms into the sleeves. "Thank you," she mumbled.

Without waiting for him, she pushed into the hall and strode toward the exit of the theater. The heels of her high boots ticked on the hard floor, and she could hear Sloane's fancy evening shoes dogging her. No doubt he was headed somewhere glamorous, like to the opera or a high-society ball. Not to a cramped three-room apartment in a West Side boardinghouse that she shared with her siblings.

She opened the door to the lobby. "Everything all right, Ava?" Gus eyed her carefully, gaze bouncing to the silent man behind her.

"Fine, Gus. Tell your sister I'll be by tomorrow. See you next week."

He nodded, and she continued out the main doors. An early evening rain had fallen during her performance, cooling the air a bit more than one would expect in midspring. The gaslight from the street lamps cast a yellow glow over the dark, wet cobblestones. Ava loved the rain. It washed the city clean and provided the residents with a reprieve from the usual odors, those of sweat, offal, and horse.

"You've acquired quite a following for these shows."

"You're still here?" She started walking, not caring whether he trailed after her. Unfortunately, his long legs had no problem keeping pace. "I'm very good at what I do, Mr. Sloane. Admit it, you were entertained."

His mouth twisted as if he'd sucked a lemon. "I was offended, if you must know."

Now at the corner, she crossed over Twenty-Seventh Street, heading south, and tried to contain her annoyance. "We don't serve champagne and caviar, so I can imagine what a hardship the evening was for you."

"I was referring to the flimflam you performed on those poor, unsuspecting people."

"Flimflam? Those 'poor, unsuspecting people' wanted a show, and that's what I gave them. There's a reason I perform in a theater, and I'm damn good at what I do."

"You take their money and pretend their dead relatives are speaking to you."

He spoke to her as if she were a criminal, his tone condescending and cutting, and blood rushed in her ears. "First of all, how are you so certain my talents are not real?" He started to open his mouth, so she stopped on the sidewalk and pointed a finger in his face. "You don't have any idea, Mr. Sloane, so save your judgment. Second, I wasn't aware that your own business practices were always so scrupulous." His eyes dimmed significantly, and she knew she'd landed a blow. "I'm sure while running a big railroad you never skirt the law or buy political favor. So save me your sanctimonious attitude."

"Fine," he snarled, leaning closer. "Run your con anywhere you want, sweetheart, but leave John Bennett alone."

Sloane was tall, much larger than she, yet she didn't back down, not for one second. She'd already let one overprivileged, handsome man try to wreck her life. No way would she repeat the mistake.

She glared up at Will Sloane. "Not in your wildest dreams do I take orders from the likes of you. Go bully someone else."

Books by Bestselling Author
Fern Michaels

___The Jury	0-8217-7878-1	$6.99US/$9.99CAN
___Sweet Revenge	0-8217-7879-X	$6.99US/$9.99CAN
___Lethal Justice	0-8217-7880-3	$6.99US/$9.99CAN
___Free Fall	0-8217-7881-1	$6.99US/$9.99CAN
___Fool Me Once	0-8217-8071-9	$7.99US/$10.99CAN
___Vegas Rich	0-8217-8112-X	$7.99US/$10.99CAN
___Hide and Seek	1-4201-0184-6	$6.99US/$9.99CAN
___Hokus Pokus	1-4201-0185-4	$6.99US/$9.99CAN
___Fast Track	1-4201-0186-2	$6.99US/$9.99CAN
___Collateral Damage	1-4201-0187-0	$6.99US/$9.99CAN
___Final Justice	1-4201-0188-9	$6.99US/$9.99CAN
___Up Close and Personal	0-8217-7956-7	$7.99US/$9.99CAN
___Under the Radar	1-4201-0683-X	$6.99US/$9.99CAN
___Razor Sharp	1-4201-0684-8	$7.99US/$10.99CAN
___Yesterday	1-4201-1494-8	$5.99US/$6.99CAN
___Vanishing Act	1-4201-0685-6	$7.99US/$10.99CAN
___Sara's Song	1-4201-1493-X	$5.99US/$6.99CAN
___Deadly Deals	1-4201-0686-4	$7.99US/$10.99CAN
___Game Over	1-4201-0687-2	$7.99US/$10.99CAN
___Sins of Omission	1-4201-1153-1	$7.99US/$10.99CAN
___Sins of the Flesh	1-4201-1154-X	$7.99US/$10.99CAN
___Cross Roads	1-4201-1192-2	$7.99US/$10.99CAN

Available Wherever Books Are Sold!
Check out our website at www.kensingtonbooks.com